# Red Sky in the Morning

# Red Sky in the Morning

❖

To Maryann —
The finest Italian cooking
North Coast publicist a guy
could have !!
Bill Hamann

## Bill Hamann

**To order additional copies of this book, contact:**
Xlibris Corporation
1-888-795-4274
www.Xlibris.com
Orders@Xlibris.com
47570

*This novel is dedicated to Cindy and Stephanie
who asked one day,
"Do you have anything new to read?"*

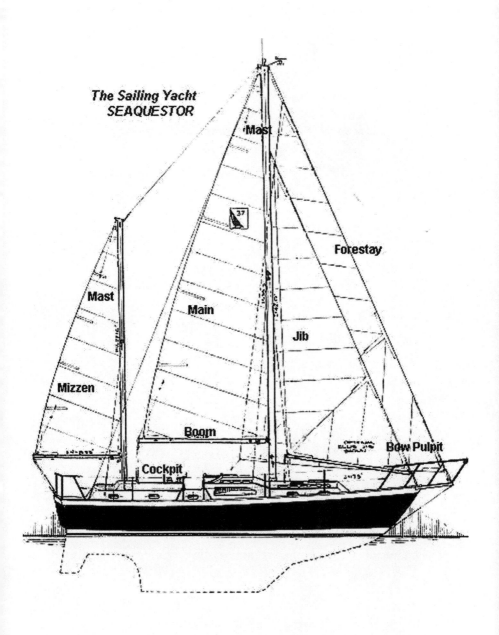

The Sailing Yacht
SEAQUESTOR

Mast

Forestay

Mast

Main

Jib

Mizzen

Boom

Bow Pulpit

Cockpit

# PROLOGUE

"Wind shift!" Susan yelled.

"I'll get the gennaker down," said Jack. "See if you can put us into the wind."

Susan was halfway up the ladder as Jack spoke. By the time he made it on deck Susan was already at the helm turning the ketch into the wind. Jack ripped the gennaker sheet out of the self-tailing winch and felt the ketch move upright as the giant parachute-like sail flapped in the strong northwest breeze. The wind had shifted more than ninety degrees and was blowing spray off a sea of whitecaps. What began as a heart-pounding alarm, became the kind of weather big boat sailors lived, and died, for.

Jack and Susan Grayson worked together like a finely tuned Swiss watch movement. In two minutes the gennaker was bagged, and Susan had winched out the self-furling jib. The maneuver was a nautical work of art.

Jack turned his face into the wind and inhaled deeply. He could smell a storm brewing before any weather radio announcement. "I think we're in for a blow, darlin'. The wind's veered another point to the north, and it's blowing spray."

"Can you tie a reef in the main and mizzen for me?" Susan yelled over the howling, gusting, spitting wind. "It'll help my steerage."

Jack Grayson adeptly responded to his captain's command then smiled at the ease with which Susan trimmed the sail after the reefing maneuver. She understood mechanical advantage and used it well. He watched her sit on the cockpit seat with one foot on the helm and the other braced up against the leeward cockpit combing. With both hands free, she was able to easily trim the sail against the gusting wind and spray washing over her back.

"That was the drill," Susan bellowed from the cockpit. "Now let's do the real thing."

*A piece of cake*, Jack thought as he finished reefing *SEAQUESTOR's* enormous flapping main sail. Then, from the corner of his eye Jack saw something fly over his head. The Vermilion Yacht Club burgee flying from the port side flag halyard had parted and the small triangular flag fluttered away like an autumn leaf. *It's really tootin' out here*, Jack thought, as he felt the ketch heel to hard over to starboard.

Jack looked aft and saw Susan in her classic three point position, struggling to ease the bulging sail. Then in a single powerful wind gust the mainspring of the Grayson watch snapped. Jack saw Susan's foot slip off the large stainless steel steering wheel. For an instant she lost her grasp on the main sheet as she jumped up to grab the wheel. Then a dozen things went wrong at the same time, as *SEAQUESTOR* tacked wildly through the wind.

What a difference an hour had made. The giant aluminum boom that earlier flexed under a friendly breeze toward Canada on a wedding anniversary cruise now whipped, and snarled, and smacked into Susan Grayson's head. Susan never saw what lunged at her as she was catapulted into the raging lake.

The starboard deck, where Jack lay stunned, was engulfed in water. He reached out feebly toward Susan's motionless body being flopped and tossed by tempestuous waves. *SEAQUESTOR* was bouncing and flapping "in irons" as she struggled for some direction from the vacant helm. Susan was only ten feet from Jack's grasp, bleeding badly from the side of her head, and buoyed by air trapped in her baggy white foul weather gear.

Jack's hand fell upon the antique cork-lined ring buoy mounted near the starboard shrouds. He knew he had to go into the water if Susan was going to survive. His gut told him the storm would pass as quickly as it had come, and that together they would survive. But his training told him to stay with the boat—to turn her around and go back to Susan. Impulse, experience, and training all tugged at him, but something deep in his soul paralyzed him.

Susan was floating but not swimming; lifeless yet not dead. Her bloody head was tilted back and her eyes closed as the wind and waves pushed the floundering ketch out of sight.

The demon heralded by an autumn morning's vermilion red sky had, at once, claimed a woman's life and infected a man's soul.

# PART ONE

*Red sky in the morning, sailor take warning.*
*Red sky at night, sailor's delight.*—Folklore

# CHAPTER 1

Jack Grayson poured a cup of strong black coffee into his thick white porcelain mug. He cupped his hands around the steaming mug and savored its warmth. As he slurped the hot brew he caught sight of the red, white and blue burgee of the Vermilion Yacht Club enameled on the side, and then slowly rotated the mug in his hands. Memories should be so easy to hide, he thought. Jack made his way toward the sun deck, but paused a moment to study his reflection in the sliding glass door. Barefoot, bare-chested, in khaki sailing shorts and Topsiders, holding a sailor's mug and gazing into the first light—a perfect reflection of how Captain Jack Grayson saw himself. *A little gray, crinkled and fat,* Jack thought. "But not too bad," he proclaimed.

As Jack looked at himself against the backdrop of the early morning sky he remembered one of Susan's favorite sayings: "Everything looks better at sunrise." He jerked the door open and the image was gone. Jack stood on the deck overlooking Lake Erie, dreading the dawn of another day alone. He had faced a year of these sunrises since Susan's death and still had found no peace.

The morning ritual cleansed Jack and focused his mind on the day's chores. This was his time to commune with mother earth.

Long ago, as a midshipman at Kings Point, he learned that the quiet moments at dawn were for listening and watching—for inhaling the essence of nature—for learning her secrets.

Just as he had done every morning for twenty five years on the bridge deck of a thousand foot tanker, Jack Grayson stood reverently on the sun deck of his home in Vermilion, Ohio, inhaling deeply and searching for a secret. The view never seemed to change—calm, beautiful first light serenity. How mysterious, Jack thought, was this volatile beauty of nature.

The great Lake Erie, an inland sea as majestic as any of the fabled seven, could at once give freedom and impose bondage; nurture love and inflict pain; spawn life and rain down death. Jack Grayson was a son of the sea, a creature of the lake. He had reveled in its energy. He had also known its fury. Now, Jack was a prisoner of the beguiling abyss. But this was a new day, and things always look better at sunrise.

Jack dressed quickly pulled on a polo shirt, poured a second cup of coffee, checked the barometer in his study, and then climbed aboard his British green Range Rover.

The sun was already bright in the early August sky as Jack backed the car from the garage and pushed the dashboard button that activated his home security system. Security hardly seemed necessary any more, but it was another familiar ritual that Jack needed.

Jack remembered how years ago a friend of Susan's, at the yacht club, had found a second life selling security systems. She had quickly persuaded Susan that with Jack spending so many months at sea, the system would help her feel safer as she sat all alone in that "big house up on the lake."

Although the specter of Marilyn Sheppard being bludgeoned to death in another big house up on the lake in Bay Village was forty years old, the mere mention of her name was enough to sell the most complicated system to the most uncomplicated person.

Jack could have put the Range Rover on automatic pilot for the five-minute drive down Liberty Avenue from the west end of Vermilion to the lagoons on the east side of the Vermilion River, but there were a few more rituals to be observed on the way to work.

The Range Rover had barely reached normal operating temperature when Jack turned left on Grand Street. He parked a few feet from the corner, and walked up to the porch of Ednamae's, one of a dozen tourist traps in the historic little harbor town of Vermilion. The Victorian house with its peaks, gables, chimneys, bric-a-brac, and massive front porch was the town's most cherished ice cream parlor. But not in the early hours after dawn.

The cafe curtains were tightly drawn across the small double hung windows. A garish plastic CLOSED sign was slightly askew in a window pane of the front door. Jack tapped the glass lightly with his academy class ring, and barely glimpsed the movement of a curtain from the corner of his eye. The ancient white painted door creaked open.

"Running a little late, aren't we Jack?"

Jack stepped inside the confection-scented foyer and stood toe-to-toe with the gran-dame of Vermilion's Harbour Towne 1837. Ednamae claimed to be the grandniece of Captain Alva Bradley, Vermilion's most prominent boat builder, captain, and merchant, who had prospered in Vermilion a quarter century after the War of 1812. His unique merchant schooner *South America* was the pride of the Lake Erie fleet in 1841. The shallow draft, centerboard, swift design helped Bradley amass a fortune by shipping farm produce from nearby Berlin Township to Canada, and to the new Erie Canal entrance at Buffalo, two hundred miles to the east.

The great Captain, it is said, brought back with him a secret recipe for rum raisin ice cream—the same recipe sought out by summer tourists each year.

But not in the early hours after dawn.

In the early hours after dawn, every Monday morning, Ednamae Bradley hosted the "Captain's Quarters." In a private dining room behind the ice cream parlor, Ednamae gathered Vermilion's few remaining Lake Captains for breakfast, reminiscence and schemes.

"Late?" asked Jack. "I don't think so." Just then the big brass Chelsea ship's clock on the mantel rang out six sharp dings of its bell. "Seven a.m.," Jack announced with a smile, then looked around the table at the council. Captain Ernie Beckett, one of the last living Master's of full rigged sailing ships, was seated at the head of the table.

Ernie was the resident manager of the prestigious Vermilion Yacht Club and adjunct curator of the Great Lakes Historical Museum, the crown jewel of Vermilion's tourist trade.

Captain Teddy "Bear" Parks, the skipper of Vermilion's last active commercial fishing boat, was seated to Ernie's left at the heavily carved oak pedestal table.

Captain Jack Grayson took his seat between Ernie Beckett and Captain Maggie Wicks. Maggie was the owner-operator of *Aphrodite*, an excursion boat that toured the Vermilion River, lagoons, and nearby coastline, thrice daily from her dock at McGarvey's Nautical Restaurant.

Captain Meg, as her passengers called her, was a feisty and controversial member of the Captain's Quarters. Ernie Beckett often barked, "How the hell can a woman be captain of a workin' boat?" Yet no one dared seriously question her credentials, least of all her growling godfather.

"Madamee, the libation, if you please," ordered Captain Beckett.

Ednamae poured a shot glass of rum for each of the captains, and then ceremoniously poured one final shot into the glass sitting before an empty chair at Captain Beckett's left hand.

"To seafarin'," Ernie intoned.

"To seafaring," the group chanted.

Everyone raised their glasses and took a small sip. All eyes turned to the empty seat.

"To Captain William Daysart," bellowed the old salt at the head of the table. "On the anniversary of your final passage, may your sails be forever full."

The group tipped back their glasses then slowly turned them upside down on the table top. Each Captain, in turn, passed the remaining shot glass of rum down the line to Jack Grayson. He lifted the dark rum high in the air as he spoke. "May your son, Will, join us at the turning of the tide."

"Here, here."

Ednamae swept up to the table with a huge steaming platter. "Rum raisin flap jacks and Canadian bacon."

"Business slow again, eh?" growled Captain Ernie.

"Not as slow as it's going to be, if that casino project down in Lorain gets approved."

"Maybe we should all learn how to deal cards," Jack said. "The governor said this project would bring in lots of new jobs." Jack could see from the hard set of Ernie's jaw that he was not amused.

"I think young Will has already learned the game," said Teddy.

"What do you mean?" asked Jack.

"I mean the kid is ready to head down the road to the bright lights of our new Gomorrah on the lake," Teddy replied. "Didn't he talk to you?"

"We haven't been doing too well lately, I'm afraid," said Jack.

"I guess I wasn't cut out to be a father figure."

Maggie reached over and put her hand over Jack's. "I know this has been an awful year for you, but it's time to stop blaming yourself. Why don't we take some time to talk this out?"

"Not now for Chrissakes!" bellowed Captain Beckett. "And not here. This ain't some damned group therapy session. We got a rescue mission underway here. We got a lad overboard—a life to save." Ernie swiped the spittle off his chin and bore into Jack Grayson with storm gray eyes. "Young Will Daysart needs savin', and we're the only people left in town who still give a damn."

"Maybe he doesn't want to be saved," said Jack.

"What the hell are you talking about Jack?" asked Teddy Bear. "Is he that far gone?"

"Some things are worse than death," said Jack. "Over in Vietnam, soldiers who were being tortured begged to die. Sometimes living hurts so much that dying looks like a blessing."

The metaphor was not lost on this circle of friends who had watched a man they loved and admired wasting away with each passing season. An uneasy silence fell upon the table, and Jack regretted his morose comparison.

"Bull shit!" croaked Ernie. "Everybody wants to live. They just need a reason. We took an oath to take care of each other, and that's what we're goin' to do."

All eyes shifted to the old sailing master.

"Now, get me another stack of those rum raisin flapjacks, and let's make us a plan." Ernie squinted up through his stormy eyebrows and whispered slyly. "Then Captain Grayson can pay a fatherly visit to young William."

# CHAPTER 2

Jack Grayson felt an irresistible foreboding as he surveyed the decaying old yacht docked behind GrayDays Marine. Halyards were slapping against the mast amid a brightening morning sun that silhouetted soaring sea gulls. It was an idyllic setting, yet in the midst of all the airy tranquility, Jack felt a claustrophobic chill. He was hemmed in by his memories and shackled by his nightmares.

Will Daysart's apartment above the marina office complex was dark and quiet. Jack guessed that Will was still sleeping off the ravages of another drug-crazed night. It was just as well, since Jack was not thrilled by his mission to carry the Captain's Quarters plan to the lad. As if searching for a stowaway, Jack looked up and down the gleaming white gel coat deck, then climbed aboard and stepped into the cockpit. He lifted out all three sections of wooden louvered hatch boards from the cabin companionway, pushed back the dark smoked Plexiglas sliding hatch cover, and descended the ladder into the yacht.

The spacious saloon of the Irwin 37 ketch now felt like a macabre nautical museum—one that Jack had not visited for a very long time. His eyes darted to the shiny brass plate mounted on the bulkhead leading to the forward cabin.

*SEAQUESTOR*
SUSAN WHEELER GRAYSON, OWNER
CLEARWATER, FLORIDA
1989

Jack ran his fingers across the engraving he had commissioned as a christening gift for Susan's new baby, one she had longed for since her first bareboat charter. In the mid-eighties Jack and Susan had taken to cruising in the Caribbean during one of Jack's winter month leaves from the Mobil Oil tanker fleet. Each year Susan arranged a bareboat charter from The Moorings in the British Virgin Islands.

Jack and Susan were able to "rediscover ourselves" each year in three enchanting weeks of sailing aboard a fully provisioned yacht. Susan's yacht of choice was the Irwin 37 center cockpit ketch. She quickly saw that this shoal draft, retractable centerboard, ketch rig was the perfect "big boat" for Lake Erie's shallow water and freakish weather. Susan was loathe to admit to anyone that she was just following the lead of old Captain Alva Bradley, who had made the same design decisions 150 years earlier.

The Irwin 37 had been a popular Caribbean charter fleet boat for years. Although measuring 37 feet on deck, the yacht with its fore triangle-enhancing bowsprit and stainless steel bow pulpit, was actually a smidgen more than 40 feet in overall length. The ketch rig, with its variable sail plans, provided easy handling with great performance in extreme wind and sea conditions. Both Jack and Susan had often single-handed the boat under full sail for short day trips. The frequent sultry light air days of summer found SEAQUESTOR slipping along under main, mizzen and an immense multi-colored gennaker—Jack's major technological contribution to the boat. But in a storm this large stable thirty ton yacht could be rigged down to a storm jib, double reefed main, and mizzen for some serious dirty sailing. When Vermilion's sloops, cutters and yawls headed for port in the face of forty knot "breezes," Jack and Susan clipped along at maximum hull speed, 8.5 knots, reveling in every gust, shift and spindrift.

Below deck, SEAQUESTOR was a cruising sailor's dream. Right amidships, at the bottom of the companionway ladder, was a warm and spacious saloon. Two upholstered settees and a large drop leaf white ash table made the saloon an ideal spot for reading, chatting, laying out lavish meals, and hosting small social gatherings for as many as eight people. Two elongated viewing ports on each side and a large overhead opening hatch gave the saloon an airy dimension that belied its actual size.

Adjoining the saloon, on the starboard side and slightly aft was the ship's galley. Susan had incorporated a gimbaled, four-burner LNG stove and oven, a small microwave, and a refrigerator/freezer/ice maker that operated off LNG/AC/DC. There was a two-section stainless steel sink, strategically placed below a nice port light that opened on deck, and about six feet of usable counter space. Everything the cruising gourmet needed was easily accessible, but was artfully laid out for a single cook; and that crew member was Jack, who had perfected a full menu of unique yachting dishes.

The major attraction of the Irwin 37 for cruising sailors, however, was not in the rigging, the sail plan, the centerboard/keel, or the sumptuous saloon. The real beauty of this yacht was at both ends. There were two staterooms on board, each with its own full bathroom and shower. This arrangement allowed a family of four to cruise in comfort and privacy.

The V-berth cabin in the bow had been young Jimmy Grayson's domain and his refuge during long summer cruises to the northern Great Lakes. The lone occupant of a cabin space for two, Jimmy was able to bring aboard his sketch pads, water colors, oils, art history books, and classical music cassettes. Jimmy preferred to lock the sliding door leading to his cabin from the saloon, then come and go through the large hatch above the berth.

Susan accepted Jimmy's reclusive artistic demeanor, Jack could not.

As Jack peered into the deserted cabin from the open doorway, he sensed that he should have opened that door much sooner. Jack headed aft across the saloon to the port side passageway leading to the aft stateroom. He stopped at the engine compartment and popped open the door. He knelt down, almost reverently, and flipped on a light that illuminated Jack's attraction to the Irwin 37—the big four cylinder 55 b.h.p. Perkins diesel engine.

Jack enjoyed sailing, but he loved machinery. Perhaps that love led him to the United States Merchant Marine Academy as a floundering Midwestern teenager. In furtherance of its mission to "train high types of individuals to become officers in the U.S. Merchant Marine," Kings Point was a first rate engineering college. Likewise, in furtherance of Jack Grayson's mission to one day have command of his own ship, he had become a first rate marine engineer and deck officer.

If there was a nautical bone of contention between Susan and Jack, it was the diesel engine. Susan was a sailing star of the first magnitude—a purist. She was as content drifting away at one knot under luffing sails, as she was beating to windward in a gale. Susan Grayson and Ernie Beckett loved preaching to the "impure" that "engines have no place on sailin' ships."

But this engine was a thing of beauty, Jack thought. It was able to propel the thirty ton yacht through the water at eight knots, faster than was possible under sail in any conditions. But the Perkins had a flaw that Jack could never remedy. It was a bugger to start. And that flaw had contributed to Susan's death, Jack remembered as he switched off the light and slammed the cover back in place.

Jack was getting depressed.

He felt dirty weather coming on.

It was time to go.

He turned around and bumped against the chart table nestled into the corner of the port side navigation station. Jack paused and surveyed the chronometer, barometer, VHF radio, radar console, and radio direction finder. He opened a sliding drawer and found his brass parallel rulers, triangle, dividers and mechanical pencil, which had been ship-christening gifts from Susan to her 1st Mate and navigator.

Jack fought the urge to handle these relics as he closed the drawer quickly yet carefully. Then he lifted the hinged chart table top and what he saw took his breath away . . .

SHIP'S LOG BOOK
*SEAQUESTOR*
CAPT. SUSAN W. GRAYSON

Jack had not seen Susan's log book since that day. Something in the volume beckoned, almost as if it wanted to speak to him. He plucked the book from its niche and folded it to his chest like a preacher carries his Bible to the pulpit. After several moments of "connecting," with log book in hand, Jack retreated to the aft stateroom—the owner's cabin—the bed he had shared with Susan.

Unlike the forward V-berth cabin, the aft stateroom was a large airy square-shaped space dominated by a queen-sized bed that Susan had adorned with a custom made soaring sea gull quilt. The cabin featured a built-in cabinet of drawers, built-in TV/VCR/STEREO rack, a cedar hanging closet, night stands on each side of the bed, book shelves at the headboard, port lights all around and a large opening hatch above the bed, "for star gazing," Susan often said. A louvered teak door near the foot of the bed led into the full bath and stall shower, also custom designed by the owner.

Jack perched himself on the edge of the bed and opened the thick leather bound log. He flipped through a precise record of weather, lake conditions, departures, passages, speeds and courses, landfalls and arrivals. This was a tale of countless odysseys and adventures, ending finally with a pathetic tragedy. The wheels were now in motion, there was no turning back, as Jack slowly leafed through the book scanning Susan's careful hand. Finally his eyes rested on the last written entries . . .

September 6, 1997
Princess Diana was laid to rest today.
May the Lord protect her as she protects those she left behind.
0530—Depart Vermilion—Dest. Port Colborne
Course: 068° mag—Speed: 5.3 kts
Weather: Part Cloudy—Bar: 30.25 falling
Wind: SSW 15 kts—Temp: 62°
0642—Sunrise
Running well under full sail & gennaker

Can smell bacon & coffee. Ummm!!
0800—Wind shifted to NW 20—gennaker down
Bar: 29.90 falling Temp: 55°
Small craft warnings for western lake
1045—NOAA Weather—gale warnings
Course: 060° mag—Weather: O'Cast
Speed: 6. 6 kts Wind: NNW 35 gusting
Storm jib, mizzen—reefing main.
She's honkin' out there.

The last log entry could not have come soon enough for Jack. He was back in the storm, and was feeling every ounce of its awesome weight. He closed the log book and bolted for the companionway. Jack decided he would finish reading the log book at home, away from the monster, away from the demons. He clamored up the ladder and was halfway into the cockpit, when he caught his shirt sleeve on the hatch track. His body jerked violently to the right and he bit his lip as the metal track tore into his flesh. The log book fell from his right hand and landed back on the sole of the saloon. Panting and sweating, Jack bounded off the floor and scrambled up the ladder. He grabbed the hatch boards and locked them down.

Some things are better left in place.

# CHAPTER 3

"Rise and shine buzzards! It's 7:30 in the great Western Reserve. Time to get up and kick ass for another day. Let's break out with a cut from Purgatory's new CD . . . where Cleveland rocks . . . WMMS!"

Young will Daysart, the heir apparent of GrayDays Marine, rolled over and fumbled for the clock radio. He ran his slim yellow-stained fingers over the buttons and dials atop the radio, then probed and analyzed until he located the volume control. Will jacked it up to the MAX, and felt the room reverberate with shrieks of Fenders and Gibsons battling frenzied drum beats. Will waited, actually he longed, for someone to shout out a complaint as distorted lyrics rattled through the walls.

The three-story century house had been the home of Vermilion's premier boat brokerage and chandlery firm for twenty years longer than Will could remember. Now it had taken on a darker role. The Wheeler family house had been the first of the lagoon houses. Although the two-and-a-half story Cape Cod style house faced Liberty Avenue on the east side of the Vermilion River, its back yard adjoined the picturesque lagoons that emerged from a natural estuary beside the river. The Vermilion Lagoons meandered from the main road to the Lake Erie shore, a mile to the north.

During the century since Susan's great grandfather Wheeler built his New England replica house on the wilderness side of the river, the old Cleveland-Sandusky trail had become a paved four lane State Route 6. The "wilderness" had become a commercial district, the lagoons had been developed into an elite housing development, and the Wheeler house had become the showroom and offices of GrayDays Marine Company.

Susan Grayson and William Daysart started the business in the family homestead that Susan's grandmother had left her in her will. Everyone in town agreed it had been ordained that these two lifelong sailing buddies would one day get together. Somehow. Somewhere.

Captain Daysart had operated a bareboat charter business in Charlotte Amalie, St. Thomas as a young man. He became enraptured by the pristine natural beauty of, what many world travelers believed to be, the most beautiful natural harbor in the world. But the rapture soon slipped away after a debilitating accident in the 1970 Newport to Bermuda race sent him ashore, and then back to his native Vermilion. But one man's curse is often another's bonanza and so it was that Susan Grayson saw another one of her frequent "golden opportunities" in the return of her sailing mentor. At first Jack Grayson was uncomfortable with a business venture that put his new bride in league with a guy, five years her senior. Especially one on whom she had a school-girl crush most of her life. The threat was all the more intense, in Jack's mind, because he was at sea for months at a time with the Mobil Oil tanker fleet. As the years melted away, however, so did the illusive threat, and Will, Jack and Susan formed a bond that any of them would have given their lives to protect.

But the Wheeler family presence had departed young William's prison, and happily so. The stodgy Wheeler clan would never have tolerated the contorted lyrics that now resounded from the top floor of the sacred house as if a coven of crazed witches were shouting incantations in tongues.

William Duncan Daysart lay motionless in his water bed, staring up at the vaulted dormer ceiling of his bedroom. He stretched his arms and legs, turned his head slowly from side to side, and surveyed the 10ft that had become his castle keep. There was a big screen television in the corner that supported a VCR, stacks of rock music videos, and a large plastic sea anemone-like novelty that continuously and mysteriously changed color. Will recalled the day he acquired this treasure at Cedar Point Amusement Park. "When you watch this do its magic, I want you to think about the wondrous things a man can do with chemistry," Captain Daysart had told his young son.

Young will had, indeed, thought about it.

There was an ancient leather ship's settee strewn with last night's clothes. A small drop leaf coffee table, littered with yesterday's junk food, looked like a toxic waste dump. An Airdyne exercise bike sat in front of the double-hung window at the end of the dormer, and a pair of Steiner military 7x50 binoculars hung from the handlebars. A large carved mahogany wardrobe with drawers and doors stood in the corner, next to an oaken school teacher's desk. The desk, presided over by a silver framed photograph of Will's mother, seemed the singular spot of order amid endless chaos. Will's eyes came to rest, once again, on the clock radio. It was 7:34 when will sat up and ran his fingers through the oily mop of long jet black hair that framed his face and fell upon his shoulders. Will's head began to bob to the primal beat of the music. He sang along. "Better . . . better off dead. Better . . . better off dead . . . than conform!"

Will swung his legs over the side of the undulating bed and sprang to his feet. He worked his way across the room to the settee, like he had so often seen Mick Jagger work his way across a concert stage. He reached under one of the old cracked brown leather cushions and withdrew a small plastic bag of vegetation. Will cleared a corner of the coffee table and deftly rolled a cigarette.

"Better . . . better off dead. Better . . . better off . . ."

Will struck a match, applied the flame, and took a long drag off the joint. He seemed to consume the smoke more than simply use it. *The wonders of chemistry,* Will mused as he stood up and played his way to the window.

The dormer window gave Will a panoramic view of the Vermilion Lagoons. Unique in all the Great Lakes, the lagoons were a boater's paradise. Each of the five navigable lagoons growing out of the Vermilion River was like a watercolor painting of Provincetown on the tip of Cape Cod. Like every product of the Vermilion school system, Will could not help but think of the town's history every time he saw the lagoons.

The Vermilion River had been a flowing spring of economic opportunity for centuries. A large dugout canoe discovered in a bog at the head waters of the river (the oldest water craft ever found in North America, circa 1,500 b.c.e., according to the Cleveland Museum of Natural History) bears testament to the river's rich history of transportation and commerce. In 1808 a village was established on the banks of' the river by the famous Revolutionary War "Sufferers" who came to the Firelands from Connecticut. These former citizens of the colonies received property rights in the Western Reserve as restitution for the homes and businesses lost to the British during the war. By 1820 the Village of Vermilion had its own shipyard and village schooner, *Ranger,* to carry passengers, farm produce, whiskey and salt along the north shore from Detroit to Buffalo.

When the Ohio-Erie Canal was begun in 1825, entrepreneurs prospected the new Firelands for harbors that might attract the trade rich terminus of the canal. Many lake captains preferred the Vermilion River because of its sheltered entrance and sandy bottom. So it was that Captain Alva Bradley chose the Vermilion River for his shipyards and shipping company, rather than the larger Black River or Cuyahoga River to the east.

The industrial revolution, the invention of the steam powered ship, the need for deep water harbors, and the choice of Cleveland's Cuyahoga River as the canal entrance to Lake Erie hastened the demise of Vermilion as an important commercial shipping port. Even Captain Alva Bradley, whose vision was pivotal to Vermilion's growth, pulled up anchor in 1868 and moved his empire to Cleveland. Thankfully, Ednamae often told Will, he left behind his mysterious rum raisin recipe.

If necessity is the mother of invention, then the prospect of a new ghost town on the Vermilion River was necessity's father. A visionary group of land developers eyed the natural beauty of the estuary beside the river. A five-year construction project, in the decade before the start of World War II, saw the erection of steel retaining walls at the banks of the estuary, the dredging of new lagoons to a controllable depth of eight feet, the subdivision of land-filled marshland between the retaining walls into building lots, and the formation of the Vermilion Lagoons Property Owners Association.

The association's first president was Susan Wheeler Grayson's grandfather. As one of the co-developers of the Vermilion Lagoons, an owner of several prime lots, and its first resident, Gordon "Percy" Wheeler had a large stake in his new neighborhood. He steam-rolled innovative property restrictions that dictated the style, size and color of all houses. He defined the maximum height of bushes, shrubs, and fences. He limited the scope of boat dock improvements at each lot's lagoon retaining wall. He assured free and unrestricted navigation for small boats throughout the lagoon network. Finally, he imposed deed restrictions that prescribed inheritance and first refusal rights before any lot could be sold.

Percy Wheeler made an exclusive club out of the once pristine estuary. Percy's snobbery reached it apogee with his creation and chartering of the Vermilion Yacht Club on the promontory of the second-most northern lagoon. With forty docks, a private clubhouse, rose garden, breathtaking view of the western lake, and a perpetual restriction against "the consumption of alcoholic beverages on the premises," the prestigious, if stodgy, Vermilion Yacht Club had become one of the last bastions of historic yachting on the Great Lakes. Now Captain Ernie Beckett was the anointed conservator of VYC's heritage, its traditions, and its flock . . . including young Will Daysart.

Will had learned his Vermilion history well. He had listened to his father and Jack Grayson tell the old stories hundreds of times. The new lagoon settlers, who ambled over to GrayDays Marine looking for a boat to buy, were delighted to have a legend or two thrown into the deal. As a kid, Will loved these stories. He enjoyed talking with customers who sought him out with questions about the sailboats. But life can be fickle. As Will looked down upon the rows of uniformly white houses, with their uniformly green shingled roofs, their uniformly painted boat docks, and their pleasurable little pleasure boats, he was lost. It was not disdain that young Will felt for the people of the historic lagoons, but detachment. Will took a drag off the numbing cigarette dangling from his lips and blew the smoke into a haze that momentarily covered the window.

"Better off . . . better off . . . DEAD!"

The song ended and Will picked up the Steiners, flipped the rubber caps off the lenses and peered down at the yacht docked in Slip No.1. The forty-foot Irwin yacht, *SEAQUESTOR*, sat quietly in the murky still waters of the lagoon. He couldn't have counted the times he sat around the cockpit table of that old boat eating Papa Joe's pizza with Jimmy Grayson. He smiled at a misty vision of his mother and Susan Grayson setting up "the boys' pizza party" on deck, while the "big kids" took their anchovies and bottle of Lonz Winery "Sailor's Red" into the cozy saloon of the ketch. Will brought himself back to the present with another drag off his weed and again blew the pungent smoke over the window.

Then something caught his eye.

Jack Grayson was scrambling off the deck of the boat. Will had never seen Jack so agitated; and he wondered what Jack had discovered on board the dying yacht. It seemed like he was running for his life. Will stepped away from the window as Jack scurried out of sight toward the parking lot. When he was certain that Jack was gone he inched his binocular gaze across the deck to the lazarette hatch. He stopped and focused the Steiners on a stainless steel five-digit thumb-wheel padlock. "All secure," he muttered to himself in another cloud of acrid smoke.

"Better . . . better off dead. Better . . . better off dead."

# CHAPTER 4

Jack peeped over a dog-eared copy of *Sail Magazine* and quickly flashed back to 1968. Dr. Meagan Palmer, Ph.D. stood before him in the doorway leading to her office. Dressed in great fitting khaki pants, deck shoes and a faded baggy Madras shirt, she was a picture of peace from the sixties. Dr. Palmer's long black hair swept back into a working ponytail which highlighted broadly set jade green eyes. She seemed to flaunt her fiery Greek-Irish heritage, lest anyone dare underestimate her.

Meagan Palmer was Jack's refuge—a safe harbor in turbulent seas. Jack had known Meagan for thirty years in myriad roles: Susan's college roommate, Cupid, maid-of-honor, sailing chum, client, confidant, crying towel, and shrink. If, as some openly criticized, Meagan was "too close to the situation" to do Jack any good, that was okay. Jack needed "close." He needed a point of attachment, a lifeline, something to hold on to. Something that was Susan.

"How the hell are *you*, Jack?" Meagan boomed as she smothered him in a benevolent bear hug.

"Pretty good, now that I've survived another encounter with the council."

"Ah yes. The mysterious meddling marauders of the Captain's Quarters," quipped Meagan. "I don't understand why you continue to subject yourself to that bunch. It must be the pancakes."

"Obviously."

Meagan poked Jack in the midsection. He leaned into her touch like an adoring puppy that had been left alone too long.

"It looks like you could afford to miss a meeting or two and get back out on the track."

"Suddenly you're a psychological fitness expert?"

"That's why they call us 'shrinks'." A quick wit and penchant for strategic self-deprecation were two of Meagan Palmer's more endearing qualities. In stark contrast to her neurotic self-effacing heiress counterparts from the Kuryakis clan, Meagan could charm your socks off one minute and pick your pocket the next. She could cry with you today and cuss you out tomorrow. She could offer a helping hand when you needed it, and turn a cold shoulder when . . . well, when you needed it, Jack recalled. Meagan Palmer had the gift and she used it well with everyone, it seemed, but her marriage partners.

Meagan's first "arranged" marriage, shortly after her graduation from college, lasted a tumultuous three years and two miscarriages. Constantine "Gus" Panopoulis found it impossible to compete with Meagan Palmer Panopoulis anywhere but in the dentist's office. That office soon became the young groom's refuge and his bordello—a situation that gave Meagan her way out. She orchestrated an annulment from the Greek Orthodox Church, and a scholarship to graduate school, all compliments of Papa Panopoulis.

Always a quick study, Meagan arranged her own second marriage. She truly loved Scott Kennedy, whom she met while doing her doctoral dissertation at Case-Western Reserve University. Scott hailed from an aristocratic family of horse breeders in Middleburg, Virginia that encouraged Meagan to get involved in the life of the hunt country. She quickly became one of the top riders on a highly competitive A-Circuit of hunters and jumping horses. Scott just as quickly retired from competition. Meagan received her doctorate in psychology. Scott did not. Meagan loved the travel, competition and parties of the horse show world. Scott craved the sanctuary of the rolling Virginia countryside. Meagan wanted a child. Scott could not. On the anniversary of their fourth year of marriage, Scott left for Ireland with a dozen steamer trunks of possessions. Meagan Palmer Kennedy did not.

Meagan moistened an index finger with her tongue and dabbed at a drop of maple syrup on Jack's shirt. "Since you've had your breakfast, and it's much too early for lunch, I presume this is not a social call."

"Not exactly."

"I hope you're not here to talk about poor little Willy Daysart," said Meagan. "What he needs is a boot in the ass, a detox program, and a halfway house. What he doesn't need is my advice."

"No. That's not it. I'll handle Will myself."

"What then?"

"Meagan, they're back."

"Flashbacks?"

"Dreams, nightmares, flashbacks. The whole nine yards," said Jack. "I feel like I'm drowning myself."

"You are," said Meagan as she put her arm around his shoulder. "Come in and sit down."

Meagan Palmer's office was like a museum of her life. There were no photographs or pictures, however. This was a museum of artifacts—of tangible things that could be handled and probed at a primal level. Jack looked around the room. On one wall hung an old Thistle sailboat's mahogany rudder, tiller and hiking stick. Beside the tiller, actually hanging off it was a cracked and worn white foul weather jacket with the words, KSU SAILING CLUB, stenciled above the left breast pocket flap. The opposite wall supported an exquisitely finished teak and brass display case with pistols poised muzzle-to-muzzle. A gold medal was suspended between them by a blue and gold ribbon. The medallion read "NCAA WOMEN'S CHAMPION—1969." Jack's glance quickly passed over the Ruger Mark I .22 caliber target pistol and rested upon the finely accurized .45 ACP—a sidearm that had saved his life more than once on the rivers of Vietnam.

Behind Meagan Palmer's ornate Louis XIV table desk and high back upholstered swivel chair, were three large framed prints of English hunt scenes, which together formed one grand panoramic view of a past life. A highly polished pair of custom riding boots with stainless steel spurs in place, stood on the matching credenza. A large Mene bronze sculpture of a mare and foal stood on the other end of the credenza—a single tricolor ribbon from the National Horse Show hanging from the mare's neck. Her office trappings announced shamelessly that Meagan Palmer, Ph.D. did not embrace defeat. She would not countenance weakness and could not accept failure. She was the perfect coach for Jack, and he found it difficult to stray too far from her reach.

As Meagan eased into her swivel chair, withdrew a leather-bound journal from her desk drawer, and opened the volume to a new blank page, her entire demeanor shifted. She placed a pair of gold-rimmed half-glasses on her nose, unscrewed the cap from an onyx fountain pen, and settled back into her sumptuous burgundy button-tufted leather chair. Dr. Palmer was poised to engage the business of the day.

"Now," she said with reassuring firmness. "Tell me exactly what happened."

"The same as before. It's the same damned nightmare that plays over and over again . . ." Jack could feel the dread of it creeping back over him. ". . . Susan going overboard; bobbing like a cork in the water. I try to turn the boat around, to get back but always lose sight of her in the spray, foam and waves. Then I wake up soaking wet and panting."

Jack barely noticed Meagan's subtle jotting of notes in her journal as he sailed back through his hellish dream.

"Okay, so what moved you to come back in this morning"?"

"I've had a pretty quiet summer," Jack said. "I never really sleep very well, but the nightmares have been gone. Now, suddenly, they're back."

"How long?"

"Two nights."

"Have you been doing anything different?"

"I wish."

"Have you changed your sleep schedule or diet?"

"Nope."

"Have you been going through old photos or videos of your summer cruises with Susan?"

"I haven't looked at those things since . . . well . . . since the funeral."

"Yes, a year ago next month," whispered Meagan, almost to herself. "Maybe that's it. Maybe your psychological clock is reminding you that autumn is near."

"I haven't thought about it."

"Hmmm. Well, do you remember what I told you last spring?"

"About needing to get back on the boat?" Jack answered.

"Precisely."

"I tried, but it just didn't work. I went there early this morning and everything came crashing down on me."

"What do you mean?" asked Meagan, totally engaged. "It felt like the boat was alive—like it was trying to consume me." Jack shook his head then stood up abruptly and headed for an escape route.

"If you walk out that door, Jack Grayson, I'll never open it to you again," Meagan screeched.

He stopped short, paused, and walked over to the wall that held the Thistle's steering gear. "Do you use this old thing anymore?" Jack asked as he lifted the sleeve of the grungy white foul weather jacket.

"No." Meagan sat down and punched the STOP button on the recorder with a quick surgical strike.

"Too tacky? Doesn't fit? What?" asked Jack.

"It was Susan's."

Jack dropped the sleeve and turned slowly toward Meagan. "No, Susan was wearing hers when . . . well, she had it on the day she fell overboard."

"Jack, Susan was wearing my coat when she died. We traded our foul weather gear at the Nationals during our senior year at Kent. Lift up the pocket flap."

Jack lifted the flap beneath the logo of the Golden Flashes and saw her name printed in faded old ink: **SUSAN WHEELER '69.** Jack ran his finger across the inscription, then dropped the flap and sat down. He struggled to avoid eye contact with Meagan.

"We did it for good luck;" said Meagan.

"I never knew."

"Just a girl thing, I guess. Anyway, we won the Nationals that year."

"Then the luck ran out," said Jack looking back to the side.

"Listen to me, Jack. Luck had nothing to do with Susan's death. You are not responsible for what happened to her. It was an accident, pure and simple and tragic, but an accident all the same. Fate took Susan from us. Fate and nothing more."

"I don't know, Meagan." I wish I could believe that. So much of that day is still so real I can't escape the agony of it all. But there are parts, like the moment she went into the water that I just can't remember."

"I can help you, Jack."

"How?"

"You need to get back on that boat," said Meagan. "You have to get out on the lake, and sail these demons out of you."

"I can't do that."

"Why not?"

Jack leaned forward in his chair. He gripped his knees and became rigid.

"Talk to me Jack. Tell me why you can't."

"I don't know Meagan. If I knew, I guess I'd be able to handle it."

Meagan pushed the RECORD button on her machine, then reached into her desk and withdrew a threefold pamphlet. "Okay. Fair enough. What do you know about regression therapy?"

"The word oxymoron comes to mind," said Jack. "Just ahead of smoke, mirrors, crystal balls, and Voodoo."

Dr. Palmer passed the folder across the table. "I want you to read the information inside this booklet. I think it will give you another perspective on some very exciting work being done right now—some work that can help you."

Jack folded the pamphlet without even glancing at it and stuffed it into his pocket. "Help me how?"

"I believe the answer to your nightmares is somewhere on that boat of Susan's. Something happened the day Susan fell overboard that is threatening you—something you're blocking out of your conscious recollection. It's all there Jack. The brain is a marvelous recorder—it stores every sight, smell and feeling we encounter. But something in each person's neurological circuitry filters the information we're able to recall. More often than not, I think, that filter spares us a lot of pain and anguish. But sometimes, like in your case, that filter denies us some vital bit of information we need to keep our lives in balance."

"And you think some hypnotic trance can remove the filter?"

"Well, maybe shake it up a little," said Meagan. "It can also put you back on the boat without actually going onboard."

Jack stood up and walked to the window. He watched the sparse mid-morning flow of boat traffic moving up and down the river past McGarvey's. He watched Captain Ernie and Maggie Wicks, on the deck of *Aphrodite* taunt each other in one of their usual boat maintenance disagreements. Jack ran his hand reverently across the glossy surface of the tiller and hiking stick he had finessed so long ago, then quietly walked over to the display case on the wall, and took the Colt .45 off its hooks. Jack pulled back the slide and peered into the chamber before snapping the weapon into firing position. He adjusted his grip, held out his arm, and formed a perfect sight picture of some unseen adversary. "Did you really shoot a 99—7x with this hog?"

"If I hadn't," answered Meagan. "That medal would have been silver instead of gold."

Jack carefully released the hammer and put the pistol back into its display case. He walked back to Meagan's desk and slid back into the hot seat. Jack searched deeply into the jade green eyes that were at once a beckoning portal and a threatening camera, poised to record his most intimate frailties. He wanted to look away, but could not—transfixed by a mesmerizing force.

"If I agree to this," said Jack. "I want you to do it."

Meagan stabbed the STOP button and leaned forward. "I don't think that would be a good idea, Jack. There's an ethical issue to consider. I've already gone farther than I should have."

"Screw the ethics."

"That's easy for you to say, Jack. I have other concerns."

"I thought I was your concern." Jack saw her expression change, and he could sense her melting down. "I'll give you a waiver."

"Okay, but you have to let me out if I see it going badly."

"Deal," said Jack.

"No consultants. No assistants."

"No problem."

Jack detected a smug little smirk on Meagan's face that ever so subtly announced her victory. *Maybe I've become a loser,* Jack thought to himself, *but I'm still in the game.* He bore once again into the green jade. "And no more tape recording."

"You're pushing your luck Captain Grayson," said Meagan as she scanned her appointment book. "We'll talk about that when I see you on Wednesday afternoon."

"Isn't that a little soon?"

"I don't want to lose you just yet."

# CHAPTER 5

Jack descended the outer staircase from Dr. Palmer's office above the Cargo Warehouse, and deeply inhaled the nor'easter that blew across Lake Erie. He reached into his pocket for his car keys then paused for a moment to check his watch. 10:35 a.m. He decided to heed Meagan's first advice of the morning and take a hike downtown. Aerobics, Jack had heard, could cure all sorts of ills, and he was certainly in the market for a cure.

It was only half a block north on Toledo Street to Vermilion's main drag. As Jack rounded the corner on Liberty Avenue he marveled at the queue of summer vacationers already standing outside the Buyer's Fair. When the wind whipped across the lake from the north, and churned the warm water into four foot waves, the "stink-potters" as Susan used to call the power boaters, walked across the bridge from Romp's Marina to indulge in Vermilion's favorite inclement weather activity—shopping.

The idyllic river harbor and picturesque lagoons were not Vermilion's only assets. Its antique shops, boutiques, jewelry stores, art galleries and ship chandlers were world class. Vermilion's old guard was provincial, to be sure, but they were also worldly. The town's movers and shakers had sailed the seven seas and traveled the world. The lagoons had long ago become an enclave for retired, semi-retired, and soon-to-be-retired corporate executives from Cleveland and Toledo. With time on their hands, money in their bank accounts, and a passion for finer things, they became the shopkeepers, merchants and dealers of their little adopted village. These "gentlemen merchants" delighted in offering only the highest quality New England style nautical artifacts, clothing, collectibles, and conversation pieces. There was not a lacquered pine trinket box anywhere in town, Jack often remarked when toying with the "Old Guard."

He promised himself that he would drop off his Rolex for its annual cleaning and tuning when he got back to the Cargo Warehouse. Jack passed by the bank and waved at the tellers who were laughing and chatting with a few customers, interrupted only briefly by a deposit, withdrawal or payment. He crossed Exchange Street and looked south at another throng of tourists standing outside the Bay Harbour Trading Company, Vermilion's premier source for "Primitive, Victorian and American Gifts and Collectibles." To the north he could see the Vermilion River and Lake Erie beyond Exchange Park. He guessed that he would soon be manning the AMVETS Post 22 French fry stand at the annual Festival of Fishes. He wondered how sales would be without Susan at the point during his shift.

The American Legion Post 397 sign caught Jack's moist eyes as he turned away from the dark images of the park. *A cup of coffee and a phone call are in order*, he thought. The Post Canteen was open every day for light meals, heavy drinking, war stories and atmosphere. It was a favorite stopping place for the boat yard and marina workers who seemed to relish entertaining the vacationers. The extra income was a welcomed addition to an ever-dwindling treasury.

"So they finally threw you out of the AMVETS and you're ready to join us in the Legion?" said a voice from behind the bar.

"Not quite," said Jack. "I served AFTER the War of 1812."

"Well, you missed a good one there," said the bartender. "Now what can I do for you sonny?"

"A hot cup of coffee, and PaPa Joe's phone number."

"I'll phone in your order Jack."

"Great. Tell Joey I want the usual ASAP, but tell him to hold the anchovies . . . on half the pizza," Jack said. "While you're doing that I need to make a call myself."

"You know where the phone is," said the burly old Legionnaire as he limped into the kitchen.

Jack walked to the wall phone and dialed Will's number. "Hey Will. I'll bet you have half the boats in the marina washed already."

"You know better than that," said Will. "I saw you here early this morning."

"Yes . . . well . . . I had to pick up something for an early meeting."

"I hope you found what you were looking for."

"Not really, but it's not important," Jack replied. "I was hoping I could get some time for a little chat."

"No can do," said Will. "I've got plans."

"It's important that we talk." Jack paused for a response but got nothing more than a faint puffing sound. "I'll swing by PaPa Joe's for a Super Supreme, and we'll have an early lunch."

"You drive a hard bargain," said Will.

"Tell Joey to hold the anchovies."

"You've got it. See you about eleven thirty." Jack hung up the phone and set a course for the grand old Wurlitzer juke box that was fabled to have been placed there by Mr. Wurlitzer himself.

The American Legion hall was an odd mélange of history and functionality. As a museum, pool room, greasy spoon, dance hall, saloon, conference center and storm refuge, the den of the old Legionnaires had no counterpart in town. The walls were full of black and white photos of boys in uniform, men on the decks of warships and under the wings of airplanes—warriors on their way to battle. Why is it, Jack wondered, that the experiences were so hideous and the memories so glorious?

Jack dropped a quarter into the mouth of the glimmering, shimmering, rainbow colored bard. He pushed "B8" almost without looking and watched the carousel of 45's spin under the searching metal claw. Dip . . . lock . . . lift . . . rotate . . . drop . . . release . . . retract. The precision movement of the machine always tweaked the engineer's side of Jack's brain. The turntable began to spin as the needle arm touched down on the dusty old record. Captain Jack Grayson held on to the glowing metallic crooner as though he were hanging on to his past. Although Frank Sinatra had died three months earlier, "Old blue eyes" gave another command performance just for Jack.

*Strangers in the night,*
*exchanging glances.*
*Wondering in the night,*
*what were the chances . . .*

Jack was lost.

"She used to dance right here on this bar," said the bartender breaking Jack's euphoric trance. "Couldn't have been more than six years old. She'd get up here and sing *On the Good Ship Lollipop*, while she tap danced to the beat. I'll be damned if it didn't feel like Shirley Temple was here in person."

Jack had heard the old stories a hundred times. Sarge Arthur, as the Legionnaires called him, made his daughter Susan a regular at the club. The constant activity, attention, stories, little jobs that grew into big ones, and secure atmosphere nurtured the little girl in untold ways that her father was unable or unwilling to provide. Susan's mother, Lorraine, had died in a difficult childbirth that left Gunnery Sergeant Gene Arthur, USMC (ret.) with the greatest challenge of his life.

The "Big War" had been just two years ended when Susan was born. America was on the move and opportunities abounded for men and women with vision, drive and determination. Gene Arthur had two out of three. The "vision" was supplied by the Wheeler Development Corporation. Gordon Percy Wheeler never quite understood what his daughter saw in her young Marine, short of his flashy Class A uniform and a chiseled body that brought it to life. But he did understand that his granddaughter was in jeopardy, with the death of her mother, and he was not about to lose the last of the Wheeler ladies. So Percy Wheeler invited his son-in-law to learn the real estate development business—from the lagoons up.

The economic priorities of World War II turned the public's attention to the war effort. By 1948 the Wheeler Development Corporation owned a third of the land in the Vermilion Lagoons, but most of it was still undeveloped. An early spring flood of the Vermilion River in 1950 devastated many of the homes in the lagoons and raised serious questions about the future of any housing development there. But the post-war fifties became a decade of explosive growth fueled by the spirit of victorious warriors who believed they were invincible—that anything was possible. The "can do" attitude of Sarge Arthur coupled to the "vision" of his father-in-law, Percy, persuaded the U.S. Army Corps of Engineers to build a flood control dam on the upper Vermilion River—a master stroke that would turn a flood ravaged folly into the most prestigious waterfront housing development on the entire Great Lakes.

But the creation of "master strokes" takes time, effort and nights away from home. So, while Sgt. Gene Arthur was struggling as a single parent, the Legionnaires adopted Susan as their own. For many of the "old soldiers" who fought in the "Great War to end all wars," and who had lost sons and daughters in Europe and the Pacific, Susan Wheeler Arthur became a surrogate child. That relationship was solidified when on the eve of Susan's "Sweet Sixteen" birthday party, her father suddenly disappeared, never to be heard of again. Incessant rumors of family intrigue were fanned by Percy Wheeler's quick move to obtain guardianship over his granddaughter.

The *piece de resistance* was a legal name change that forever pruned the name "Arthur" from the Wheeler family tree. Susan grew up at the American Legion Hall tap dancing, singing, cleaning, bussing tables, cooking, bookkeeping, refereeing, listening, laughing, and crying with the biggest family a kid could have. It was the Legion Hall where Jack and Susan held their wedding reception. It was the Legion Hall where the Grayson's held their "public" birthday parties. Now it was the Legion Hall where Jack came to find his family.

"God, how I miss her," Jack said as he turned away from the juke box.

"We all miss her Jack," said the bartender.

"The good part is that we had her for 49 years . . . a great 49 years. And we still have her right here with us."

Jack sipped his black coffee and scanned the rows of photographs hanging everywhere. The family wall was dominated by pictures of Percy, Sarge, and Susan . . . and Susan . . . and Susan.

It was like a scrapbook of her life, and of her death. Jack became transfixed upon a watercolor of himself laying Easter lilies on Susan's grave in the Wheeler plot of the historic Vermilion Cemetery. A loud buzzer from the kitchen broke his trance.

"They're fishing your anchovies out of the oven," yelled the bartender. "You'd better get over there."

Jack threw a dollar bill on the bar and started for the door. Halfway there he turned around and asked, "When's the last time young Will Daysart stopped in?"

"Haven't seen him for months, thank goodness. The kid is trouble."

"So I'm told," Jack said as he left.

Jack hurried past the Chamber of Commerce, across Main Street then north across Liberty Avenue to Higgins Pharmacy. He was tempted to stop in for an old fashioned cherry phosphate at the soda fountain, but checked himself. Duty called. West on Liberty Avenue past the Old Prague Restaurant and Jack could smell the aroma of sauerbraten wafting from the strategically placed kitchen vent. Right next door was PaPa Joe's.

Joey Mariano may have been the only person since Captain Alva Bradley who came to Vermilion strictly to make money. After a nasty family feud that left Mariano's Family Restaurant in ruins (that's how Joey Mariano described his brother's management of the family shrine) Joey opened the first pizzeria in Vermilion. Thirty-two years later, PaPa Joe's was an institution. There was no delivery, no table service, nowhere to sit, and not much room to stand around and gossip. There was only the pizza. "The best damned pies on the North Coast," Joey often said.

The only known PaPa Joe's menu innovation in history came in the mid-eighties. For over twenty years pizza was the one and only fare, painstakingly fashioned in six, ten, fourteen and twenty inch rounds. "Square pizzas are for squares," Joey would bellow when a naive vacationing yuppie tried to order pizza by the foot. After more than one unpleasant encounter Joey's daughter and co-proprietor, Angie, "got daddy a little buzzed on Bardolino Classico," and cajoled him into adding crisp garden salads and freshly baked pies. The latter became so popular after Svenson's Bakery closed, that July 4, 1990 saw a new sign hung above the small storefront: PaPa Joe's Pizza & Pies.

A tell-tale warning bell jingled as Jack Grayson pulled open the front door. At the same moment a buzzer sounded on the large stainless steel pizza oven.

"Do you time EVERYTHING so well, Captain Grayson?"

Jack felt a rush of blood to his face, as he hesitated a moment at the open door and stammered, "I do my best."

"I'll bet you do," said Angelina Mariano as she scooped a twenty-incher off the hearth, and deftly slid it on to the wooden counter behind her.

A few moments of silence allowed Jack to get his composure, step inside the shop, and slip up to the counter. Although "39ish," Angie could have passed for a woman in her twenties. Dressed in Gianni Versachi jeans, a loose fitting green surgical scrub top, Vermilion's obligatory boat shoes, and a greasy stained red apron, Angie looked like a college kid working the boardwalk in Ocean City. Her shoulder length black hair was tied back in a ponytail and adorned with a long scarf sporting the colors of the Italian national flag. She could have been a walking scoop of Spumoni ice cream, Jack thought. Then he suppressed the image.

Angie put a white cardboard pizza box on the counter in front of Jack, who was already fumbling for his wallet. "I see you and Will are eating in today."

"How did you know that?" asked Jack.

"Half an order of anchovies is definitely not your style."

"Is there anything the good citizens of Vermilion don't know?"

"I don't think so Jack, but I'm always willing to learn."

Jack laid a twenty on the counter. Angie rang up the $15.95 sale on the ancient brass NCR cash register, deposited the $20 bill, and counted out the change. Jack held out his hand for a moment, and Angie steadied it from underneath while she pressed the wad of paper and coins into his damp palm.

"Where's Joey this morning?" asked Jack.

"The same place as every Monday morning lately—St. Angela's in Cleveland. He drives into Little Italy every Monday morning for early Mass and breakfast with his *paisan*."

"I didn't know that," said Jack.

"I'm just full of surprises."

Jack tried to pull away gently, but Angie clamped down and leaned across the counter.

"We're never very busy on Monday mornings you know. Daddy told me to close up and enjoy myself once in a while. What do you think?"

"You should probably take his advice, Angie." Jack pulled away, stuffed the change in his pocket, grabbed the pizza box and headed for the door.

"Why don't you stop in again next week?"

Jack heard Angie's words trailing off behind the-sound of the warning bell jingling over his head and was relieved to find himself amid the sanctuary of the tree-lined public street. In the year since Susan Grayson's death, Jack had become Vermilion's "most eligible bachelor," a label he had grown to despise. He was still astonished that within a fortnight of the funeral of their princess, the townsfolk had begun to whisper of matchmaking.

Jack first got wind of the gossip at a Vermilion United Methodist Church potluck supper. As a church trustee he couldn't avoid the quarterly ritual. After the potluck, the gossip spread to the yacht club, the Legion Hall, the AMVETS Lodge, and even the sacrosanct Captain's Quarters.

Maggie Wicks carried the message which surprised even Jack: *I had lunch with Angie Mariano the other day . . . She's worried about Joey's health . . . She said he's spending more and more time at that old church in Cleveland . . . She's afraid there's something wrong; that he's not sharing with her . . . I'm concerned about what will happen to her when her dad dies . . . She never seemed interested in marrying again after Tino's accident . . . Jack, maybe you should make an overture . . . It would be good for both of you . . . She's such a lovely girl.*

Jack had even heard himself described as "Prince Charles without the baggage." The historical allusion couldn't be avoided. Susan had died on September 6, 1997—the day of Princess Diana's funeral in London. Jack and Susan sat up, with the rest of the world, at 3:00 a.m. to watch BBC live television coverage of the procession to Westminster Abbey. They cried together when Diana's brother, Earl Spencer, ended his eulogy with the words:

> *I would like to end by thanking God for the small mercies he has shown us' at this dreadful time; for taking Diana at her most beautiful and radiant, and when she had so much joy in her private life.*

Jack would later copy those words from an old newspaper clipping and wonder when, or if, he would ever be able to thank God for "small mercies." The paradox was that although Charles, Duke of Windsor and Jack Grayson shared the burden of living as widower princes, nobody in the realm wanted marriage and happiness for Charles, while everyone in the hamlet encouraged liaisons for Jack.

Back inside PaPa Joe's Pizza & Pies, Angelina Mariano watched Jack Grayson dart across Liberty Avenue. Her smile turned taut as she lifted the telephone receiver off the wall next to the counter. Her highly polished red finger tips tapped out seven digits without hesitation. After one ring, Angie heard a click and a voice: "Yeah," she replied. "He's on the way."

Jack broke into a slow jog across Main Street, past Exchange Park, between some parked cars, and south across Liberty Avenue. Before he reached Buyer's Fair he slowed to a walk, then, to a shuffle as he breathed shallow, fast breaths and felt his heart pounding. Meagan was right, he thought. *I need to get back on track . . . back on the track . . . whatever.*

# CHAPTER 6

Will Daysart carried the large plastic bucket, long-handled boat brush, and bottle of boat wash off the deck of *SEAQUESTOR*. He stowed the bucket and bottle then snapped the boat brush into large clips on the side of the huge wooden dock box. He checked his watch again. 11:20 a.m. Angie's phone call alerted him that Jack should be arriving any moment, so he grabbed a white plastic water hose and gave the gleaming white ketch a final drenching.

Will was reeling in the hose near the water faucet when Jack Grayson carne through the back door of GrayDays Marine. He was carrying a 20 inch square box. "As long as she's all scrubbed up," said Jack. "Let's have lunch on board. For old time's sake."

"Damn Jack. I just hosed her down. Let's go inside."

"A little water never hurt anyone," said Jack as he hopped on board. Meagan Palmer would be proud of his crossing this hurdle he thought. "Grab a towel and we'll wipe down the cockpit."

Will winced at the command but dutifully reached into the dock box for a large old beach towel. He followed Jack on board and quickly wiped down the gel coat seats in the spacious cockpit forward of the mizzen mast. As Jack lifted the teak table into position from its hinge on the steering pedestal, Will subtly balled up the towel and flipped it over the padlock on the lazarette hatch near the stern.

"You've kept her looking smart," Jack said as he scanned the deck fore and aft.

"How's everything down below?"

"You ought to know," Will smirked. "You've been down there more recently than me. I haven't been on board for weeks."

Will's lack of deference peeved Jack but he avoided the confrontation needed to drive home the point. This was neither the time nor the place to pick a fight, he reasoned. Instead he flipped open the top of the pizza box and handed Will a large slice of the pie. "I guess if anything goes wrong, she'll tell us—one way or another."

Seamen have a need to anthropomorphize their ships that few landlubbers understand. Seafaring is a desolate and lonely life, perhaps the more so because desolate and lonely men so often find refuge there. Yet even these outcasts crave a point of attachment, some relationship that is secure, if not entirely predictable. The mistress conjured up by seamen in the form of their ships could bring them sustenance, tranquility, structure and safety. She could also bring danger and tragedy.

*SEAQUESTOR* had become the tragic mistress in Jack Grayson's life. She had betrayed him, abused him, and stolen from him. Such thoughts were not uncommon among sailors in their fragile relationships with ships. The lore of the sea is laden with superstition and taboos, signs and jinxes—of curses to be avoided. This jealous mistress of Jack's, many believed, had killed and would necessarily kill again. She was forever tainted and never again to be trusted except by the foolhardy or uninformed. In the small boating community of Vermilion the word was out, the curse was known, and the warning was heeded by all. There were no buyers to be found, at any price, for a 40 foot ketch whose beauty was legendary, but whose soul was as ominous as an autumn fog over the shoals of Long Point.

Jack remembered how the Bay Village house where Marilyn Sheppard was murdered was on the market for nearly five years. He recalled the eerie feeling he had driving down Lake Road beneath the towering red oak trees, past the ancient Lakeside Cemetery near the Sheppard house, much like Ichabod Crane stealing through *Sleepy Hollow.*

Jack recalled a recent national news broadcast reporting that "one year after the death of little beauty queen, Jon Benet Ramsey, the family home in Boulder, Colorado still has not been sold." The child beauty pageant star had been beaten, sexually assaulted, tortured, killed and buried in the basement of that house. He thought as he watched, *who the hell would want to buy such a place?* Demons are fine in the movies, but not in real life.

Jack chomped down on a large slice of pizza that featured two crusty anchovies on the end, while Will carefully plucked a salty sliver off his slice. He smiled as the kid flipped the contaminant overboard. Jack resisted the temptation to reminisce and got down to business. "When was our last inquiry on the boat?"

"Seven, maybe eight weeks ago."

"Got any ideas?"

"Yeah, sail her out into the lake and open the seacock," Will said.

"I'd still know where she is." Jack started on his second slice of pizza. "Besides, I told you I'd never sail this boat again."

"You also said you'd never get back on her again. But here you are."

"Things change. Memories fade."

"You know, Jack. Life gets easier when you just kick back and let it happen."

Jack was surprised by Will's insight. The kid had struck a note and Jack was beginning to feel old wounds throbbing, but he didn't want to cut off the dialogue. It was the most he and his god son had talked for a year—since the funerals.

"Will, I've kicked back about as far as I dare, and it's not working for me. Coming back on board is part of my therapy."

"So, you've been to see the all-knowing, all-seeing Dr. Palmer again."

"News travels fast," Jack said as he finished off the last crust.

"We're starved for excitement around here. Especially something trashy."

Jack let the barb pass. Some day the kid would understand. One day when he was older and lonelier. But for now Jack backed away from the hot grudge that Will carried against Meagan Palmer for past indiscretions.

Dr. Palmer asked about you."

"I doubt that," said Will.

"I'm sorry you feel that way, but I really didn't come down here to discuss Meagan Palmer."

"And I don't think you came here to get an update on my efforts to sell this barge," said Will as he closed the top on the empty pizza box.

"You're right Will. I didn't."

Will leaned back into the corner of the cockpit seat and propped his feet up on the yacht's large stainless steel helm—a gesture that grated on Jack like fingernails dragging across a chalkboard. Jack knew the kid felt a lecture coming, so he simply took a deep breath and eased into his mission. "I know you haven't been happy here since your Dad died . . ."

"That's an understatement," said Will interrupting.

"Please let me get this out Will." Jack ignored the annoying little gesture of mock condescension that Will displayed. "I know it's been rough for you here without your father. I miss him too. I also know that I could have supported you more, tried to be more of a father figure to you. But with Susan's death so soon after your Dad's, I just couldn't pull myself together. Susan was ready to teach you. She believed that if you threw yourself into this business you'd grow to love it like she and your Dad did. I loved watching Susan do what she loved, and what she had a passion for. But after she died I realized this wasn't for me. I had done my thing and enjoyed my career. But after, twenty years at sea it was time for me to think of someone else. That someone was Susan. I devoted my life to her and to everything she loved. When she drowned, I drowned along with her . . . I'm still drowning with her." Jack grabbed a napkin off the cockpit table and turned away.

Will's gaze was now transfixed on Jack. He moved his feet off the helm, wrapped his arms around his knees, and did not speak.

"Will, I'm telling you these things because I want you to know why I let you down. It's not an excuse, and I'm not looking for forgiveness. I just have this feeling that in many ways you've suffered just like me. I know how close you were to your Dad. I know how much you tried to please him and help him. It was a special quality of yours that we wished our Jimmy had . . ." Jack looked away again and ran his fingers through his hair, then continued. "But people are different. Sometimes it just takes us too long to appreciate the beauty of those differences. You and I loved those differences in Susan and your Dad. We lived our lives through them and for them, but now they're gone and we're left here to pick up the pieces and make some sense of our lives. We're actually much more alike than we've been willing to admit lately."

Jack knew that he had will's attention. His instincts told him he had the kid on the ropes, so he moved in a little closer. "It's time to make some changes, and we've come up with an idea we think you'll like."

"We?" Will asked. "We who?"

"People who care about you."

"The Captain's Quarters?"

"Your father's friends."

"My keepers."

"Your new partners," said Jack.

"I can't wait to hear this one," said Will as he leaned back into the cockpit and put his feet back on the wheel.

"What's the biggest tourist attraction on Lake Erie?"

"I didn't know this was going to be a test."

"Come on Will, humor me for a moment."

"Okay. The islands, I guess."

"You guess right," said Jack. "Now which of the Lake Erie Islands is the biggest draw?"

"Put-In-Bay."

"Close enough. South Bass Island." Jack could see the nautical chart in his mind. In the far western end of Lake Erie, between Point Pelee on the Canadian shore and the Marblehead peninsula in Ohio are strung the pearls of Lake Erie. Five large islands form an inland archipelago starting in the north with Pelee Island. Six miles southwest of Pelee lies North Bass Island, followed by Middle Bass Island a mile to the southwest, and South Bass Island two miles farther south. Kelly's Island, seven miles to the east of South Bass, and due south of Pelee Island completes the necklace.

"Why South Bass Island?" asked Jack.

"Put-In-Bay, the boat docks, the yacht club, the Wooden Nickel Saloon."

"And?"

"And what?" asked Will moving his feet off the steering wheel.

"History," Jack said as he reached into the companionway and came out with a tattered old scrapbook in his hand."

"Where did you find that old relic?"

"It was one of the 'treasures' Susan would never part with, said Jack as he tossed the book to Will. He watched as Will carefully opened the cover and spied the title page.

The Battle of Lake Erie
By Willie Daysart

"I remember when Susan took me out to the monument so I could do what she called a 'real live' report for my ninth grade history class. She told me that history didn't make much sense unless we learned how to live with it."

Jack wondered how Susan would rate his success at "living with history" lately as he pondered the reverent, almost weepy quality to Will's voice. Jack sensed that he was losing momentum, so he grabbed the book off Will's lap. "Tell me what you remember."

"What? About the trip with Susan?"

Tempted though he was to hear the story, Jack stayed his course. "No. I want you to tell me about the battle."

"Well, once I got rid of the 'Willie, things started to look up for me."

"Come on Will. Think back and give me the set up for the battle."

Will gazed off into the distance, toward the islands, and began. "It was in the fall of 1813."

"September 10th," Jack interjected.

"The British were messing up American shipping in the Atlantic Ocean, and were kidnapping American sailors to serve on their warships. Some congressmen from the Western Reserve wanted to get revenge by invading that little part of Canada just across Lake Erie."

"They called it Upper Canada back then, and it held some of the best farm land in all the Great Lakes."

"Right," said Will.

"But the British Navy was up in the Detroit River . . ."

"At Arnherstburg."

"Yeah . . . they controlled the lake. So President Madison sent Commodore Oliver Hazard Perry to Lake Erie to wipe out the British."

"The only problem was," said Jack. "That Perry was only 26 years old, about your age, and had no ships."

"That's right. I remember now. He built a whole fleet down in Erie, Pennsylvania."

Jack turned a few pages in the scrapbook and read aloud. "Perry built nine ships in only six months and floated them across a sandbar in the fog to slip past a British blockade." Jack looked up and said, "That alone should have made him famous." Will got back into the battle. "Perry's big ship was the *Lawrence* and he had another large ship called the . . ."

"Niagara," Jack said. "Which he put under the command of Lt. Jesse Elliott, who almost sunk the whole British fleet."

"Give me the names of the British ships," Will asked, now fully caught up in "living" the event.

"Captain Barclay's flagship was the *Detroit* which had about 20 heavy canons. The other large frigate in the British fleet was the 17 gun *Charlotte*. Perry took on the Detroit and left the Charlotte to Lt. Elliott." Jack paused for a moment and handed the scrapbook back to Will. "Now tell me about the battle."

Will turned through a few pages and said, "I have to read this to you. I worked on these four paragraphs all night."

"As soon as the British fleet of six ships was in sight, west of Middle Bass Island, Perry led his ships through a horrific barrage of British long guns. The *Lawrence* was bruised and burning as she broke through the perimeter of British ships and unleashed a crackling fusillade of smaller but more plentiful canons. The *Detroit* was wounded as Perry looked astern for support from Lt. Elliott in the Niagara. Victory was within sight.

The same extreme circumstances that forged Commodore Perry, also defined Lt. Elliott. Whether from incompetence, terror or cowardice, the young Lieutenant failed to advance into the battle, a failure that sealed the fate of the *Lawrence*. When Captain Barclay saw that Perry was trapped alone inside his battle line, and that Lt. Elliott was not engaging, he trained all his guns on the *Lawrence*. Under heavy fire from both of the large British frigates, Commodore Perry soon had to abandon his burning and sinking flagship."

"Now comes the really great part," said Will.

Jack was as deep into the battle as Perry and Elliott, and hung on every word from Will's old project.

"Oliver Hazard Perry struck his battle standard, a crude homemade flag with the words *Don't Give up the Ship*, jumped into a row boat and pulled across the battle line to the *Niagara* which still had not fired a shot. On the quarterdeck, as Perry took command of *Niagara*, Lt. Elliott asked 'How is the day going?' Perry answered curtly, 'Badly enough,' then he turned the *Niagara* around and sailed her into the battle.

Will paused again and looked around the cockpit, like he was searching for something.

"What?" asked Jack. "Come on let's hear the end of the story."

"Do you have something left to drink?"

You must be related to poor Lt. Elliott," Jack quipped as he flipped a can of Pepsi to Will. He watched Will pop the top, take a long drink and gasp. Finally, Will seemed ready to end the battle.

"Just after Perry abandoned the *Lawrence* the wind shifted and pushed the two wounded and burning British frigates together. The big ships became tangled and tethered together. For a few minutes Barclay could not separate the ships and could do nothing to aim his guns toward the remnant of the American fleet that was bearing down on him under a fresh breeze and full sail. Perry unleashed a ferocious fusillade from every gun left in his tiny fleet. The British quickly surrendered rather than be killed. The Battle of Lake Erie was over."

Jack slowly broke away from the story that had transported back almost 200 years to the scene of the battle. "You said you worked on those pages all night?"

"Sure did," said Will triumphantly.

"Hmmm. Somehow those words don't sound like you in the . . . what was it? The ninth grade?"

"That's just what aunt Susan said. Okay, so maybe I copped a few lines from some history book. So what?"

"It's piracy, Will. You didn't just "cop" a few lines; you stole them and used them as your own without giving the author credit. I think that's called plagiarism.

"What a naughty little boy, I was. Maybe some good day I'll find out who wrote that stuff and correct the record."

"Anytime you start telling the truth is a good day," said Jack.

Will thought about that for a few seconds, but decided not to take the bait. Instead he looked up at Jack and consumed the rest of his Pepsi. Then he smiled and said, "Now it's test time for you."

"Okay, hit me with your best shot."

"What message did Commodore Perry send to General William Henry Harrison after the battle?"

Jack stood up and struck his best actor's pose. "We have met the enemy and they are ours. Two ships, two brigs, one schooner and one sloop." He took a deep theatrical bow that got a chuckle out of Will.

"How did you know that?

"It was part of my Plebe knowledge at the Academy," Jack said as he twirled his large class ring around his finger. "The upper classmen forced us to learn all sorts of trivial facts that seemed useless—until now."

"I'm missing something here Jack. Where is all this going and what does it have to do with me?"

"Hang in here with me a few more minutes," Jack said.

"To commemorate Perry's victory over the British the State of Ohio built that grand old limestone monument that Susan took you to see for your report. That monument and all the history that surrounds it draws thousands of tourists to the island every year."

"So?"

"So, how do tourists get to South Bass Island?"

"By boat."

"From where?"

"Sandusky."

Jack could see a spark of interest in Will's eyes, so he pressed on with his little history game.

"Have you ever driven from here to Sandusky, and then hopped the ferry to Put-In-Bay?"

"Yeah," said Will. "Last summer Angie . . . uh . . . yeah; I met some of my friends over there."

*Angie huh? This one gets around more than I imagined* . . . Jack smiled inside. But that discussion was for another day so Jack let the slip-of-tongue pass without comment. "How long did it take to make the whole trip—door to dock?"

"About two and a half hours, by the time I parked the car, got my ticket, waited for the ferry and crossed over to the island."

"That's about average," said Jack.

"Now, how long does it take to get there from Vermilion by power boat?"

"About ninety minutes—dock to dock."

"Bingo!" said Jack. "Your keepers, as you call them, want to run a tourist boat from here to South Bass Island."

"So?"

"They . . ." Jack leaned forward. "WE . . . want you to run the business."

Now Will was standing, with his hands on the ketch's helm. He was quiet for several moments, and Jack delighted in the vibrations from the machinery grinding in the kid's head. "I can't run a passenger boat," said Will. "You know that I don't have a license. I don't want to get a license. Hell, I don't even like boats."

So it was finally out, Jack thought. Everyone in town seemed to know that young Will Daysart had no interest in the boat business, but no one wanted to face it. What else was the kid going to do to support himself they grumbled? *The marina and historic house are landmarks. They have to be maintained, and Willie Daysart will simply have to rise to the occasion. So much for community wisdom.* With the passage of each month the house looked worse, the business saw fewer customers, and Will drifted farther from the nest.

"We know that." said Jack. "And that's the beauty of the plan. Maggie Wicks will run the boat, and you'll run the whole tourist operation from the island."

"Tourist operation?"

"The whole enchilada. The boat dock, reception center, restaurant, golf carts, bicycles, maps, tour guides, gifts and trinkets. What do you think?"

Will stepped out of the cockpit and on to the deck. "I think you're all crazy, that's what I think. And I have to get out of here. I have an appointment in Lorain."

Of course the kid was right, Jack thought as he stayed put in his seat. But there was more going on inside young Will Daysart than was betrayed by his hasty outburst. *Don't give up the ship*, he thought to himself. "Will you at least think it over?" asked Jack.

"Sure. Why not? It's not like I have a whole lot to lose."

Jack watched the flippant youngster jump off the boat, and remembered how often he had just as casually remarked, what have I got to lose? A damp chill fell over him as he sat alone again on Susan's ketch. For a moment he considered going back down into the cabin to retrieve the log book he had dropped earlier in the morning. He walked over to the companionway and began to dial in the combination lock sequence. Before he could finish, a sense of dread and panic overtook and froze him.

The demons were awake.

# CHAPTER 7

Down on the Vermilion River, alongside the dock at McGarvey's Nautical Restaurant, on the deck of *Aphrodite*, a meeting between Captain Maggie Wicks and Captain Ernie Beckett had reached critical mass. These two volatile personalities had been too close for too long.

"I don't know how in the hell you could let this happen," barked Ernie Beckett, the road map of tiny broken capillaries in his face radiating fuchsia.

"I didn't LET it happen Ernie," volleyed Maggie. "It just happened and then I discovered it."

"That's what Eleanor used to say when her car stopped after the oil pressure light had been on for a week."

"Don't patronize me with that sexist bull shit."

"Then stop talking like some hurt little girl," growled Ernie. "And start taking responsibility for your ship."

"Start? Did you say START taking responsibility?" yelled Maggie, now nose-to-nose with the old sailing master. "You're really starting to piss me off."

Maggie Wicks had a point. She had no problem taking on responsibility, and she had no problem dressing down anyone who questioned her capabilities. She had done it many times in the past. After graduation from Heidelberg College in Tiffin, Ohio with a degree in music education, Maggie Wicks discovered she had made a dreadful mistake. She could not bear the thought of wasting away in front of some eighth grade band during the day and dying a little more with each sour note in the parlor while she gave piano lessons at night. She had watched her mother do that.

So at the age of twenty-two years, on April 15, 1970, Margaret Elizabeth Wicks filed her income tax return, in person, at the Internal Revenue Service booth in the bustling lobby of the Celebrese Federal Office Building at Ninth & Lakeside in Cleveland, then walked north on Ninth Street to give herself a birthday present—one she would never forget. She charged into the District Headquarters of the United States Coast Guard and enlisted.

Maggie Wicks was a product of the turbulent liberating sixties. Rather than "buck the system," however, she opted to work for changes from the inside.

She wanted adventure, excitement, challenges, and more than anything she wanted to make a difference—to leave her mark on the world by helping people. Since "HELP" was the mating call mariners used to attract the Coast Guard, it was just what Maggie was looking for. She also knew that the United States Coast Guard was the first of the armed forces to give women real opportunities for command positions on fighting and rescue ships.

After a week of physical and psychological examinations, followed by a battery of officer aptitude tests, Maggie was accepted to Officer Candidate School in New London. Nineteen weeks later, Ensign M.E. Wicks accepted her commission with a snappy salute to the Commandant, and a wave to her mother in the reviewing stand. Maggie immediately applied for sea duty and was promptly assigned as a supply officer on a Coast Guard cutter patrolling the Bering Sea and Aleutian Islands from her base in Juneau, Alaska.

But Maggie Wicks did not see herself forever passing out dungarees and heavy weather gear, so she studied and snooped and learned everyone's job. Fitness reports were glowing, and the Coast Guard quickly realized it had a rising star in its grasp. An aptitude for organization and navigation landed Lt.(jg) Wicks in an assignment as navigation officer aboard a drug patrol boat out of Miami—a post she held for 14 months. A promotion to full Lieutenant led to a billet as Executive Officer on a 105 foot cutter berthed in Woods Hole, Massachusetts.

Maggie would remain second in command of the *TICONDEROGA* for a year, and ready for a ship of her own, when disaster struck. *TICONDEROGA* was called out to the Grand Banks late in September for a rescue effort on one of the local fishing fleets that was being pummeled by an autumn storm. After steaming for two days in forty foot waves, the rescue team spotted one of the trawlers listing badly, without power, and taking on water with each new wave that carried over her deck house.

As second-in-command, Lt. Wicks donned her survival suit and went on deck to supervise the rigging of a breeches buoy that would run from the *TICONDEROGA* to the bridge of the wounded trawler. The breeches buoy was basically an old fashioned running clothes line with a pulley on each end and a pair of canvass drawers hanging off the line. The idea is to shoot a line to the sinking ship, pull over and secure one end of the rig, then load one seaman at a time into the breeches and haul them back to the rescue craft. The maneuver was one of the oldest known to seafaring. It is a delicate maneuver in gale force winds, but necessary when small rescue craft and helicopters cannot be launched. The chances of plucking men out of the cold North Atlantic under these conditions was slim to none, so the breeches buoy became the fishermen's only hope of survival.

Maggie tied herself off on a deck stanchion—the standard drill in heavy weather operations—and directed the procedure from the weather deck of the cutter. When TICONDEROGA had maneuvered within a boat length of the trawler, Maggie signaled for the Lyle gun to shoot a line to the fishing boat. On the first shot of the small canon, a coiled polyester line ran out to the sinking ship and was quickly retrieved by the stranded crew. Within minutes the fishermen succeeded in securing the wooden block and sheave that held their "clothes line."

Just as the first transfer began, a rogue wave appeared out of nowhere. The sixty-foot breaker crashed over the windward side of TICONDEROGA. Working off the leeward side of the cutter, Maggie never saw it coming. She was swept over the side of the ship but was secured to the deck by her harness and ten foot tether. That was the good news. The bad news was that as the ship rolled, Maggie was beaten against the leeward side of the ship's hull like an orange ball on a rubber band smack . . . smack . . . smacking a paddle. By the time Maggie's crew pulled her back on deck, she was unconscious and bleeding heavily from her mouth and nose. She had nearly been thrashed to death.

It was astonishing, she later thought, how quickly the fisherman can become the fish. Three months of rest, repair and rehabilitation in a Navy hospital, a commendation for valor, a promotion to Lieutenant Commander, and a medical retirement ended Maggie Wicks' dream of command—almost.

Aphrodite was not a Coast Guard cutter, but she was a vintage eighty foot Sparkman & Stephens yacht, custom-built in the early fifties as a Wall Street financier's Hudson River palatial barge. And now, she too was wounded.

"Pissed off, are you now?" said Captain Ernie Beckett. "That's good, because that's when you do your best work."

Maggie's eyes betrayed her rage, as she leaned in, ready to fire the next volley. But then her glare slowly softened in the aura of Captain Beckett's widening smile and raised eyebrows. Years at sea, in command of men who were often tested to the limits of their endurance, had given Ernie credentials in clinical psychology unmatched by most universities.

"Okay. Fair enough. I forgive you, you old coot."

"I'm long past forgiveness, lady."

"Don't be so sure," said Maggie.

"Now, what are we going to do about this little leak?"

"You're going to run down to Toledo on one engine, get hauled out, have them pull the shaft, straighten it out or replace it, and get back to work."

"It's not that simple," said Maggie. "I already talked to the yard and they can't haul the boat for a month." Maggie detected a glint in Ernie's eyes when he realized she was a small step ahead of him.

"What about Detroit?"

"They're behind on a big repair contract for Cleveland Cliffs and can't get to me anytime this year."

"Hell, if you wait for Toledo the season will be over by the time you get back into the water," said Ernie.

"Maybe not," said Maggie. "I don't think the shaft is bent. It looks to me like a nut sheared off, and then the shaft vibration cracked the stuffing box."

"Not likely. I think you hit something, bent the prop and then the vibration shook everything apart."

Maggie knew a little something about engineering herself and realized that either scenario was possible. The stuffing box is a steel cylinder containing greased sisal or hemp packing that compresses around the engine's drive shaft as it exits the hull of the ship. The cylindrical box has a large clamp around it that is tightened with a stuffing nut, until water flow from outside the hull is nearly stopped. A water trickle mingled with the greasy packing material lubricates the turning shaft. When the nut is too tight the packing heats up from friction and burns, often damaging the drive shaft. If the nut is too loose, unwanted water ends up in the bilge straining the pumps and sometimes even flooding the ship.

Maggie set her jaw again, and took a deep breath. "Ernie, if I had run over something, or hit bottom, I would have felt it. I was taking on water before I felt the vibration."

"Well, the bottom line is the same. You can't run that starboard engine until the stuffing box is repaired and you know the condition of the propeller shaft." Ernie turned his face into the wind, took a deep breath and continued. "And you can't do that until you get her hauled out. By then we're liable to lose the kid and the deal."

"Listen," said Maggie. "I wonder if Jack Grayson still has his SCUBA gear. Maybe he'll get in the water and take a look to see whether the prop or strut is damaged."

"Scuba gear? Sure he has it. He also has a boat, a boat business, a Master's license, and a house on the lake."

"The point being?" asked Maggie.

"Everything in Jack's life is floatin' in water. Everything except Jack."

Maggie cringed as Ernie leaned over the rail and dribbled a gob of nasty dark spittle that had formed from the disgusting tobacco he always carried somewhere in his cheek.

"You really are a nasty old man."

"Maybe so. But I'm also right about Jack Grayson. I've seen it too many times before to be wrong."

"Seen what?" "The fear that eats a man alive from the inside when he's had a scrape with death."

"Jack has already faced more danger and death than most people ever read about," said Maggie. "He got the Navy Cross for his service in Vietnam."

"Yeah. But that was thirty years ago. He was young and had nothing to lose." Ernie squinted through his weathered eyes at Maggie. "You know the feeling don't you?"

For the first time Maggie could remember, Ernie seemed to acknowledge her work in the Coast Guard and the near-death experience that sent her back home. She stood a little taller and beamed a little brighter at the backhanded compliment. All at once Maggie Wicks felt that she and the ancient mariner in front of her shared common ground.

"I get your drift," said Maggie. "After my accident it took a very long time for me to get back on the deck of a ship. Even now when a storm rolls over the lake, I start to breathe a little heavier." Maggie was lost in the confused sea of her memories; a sea that at once beckoned her and warned her away. She was feeling that same combination of exhilaration, doubt and anguish that all adventurers feel in their inevitable moments of desperation. These were feelings she would never want to extinguish—of events she would never want to repeat.

"So what did you do about it?" Ernie asked breaking the trance. "Do about what?"

"Your fear about getting back on a ship?"

Maggie smiled at the little thrill of being swept into the web that the master manipulator had spun. "As I recall, you made me an offer 'I couldn't refuse.'"

"Exactly. So let's take your idea about the scuba gear and see if we can encourage Jack to get his feet wet again."

"And if he refuses?"

Ernie spit over the rail again. "We'll just have to make him an offer HE can't refuse." Ernie put his whiskered chin into the wind and inhaled deeply. "Invite him down here for a chat."

"I'll call him tonight," said Maggie. "After he's had a chance to talk to young Will."

"Okay, but I think I'll stop over at the marina and soften him up a little bit."

# CHAPTER 8

"You look like you've just seen a ghost," Captain Ernie Beckett said as he approached Jack Grayson on the pier alongside *SEAQUESTOR*.

The old salt had uncanny instincts, Jack thought as he fought to regain his composure. He wondered what it must have been like sailing with Captain Beckett in the old days—the days before all the gadgets and electronics—the days when a seaman had nothing to rely on but his experience and his instinct. Ernie was one of the last of an exclusive class of mariners that were slowly becoming extinct, and Jack treasured every moment he was near the "Old Man."

"No ghosts," said Jack. "Just memories and too much pizza." Jack regretted his deceit, but was not in the mood for a relevant discussion.

"Shame to see a boat sit there like that, wasting away," said Ernie. "Somethin' unholy about it."

"She's been on the market since the ice melted off the lake, and we haven't had a single serious offer."

"Boat's tainted," growled the old man. "She's got a gremlin in her."

"You don't really believe that do you?"

Captain Beckett did not answer immediately. He just stood there slowly surveying, the ketch with wary knowing eyes. Then Jack felt Ernie's eyes boring into him. "We both believe it Jack. Trouble is you don't trust yourself anymore."

The old sage had struck a chord, a sour one, but Jack dismissed his urge to lash back. Ernie Beckett's instincts were as sharp as ever, Jack thought, and his own were still drifting in the fog. Better to wait for a clearing. "I'll bet you didn't come down here to talk about this old boat," Jack said. "Why don't we go up to the office and get a cup of coffee."

"You're the captain down here," said Ernie. He put his tattooed arm around Jack's shoulders and led him back to shore.

The business office of GrayDays Marine occupied about half the second floor of the century house—the back half. Susan much preferred the serene view of the lagoons to the frenetic scenes on East Liberty Avenue. A large double sized partner's desk sat against the back wall of the building, between two large mullioned windows overlooking the boat docks. Each of the two executive desk chairs sat abreast one of the windows, giving Susan Grayson and William Daysart a panorama of ever-changing beauty that Monet could not have duplicated.

Ernie Beckett sat in the long-deserted high-backed leather button-tufted chair once used by Captain Daysart. As Jack poured two mugs of strong black coffee he realized that even young Will could not bring himself to sit in his father's chair. Jack set the coffee mugs on the desk and melted into Susan's low back upholstered swivel chair. A hint of Chanel still lingered there.

"What did the kid think about our plan?" asked Ernie.

It was just like the old salt, Jack thought. Cut right to the chase. No monkey business. "He said we're all crazy."

"Did he now?"

"That's what he told me."

"He's right you know," said Ernie after sloshing around a gulp of hot coffee in his mouth. "We're talkin' about startin' up a tourist business with a leaky old boat, two old men, and a captain who's afraid to sail out on the lake."

Jack had to give the old boy credit. He was persistent. But Jack was not going to take the bait—was not going to get into his problems. Not now anyway. "I guess Will's smarter than we gave him credit for," said Jack. "So where do we go from here?"

"We follow our course. That's why we strike a line on a chart—so we have some way to go. Christopher Columbus was crazy, they said. Orville Wright had his head in the clouds. Edison was a daydreamer. Hell, some people even think I'm one link short of a full anchor chain."

Ernie did have a sense of humor, Jack thought. More importantly, he knew when and how to use it. Ernie had a lot of weapons in his arsenal. He could disarm you with his anger, impale you with his knowledge, or lift you up with his wit.

"You've put us in some pretty great company. But even the great ones fail once in a while. It could happen to us."

"Not if we stay the course," said Ernie. And that's what I mean to do."

"I have to admit that I saw a little spark of interest in Will before he jumped ship and headed for Lorain," said Jack. "We may just turn him around after all. He just needs a little time to check out his other options."

"Which are?"

"None that I know of," said Jack. "But he's got something going, and I don't like the smell of it."

"Okay then. Until we know more, let's proceed as planned," said Ernie. "You'll have to turn on that fancy computer of yours and type up a plan for the bank. I made the rounds this mornin' and everyone's on board. Teddy Bear 'ill throw in his land on South Bass and said he can even refit his boat for passengers."

Jack was sure that Ernie had missed the skeptical look that surged involuntarily across his face.

"Maggie 'ill patch up her ship," Ernie continued without missing a beat. "It'll get us through a season or two until Teddy's refit is done." Ernie paused to spit into a waste can beside the desk. "Which reminds me Maggie's gonna call you later for a little consultation."

"What kind of consultation?" asked Jack, smelling the faint odor of a rat somewhere on board.

"Somethin' mechanical I think. She'll explain it." Ernie moved quickly to change the subject. "With the kid runnin' things out on the island, and you throwin' in your credit, we can't lose."

"Right, Ernie. We can't lose . . . can't lose anything but two pieces of floating junk, a useless plot of barren land, and everything I've saved my entire life."

"Okay, okay. We'll let you keep your pension plan out of the deal," said Ernie. "But I'll tell you something. I liked you a hellava lot more when you weren't afraid to take a few risks."

"And what about you? What are you contributing?"

"I'm organizing the whole thing."

"Will's right," said Jack. "We are crazy, every last one of us."

*     *     *

"Do you think I'm crazy or something?" Will yelled out desperately. "Why would I take your money?"

"Because you're a fucked up smart ass little dope head."

Will Daysart stood before Paddy Delaney's heavily carved mahogany desk like Brer Rabbit facing the briar patch. He was searching for a way out, but all he could see were thorns. It seemed so easy when Angie Mariano brought him in a year ago. It was a way to "earn some quick freedom money" and get out of Vermilion forever. When the shock of his dad's death began to wear off Will decided to sell GrayDays Marine, take the money and run. He thought he might even hook up with Jimmy Grayson out in Sausalito. Then the harsh realities of business set in. All of his father's assets were tied up in the business and Jack Grayson, who inherited Susan's half, refused to talk about a sale or buyout.

"The only person in town who seemed to understand his predicament was Angelina Mariano, who had snuggled up to him one night in a college bar near Tiffin. During the next four hours Angie explained the dynamics of college sports betting to young Will. There were millions of dollars to be lifted from the deep pockets of college students exiled to boring Midwest liberal arts colleges by affluent jet-setting parents. Angie didn't have too much explaining to do however. Will had laid down a bet or two while visiting college friends down in Columbus at the Ohio State University campus.

Angie explained how he could "work the other side of the table," the side that transformed him from buffoon to bookie. Will delighted in Angie building him up with the great money . . . loads of fun . . . parties every night . . . cash and carry . . . make a boatload of money and split, arguments that delighted him and sucked him into the scheme. She had told him he could even "peddle a little weed" to get close to the students, and "hold on to the leftovers for home use."

Angie convinced Will that he was already a good salesman, that he already knew what he had to know to make a fortune. What Will didn't know was that the campus betting game had reached the pristine bedroom communities of the Firelands. What he could not have known was that Paddy Delaney owned the game. Now the game had turned nasty.

"Mr. Delaney, I admit that I took some of the grass, maybe too much of it, but it was just . . ."

"I'm not talking about marijuana," said Paddy. "I'm talking about cash, my cash." Paddy lunged out of his chair and leered over the desk at his prisoner. "What? I don't pay you enough to go out, get high, get a little college pussy, and take a few bets?"

"You've been real good to me Mr. Delaney. That's why . . ."

"That's why you've been skimming off the top?"

Will's queasy stomach was suddenly erupting through his arm pits, throat and brow. "Well, maybe I was a little strung out."

"Shut up!" Paddy Delaney let Will stew in his own juices for several silent moments. "I know exactly how much you stole from me. I know exactly when you took it . . . how you took it . . . and where you stashed it. Now, I also know that you're a weakling and a liar."

I'll give it all back to you Mr. Delaney if you'll . . ."

"No. I'll take my money off that sailboat behind your house . . . just after I drop your pathetic ass in the Black River."

Will lost it. He broke down into low guttural sobs. He felt warm tears oozing down his cheeks and chin. He couldn't look at the demonic smirk radiating from Paddy Delaney's red freckled face. He knew, for the first time, that he was looking straight in to the face of evil.

"Take him up to the roof and throw him off," said Paddy to the two grizzly lieutenants stationed in the back of his large gloomy office in the old Broadway Building. "Then strip him naked and dump him in the river."

Will was numb. He was losing consciousness as he heard himself pleading for his life somewhere off in the distance. Something told him he was outside. The warmth of the sun was on his face. A friendly lake breeze erased the perspiration from his brow. He was at once paralyzed with fear and strangely at peace. Maybe this was how Karla Fay Tucker felt as Texas prison guards strapped her to the lethal injection table. Then the execution began.

Dragged to the edge of the roof.

Strong hands on his ankles and feet.

The Black River rushing toward him . . . yet he seemed not to be falling.

A telephone ringing.

Footsteps on the gravel roof.

"Yes Sir Mr. Delaney. Right away."

Tension.

A muttered feeble prayer.

A few minutes later Will Daysart was again staring at the briar patch; snatched from the clutches of certain agonizing death.

"I'm going to cut you a little break," said paddy Delaney. His steely blue eyes left no question about future consequences of another breach of trust.

"Anything you say Mr. Delaney. I won't disappoint you."

"I know that," said the devil. "And as a gesture of my faith in your loyalty and resourcefulness you can keep the . . ." Paddy shuffled some papers on his dark altar, put on his half glasses and continued. ". . . twenty four thousand three hundred and twenty five dollars you appropriated. We'll call it an advance."

Will was fully conscious now and vaguely recalled something his father had told him in Sunday school about making deals with the devil. But he was too far down the slippery slope of deceit to pull away.

"Is that boat behind your house still for sale?"

"Yeah . . . yes sir," answered Will.

"I just bought it."

"Right. I'll do the paperwork . . ."

"I won't be needing that."

"Okay," said will. "I understand."

"You don't understand anything. You understand only what I tell you to understand. You got that?" Paddy's lieutenants inched toward Will.

"I understand . . . yeah . . . uh, yes. I've got it."

Paddy Delaney dismissed his lieutenants with a brisk wave of his hand, and was alone with Will. "Sit down."

Will took a seat in the one leather side chair across from Paddy's massive polished desk. He locked on Delaney's piercing eyes as if he were in the grip of Dr. Mesmer himself.

"You're going to transport some very sensitive cargo to Canada," said Delaney.

"Mr. Delaney, do I need to know what kind of cargo?"

"That's better, Will," said Paddy as he smiled and leered over his half glasses. "Very sensitive cargo." Will shuffled in his seat. "How long will it take to sail that boat of yours . . . of mine . . . to the Welland Canal?"

"I don't know. Maybe two days."

Paddy flipped through his desk calendar, then turned back a few pages and made a large black check mark. "Have the boat ready to sail on Saturday, September 5th."

"I can't sail that boat alone. I mean I've never . . ."

"Shut up and listen to me," said Paddy. "Every Tuesday and Thursday morning for the next three weeks, you will receive a delivery from Malta Marine. The truck will arrive at your marina promptly at 7:30 a.m. The parcels will be addressed to your personal attention. You will be present to accept delivery."

"What if . . ."

"Don't interrupt me," exhaled Paddy. "You will unpack the parcels and store the contents on the sailboat in a customary place."

Will was feeling more uneasy with each shadowy statement. He began to squirm around in his chair, hoping to find a position that would ease his increasing discomfort. "Excuse me Mr. Delaney, but is there a . . ."

"Shut up and listen."

Will squeezed his legs together and took a deep breath, wondering when Paddy Delaney would put him out of his misery.

"At 5:30 a.m. on September 5th, my captain will arrive to take delivery of my boat. You will ensure that all cargo is safely stowed on board, that the boat is fully rigged and fueled; and that Lake Erie navigation charts are in place."

Paddy removed his glasses and returned the desk calendar to August 10. "Do you understand what I've said?"

"Yes sir. I've got it."

"Do you understand what I've said?"

*Is this a trick question?* Will wondered, but he didn't think about it too long, before blurting out an answer. "Right."

Paddy reached into a crystal bowl of walnuts on his desk, and began to squeeze the nuts in his hand. "Will, I want to know if you *understand* what I've said." Paddy released his grip, without ever losing eye contact with his prey, and Will watched the shells and nut pulp fall to the floor.

"Uh . . . okay. Yes, I understand Mr. Delaney."

"You're a smart kid Will. Be smart about this little job I've given you." Delaney stood up and pushed a small button on his desk. "The bathroom is at the end of the hall."

Will was grateful and embarrassed all at the same time. The door opened and the death squad reappeared. Will eased out of his chair and headed for the hallway.

"And one more thing Will," said Paddy Delaney. "I never want to see your face again."

For the first time all afternoon, Will was relieved by something Paddy Delaney had told him.

# CHAPTER 9

By the time the last page of the "Historic Cruises Business Plan" shot out of the laser printer it was 10:30 p.m. Although his heart had not been in the project at the start, Jack found the old momentum rise during six hours of productive solitude amid the trappings of a life he had not enjoyed for almost a year.

Like all mortals, Jack Grayson had his weaknesses, but the ability to focus was not one of them. Once put on a mission he had the tenacity of a Moray eel. Jack stuffed the sheaf of papers into a manila envelope, switched off the computer, and for the first time all evening wondered why Will had not come home. Then he remembered another one of Susan's admonitions: *These boys aren't crewing some ship you command, Jack. Give them a little space.* Jack and Susan never could agree on just what "a little space" meant in their compact world.

Captain Grayson grabbed a yellow Post-It Note and scrawled, "I hope you had a great time. Call me in the morning! Jack."

On the way out the back door, Jack stuck the note on the bulletin board.

\* \* \*

Jack spied the large lighted sign for Ednamae's Ice Cream Parlor and glanced at the dashboard clock: 10: 45 p.m. He still had time to get a triple scoop for the voyage home. Besides, he thought, *there's something tidy about beginning and ending a day in the same spot.* No loose ends. Circle complete.

The precise rack and pinion steering of the Range Rover responded flawlessly to an emergency right turn at Liberty and Grand. Fortunately the disk brakes were also at optimum efficiency, for as soon as he turned the corner Jack was blinded by oncoming headlights. He slammed both feet into the brake peddle and skidded to a halt. The two vehicles were eyeball to eyeball with engines panting. Both drivers' doors flew open, and Jack charged between the bumpers to chastise the nut who had nearly hit him head-on.

In the dim glow of the ice cream parlor sign, Jack glimpsed the imprint on the door of the blue Ford Escort station wagon: GrayDays Marine. "Damnit Will, why the hell are you driving on the wrong side of the street? Are you drunk, high, or what?"

"Ednamae's closes in fifteen minutes and I was going to slide into that parking space right there."

"Well, you lucked out this time," said Jack. "But one of these days you're going to pay for your shortcuts."

"Right you are Jack, as always, and tonight's the night. Let me have this parking space and I'll buy the ice cream."

Despite the gaff, Jack choked back a chuckle. As angry as he was at the moment, he had to admit to himself that Will Daysart had the touch—just like his old man. He was a charmer when he was in the mood.

"Okay. I'll park in the back and meet you inside."

Ednamae was already clearing out the remnant of an unusually large Monday night crowd when Will and Jack bellied up to the counter. "Running a little late aren't we boys?"

"Yes ma'am," said Jack. "But we've had a real bad day." Jack nudged Will and continued. "We have had a bad day haven't WE Will?"

*You really have no idea,* Will thought to himself, but opted to play along. "Yes we have. And we need something special to settle our queasy stomachs."

Jack marveled that will actually looked queasy while staying in character.

"You're in luck tonight," said Ednamae. "I have a lot of extra cleaning up to do, and since I *kinda* like you two I'm going to let you find a table and stay a while."

"Okay, I'll have a double scoop of . . ."

"No, no. Beggars can't be choosers. Your money is no good here tonight. Now go sit down—after you've wiped down the tables in there."

The beggars headed for the parlor as ordered, and chuckled about how the wily old Ednamae seemed always to have an ulterior motive. "Who would ever want to leave an intriguing little town like this?" Jack asked Will, with a smirk on his face.

"Funny you should ask. That's just what I want to talk to you about."

"You have my undivided attention," said Jack.

"I'm moving to California."

"Why's that?"

"There's nothing here for me," said will. "I feel like I'm suffocating—like if I don't get out of here I'm going to die."

"Or end up selling history tours on South Bass Island?"

"It's all the same."

"Come on Will, I don't think you're giving this new plan of ours a fair chance." Jack glanced at his Submariner. "Hell, it's only been about ten hours since we sat on the boat and talked about all of this."

"Ten hours that seem like a lifetime," Will said woefully. "Jack, you know I'm the only person in my high school class who still lives in Vermilion?"

"That's because they all went off to college or the military." Jack wished he had not fired that cheap shot as he saw the anguish pour from Will's eyes. "But they'll be back."

"Sure they will, when their lives are over. This is not a town where you come to live. People come here to die. Just look around. Everyone we know is either waiting to check out or already gone—like Susan and Dad. Look at yourself, Jack. What are you waiting for?"

Jack was taken aback. But he knew he had it coming. One good slap in the face deserved another.

"A small banana split for Captain Grayson who, I'm told, is now in training. And one Full Rigger Rum Raisin Sundae for young Will, who definitely needs the calories," said Ednamae as she swooped down upon the drifting life raft.

"Thanks for sparing me," said Jack. The double entendre was clear to everyone.

"Now, you boys just take your time and I'll bring each of you a nice cup of tea in a little while." As Ednamae turned away she gave Jack a playful bop in the head and said, "Now be nice."

The castaways enjoyed a few moments of tactical silence as they dipped into their custom prepared confections. They both sensed that the next opening line would be critical, and neither seemed anxious to reopen the dialogue. Jack looked across the table at his godson and, although he bore no resemblance to Jimmy, saw his own son sitting across from him. He wished that somehow he could have been sitting down with his son, talking about . . . well, just talking.

"I really do understand your urge to leave," said Jack in his most compassionate tone. "Your dad and I both left home before we were your age, and God only knows that Jimmy wasted no time getting out of Vermilion. It's just that it seems a lot easier to go, than to let go."

Jack could see that Will was trying to figure out the drift of his new attempt at sensitivity. He studied Will's deliberate and focused attention on the gargantuan sundae, then decided to press on and encourage some response. "Where in California will you go? What will you do?"

"Do you remember the keyboard player from our high school band?"

"How could I ever forget Shawnee Fredwest?" said Jack.

"I thought you and Jimmy would end up killing yourselves over that girl."

"If we only knew then what we know now I guess both of us could have lost a little less sleep, huh?"

For a moment Jack found himself smiling at Will's light hearted allusion to Jimmy's sexuality. Too bad he couldn't have smiled about it back then. *Why do we always try so hard to mold our kids into our own imperfect shells?* Jack wondered.

"Anyway," Will continued, "Shawnee bought into this music video production company in L.A. and says they're doing some really great stuff. She told me they have more work than they can handle, and asked me if I'd ever consider leaving the "nest" to see the bright lights and palm trees.

"And you said?"

"The nest is a little cold and lonely these days. I asked her to give me a month to wrap up everything here."

"Hold on now, Will. Shouldn't you give this a little more thought before you chuck your life here?"

"The only thing I have to lose here IS my life," said Will.

"What happened to you today?"

"What do you mean?"

Jack had Will's full attention now. His godson put down his spoon and no longer seemed interested in ice cream. "What I mean is that all of sudden you're talking about death and dying instead of living. This morning I thought I saw a glow in your eyes. Now it's gone." Jack leaned forward on his elbows. "So what are you afraid of?"

Jack thought that Will looked like young Tommy Smothers who had just been broadsided by his brother with a question he knew he didn't want to answer. Will was squirming. A few uneasy moments of silence passed as Will looked at everything in the room, everything except his inquisitor

"You know what I'm afraid of Jack."

"I'm not so sure."

"Well I've already told you."

"I know what you told me," said Jack. "What bothers me right now is what you haven't told me." Jack edged forward. "Come on Will. Give it up. Let me help you."

"There's nothing to give up. I'm just sick of being stuck in this lame ass town." Will dug back into his sundae. "So I'm leaving. I'm going to California. And that's final."

"What about the business?" asked Jack. "What about the boat? You can It leave until you sell Susan's boat."

"Oh, didn't I tell you?"

"Tell me what?"

"I sold *SEAQUESTOR* today."

"What? Who bought her?"

"Mr. D . . ." Will pulled up short. "You told me you didn't want to know the details."

"I lied."

"Sorry, Jack. It's a done deal."

"Is that what you were doing in Lorain this afternoon?"

"Sort of. But the boat's not going to Lorain. She's going to some guy up in Port Colborne. I thought that would be far enough away from here to suit you."

Now Jack was speechless. He hadn't seen this one coming. As much as the boat had been a stain on his memory of Susan, an albatross that endlessly circled his life, it was also an icon of better times. In a macabre way, Jack felt anchored and secure with the ketch bobbing gently in the lagoon behind GrayDays Marine. Now his anchor chain was being cut, and he was uneasy.

"I will tell you this," Will continued. "It's a straight cash deal. No survey and no warranty. Strictly as is."

"You must have given her away," said Jack.

"In keeping with your instructions I can't divulge the price, but I will tell you that it's enough for you to buy out my half of the company."

"So you dumped Susan's boat, slapped all of us in the face, and now you're free to go," said Jack. Is that it?"

"Free to go on, Jack. Just free to go on living my life on my terms."

"So, in one murky mid-afternoon deal we're both getting rid of old baggage." Jack muttered, almost to himself. "When is the delivery?"

"September 5th."

"Jesus Christ, Will. That's the day before Susan's . . ." Jack couldn't manage to finish the sentence.

"It was the buyer's call. Maybe the new captain will have better luck with her."

*Luck?* That was the beauty of youth, Jack thought. There was always a way out—an escape hatch for any situation—always a way to rationalize coming up on the short end of the stick. But then we grow up and find all the rationalizations are gone.

*Life is a bitch* . . . Jack said to himself, remembering a pickup truck bumper sticker passing through town . . . *then you die.*

*   *   *

Back at home, Jack lay back on the overstuffed sofa and gazed out upon a brilliant August moon that painted a wide river of light from heaven to hell. He took a long drink of the *Martell VSOP* in his large Waterford crystal snifter. He seemed to wallow in the emptiness of the castle that had become Devil's Island. The tumultuous events of an endless day reeled through Jack's mind like an old *Movie Tone* newsreel. Hazy black and white images compressed into high-impact vignettes coursed through his brain like some virtual reality game.

In a scant eighteen hours Jack Grayson had relived a lifetime, and in the process he had traveled from heaven to purgatory, and then to the depths of hell. Now he was back in Susan's beloved Vermilion, a place that proved it could become anyone of those without warning. How fickle and fragile life is, Jack thought as he pondered the events of the day. It didn't take much to alter the course of a man's life journey. A gust of wind, a lightning strike, an unkind word, an untimely remark, a lie, a rebuff, an unfair judgment, a sudden storm, a lapse of attention, a mistake, a . . ."

Jack finally gave way to the unconscious-subconscious state that held so many secrets. Perhaps this night the moon goddess who plied the river of light outside his window would solve the riddle that plagued his life—a riddle that neither a trip to heaven nor hell had been able to answer for him.

And so for a restless few moments Captain Jack Grayson dreamed.

# CHAPTER 10

Tuesday morning started with a bang for young Will Daysart. Remarkably, he had slept the *sleep of the dead* after his near death experience on the roof of the old Broadway Building the day before. Now the grim reaper was back, Will thought as he crawled over the sleeping Angelina Mariano and peered down to the parking lot at the Malta Marine delivery truck.

The digital clock read 7:30 a.m. and, just as Paddy Delaney threatened, the driver was unloading large cardboard boxes from the back of the van. It must have been the banging of the truck doors in the normally quiet back parking lot that raised Will from the dead.

He pulled on his faded jeans, the ones with the knees missing, and his black stretched-out and faded Metallica tee shirt. He slipped into his seasoned white-soled boat shoes, a small concession to the business image, and bounded down the creaky old stairs of GrayDays Marine.

Will arrived in the rear parking lot just as the truck driver was pulling the rear cargo door closed. The final crash of the metal door reverberated through his head like a bad chord on a Fender electric guitar. Without a word the starched pressed uniformed driver thrust a clipboard at Will's midsection.

The shipping invoice was addressed to *William Daysart c/o GrayDays Marine Co., Vermilion, Ohio.* Will cringed at the sight of his father's name. He felt as if the "old man" was standing there looking over his shoulder. A one line entry on the bill of lading described *TWO (2) BOXES OF TWO (2) EACH X-LARGE YACHT FENDERS—PREPAID.* Will scrawled his signature on the document and handed the clipboard back to the driver. Not a word had yet been spoken as the driver pulled a pink NCR copy of the shipping notice from the clipboard and handed it to Will. The driver quietly stepped up into the cab of the truck, then paused and looked back at Will. "Watch your back kid."

Will's eyes followed the truck up the driveway alongside the office, and watched it as it turned left on East Liberty Avenue and sped off toward Lorain. He stuffed the pink slip into his jeans pocket and examined the two large cardboard boxes sitting on the pavement next to him. They were identical—tall, brown, unmarked, and sealed on the top and bottom with clear plastic packaging tape. Each box looked to be about two by three feet.

Curiosity mixed with a bit of confusion got the best of Will. He vividly understood Paddy Delaney's instructions to stow the cargo on the sailboat in a "customary place," but there was no customary place to store large cardboard boxes on a sailboat. So he reached into his pants pocket and took out the Swiss army knife that had been a birthday gift from Jack Grayson. Will easily slit the plastic tape on one of the boxes, opened the flaps and looked inside.

True to the description on the pink slip, the box contained two large white yacht fenders. Will ran his fingers across the familiar rubber-like surface of these typical link sausage shaped yacht fenders. Each fender was flattened on both ends and had a large round metal grommet punched through the thick flat surface. Short lines would be attached through the grommets, so that the fenders could be hung off the deck of a boat, between the fragile wood or fiberglass hull and the abrasive immovable wharf. Will had seen and used these fenders hundreds of times. All boaters had. The hollow air-filled interior of the tightly sealed fenders gave a nice protective cushion to vulnerable boats. This type of fender came in all sizes, but these were the very large ones—12 inches in diameter and 36 inches long.

Okay, the "customary" storage riddle was solved, Will thought. These large fenders are usually stored in the lazarette hatch on deck, at the stern of the boat, where they are easily accessible for docking. But why the hell would Mr. Delaney want to transport rubber boat fenders to Canada, will asked himself as he reached down to pick up one of the boxes.

His question was answered instantly.

Well, almost.

Will grunted as the box seemed unwilling to break loose from the pavement. "What the hell?" Will said out loud as he stood up and looked down at the box. His deep memory bank told him in a microsecond that the fenders should weigh no more than five pounds each. He had often carried six of them at a time from the storeroom to a car or boat of some waiting customer. He reached inside the open box and, with great difficulty, pulled one of the fenders onto the driveway.

Instinctively, Will knelt down with one knee pressed against the fender. It was the standard drill to test for a break in the air seal that provided the cushion. This fender, however, did not cushion. It did not collapse. It did not give at all. Will knew this was not some new design. Something other than air filled the space inside the rubber membrane. "So, this is the cargo," Will mumbled to himself as he reached again for his open Swiss Army knife.

"Do you need a hand?" Will nearly stabbed himself at the shrill noise behind him. He dropped the knife and jumped to his feet and, in one motion, executed a perfect 1800 pivot.

"Jesus Angie," he yelled. "You nearly scared the shit out of me."

"I'm sorry Will. I thought you heard me. I wasn't exactly sneaking up on you."

"I know. I guess I'm a little jumpy lately. I've been trying to get off my early morning weed ritual and I'm a little strung out."

"Maybe you need a substitute," Angie said as she grabbed him in the crotch. "Why don't you put your little toys away and come back upstairs? I think I can take the edge off your habit."

Will marveled at how quickly Angie Mariano could get his attention. She seemed to have an insatiable appetite. Will couldn't believe that only six hours ago he commented that his *schwanz* wouldn't be stiff again for another week. But as Will felt Angie's aura engulf him, he knew that she was the kind of girl that could make a liar out of any man. He could see her dark nipples erupting through the long pink "Sex Pistols" cotton nightie she always carried in her Papa Joe's tote bag. As she emitted an odd mixture of Arpege and oregano, Angelina Mariano gave a new dimension to the term "home delivery."

"Hmm . . . Let's see," said Will. "Should I work or should I play?" He paused a moment and scratched an itch. "You drive a hard . . . very hard . . . bargain. What the hell, this will wait. Let's go."

Angie pushed Will away. "Pick up your toys first. I'll go up to the loft and prepare a special treat for you."

Will watched Angie disappear through the back door, his eyes fixed on her like a colt whose mother had just been led away. He quickly retrieved his open knife from the ground and slit open the second cardboard box. Will felt a new surge of energy as he carried the mystery-stuffed fenders on board the boat.

\*   \*   \*

Angelina Maria Mariano stood in the dormer window of the third floor loft and watched her pitiful little drone do her bidding. She dialed seven digits into the cordless telephone and heard the familiar "talk to me" after one ring.

"He opened the boxes," she said.

"Yes, he's curious," she replied.

"He started to."

"No, I handled it."

"He's taking them on board right now."

Just before hanging up the phone, Angie simply said, "No problem."

*   *   *

"Hey Will, are you up there?"

Will glanced at the clock. It was 10:15 a.m. He looked around his room at the steeply angled rays of sunlight pouring through the window. Angie was gone, but not forgotten. *I must have dozed off,* he thought.

"Will Daysart. Rise and shine. All hands on deck."

It was Jack Grayson, Will realized as he struggled to his feet. "Yeah Jack. Hold your horses. Let me get out of the can, and I'll be right down."

The last thing Will needed this morning was Jack Grayson snooping around. He grabbed the Steiners off his exercise bike and looked again at the padlock on *SEAQUESTOR*'s lazarette hatch. It was kind of ironic, Will thought, that his illicit skimming of profits and Paddy Delaney's mysterious new yacht fenders ended up in the same compartment of a boat that for years had stood for "doing the right thing the right way." If Jack ever found out what he was doing, even California wouldn't be far enough away to save him.

Will had always looked up to Jack, despite the obvious problems he caused for Jimmy. During his final high school years, while his own father was dying, Will couldn't bear to watch his dad's pain and decay. He seemed ill-equipped to be of any real comfort to him. So he adopted Jack as a sort of surrogate father. It hadn't been all that difficult really, since Jack was desperately searching for a son he could relate to.

With Susan and Jimmy spending so much time with his father, Will was able to form a special bond with Jack. They threw themselves into the business, each of them happy to have the diversion. Will learned the fine points of diesel mechanics, engine repair, sail rigging, mast tuning, and navigation electronics. Jack learned something about being a father. For everyone concerned, it was a good deal.

Then all of a sudden the deal went bad.

Will's dad died alone, in the middle of the night, while Will was shacked up with Angie. Susan Grayson was swept away by an angry lake. And just as tragically, Jimmy Grayson was driven away by his own father. It had been a miserable and tumultuous year, but now things were changing, Will thought. For better or worse.

"Come on Will," yelled Jack from downstairs. "Let's get going. I want to start getting our things off *SEAQUESTOR* and I need your help."

Jack stood in the cockpit of Susan's yacht and, without thinking twice, dialed the numbers 9-8-6-8 into the brass thumb wheel type combination lock. Then he stopped to think. This may be the last time I ever use these numbers again. Jack was a gifted mathematician, but had a terrible memory for numbers. He remembered Susan telling him when she first snapped the new lock on the hatch boards of the cabin companionway; I hope you won't have any problem remembering our wedding date. But if you do, just look inside your wedding band.

Jack now knew that he could never forget their wedding anniversary, a beginning so inexorably linked to an ending. But just the same, he kept his wedding band in place, and vowed never to take it off.

Jack pulled out the four louvered hatch boards and laid them on the molded fiberglass cockpit seat. He swung his feet over the lip of the hatchway and started down the companionway into the saloon. Then he froze in his tracks.

Lying on the beautifully finished teak and holly sole, under a single beam of sunlight streaking through a port light, was Susan's log book—the one the boat had reclaimed at the end of his last visit there. Jack was overcome with such a crushing sense of foreboding that he could not move.

"What's wrong?" asked Will, a bit impatiently.

"Nothing. Just a flash from the past." Jack turned around, fighting the urge to abandon ship. He thought about what Meagan would tell him, then looked down toward the dock and shouted, "Grab those boxes and my tool kit and bring them down."

"Go on in and I'll hand them down to you," said Will. "You take care of your stuff inside and I'll clean out the cockpit lockers and lazarette."

"Leave whatever is in there. It's Just cockpit cushions, winch handles, a couple of fenders, a spare anchor, and our old trailing line." Jack grabbed his tool kit and started down the ladder. "All that gear should stay with the boat."

"It won't hurt to double check," Will said. "Besides, the buyer should have a complete inventory . . . and I may have to replace a fire extinguisher or life jacket to meet Coast Guard standards."

Jack looked up at Will with a huge smile. "Nice. Very, very nice. I guess you DO know a thing or two about yacht brokerage after all."

"Hey, I've been running this place alone for the last year, and she hasn't gone down yet."

Now Jack could see that Will was beaming. For a moment he felt like he was talking to a business partner, rather than some wayward kid who needed "savin'." He decided to capitalize on the mood. "And on top of all that, you sold Vermilion's most unsalable property—the boat with the *curse* as Ernie Beckett calls it."

"There's another reason I'm getting out of this town."

"What's that?" asked Jack.

"Too many goofy old superstitions that keep everyone shackled to the past.

"Now pick up your icons," Will snickered. "And I'll take care of the equipment on deck."

"Aye, aye Captain Daysart," said Jack as he watched young Will step out of sight. He saw a spark in the kid and also a release in himself that he had not noticed for many months. Maybe it was the boat after all, he thought. Maybe the sale of *SEAQUESTOR* was the lynch pin that would resolve both of their problems. Maybe the departure of the cursed yacht would free Will from Vermilion, and free Jack from painful memories that now seemed nearer and nearer the surface.

Jack felt none of the foreboding of dread that had consumed him earlier, as he packed mementos, books, and papers into the few large boxes he brought along. Neither did he have any sense of finality as he purged the boat of its accumulated stash of trinkets and treasures. Jack determined that he would not venture into the boat again. He had done his work. He had struggled with whatever force had kept him away for a year and now felt comfortable as he prepared to let go once and for all. But to whom?

True to his word, and to their deal, will had not given up a single detail of the mysterious sale, save that the yacht was destined for Port Colborne. Jack knew that the Canadian port was probably just a transfer point to some more distant home port, perhaps in Lake Ontario, Nova Scotia, the Chesapeake, or Florida. It didn't really matter to Jack, yet something Will said about the deal nagged at him.

Who would pay six figures for a yacht and not demand a trial run, marine survey and some kind of warranty? It all seemed too good to be true, as Jack remembered the old adage about such things. He determined to snoop out the identity of the mystery buyer.

*     *     *

Of course Will knew that Jack was right about all the gear left in the lazarette hatch. He was more right than he could know, will thought as he propped open the hinged hatch cover and knelt down to take stock of his dilemma. How would he keep the snooping Jack Grayson from finding out about the new supply of boat fenders? Will had no idea how many of them would be delivered during the final three weeks before the unidentified "Captain" would arrive to take delivery. If Paddy Delaney had been true to his word, a good bet Will thought, then there was likely to be another twenty new rubber boat fenders delivered by the end of Paddy's "every Tuesday and Thursday morning." He peered down into the deep dark cavernous lazarette and tried to visualize two dozen of the big fenders inside. It would be tight, he thought, as he pulled the other gear out onto the deck, but would fit snugly if he moved or trashed out a few pieces of nautical gear.

Will could move the spare stern anchor and coiled line into the fish locker up in the center cockpit. The four old life jackets could go since the new Captain would be alone and would certainly bring his personal survival gear. The large foam fire extinguisher which, Will noted was out of date but still charged, could go into its bracket on the steering pedestal. A large burgundy canvas bimini top and aluminum poles would be transferred to a locker in the forward vee-birth.

Finally, Will fisted onto a large long coil of Dacron braided line that had been dirty, wet, and cared for badly. At one end of the line was tied a large old Clorox bottle. Duct tape had been wound around the bottle handle and body to keep it from breaking under the strain of being dragged through the water on long voyages. This, Will remembered, was Susan's "trailing line." He recalled hearing his father and Captain Ernie kidding Susan about her funny little precaution against "being lost at sea." He couldn't remember anyone laughing since her death. He was ready to throw the whole moldy mess over the side to the dock, when he decided it would make a nice distraction from the neat stack of sparkling white fenders that might otherwise attract closer inspection. Will kicked the mass of line and plastic back into the hatch and smiled as it covered the four new fenders deep in the bottom.

*In less than three weeks it will be over*, Will thought as he snapped the lock back on the hatch. *Music to my ears.*

# CHAPTER 11

The late August sun had just winked over the horizon as Jack lugged his old sea bag across the deserted parking lot at McGarvey's Nautical Restaurant. It was early but today's mission was best suited for the early hours, and he didn't want to attract any more attention than necessary. His gait across the pavement looked more like the condemned man's march than that of an agent in a select operation that "only one man in Vermilion can handle." Maggie's words hung in his mind like a mysterious fog, as he rounded the corner of the building and stepped onto the dock where *Aphrodite* was tied up.

The uncommon desperation in Maggie's voice left him no option but to agree. Such was the mutual oath of the Captain's Quarters. Teddy Bear Parks, Captain Ernie and Maggie Wicks were seated around a large table on the fantail of *Aphrodite*. Maggie, who was facing Jack's expected entrance point, stood up when she spied him rounding the turn. She hawked out through the calm, "If you're going to get the last apricot Danish, you'd better hustle it up."

Just as Jack reached the stern of the excursion boat, Teddy Bear reached over the rail. "Give me your bag," he said. Jack and the others laughed aloud as Teddy grabbed the sea bag and was nearly dragged over the low steel railing. "What in Davey Jones' locker do you have in this thing?"

Jack hustled up the gangway without missing a step and headed aft. "You're lucky I only packed my small tank."

Teddy put the bag of diving gear down on deck as Jack sat down and reached for the large flaky apricot pastry. Maggie was already pouring his coffee from a large brass pot. "I thought we'd best eat light this morning," said Maggie. "Then we'll have brunch at McGarvey's before the crowds arrive. My treat."

The local movers and shakers in Vermilion tended to congregate and socialize very early, or very late, to avoid the endless throng of tourists, vacationers and seasonal boaters who consumed the hamlet every summer day from 9:00 a.m to 9:00 p.m. Early morning on the Vermilion River was for the locals, and most of them agreed it was the best time. The restaurant was still dark, usually seeing no life until about 10:00 a.m. when the kitchen crew arrived to begin preparing lunch. Today, however, Maggie had arranged for her favorite chef to "layout brunch on the patio at four bells sharp," ten o'clock.

Across the river some workmen at Parsons Boat Yard and Moe's Marine were hauling out ladders, scaffolds, tools and anti-fouling bottom paint for the morning's scheduled chores. The resident big boat population of more than a hundred yachts in the river and lagoons kept Vermilion's two boat yards backed up all summer long. Unfortunately neither of them had haul-outs large enough for *Aphrodite*, and neither had any facilities for underwater repair or inspection. Normally, these major jobs on large vessels were done in dry dock, either in Toledo or Detroit.

Farther up river the Vermilion Boat Club was quiet after a night of hard partying after the usual mid-week Tartan Ten races on the lake. Jack spied an aproned waiter a bit out of place on the patio of the French Restaurant, wielding a hot water hose against the spillage of "fine continental sauces" on old brick. Jack made a mental note to set up a dinner date with Meagan Palmer. She refused to take any payment from him for her consultations, and he felt obliged to make some gesture.

"Okay," said Jack. "Tell me exactly what we're up against."

Maggie leaned forward and put her elbows on the table. "Two days ago I noticed that the bilge pumps were running more than usual so I went down below to . . ."

"For chrissakes Maggie," interrupted Ernie. "This ain't some soap opera. Spare us the suspense and get to the facts."

Maggie was clearly exasperated as she bit her lip, took a slow sip of coffee and continued. "I pulled up the floor plates in the engine compartment . . ."

"She ran over something in the river and cracked the stuffing box," Ernie bellowed.

"Let's not go back to that," said Maggie. Jack glanced at Teddy Bear and could see that he was enjoying the joust as much as he was. It was the usual bill-of-fare on board *Aphrodite* with these two. Neither of them dared interrupt the entertainment. "We don't know what happened," said Maggie.

"Well lassie, we do know that the damned stuffin' box is cracked," growled the old man. "And before I patch it up we need to know if the shaft or strut is damaged." Ernie launched a disgusting dark wad from his mouth and Jack watched it plop into the glassy river. "Is that about it?"

"Yes Ernie, that's just about it." Maggie sat back in her deck chair and crossed her dark tanned arms tightly across her chest.

"And the dry docks in Toledo and Detroit are booked for the rest of the season," added Teddy Bear. "No more haul-outs."

"She can't finish the season on one engine," said Ernie. "I told her to pack it up and take an early winter vacation, but she's had some vision that everything below the waterline is okay." Maggie seemed ready to erupt but then Jack thought he saw the slightest hint of a wink from her eyes as Ernie carried on. "I told her I wouldn't touch the damned thing unless she could find some sap to jump into the river and check it out." Ernie spit over the rail again. "And then you showed up."

Jack knew he was being handled, but as Maggie had detailed the scenario to him the night before she had made a credible case and she did seem to be in a hopeless situation. Not only did she need a diver, she needed a marine engineer. Jack knew he was the only person within 100 miles that filled the bill.

"I brought down my big underwater light," said Teddy. "When Maggie told me what she asked you to do, I knew you wouldn't have more than a foot of visibility without a light."

"And if we don't start divin' before the boat traffic picks up on that river," growled Ernie. "You'll not see anything down there through all the mud that the props kick up."

"Let's do it then," said Jack abruptly. The expression of bravado surprised even him. It was true that he hadn't been in the water for a year, and hadn't had his scuba gear on for a year before that, but it was a simple, short, shallow dive that shouldn't take more than fifteen minutes to complete. Deep down he sensed that he didn't want to go into the water again, but this was not much more than a short bath.

Jack pulled his Polo shirt over his head and dropped it on his chair, then released his belt and let his baggy khaki shorts fall to his feet. He took a short step forward out of the shorts, and launched them into the air with one fluid kick. No wasted motion. No useless movements. As he stepped out of his Topsiders, Jack looked at Teddy. "Open my bag and hand me my BCD."

Jack's buoyancy compensation device was a synthetic mesh sleeveless vest that held the air tank and allowed the diver to divert compressed air into and out of the jacket to establish neutral buoyancy underwater at various depths. When deflated, the BCD allowed the diver to sink, and when air was pushed into the vest, the diver rose to the surface.

Jack slipped the vest on and felt the tug of the small 20 minute compressed air tank he had selected for the dive. He knew the inspection would take only a few minutes, and the smaller tank would be easier to deal with in the tight confines between the dock and propulsion gear of Maggie's ship. He connected the short inflator hose to the BCD, then pulled the longer regulator hose over his shoulder and held the breathing regulator in his hands. "Maggie, you want to turn on my air?" Maggie, who had once been a certified diver, opened the air valve at the top of the tank. Jack felt the hoses stiffen to the surge of compressed air. He was reassured to feel Maggie back-off the opened valve a half-turn to avoid the possibility of freezing up. The woman was a pro.

Jack quickly tested the flow of air in and out of the BCD, and then put the silicone and stainless steel regulator in his mouth. After a few short breaths he was satisfied that his life support system was functioning properly. He felt as though he had never been away from the scuba diving he had once enjoyed so much. It was kind of like riding a bike, he thought.

"Teddy, hand me my weight belt, fins and mask," Jack said at the end of his mechanical check. He turned to the stern rail of *Aphrodite* and saw that Ernie had already opened the gate through the railing and was standing on the swim platform near the edge of the water. Jack climbed down a short inclined ladder to the platform, while Ernie steadied him against the unbalanced weight on his back. Jack sat down on the platform and swung his feet into the water. He was happy to feel the cool water on his legs. There had been no rain for a week, and Jack was pleased to be able to see his feet through the usually brown murky water.

Teddy Bear handed the mask and fins to Ernie, who passed them along. Jack slipped on the long black rubber flippers and then spit a few times into his mask. The saliva coating on the inside of the glass prevented it from fogging up with condensation. Finally, Ernie handed the stubby waterproof underwater light to Jack.

"I tested it myself, and it's workin' fine," said Ernie.

Jack nodded, slipped the mask over his face and said, "I'll be back in five minutes."

The first thought Jack had as the water closed over him was that something did not feel right. He had been diving in Lake Erie before, but never in the river. He quickly realized that the source of his uneasiness was the lack of visibility. Caribbean divers have no difficulty seeing a hundred feet in the pristine ocean waters of the tropics. Even the northern Great Lakes and deep cold waters of Georgian Bay allowed visibility of fifty feet on bright sunny days. But Lake Erie is often called the "cesspool" of the Great Lakes.

Back in the seventies Jack and Susan had become active in a North Coast Preservation League effort to "Save the Lake!" Biologists and ecologists had declared the lake dead after the oil slicked Cuyahoga River in Cleveland caught fire. If the sight of burning water inspired the late night television comics, it also mobilized local groups of boating, fishing and lake history enthusiasts. The community-minded Graysons raised money to fund ecological water quality studies. They lobbied state and national congressmen for clean water legislation targeted at Lake Erie. But there was huge pessimism in the scientific community, and for good reason. Jack and Susan quickly learned that they were all fighting an uphill battle against geography.

Water from Lake Huron rushes southward under the so-called "Blue Water" International Bridge between Sarnia, Ontario and Port Huron, Michigan. On its journey to the sea the originally pure blue water of the upper lakes pales and becomes murky as it passes down the St. Clair River, through a lake in the St. Clair Flats, and past Windmill Point at the top of the Detroit River. For 28 miles the water runs the gauntlet of some of the most heavily industrialized shoreline in the country. In the process it gathers innumerable pollutants from factories, sprawling cities, sewers, high-rise apartments and suburban housing. It plows through the flotsam and jetsam of pleasure boaters and commercial shippers, past and present. The swift current through the St. Clair and Detroit Rivers have, for millennia, carried sand and silt from their banks and bottoms for deposit into Lake Erie.

So it is, Jack quickly learned, that Erie's waters swirl in a shallow basin that holds jealously onto whatever, or whoever, passes through it. Tributary rivers flowing into the lake contribute to the problem, especially as irresponsible and under planned industrial, urban and suburban development rise along their banks. With average depth contours a mile off shore of only thirty feet, a mean depth of ninety feet, and a deep sounding of only 210 feet off Long Point, Lake Erie is 1,000 feet more shallow than Lake Superior to the north. The murky water is often churned by violent storms and flows in a frenzy down the Niagara River, under the Peace Bridge, past Squaw Island, over the great Niagara Falls into Lake Ontario and eventually through the St. Lawrence River to the Atlantic Ocean.

But the often meager natural flow could not keep pace with the environmental havoc inflicted by man. Despite local clean-up efforts, industrial and urban waste controls, and legislation, the Great Lakes family's most southern child seemed doomed—that is until Mother Nature hitched a ride on a "salty."

Pure environmentalists believe that nature will always find a way to preserve itself. Jack believed it himself, but could never have foreseen the simple solution that appeared. Since the opening of the St. Lawrence Seaway and locks that allowed world shipping to enter the Great Lakes at Port Colborne, salt water ships from the seven seas found their way into Lake Erie. Salt water ballast that stabilized these vessels against the deep waters of the ocean was often pumped into the shallow lake to ease their passage into the ports of Buffalo, Cleveland and Toledo. That salty ballast water carried with it "Mother's" little cleansers, the Zebra Mussel.

As manmade pollutants decreased and the Zebra Mussel population increased through the eighties and nineties, the Lake was born again. The tiny mollusk, with its continuously operating biological filtration system, accomplished what man, machine and money never could have. The offshore waters of Lake Erie became clear again. But onshore, and in the rivers flowing into the lake, there was still the timeless accumulation of sand and silt. Jack Grayson now found himself in the grip of it.

The light Teddy provided made a big difference. Still, only five feet under the surface and in the shade of the dock, the visibility with the light, Jack judged, was no more than three feet. Suddenly, Jack glimpsed one of *Aphrodite's* propellers just above his head. He realized he was too deep and must have been stirring up silt from the river bottom with his diving fins. He gave the BCD inflator a short burst of air and rose slightly to where his face mask was at the same depth as the prop. Now he kept his feet quiet so as not to compound his visibility problems. Jack grabbed the starboard shaft strut with his right hand while holding the light in his left. He shook the assembly, then grabbed the prop itself and tried to move it from side to side. Nothing. Everything seemed in tact. Maggie was right, he thought. There were no signs that she had run over anything.

Jack moved closer to the propeller shaft. He sighted along the short five foot extension of the shaft from the hull to the supporting strut and could see no evidence of damage. He decided that as long as he was in position he would slip to the other side of the ship and check the port side propeller assembly—just to be on the safe side. As he began to slip under the hull he got hung up. He twisted and jerked his upper body, the wrong thing to do he would later recall, as he felt the rush of air past his mask. One startled moment was all it took to lose his grip on the light.

Instantly Jack was in a frenzied and noisy maelstrom of bubbles, water, bottom silt and darkness. He also had the sensation that he was falling—a sensation he confirmed as his fins plopped into the powdery bottom of the Vermilion River. Something on the bottom of *Aphrodite* had disengaged his inflator hose and the air in his BCD spilled out, sending him to the bottom. Although he could still breathe through his regulator, he plummeted into a panic attack.

Jack was in dark water, being pulled to the bottom, and seemed unable to help himself. Somehow he felt he had been here before, like he was revisiting an episode in his life. He tried to scream, but could only mumble deep guttural grunts through the mouthpiece of his breathing regulator. His mind screamed what his voice could not:

*Somebody help me!*
*Please help me, I'm drowning!*
*I can't swim!*
*Save me!*

Something grabbed Jack's shoulders and spun him around. He thrashed and pulled away from the human-like hands that tugged at him from somewhere in the darkness. Were his eyes closed, he wondered as he strained them wide open to see nothing but a galaxy of brown luminescent bubbles streaking past his mask? It was like being trapped inside a can of Pepsi with some fantasy monster. Jack didn't know whether he was up or down, near the ship, or in the river channel. But he did sense that his air supply was about to end . . . and the thought of drowning paralyzed him.

The monster was back, grabbing and turning him. It had control of him, pulling at his waist. He pushed and fought, though he still had not seen his adversary. Suddenly he was whisked upward by his captor. As his head broke the surface the monster ripped his mask away. Daylight!

"Jack, Jack," a voice screamed. "Help me out here. You're all right."

It was Maggie Wicks who pulled the regulator from his mouth and now yelled directly into his panic stricken face. "I'm with you Jack. It's okay. Calm down now and let me get you back to the ship."

Ernie and Teddy Bear stood on the swim platform and pulled Jack's limp exhausted body on board like fishermen landing a yellow fin tuna. Maggie treaded water until Jack was aboard then climbed the swim ladder out of the river. She sat down next to Jack, who was again seated on the edge of the platform, after Teddy had helped him remove his diving gear.

"What happened down there Jack?" Maggie asked softly as she put her arm around his shoulders.

"I snapped a hose on my BCD and dropped like a rock to the bottom." Jack was clearly shaken as he looked up at Teddy. "I guess I lost your light. Sorry."

"Why didn't you just drop your weight belt and swim to the surface?" asked Maggie citing the standard drill.

"I couldn't see a thing. I was totally disoriented. Then it seemed like I was somewhere else." Jack looked sadly out into the river. "I had no idea where I was or what I was doing. I've never felt so helpless."

Maggie looked away from Jack and whispered to Ernie, "Give Meagan Palmer a call and see if she can come down here right now." She could see from the look on Ernie's face that he would simply have given Jack a shot of Bourbon and a boot in the ass.

"Just do as I ask," said Maggie with a command presence that left even the old sea dog little option but to comply.

Jack had just laid back on the deck chair and closed his eyes when he sensed someone in his space. He squinted one eye open as if he really didn't want to see what was there, but was glad that he forced himself. Meagan Palmer was standing beside him. The strong back light from the morning sun gave her a mystic quality that perfectly capped off the horrific experience in the river. She looked like his guardian angel. "Are you here for the cruise?" he asked.

"Not bad for a guy who was just dredged out of the river," said Meagan. She sat down on Jack's deck chair and took his hand in hers. Jack felt a surge of electricity course through his depleted body. "I had just arrived at my office and was opening the shades when I saw Maggie dive into the river. I figured it was a little early for a swim, so I waited and watched a few moments. Imagine my surprise when she came up with you." She smiled broadly and continued. "And, well . . . you know what a snoop I am, so I decided to come down and see what was happening to my most intriguing patient."

"I had hoped I was your only patient."

Meagan flinched as Jack dragged her nearer that nebulous boundary between ethics, friendship and . . . She denied the thought. "Just tell me what happened Jack."

"I nearly drowned. That's what happened." Now Jack was sitting up, once again fully alive. "I can't believe that after thirty years of diving I had a panic attack in fifteen feet of muddy river water."

"Describe what you felt."

"Disoriented. Helpless." Jack shook his head in abject disappointment. "I didn't have a clue where I was or what to do. I had this weird feeling that I was somewhere else."

"Where?" asked Meagan, bearing in.

"I don't know, but it wasn't in the river. It was one of those feelings you get every once in while that you've been somewhere, or done something before."

"Like Yogi Berra's deja vu all over again?'" quipped Meagan in an attempt to conceal her concern.

"Yeah, something like that," said Jack with a hint of a smile.

Meagan's well-timed bit of humor calmed Jack and the threat of his near-death experience seemed to flutter away in a moment of silence.

"Well . . . I can't earn any money down here with you freeloaders, so I'd better get back to work. Don't forget our appointment this afternoon," said Meagan lightheartedly as she stood up to leave.

"Can't we postpone it for a few days?" pleaded Jack.

"Under the circumstances, I think not."

Meagan leaned down until she was eye-to-eye with her subject. "Actually, this is the best possible time to take a big step forward. Something inside of you is trying hard to get out. We might as well give it a hand." The look on Meagan's face left no room for negotiation. Whatever she was after, Jack knew she would not be denied.

"Should I bring the ice cream?" he asked with a smile.

"No, but you might consider a life jacket."

# CHAPTER 12

"Jack, I want you to relax, let yourself go," said Dr. Meagan Palmer in her quiet darkened office. "Just lay back and practice some long slow rhythmic breathing. Close your eyes and think of the sun sinking below the horizon on a quiet calm summer evening."

Jack had his doubts about what this *hocus pocus* would accomplish. In fact, he was certain he could not be hypnotized or put into any kind of trance. But it felt comforting to be near Meagan and maybe, he thought, that was enough therapy.

"Now, open your eyes and watch the crystal on my desk," said Meagan.

As he looked up into intense green eyes that shimmered the reflection of drawn window shutters, he could think of little else than diving deep inside them. If Jack's nightmares were becoming more persistent, so too were his thoughts of Meagan. Thoughts that were more, or less, than clinical. He watched a large faceted crystal turn slowly to the left, then back again to the right, almost one full revolution each cycle. He glanced upward at Meagan and caught her eye as if to tell her, this is not working.

"Concentrate on the crystal, Jack."

One turn to the left . . . one turn to the right . . . sparkling colored light . . . to the left . . . to the right . . . left . . . right . . .

"You are following the sunset, sinking ever so slowly from the sky," Meagan whispered. "Dimmer and dimmer. Darker and darker as it slips away . . . slips away . . . slips away."

Jack felt deeply relaxed, yet not asleep. He could see the turning crystal but could not distinguish its facets. There was nothing in the room but Meagan's soft whispering voice.

"Jack, the next time you hear the word 'wake' you will open your eyes. When you open your eyes the journey will be over. You will remember every detail of your voyage, but when you open your eyes the voyage will be in your past. You will be in the present. Do you understand me, Jack?"

"Yes."

"I want you to go back to September 6, 1997."

"Yes."

"What is happening?"

"Susan and I are watching television. There are horses and guards and crowds of people. Prince Charles and his two sons are walking behind a hearse covered with flowers. The Princess is dead."

"Move ahead to sunrise, and tell me what you see."

"Susan is writing in her log book."

\* \* \*

"The sun is up at 6:42—right on time, we're steady on course 068°, the wind is steady from the south southwest at 15," yelled Susan from the cockpit. "And I'm ready for some of those eggs and bacon."

Jack pushed a steaming cup of coffee, cream and sugar through the hatch and felt Susan's ice cold fingers as she grabbed the steaming yacht club mug. This will have to hold you for now, Captain. Breakfast in fifteen minutes."

The ship's clock was dinging out six bells when Susan set the autopilot, slipped down the companionway and slid onto the settee behind a plate of scrambled eggs, Canadian bacon, toast and orange marmalade. She still moves like an eighteen year old, Jack thought as he sat down across from her at the slightly tilted table.

"Nice touch," Susan said.

"What's that?"

"The Canadian bacon. I thought you didn't like it."

"Ah yes, but *you* like it my Captain," said Jack. "And this is *your* wedding anniversary cruise."

"Au contraire *mon cherie*," said Susan. "What's mine is also yours."

Jack leaned in at the touch of Susan's hand on his leg. He delighted that after twenty years he still got a tingle. He had to get rid of the tingles however, if he stood any chance of getting his fair share of the eroding mound of scrambled eggs. Susan had a good appetite that became ravenous sailing before the wind toward her favorite destination, Port Colborne, Ontario.

After the dishes were cleared, Susan poured the last of the breakfast coffee into the two mugs and said, "Let's have a little chat."

"Have I been bad?"

"Of course," Susan quipped. "But there's always hope of redemption."

"Certainly. But at what cost?"

"Jimmy wants us to come out to California for a few days."

"Us or you?" Jack saw the pain flash across Susan's face and quickly regretted the gaffe. "I'm sorry."

"Not good enough Jack. If you're really sorry then you have to do something about it. You're long overdue." Susan paused and inched away from Jack. From her new angle of attack, he couldn't avoid looking into her eyes. "Jimmy has made an overture, and now the ball's in your court . . . in OUR court. And to answer your first question your son asked for US. He loves you Jack, and he's proud of you. All he wants is for you to be proud of him."

Jack was trapped. Susan had snared him in her cunning little web, and now he squirmed as she circled him. "It's not Jimmy," he muttered. "It's his lifestyle." "Jimmy *is* his lifestyle, Jack. You've just never been willing to accept that you've always wanted him to be something different than he is."

"Something more."

"Something less."

Jack felt Susan's hand on his—caressing, reassuring, soothing, encouraging—as she continued. "To ask Jimmy to be someone he's not will certainly make him something less—if he listens. You, better than anyone, know that." Jack was squirming. "Kings Point rather than Rutgers. Mobil Oil rather than law school. Susan Wheeler rather than . . . what was her name?"

"I don't remember," said Jack with a smile.

"Good. Now forget whatever it was you planned for Jimmy's life and enjoy your son for the beautiful, sensitive, artistic person he is."

"Daughters are supposed to be beautiful, sensitive, and artistic," said Jack. "Sons are supposed to be . . ." Jack pulled his hand away and looked around the cabin.

"What Jack? Sons are supposed to be exactly what?"

"Straight would be good for starters."

"And I wish he had my eyes and your hands," said Susan.

"I'm not talking about body parts. I'm talking about masculinity."

"Oh really?" asked Susan. "Whose?"

Jack was headed for the end of the settee when the ship's clock sounded eight bells. *Saved by the bell*, he thought. Then all hell broke loose.

The boat lurched to starboard and threw Jack into the corner of the settee, next to Susan. The yacht club mugs crashed into the starboard port-light and shattered on the cabin sole.

"Wind shift," Susan yelled.

"I'll get the gennaker down," said Jack. "See if you can put us into the wind."

Susan was halfway up the ladder as Jack spoke. By the time he made it on deck Susan had disengaged the autopilot and was already at the helm turning the ketch into the wind. Jack ripped the gennaker sheet out of the self-tailing winch. He felt the ketch move upright as the giant red, white and blue parachute-like sail flapped in the strong northwest breeze. The wind had shifted more than ninety degrees. From the endless whitecaps on the water Jack estimated the wind speed to be over thirty knots. He knew the boat was in no danger. On the contrary, this was the kind of weather big boat sailors lived, and died, for. But a sail change was in order. Jack gave Susan thumbs up and walked forward to douse the chute.

Unlike its big brother spinnaker, the gennaker was a cruising sailor's dream. This light air, down-wind sail had most of the performance benefits of a spinnaker without the hassles of a supporting pole and two sheets that required constant trimming by two crewmen. The gennaker foot was secured on the deck end of the forestay while its head was hoisted to the top of the mainmast by a special halyard. The clew end of the large triangular cut sail was trimmed on one side only by a lightweight sheet much like any large jib. The gennaker, however, was deep cut with an enormous draft that gave it the look, size, feel and performance of a classic spinnaker. The sail was trouble-free running downwind, but on the gusty broad reach *SEAQUESTOR* had assumed after the wind shift, the gennaker could drag half the deck under water and seriously test the strength of the mast rigging.

Jack positioned himself inside the sturdy stainless steel bow pulpit that grew out of a stubby teak bowsprit anchoring *SEAQUESTOR*'s forestay. He gave Susan a nod and watched her cast off the gennaker halyard from its cleat on the cabin top. She maintained slight tension on the halyard while Jack gathered armfuls of fabric which he stuffed into the "turtle" secured on deck at the forestay. Jack and Susan worked together like a finely tuned Swiss watch movement. In two minutes the gennaker was bagged, and Susan had winched out the self-furling jib. The maneuver was a nautical work of art.

\*     \*     \*

Meagan Palmer made a note to talk to Jack about Jimmy. She had promised Susan she would find a way to broach the subject with Jack, but somehow that mission had been lost along with Susan. The session was going longer than Meagan had expected. It was as though Jack were enjoying himself on his little voyage back into the past. Meagan realized it was time to move ahead—time to raise the stakes.

Meagan pushed the RECORD button on her machine and returned to Jack's side. "Jack, I want you to move ahead to the storm. When did you first sense trouble?"

*     *     *

Jack turned his face into the wind and inhaled deeply. He could smell a storm brewing before any announcement came over the radio. It was his special gift. Ernie Beckett had it too. Most sea captains did, and it drove everyone around them a little crazy to hear the two "old men" make their uncanny predictions.

"I think we're in for a blow, darlin'. The wind's veered another point to the north, and it's blowing spray." Susan checked the time, course, and the boat's speed, and then recorded the data in her log book. The time was 1045, Jack noted as he came back on deck with Susan's old white sailing slicker, and put it into her hand. He saw that Susan had already furled the jib on the forestay, and was now fighting a heavy cumbersome helm

"Can you tie a reef in the main and mizzen for me?" Susan yelled over the howling, gusting, spitting wind. "It'll help my steerage."

Jack waited for Susan to ease the mizzen sheet until the sail luffed gently, then cast off the halyard and watched the small sail creep down the mizzen mast. The slightest wind in the sail made it impossible to haul down, so he asked Susan to payout the rest of the sheet and spill the wind out of the sail.

He pulled the bolt rope down the mast track until the reef points attached along the horizontal axis of the sail reached the boom. He furled the loose Dacron around the boom, and then secured it with reef ties extending all the way out to the end of the boom. When the tying-off was completed Jack went back to the mast, winched up the mizzen halyard and cranked the wrinkles out of the luff of the shortened sail.

Jack smiled at the ease with which Susan trimmed the sail after the reefing maneuver. She understood mechanical advantage and used it well. He watched her sit on the cockpit seat with one foot on the helm and the other braced up against the leeward cockpit combing. With both hands free, she was able to easily trim the sail against the gusting wind and spray washing over her back.

"That was the drill," Jack yelled to Susan. "Now let's do the real thing."

Jack waited for Susan to ease the main sail sheet, then he hopped up on the top of the deckhouse and headed for the huge main mast.

Cast off the main halyard.

Cast off the main sheet.

Pull down the bolt rope.

Gather up loose sail cloth.

Tie in the reefs.

Wink at the helmsman.

A piece of cake, Jack thought as he finished the procedure and walked cautiously back to the mast to winch up the shortened main sail.

A couple of brisk cranks on the winch handle and the bolt rope was taut. From the corner of his eye Jack saw something fly over his head. The Vermilion Yacht Club burgee flying from the port side flag halyard had parted and Jack watched the burgee flutter away like an autumn leaf. *It's really tootin' out there*, he thought.

Jack could feel the boat heel to starboard as he tied off the main halyard. He looked aft and saw Susan in her classic three point position, hauling in the main sheet to trim the sail. He had taken only one step when the mainspring of the Grayson Swiss watch snapped. Jack saw Susan's foot slip off the large stainless steel steering wheel. For an instant she lost her grasp on the main sheet as she jumped up to grab the wheel. Then a dozen things went wrong at the same time.

The main boom swung far out to starboard.

The boat lurched into the wind.

Jack lost his balance and fell off the deckhouse.

Susan strained forward to find Jack.

The boat tacked through the wind.

The jib sheet jammed in its cleat.

The main boom swept across the deck.

Jack screamed to Susan.

Susan strained to hear him.

She never saw it coming.

The steel boom smacked into her head.

Susan Grayson was launched into the raging lake.

The port side deck, where Jack lay stunned, was engulfed in water. He reached out feebly toward Susan's motionless body being flopped and tossed by tempestuous waves. *SEAQUESTOR* was bouncing and flapping "in irons" as she struggled for some direction from the vacant helm. Susan was only ten feet from Jack's grasp, bleeding badly from the side of her head, and buoyed by air trapped in her baggy white foul weather gear.

Jack's hand fell upon the antique cork-lined ring buoy mounted near the starboard shrouds. He knew he had to go into the water if Susan was going to survive. His gut told him the storm would pass as quickly as it had come, and that together they would survive. But his training told him to stay with the boat—to turn her around and go back to Susan. Impulse, experience, and training all tugged at him, but it was something deep within that paralyzed him.

*     *     *

Meagan jumped as Jack suddenly screamed, "I'm drowning. Someone please help me. I'm drowning." She watched in horror as Jack grabbed at his throat and coughed and gagged as though he were actually going under. But she thought he had stayed with the boat.

"Where are you now Jack?" she asked him.

"I'm in the quarry," Jack yelled. "Hurry. Help me. I'm drowning."

Meagan noticed a different, high-pitched, childish quality to Jack's voice. More than the setting had changed. "How old are you Jack?"

"I'm only eight," he screeched. "I'm only eight, and I can't swim. Help me. Please help me."

Jack was panting, almost hyperventilating, Meagan observed as the magic word that would end it all was on her lips. He was sweating, drowning in his own perspiration. Meagan fought off the urge to yell out, Do something, Jack! Take control. React!

Meagan touched his hand and wiped his face. "I'm here with you Jack," she said calmly. "You're not drowning. Breathe deeply. Feel the air in your lungs." Meagan watched Jack calm down again. He was at peace, but Dr. Palmer had opened a closet door she was not ready to close. She charged ahead.

"You're still on the boat Jack. You're in the storm. Susan has fallen overboard. I want you to think Jack. What did you do after Susan went into the water?"

*     *     *

On the way to the cockpit Jack grabbed the yellow plastic horseshoe buoy from its cradle on the lifeline and tossed it toward Susan. He could see her red hair atop the old white foul weather jacket that had brought her so much good fortune in days gone by. *The drill. Remember the drill*, he said to himself as he climbed over the combing into the cockpit.

Jack cleared the fouled sheets and cast them off so they would run free. He had to stop the boat. Jack put the helm down and felt the ketch round up into the wind. The sound of the sails flapping against the gale was deafening, but at least the boat was back in Jack's control. He glanced astern and could still see a dot of red and white bobbing in the maelstrom. The yellow horseshoe had taken flight and was almost out of sight—useless. The engine, he thought. My Perkins diesel will save her.

Jack turned the key.

Nothing.

He looked to the stern.

Nothing.

He screamed, "Susan . . . Susan."

Nothing.

Jack screamed . . . and screamed . . . and screamed.

"Wake . . . wake . . . wake," Meagan said softly. "Come on Jack. Wake up now. Come back to me. It's all over. The storm has passed."

Jack felt the warmth of a porcelain cup in his hands. He smelled the familiar aroma of blueberries. He looked into beckoning green eyes of Dr. Meagan Palmer, and suddenly felt secure. "I was so close to her, Meagan. So close."

"Here, sip some of this tea. It will settle you down."

"Why doesn't this feel like therapy?"

"That was the hard part, Jack. Now we can start breaking it down."

"I'm broken down as far as I care to go," said Jack as he sat up on the sofa and slurped his herbal tea.

"You're hurting, but you're not at the bottom of the pit. Not yet."

"When?"

"That's going to be up to you, Jack. Only you can see what's at the bottom. Take a couple days off and I'll see you Friday."

\*       \*       \*

When Meagan Palmer sat down at her desk to make some notes about the stormy session with Jack, she knew she had the key—a part of the story she had never before heard from Jack. The question that twisted in her gut was whether she could turn that key. How do you tell a man that his own fear killed his wife, she asked herself? Would that knowledge be more destructive than his murky nightmares, Meagan wondered.

Dr. Meagan Palmer had her work cut out for her, and she loved it. That love affair, she remembered, began one unforgettable spring break in Myrtle Beach when Meagan picked up a copy of Irving Stone's controversial best seller *Passions of the Mind.* The highly dramatized treatment of the life and work of Sigmund Freud had become the passion of her mind. During graduate school she became enthralled with Carl Gustav Jung's notion of a "collective unconsciousness" available to all of us somewhere deep within our psyches. Sometimes during our altered states of consciousness, in which Meagan herself often existed, we become aware of knowledge that no amount of bookish education could ever supply. She understood that by bringing the collective unconscious to the surface she would no longer merely observe and reflect the material world, but could create a new reality of her own.

Extensive recent reading in professional journals confirmed for Meagan that the emergence of emotional symptoms from Jack's dreams, and his obvious panic black-out in the river, were not the beginning of his problem, but the cracked door leading to a resolution of a hitherto unresolved traumatic episode.

The quite unexpected deep regression into a near drowning even in Jack's childhood, Meagan wrote, provides the crucial key to unlocking his deep psyche and setting him free from his nightmares.

The difficult question for Meagan was just how and just when she would use this new found key from Jack's past.

Jung taught that in psychotherapy the task of the therapist is to mediate, for the patient, a contact and exchange with his inner self. This contact alone, Jung believed, would then guide the patient through an individualized transformation and healing. The wisdom for change and rehabilitation, Meagan recalled, comes from the collective conscious which far surpasses any knowledge the psychotherapist may have.

Intellectually, Meagan understood Jung's lessons, but still she was frustrated at not being able to explain why Jack's long buried memories were surfacing now. Even more, it was part of her nature to want to act on this knowledge—to force an encounter, and thus a resolution. But how?

As she scrawled her notes, thoughts and questions in Jack's file she wondered how long she could sit back and wait for Jack's mind to connect his childhood fear of drowning to the adult fear that paralyzed him when he needed to act to save Susan.

Jack clearly had no recollection of his near-drowning in the quarry. Given his precise technical mind set, he would have great difficulty in accepting this "hocus pocus" as an explanation for his nightmare. The next logical leap of ascribing that latent fear of drowning to his failure to save his wife was a leap Meagan was not excited about taking. And yet an encounter with a psychological profile like Jack's was what most excited Dr. Palmer about her chosen profession.

Paradoxically, it was not the collective unconscious wisdom that surfaced in Meagan and terrified her. She couldn't bear the thought of hurtling the man she loved.

# CHAPTER 13

Will looked out the window of his loft at the vermilion sun just sneaking over the rooftops of the lagoon houses. It was so perfectly round and brilliant against the backdrop of the late August sky that it reminded him of a huge Japanese flag. There was not a leaf fluttering in the quiet lagoons, and Will could feel the onset of another of what his Dad called the "dog days of summer." It was going to be another day when the misery index would creep like molten lava toward two hundred.

The great lake had been in the stagnate grip of oppressive heat and humidity for a week. The absence of any wind, save the brief morning lion-shore" breeze and its evening counterpart caused by rapid heating and cooling of the land against the unchanging 78° lake, gave most sailors an excuse to sleep in or walk into town for a leisurely breakfast at Mike's Freestyle Cafe or Ednamae's. But the defiant sailing junkies would soon be rigging up for a one-hour fix under sail, hopelessly becalmed again until evening. Even the fishermen stayed away from Lake Erie during these dog days, when swarms of flies were biting and fish were not.

The only major activity on the river today, Will figured, would be the usual Saturday morning exodus of "stink-potters" from Romp's Marina, down the river, and westward to Cedar Point, Kelly's Island and Put-In-Bay. The islands sucked pleasure seekers into their harbors like a brisk ebbing tide. Will had often joined these pleasure seekers, much to the chagrin of his father, who never seemed to understand why Will couldn't make it back for work on Monday mornings "like everyone else." Of course "everyone else" didn't make it back—just those types that his father approved of. But that was in the past, Will told himself, and today neither memories nor "dog days" would get the best of him. Today the world looked much like the old Japanese flag—invincible.

The last of Paddy Delaney's deliveries had been made two days earlier and the two dozen pristine fenders were tucked into *SEAQUESTOR*'s lazarette. Will got a small knot in his gut when he had placed the last four fenders through the hatch and saw how perfectly they fit. There really were no secrets in Vermilion, he remembered.

The boat was scrubbed and stocked and fitted out for delivery in a week, and Will was delighted, if not surprised, that Jack had stayed off her since his last pack-up. Will had earlier declined Jack's offer to have a friend of his transport Will's furniture and keepsakes out to Los Angeles by claiming that Shawnee had advised him to "travel light." Will was determined to make a new start, and he would begin by leaving Vermilion and all of its trappings behind. The one exception he made was the school teacher's desk and its contents that would "hitch a ride" on a moving van leaving the lagoons later in the week. At the last minute, Will also packed his magical multi colored plastic sea-anemone from Cedar Point.

Will remembered the stunned look on Jack's face when he pushed a Bank of Canada Cashier's Check for $150,000 (U.S.) across the table. Jack and Will had been reviewing the details of the buyout of GrayDays Marine. Will knew that Jack would not stand in his way, and that he had anticipated throwing in extra cash to make the purchase, after the boat sale proceeds were deposited. Then came the delightfully puzzled look on Jack's face as he blurted out, "Who bought her the Sultan of Brunei?" Will also remembered his own surprise when he learned that Attorney Joe Ryan had valued will's half of the business a week earlier at exactly $150,000.

In a week it will all be over, Will thought as he sat back or the old settee. He would soon swim out of the tiny fish bowl that had so constrained his life, and float free in a west coast sea of a million nameless faces. Strangely, Will now enjoyed the easy moments of solitude that allowed him to reflect—something he hadn't done much of in the past. For the first time in several years there was no music, no smoke, no clutter and no pressure—just an uncommon peace that suddenly spoke to Will and told him that his life was about to change.

*     *     *

Across town Jack Grayson saw the rising sun quite differently. As he sipped strong black coffee on the rustic wooden deck that overlooked Lake Erie he was refreshed by the light morning breeze spilling past his face—a face that described turmoil better than a Van Gogh portrait.

In the two weeks since his freakish diving accident his unhappy but secure little world had become totally insecure. He had quickly sold his diving gear, against Meagan's advice, and donated the money to the American Legion. It seemed a suitable repository for another relic of his past. He had become frustrated with the biweekly therapy sessions Meagan had insisted upon. It seemed to him that she was overreacting to some bad luck, and her idea that the episode was a "panic attack" had put them at odds. Panic was not in Captain Grayson's procedure manual. Yet, despite the tension, he could not bring himself to end the sessions, believing that Meagan was trying to tell him something, to lead him to some essential truth in the way shrinks do that sort of thing.

Will's announced departure had sunk the "History Tours" project with salvos that would have put a smile on Commodore Perry's face. Not only did the Captain's Quarters lose its reception center operator, it lost its motivation—at least most of it. *Without a "life to save," what was the point?* But then, the denial of the loan application at the bank didn't help matters either. Jack was surprised at his own disappointment over the loan rejection letter, since he had never felt any excitement about the project. Maybe, he thought, he just didn't like losing.

Then there was the matter of GrayDays Marine. He had satisfied himself over the last year that he didn't want to run the business, yet he couldn't agree to sell it off when Will's father died. Now he was stuck with the reality that as the sole owner he would have to make a go of it, at least until he could sell it, or take a quarter million dollar loss.

Everywhere Jack looked he saw another obligation, another snare, and another trap. As he watched the red sun rise into the humid haze, and felt the sticky film of sweat mounting on his face and arms, he saw nothing ahead but another dog day.

*    *    *

Angelina Mariano paused in the entrance way of the Renaissance Hotel in the old Broadway Building as if she were waiting for someone or something. She took a Benson & Hedges 100 out of a monogrammed cigarette case and lit it from a small butane lighter built into the edge of the case. She inhaled once deeply, then dropped the cigarette and crushed it under her black patent leather high, high, high heeled shoe. She unpinned her hair, shook it out as it dropped to her shoulders, then tied a bright Gianni Versachi scarf around the flowing ebony ponytail she formed. She was aware of the inquisitive eyes focused on her from somewhere inside the hotel lobby, but was used to the feeling. She even enjoyed it a bit.

The familiar clanging of bells followed by a whining siren caught her attention. She bolted quickly from the doorway and hurried around the corner to the edge of Lorain's famous old Bascule Bridge. She trotted awkwardly up the slightly inclined bridge sidewalk and waved frantically at the bridge attendant high in the control tower. Cars were lined up at the gate behind her as she reached the crest of the bridge and stepped over a steel edged crack. She was only two steps on the downgrade when she looked behind her and saw the man in the dark suit running up the slowly inclining sidewalk as if his life depended on crossing the bridge. It probably did, she thought as she waved to him and smiled just long enough to see him disappear behind the towering mass of concrete and steel. Angie whisked off her shoes, stuffed them into her tote bag, and scampered off the bridge ramp to the line of waiting cars at the end of East Erie Avenue.

Angie crossed the road and paused at the old bronze plaque that commemorated the building of the bridge by Roosevelt's WPA in 1934. Angie looked up as the craggy old bridge tender leaned out the window of the control booth.

"Why in the hell do you do that Angie?"

"You know how much I crave attention," she shouted skyward.

"You'll get a lot of attention at your funeral young lady."

"Oh, go on now you old coot. I knew you wouldn't leave me stranded up there."

"Well don't do it again," the bridge master yelled down through the sirens. "We're both getting too old for this."

"I promise," Angie yelled back then blew him a kiss.

Maybe he's right, she thought as she wiped the sweat off her face and neck. It was only 8:00 a.m. and already the heat and humidity of the day was getting to her. She had been pulling that little stunt for years and had never before broken a sweat, but today there was more at stake than usual.

She did not want to be followed by Paddy's goons this morning, so last night she had parked her car at the old Lorain Yacht Club across from the Coast Guard station and walked up the hill and across the bridge to the hotel. Angie had planned her escape like the pro she had become. She watched the huge Cleveland Cliffs ore boat beat slowly up the Black River and under the large archway created by the two cantilevered halves of the Bascule Bridge. Angie had not seen one of these leviathans pass under the bridge for years, and wondered why it was making the unusual trip. U.S Steel had long ago constructed self-unloading ore docks on the north side of the bridge and had abandoned its old Hewlett unloaders down river at the mill. The new lake fleet of thousand footers now unloaded their cargo of Taconite iron pellets, from the Mesabi Range in Duluth, Minnesota, at a highly mechanized conveyer station just inside the harbor entrance.

Angie waved to the men on deck and followed the ship's progress upriver for a few moments. She glimpsed the deserted old American Shipbuilding

Company dry docks once owned by George Steinbrenner, Senior and Junior. Long devoid of any shipbuilding activity the property, now owned by Paddy Delaney, would one day, he speculated, become his Shamrock Casino and Marina. Although Cleveland's power brokers with the help of Governor George Voinovich, had twice defeated Paddy's initiative for casino gambling legislation, it was election time again and Paddy had assembled an immense political war chest to buy the support he needed in Columbus.

Paddy had gained quiet momentum for his project in the late eighties when he narrowly missed approval of his plan in a statewide election. Even Paddy was surprised at how quickly a coalition of North Coast business leaders—"Shooters, Hooters and Coasters," he called them—rose up and proclaimed the evils of a casino on the lake. These entrepreneurs were, Paddy understood, less interested in morals than in the survival of their own restaurants, bars, clubs, museums and amusement parks. But still, they had found an issue that conservative downstate Ohio voters could get close to, and they capitalized on that issue in the final days of the campaign.

But Paddy Delaney is a patient man, and so it was ten years after the opposition had dubbed the old shipyard "Delaney's Dump," he was ready to strike back and claim his fortune. It was all just matter of getting his dirty cash into the right pockets.

Angie had keen powers of observation and had learned more about the "Irish" than any of them would want to admit. But in the beginning her motives were more pure. She believed the casino was a good idea for an area blighted by the erosion of industry to foreign countries and to the south. In fact she thought it was such a good idea that she worked her way into the inner sanctum of Paddy's empire and helped him generate the money he needed, albeit on the backs of college students and their naive parents. All of a sudden, however, Angie's dreams of life in a glitzy, fantasy world that would grow out of the ruins of a bygone era had turned as smelly and dark as the old rusting shipyard.

Now she was scared.

She estimated that she still had ten minutes before the bridge would close, and she guessed that her pursuer had given up. Still, she opted to end her reminiscences and complete her escape. She needed only a brisk five minute hike in bare feet to arrive at the red Alpha Romeo Spyder that complemented her image. The car was one of a kind in Lorain County and it helped to set her apart from the "common folk." The car was an easy conversation piece for the unwary college students she snuggled up to as a "political activist." Angie pushed the electronic entry button on her PaPa Joe's key chain, decided to leave the rag top up, slid into the driver's seat, fired up the engine and in two exhilarating minutes was purring down Colorado Avenue, past the shipyard gate, and speeding toward the high-level bridge. She dared not risk traveling the direct route to Vermilion across the Bascule Bridge, down West Erie Avenue and out the Lake Road. Instead, she would take her time wending through the old ethnic neighborhoods of the dying little city.

As she crossed the bridge at 21st Street she looked north and saw the mammoth ship rounding the final bend at the steel plant ore docks. Her earlier puzzlement at its passage under the bridge was resolved when she saw the large tents, banners, and crowds of finely dressed dignitaries standing by. Angie couldn't imagine what there was to celebrate in Lorain these days, but knew that sometimes you have to make the best of your circumstances.

When she eased off the bridge and crossed Broadway, she plucked the cellular phone from its perch and punched a single digit on the speed dialer.

*     *     *

Will's thin hard muscled body was statuesque under a refreshing waterfall in the bathroom of his loft, but his head was already on Ventura Beach looking out over the great Pacific Ocean, when he heard the telephone ringing. Normally this intrusion into his fantasy world would have upset him—but not today. For the first time in his life he had a plan, one of his own making. He also had the means to carry it out. For as long as he could remember his future had been in a box that someone else carted around. First it was his father, who seemed to want a clone rather than a son. Then Jack Grayson shackled him to GrayDays Marine with a guilt trip about "obligation and tradition." When Jack abruptly abandoned the box in the lagoons, Angie Mariano picked it up and sold it off to Paddy Delaney.

Will now felt he had redeemed himself, that he had taken the little box that held his life in check and had forever broken out of it. But he could never have foreseen the twist of circumstance that had liberated him. Contrary to all the confining Puritanical doctrine shoved at him as a kid, something very good had risen out of the personal Hell he had descended to. Nothing—nobody—would ever defeat him, or box him in, again.

A soggy trail of footprints and puddles tracked Will out of the shower and into his room. He quickly wiped the water off one arm and snatched his cordless phone off its base. "GrayDays Marine," he answered.

"We have to talk."

"That's what these things are for." As quickly as the words left his lips he regretted them. But then Angie Mariano was no longer in his play book. They had agreed that it was time for both of them to move on, or so he thought. Now he was fighting back a surge of aggravation that surfaced at the threat of a final tie that would not be broken.

"Don't be cute," said Angie. "I need to see you right away."

"I'm really stacked up today. I was just on my way out the door."

"Go back inside and close it then. I'll be there in twenty minutes."

"I don't think that's a good idea. We said our goodbyes, and I just don't see the point in going backward."

"The point? You want to see the point?" Now Angie was screaming through the phone. "How about the point of a knife?"

"Are you crazy or something?" Will had been on the receiving end of Angie's Mediterranean ire before, but she had never before threatened to hurt him, although he always sensed she was capable of it. "What are you talking about?"

"They're going to kill you."

"What? Who?"

"The Delaneys."

# CHAPTER 14

It was 6:35 a.m. on Monday morning when Jack whisked past Ednamae's. The misery index; that so dampened everyone's spirits over the weekend, had finally slipped to a tolerable level with the arrival of an enormous Canadian high that now caressed Lake Erie. The early morning near-shore weather forecast that was broadcast by NOAA Weather Radio called for ". . . a high temperature of 78° with relative humidity at 60%. Lake winds will be from the north northwest at 10 to 15 knots and wave heights less than two feet." A good day for taking care of business, Jack thought as he squinted into the bright yellow sunrise.

Jack had spent much of the previous Saturday morning with Will Daysart and Angie Mariano. Will's frantic telephone distress call at once delighted him, elevated him from his mounting depression, and horrified him. His first instinct was to go to the police, but Angie had enlightened him about uncertain complications inherent in such a move. Paddy Delaney's reach, it seemed, dipped deep into the Lorain Police and Fire Departments, City Council, and the County Sheriff's office. And, of course, Will wasn't squeaky clean either.

Jack slowly came to realize that this incredibly weird scenario needed a more creative approach—a brain trust of wisdom. So he ordered that Will lay low for the weekend, that Angie stay away from the lagoons, and that Will present his dilemma to this morning's meeting of the Captain's Quarters. Angie had scoffed at the idea, and Will railed at the suggestion that the group of "old fogies" would be able to do anything meaningful for him. But he was clearly alone and visibly frightened. Jack knew that it is usually during those desperate episodes of our lives that we scurry back to the nest for nurturing and protection. And on this last day of August the Captain's Quarters were the only family Will had left.

Will had readily agreed to leave his car parked in its usual spot at the front of the building, and to drive his twelve foot Avon inflatable dingy down the lagoon and across the Vermilion River to Parson's Boat Yard—the designated rendezvous point. Jack didn't know whether Will was being watched, but sensed there was no point in arousing any more suspicion than necessary.

Meagan Palmer's office lights were on, Jack noticed, as he slowed down at the Cargo Warehouse and crossed Liberty Avenue to enter the narrow driveway into Parson's Boat Yard, just west of the bridge. The yard was still as Jack carefully maneuvered his Range Rover down the steep incline to river level. Will was nowhere to be seen. Jack checked the dash clock and confirmed that he was on time for the planned 6:45 a.m. pick up. "Where the hell are you?" Jack whispered as he killed the engine and stepped onto the oily gravel. There was an eerie cemetery quiet in the boat yard that quickly caught Jack's attention and activated his memory cache.

Boat yards have an ambience about them that Jack had loved since his first visit to Derektor's Boat Yard in New York. The legendary boat yard, nestled on City Island in western Long Island Sound, had been the birthplace of a score of ferocious ocean racing yachts of the nineteen fifties and sixties. Jack had delighted in his frequent visits to Derektor's for specialized repairs on Kings Point's aging fleet of big ocean racers. In his final year at the academy, as a First Classman, Jack had captained the ocean racing team. Overseeing the maintenance of the yachts was one of the Team Captain's responsibilities, but Jack saw it more as a very special perquisite.

It had been thirty years since his first boat yard encounter yet he was immediately beamed back as he consumed the sights and smells of Parson's not-so-legendary little yard. He walked slowly past stacks of ancient wooden and modern steel pipe cradles that nestled some of Vermilion's finest sailing yachts during the severe North Coast winters. He ran his hand reverently across the crusty bottom of a sailboat resting on her cradle for some mid-season repair. He inhaled deeply of the distinctive comfortable aroma of bottom paint, spar varnish, gel coat, epoxy, grease and Dacron that congealed to form the common signature of every working boat yard.

For an idyllic moment Jack felt young again. Then he remembered the morning's mission and resigned that although his youth had long since sailed away, never to return, he had a chance to help Will salvage his.

At river's edge he scanned the row of twenty docks jutting into the river from the retaining wall of the yard. Just as in the days of old Captain Alva Bradley, the Vermilion River was an enduring asset, not a foot of which could be wasted. Fees for winter storage on cradles parlayed into income from prime summer dock space for yachtsmen lucky enough to rise to the top of a perpetually long waiting list. The small row of docks between Parsons' haul out slip to the north and the Liberty Avenue Bridge to the south, were even more coveted for their easy access to inevitable seasonal maintenance and repairs.

Every dock was full, Jack noted, and still there was no sign of Will or the GrayDays dingy. Maybe he overslept, Jack thought as he turned back toward the Range Rover.

He paused for a moment to fawn over a rare old mahogany yawl suspended in large padded canvas covered slings over the haul out slip. Jack admired the beautiful lines of what looked like a Nat Herreshoff design from somewhere "Down East." *They don't build them like that anymore,* he said to himself. He didn't recognize the yawl and thought he would like to meet her owners, perhaps inspect her more closely, so he walked to the edge of the slip to check out the transom for a name and home port. As he walked slowly along the port side his eyes followed the long graceful sweep of the keel down to the water. Then he saw it.

The little gray and yellow Avon dingy was bobbing quietly in the corner of the slip under thirty tons of mahogany and teak hanging precariously overhead. Jack squinted into the shadows and saw Will stuffed under the bright yellow dodger that covered the bow. His heart sank just as his worst fears erupted. He took command of his emotions and chided himself for getting caught up in the eerie spell of the deserted yard. He scooped up a small handful of greasy stones and heaved them at the dodger. Will twitched then jerked himself up a click at the sound of the aerial barrage.

"Hey sailor. Rise and shine." Will struggled to get his bearings as he crawled slowly onto the yellow plastic seat and tried to squeeze the bright morning sun out of his eyes. "You look like a derelict from a shipwreck," Jack quipped.

"Actually, I feel like the one who didn't survive."

"How long have you been down there?"

"Since about midnight," Will rasped. "I couldn't get to sleep in that house, so I decided to camp out."

Jack couldn't blame the kid for being scared. He had tried to reassure him that if Angie's information was correct, which he doubted, Paddy wouldn't try anything until *SEAQUESTOR* was gone at the end of the week. But it seemed that Will had no faith in a logical analysis of an illogical mess.

"Come up out of there," said Jack offering a helping hand. "You can wash up before breakfast at Ednamae's. We don't want to keep the Captains waiting."

\*   \*   \*

The old Chelsea ship's clock was just striking six bells when Jack and Will entered the parlor. Everyone sprung out of their chairs at the sight of the duo, and Ernie Beckett growled the unmistakable expression oozing from all of their wide eyes. "What in the hell happened to him?"

Jack put his arm around Will's shoulders and smiled. "He just came off the midnight watch."

Ednamae scurried out of the kitchen and took Will by the hand. "Come with me, Will. Let's scrub up a bit before morning inspection. You're going to be playing to a tough crowd."

The group eased back into their chairs and Jack took his usual seat next to Captain Beckett. They watched him pour a cup of steaming black coffee. He knew he had stunned them with Will's unexpected appearance but wanted to let them pant a while longer.

"So, what's new in your life Captain Grayson?" asked Maggie Wicks from behind a bone china coffee cup clutched between both hands.

"Why do you ask?"

"Well, I thought that since you asked Meagan to join us this morning . . ." Maggie put her cup down with a dramatic pause then smiled into Jack's eyes. ". . . that perhaps the two of you might have some announcement to make."

Jack felt blood rushing into his face after being blindsided. He hadn't seen that one coming, and felt the conscious helplessness of a person who had been stun-gunned. He turned quickly toward Meagan, who had one of those "you asked for it" looks on her face. Then, as only Meagan Palmer could, she came to his rescue. "Contrary to rampant speculation and rumor," Meagan began. "I want to assure everyone that no, I am not pregnant with Captain Grayson's lust child."

"Yes, well . . ." began Ernie with uncommon decorum. "I'm so happy you've straightened that out for us . . . I mean cleared that up."

Teddy Bear erupted into a belly laugh that infected the rest of the group. Even Maggie, whose incessant meddling had been splayed, found herself chuckling at this unexpected moment of comic relief and said, "Ernie, you DO have a way with words."

"Sometimes things just pop out . . ." Ernie started to say when Teddy and Meagan lost it. In an instant the whole table was out of control.

"Did I miss something?" asked Ednamae as she walked into the melee.

"Just another episode of *As the River Rolls*," said Meagan.

"I should be rolling into the kitchen so I can get our breakfast on the table," said Ednamae.

"No. Please sit down a minute," said Maggie. "Let's find out what Jack has to discuss with us and our two special guests."

All eyes turned to Jack, whose mood had turned serious. "I wish it were as simple as a lust child," he said. Jack now had the full attention of the group. His quick wink to Meagan, he knew, had not been missed by anyone. "But I think Will should explain."

"Why don't you give us a preview?" said Teddy Bear.

Jack took a moment to assess the dynamics then unloaded. "Will's life may be in danger."

"What? Is he sick or somethin'?" Ernie asked.

"No," said Jack. "He's healthy enough. But he's gotten himself mixed up in something very nasty and has nowhere else to turn."

"My God Jack, just spit it out," demanded Maggie. What's the problem?"

"Paddy Delaney is planning to kill him." Jack watched the expressions around the table simultaneously turn to disbelief. But no one uttered a sound nor spoke a word. "At least that's what Angie told him."

"Angelina Mariano?" said Ednamae. "How could she possibly be mixed up with that Delaney scum?"

Jack saw Meagan shift slightly in her chair, and give him a curiously negative nod of her head. Then he turned to the archway and saw will standing there quietly. "It's a long story," said Jack. "I think Will should tell it." Jack stood up and motioned to him. "Come sit down Will."

"Why don't you go and get breakfast on the table?" Ernie growled to Ednamae.

"Breakfast will wait, Ernie. I'm not going to miss this," Ednamae said. "Just take your time Will, and tell us what's going on."

"What's she doing here?" Will hissed as he pointed his finger at Meagan Palmer.

"You need all the friends you can find," said Jack. "And whether you accept it or not, Dr. Palmer is a friend. We're all friends and we want to help you out."

"Yeah, well I'm not crazy and I'm not going to let her check me into an institution somewhere."

"Listen up matey," said Captain Beckett glaring into Will's darkened eyes. "No one's checkin' you in anywhere. You best take us or leave us as we are. It's your choice."

"He's all right Ernie," said Jack. "He's had a bad weekend and is a little panicky. He'll be okay." He looked at Will with firm but pleading eyes and said, "Go on Will, just start at the beginning and tell them the story you told me."

They were spellbound and quiet for half an hour as Will poured out an ugly story of gambling, drugs, sex, deceit and lies. Jack could see that his provincial group of conservatives was wounded at the revelation that the sordid world of tabloids and cable news had tainted their pristine village. Then, over mounds of rum raisin flap jacks, the questions began.

Maggie was dismayed that her alma mater in Tiffin, a bastion of culture and enlightenment she had known and supported for years, had become a refuge of vice and deception ruled by demons rather than deans. Ednamae was crushed to find that the landmark Wheeler house had become little more than a "hovel and opium den." She was horrified to learn that the ebullient Angelina Mariano was nothing more than a "narcissistic hussy." Teddy Bear Parks was shocked to discover that this seemingly timid orphan kid actually led the secret life of a gambler, confidence man, hustler, sex machine and scam artist. That he dared to scam Paddy Delaney transcended shock—it felt like a level 6.5 earthquake to Teddy.

Only Meagan Palmer sat back quietly and pondered the mixed blessing of being right again. She had seen Will's demise looming before his father died. She had made several attempts to intervene, only to have her suggestions maligned by both Daysarts, junior and senior.

Jack lamented the smug look of righteousness on Meagan's face, and regretted that the image was having its obviously desired effect on Will. He felt a storm brewing. The questions finally dried up with the morning's maple syrup and coffee. Will seemed near an exhausted melt-down when he lashed out one more time.

"So what is Dr. Palmer doing here?"

Jack quickly scanned faces that seemed equally puzzled at the presence of the quiet Dr. Palmer. "Why don't you tell them Meagan?"

"Paddy Delaney is my uncle."

# CHAPTER 15

"How could you do that to me?" Meagan screeched. She had put Jack in the hot seat in front of her desk and was now circling him like a Peregrine Falcon in the hunt.

"Would you have come otherwise?"

"That's not the point," Meagan spat.

"That was exactly the point. I needed you to be there and I didn't think I could tell you . . ."

"The truth?" she interrupted. "I don't appreciate being handled like some school girl."

"And I don't appreciate being spanked like a naughty little boy."

Meagan stopped in her tracks and turned to Jack. Her face contorted slightly with the erratic squinting of her eyes. She ran her fingers through her hair as if to straighten it back into a place it had not left.

"Touché."

"Why don't you sit down, take a deep breath, and let's talk this out."

Meagan didn't relish being ordered about in her own office, but recognized the flag of truce that had emerged. She glided behind her gilded desk and slid into the comfort of her large caressing chair. The presence of a desk between her and Jack seemed to draw Dr. Palmer back to her usual office demeanor where she did what psychologists do best. She waited and watched.

"I really am sorry for not being candid with you," Jack began. "I had no idea the meeting would upset you so much."

"Didn't you think that perhaps I wished my relationship with Paddy to remain private?"

"Actually, no. It never occurred to me."

"How did you find out anyway?"

"Susan mentioned it years ago."

"Did she also happen to mention that I haven't seen him for thirty years and never want to see him again?"

"Meagan . . . I didn't know."

"Well now you do, so back off."

"But we have a crisis here and your relationship with him could . . ."

106

"My relationship with him could do nothing—absolutely nothing." Meagan fired emerald lasers at Jack. "I will not see him. I will not call him. I will not write to him. I will not contact him in any way for any reason."

"But Meagan, this is a life and death situation."

"Yes it is."

Meagan swiveled her chair toward the window and gazed out toward a buzz of activity that now seemed in another world. Jack had resurrected animus that she had not felt since she was a teenager. She was disappointed in herself for allowing feelings so long buried, and she thought resolved, to erupt so quickly and violently. Since college she had always been in control. She couldn't live any other way—couldn't possibly go back. Her life had been sailing blissfully along on the currents of a Utopian sea she had created. She was healthy, happy and successful. She had, for the first time in years, felt stirrings that might have begun something lasting and comfortable with Jack Grayson. Now, like most Utopian seas—one's conjured from our peaceful dreams—a serpent had risen out of the blue to turn her fantasy world into her Inferno. Meagan jumped at the touch of a hand on her shoulder.

"Maybe you can think this over tonight and find a change of heart tomorrow," said Jack. "Frankly, without your help I'm scared."

Meagan did not speak, and did not look up. She just gazed into nothingness and waved a dismissing hand. Somewhere in the distance she heard a voice say, "I'll call you."

\*    \*    \*

Jack's mind was whirling as he tried to process the bizarre and violent reaction he had just endured. Nothing in his past encounters with Meagan gave him a hint about Meagan's vehemence towards her uncle. She was obviously wounded and hurting—the last things he wanted for her. Now he hoped he could find another way to deal with Paddy.

A part of Jack's problem, he knew, was that he just didn't have enough information. Why did Paddy want Will dead? Was it just the gambling money Will skimmed? How did Angie find out what Paddy was planning? What is in those heavy new fenders in SEAQUESTOR's lazarette? Why were the fenders to be sailed to Port Colborne? Why had Meagan reacted so violently about her relationship with Paddy?

Jack had always been driven by information, facts and logic. Now he had to have some answers. He wheeled the Range Rover into a hasty, illegal U-turn, and set a course for PaPa Joe's Pizza & Pies. Angie Mariano had delivered the first hard fact. Maybe she could be encouraged to tell something more.

*   *   *

It had been years since Jack Grayson had maneuvered a small boat through the lagoons. As he stood at the steering console of the little Boston Whaler he had borrowed from Parson's, he delighted in how comfortable he felt. He decided that small boat handling was like riding a bike. Angie Mariano sat quietly in the bow section looking attentively from side to side like a sailor in a crow's nest.

Jack had gone to Angie for information and got more than he had bargained for. She believed the fenders were full of cash—dirty money from gambling—perhaps as much as a million dollars. The money, she thought, was destined for one of the big national casinos in Windsor, Ontario. But Windsor was only a short trip over the western end of the lake and up the Detroit River. So why were the fenders going to Port Colborne? Angie didn't know but she did hear that Will was being watched night and day to ensure his compliance with Paddy's instructions. She also overheard that shortly after the departure of the yacht with Paddy's hired captain, Will would also be dispatched, never to be seen again. Was all this worth a million dollars in dirty money, Jack wondered? He didn't think so, and suspected there was something else loaded on board. But what? And why?

He knew that Will had planned to spend the day at GrayDays making some front entrance repairs Jack had begged from him. If Will was being watched, then the lagoon side of the property would be unobserved.

Jack had become increasingly wary of Angelina and her motives, so rather than trust her notoriously absent discretion, he opted to take her along—as insurance. They would pull alongside SEAQUESTOR, go on board, move one of the fenders from the lazarette to the saloon, and inspect its contents. Jack had to know what he was up against if he was to have any chance of reversing Will's bleak forecast.

The five minute motor cruise across the Vermilion River and into the South Lagoon was uneventful. Jack was surprised at the casual facility with which Angie tied the Whaler abeam of Susan's yacht. As Jack shut down the outboard motor, Angie climbed on board, then unsnapped the pelican hook gate through the port side lifeline and leaned over to give Jack a helping hand. Angie had a subtle ability to make him feel old, but he took her hand anyway, and was yanked upward with a display of strength that surprised him again.

Jack gave Angie the 9-8-6-8 combination for the companionway lock, while he walked aft to the lazarette hatch. Jack hadn't previously noticed the small lock that now secured the lazarette, and hadn't a clue to its combination. As Angie removed the hatch boards to the main cabin, Jack rummaged through the cockpit gear locker and grabbed a long stainless steel marlin spike. One quick twist of the spike in the shank of the lock and Jack was in. He knelt down and pushed aside the tangle of Susan's trailing line until he uncovered one of the new white rubber fenders. He strained to pull one free and grunted what felt like a thirty-pounder onto the deck. He closed the hatch, replaced the sprung lock, and told himself to call Will later and have him replace it.

"Incoming," Jack yelled down to Angie as he tossed the fender through the companionway opening. By the time Jack descended the ladder into the saloon, Angie was already sitting on the cabin sole with the white fender lodged between her legs.

"I guess the first man who told me I had money between my legs knew what he was talking about wouldn't you say?"

Jack was always disarmed by Angie's crude candor. He doubted that he had ever been, or ever could be, so unabashed. "I guess we'll find out in a minute."

"Sounds exciting Captain," said Angie with a twinkle in her eyes. "I'm already breathless."

Jack knelt beside Angie's outstretched leg and opened his Swiss Army knife. Like a skilled surgeon beginning a routine appendectomy, he carved into a welded seam of synthetic rubber. He heard the slight whoosh of air as he punctured the case, and felt the rubber collapse under the weight of his hands. Jack cut a slit about a foot long then set down his knife and pulled open the gaping wound. "Reach inside and pullout whatever you find," he told Angie.

"Told you so," Angie said as her hand emerged with a banded stack of currency.

"How much is there?"

"The band says $25,000," said Angie.

"That can't be right," said Jack. "Let me see it." Jack released his grip on the fender and examined the stack of bills. They were all one hundred dollar bills, well-circulated, but neatly flattened and well compressed. He flipped through the edges and did a quick count—250 bills. "They must have bundled these somewhere other than a bank," Jack said.

"No kidding," quipped Angie with a look that made Jack feel like a dunce.

"How many bundles do you think are in there?" he asked.

"Let's take them out and see."

To his astonishment, in less than five minutes, Angie had pulled out and plunked down forty bundles of cash—a cool million dollars, Jack calculated.

"My God Jack., how many of these fenders are back there?"

"Two dozen according to Will."

"So little Willie Daysart has become the $24 million man," said Angie.

"No wonder Paddy is taking no chances."

"What do you mean, Jack?"

"He's taking this stuff to Canada on my boat, through my company, and through a port we've visited dozens of times. With the right captain and the right story, Canadian Customs won't suspect a thing."

"Even so," said Angie. "It seems like he's taking a big risk with so much money."

"Yeah, but he's already hedged his bet."

"How?"

"Will asked me to FAX the transfer papers and a personal note to a friend of mine in Canada."

"Who?"

"The Chief Customs Inspector at Port Colborne."

"Paddy doesn't miss much," said Angie. "Losing is not something he handles very well."

Jack marveled at the length of Delaney's reach and the depth of this knowledge. Suddenly Jack was feeling like he was in over his head, and needed to find a sensible way out. This was no time to be inventive, he told himself. Sometimes it's better to cut and run. "Start replacing the cash bundles—all of them," said Jack. "I'll be right back."

Jack bounded up the ladder and plunged back into the cockpit gear locker. As he pushed and probed for the old tube of synthetic rubber bonding compound he stumbled across one of Susan's old disposable cameras. His heart sank at the recollection of the hundreds of candid surprise snapshots Susan got over the years.

He noticed that the camera was still loaded but had only one shot left. When Jack reappeared at the hatchway Angie was still on the cabin sole stuffing the cash bundles back inside the fender. "Angie. Smile," Jack said. When she looked up, Jack flashed a final shot from Susan's camera.

"What was that for?" Angie yelled.

"Just a little insurance policy."

*     *     *

Dr. Meagan Palmer was drawn out of her trance by the subtle electronic ringing of her telephone. Beams of jade green scanned the room as if searching for some anchor point. When her eyes came to rest on the mantel clock, she sat upright with a start. 4:15 p.m. She had not moved from her desk chair for more than six hours. She had seen no one since Jack's departure and had seemingly done nothing to resolve her inner conflict, yet as she returned from a self-imposed altered state of consciousness everything was crystal clear. Meagan swiveled her chair around to the desk and picked up the ringing telephone.

"Meagan?" Are you there?"

"Yes Jack, I'm here."

"About this morning . . ."

"You don't need to go into it. I'm fine."

"Fair enough," she heard Jack say with a soft tone of relief in his voice. "I've made dinner reservations for us at *Chez François* tonight, if that's okay."

"Yes Jack. Of course. That's fine."

"Great. Then I'll pick you up the light side of nine."

"Not necessary Jack. I'll meet you there."

"Meagan, are you sure everything is all right?"

"Never better. I'll see you at nine."

Meagan carefully put the phone down then turned her attention to her old pistols hanging on the wall. "Paddy you rotten sonofabitch," she yelled. "It's payback time." The pistols were like a post hypnotic suggestion that triggered six hours of self-therapy into reality. It was uncle Paddy who had been Meagan's motivation for becoming a national champion marksman. Now he motivated her thoughts again.

When Meagan had returned from Paris to enroll at Kent State University, following the death of her mother, she had been obsessed with the idea that the sweet aroma of black powder would neutralize the stench her uncle had left on her.

Paddy Delaney, the wealthy benevolent uncle, had taken his "favorite niece" on cruises in the Caribbean, ocean crossings to their beloved Ireland, holiday excursions to the Greenbriar Hotel in White Sulfur Springs, the Breakers in Palm Beach and Caesar's Palace in Las Vegas. Together they had visited the most prestigious bright lights of the world, and together they had also glimpsed the most obscene dark corners of Hades.

Meagan was thirteen years old when Uncle Paddy snuggled in beside her in a first class cabin of the Cunard Lines *Queen Elizabeth* on an Atlantic crossing to the Mediterranean. Meagan remembered how Paddy caressed her and told her she would always be his "secret queen." But with time the caresses turned to kisses and the kisses to more intimate "lessons that a lady of the world must know to make her way." At the coming of her sixteenth year, when Susan Wheeler was enjoying her sweet sixteen party, Meagan Palmer had become a not-so-sweet concubine—a role she had despised from the opening act.

She remembered how, when her mother discovered the truth, she just looked the other way and tried to drink away the shame. It simply would not do to challenge the family patriarch and newly discovered treasure trove, she was told. The Palmer's owed their lives, their jobs, their wealth and security—even their daughter—to dear Uncle Paddy. No one must know the truth. The family image must be maintained, Meagan was reminded time and time again during her mother's infrequent semi-sober lucid moments.

But the darkest secrets of our lives often surface in the delirium of sleep. And so it was, Meagan recalled that her father charged into her room early one morning and woke her from her own fitful slumber. After an hour of tearful sobbing, Meagan confirmed the horrid truth of the nightmarish story her mother had innocently revealed. Then she watched her father suffer a living death. Even in his heartache, however, she could not embrace him. It would be many years before Meagan could allow herself to give any man a loving embrace.

She would never see her father alive again. An hour after he left the house to confront his brother-in-law, he was found dead on the bank of the Black River beaten and shot between the eyes. The killer was never found, and three months later the investigation was closed. But not for Meagan.

The *Lorain Journal* ran several stories about the cohesive spirit of the Delaney clan who rallied together behind Meagan and her mother in their time of loss and grief. The paper extolled the virtues of Paddy Delaney who funded a half-million dollar trust fund for his sister and niece to live in Paris, where they could "forget the cruelties of man." But Meagan Palmer would never forget the cruelty of the man who had taken her father, her mother, and her innocence. One day she would make him pay.

Fear, however, can be a powerful sedative. Paddy Delaney was a frightful man who, cloaked in his own fearlessness, bent people to his will. In her quest for redemption, Meagan had concocted scenarios where one .45 caliber round in her locked and loaded pistol would bring her uncle to his knees and see him beg for his life—a life that his "queen" would hold in the grip of her determined hands. But it was not to be, and with the passage of time her burning hatred cooled.

Meagan had established a satisfying life and had retrieved a large measure of her self esteem. She had interred Paddy Delaney in a chamber deep within a dark corner of her soul. But now, like the mythical vampire of Transylvania whose wooden stake had been excised by some unwary passerby, Paddy Delaney was back. Ironically, it was Meagan's providential liaison with her patient, friend, and lover who had laid the demon back at her doorstep.

# CHAPTER 16

*Chez François* was closed to the public on Monday evenings. But the public did not include the townsfolk of Vermilion. Much of Vermilion's mystique sprang from the cohesion of its resident conservators. That unique cohesion was maintained during the hectic summer tourist months with never publicized "accommodations" to the ruling gentry. There were special weekly candlelight services at St. Mary's Catholic Church and the Vermilion United Methodist Church, "before and after" hours shopping at Vermilion's finest shops, and quiet dining alongside the river at *Chez François*.

Jack sat alone at the corner of the grand old bar rumored to be a relic from one of Lake Erie's long gone passenger ferries that steamed from Buffalo to Detroit at the turn of the century. He had arrived at eight thirty and was enjoying the familiar tang of his Pink Gin—a simple concoction of Bombay Gin and Angostura Bitters he had discovered as a midshipman on his required round-the-world sea year cruise. He swirled the bittersweet gin in his mouth and listened to a familiar medley of "requests."

Gary Ryan, one of Cleveland's most sought after piano lounge players, had been playing quiet Monday evenings at *Chez François* as long as Jack could remember. He and Susan rarely missed an opportunity to sip a Saint Emilion Bordeaux and listen to Gary play their songs. *Strangers in the Night, Through the Eyes of Love*, and *The Theme from Romeo and Juliet*, had become standard Monday evening fare as nourishing to the soul as Chef Jacques' Chateaubriand was to the palate. Jack felt comfortable and safe in what he knew was little more than another shrine to his life with Susan. He looked across the room to their regular table next to a window overlooking the river, beautifully set for two for the first time in a year. "A sight so splendid for me," according to Maitre'd Henri.

It was just a whisker past nine o'clock when Jack crunched the ice out of his second pink Gin and listened to the final chords wafting from the Steinway grand as Gary Ryan crooned, ". . . since I found you, looking through the eyes of love." Jack dropped a ten dollar bill into the large snifter sitting on the corner of the piano and walked to his table. He sat with his back to the window so he would not miss Meagan's entrance.

Just after settling into his chair he heard the familiar blast of *Aphrodite*'s fog horn. Within the crimson aura of the wheelhouse Jack could see Maggie Wicks piloting another group of tourists from McGarvey's through the river and lagoons on her popular "Sunset Cruise." He grinned at the realization that Ernie Beckett, the crusty old salt from yesteryear, had somehow jury-rigged the fragile stuffing box on the excursion boat and gotten Maggie back underway. Jack hoped he would remain so resourceful in his eighties.

All of a sudden the piano man switched from his new arrangement of *Les Bicycles des Versailles* to the familiar chord progressions of *My Wild Irish Rose*. Jack looked up and saw Meagan Palmer float through the door in a sea of shimmering turquoise satin. She glided straight to the piano and placed a single yellow rose in Gary's snifter, then gave him a friendly "continental" kiss. Henri quickly intercepted her and Jack smiled again at their hugely theatrical exchange of hugs and kisses. Jack did not move but allowed his eyes to follow Henri and Meagan as they made their way through the rustic old twine house.

The historic building, now occupied by *Chez François*, had once been a shop where fishing nets were hung to be dried, inspected and repaired. A thoughtfully loving restoration of the decrepit structure had preserved the old bricks, crumbling mortar, hand-hewn wooden beams and oak planked floor now reminiscent of a bistro on the Left Bank of the Seine. Burgundy linen tablecloths, white tented napkins, candlelight and fresh flowers adorning each table provided a dining ambiance that stood unmatched on the North Coast. It was a special setting for special relationships. Assuredly so on Monday evenings, when all gentlemen wore formal dinner jackets and all ladies dressed to the nines.

"Captain Grayson," announced Henri. "Your most lovely dinner guest has arrived." Jack stood up and bowed to Meagan's coquettish curtsy. Then like a squall line rising in the west, Captain Grayson saw Meagan's demeanor change.

"Jack if you don't mind, I'd like to sit over there."

For a moment Jack was speechless. Henri must have sensed his dilemma and with the skill of a seasoned Parisian restaurateur, rose to the occasion.

"But of course," he said. "How stupid of me. Madame your table is ready over here, just as you requested."

Jack turned his attention to Meagan who smiled just a bit and said, "My treat."

Now Jack fully understood that the evening would not be going as he had planned, a realization that was confirmed when Meagan asked Henri for a bottle of her favorite *Pouily Fuisse*. Rather than sail blindly into uncharted waters, Jack fell back on his training. He sat quietly watching, waiting, and assessing. He was drawn toward, yet curiously unnerved by, Meagan's eyes, luminescent in the glow of candlelight against the backdrop of her stunning turquoise gown.

Meagan had never, in Jack's experience, looked so elegantly seductive. Her silky black hair was pulled back and upward into the style of a French twist that was secured with a jade and gold arched comb. The theme continued through perfectly shaped ears pierced with matching jade and gold earrings, down her long tanned neck to a surprisingly robust cleavage adorned with a large jade and diamond pendant suspended on an elegant braided gold chain. Meagan's jewelry ensemble paused with a simple gold bracelet on her left wrist, and then gasped with a dazzling diamond and jade ring on her right hand—a perfect mate to the pendant.

The unmistakable eastern Mediterranean motif, facing Jack, was at once enchanting and foreboding. It was almost as though he were sitting across the table from a strange seductress in a foreign land. Although Jack's defense sensors were operating, the subtle fragrance of jasmine interfered with his ability to discriminate the multitude of signals he was receiving. In a scene reminiscent of a Bogart and Bacall movie, the magnificent couple sat quietly in the candlelight measuring and assessing each other like prizefighters preparing to do battle. After Henri had poured their chilled white wine, Meagan raised her fine Austrian crystal flute, then leaned across the table provocatively and said, "I want to offer you my apology."

"Meagan, that's not necessary. I had no right to presume . . ."

"No you didn't," she interrupted. "But that still does not excuse my outburst. I should have controlled my emotions."

A darkness so deep that it made Jack shudder for a moment, fell upon Meagan's eyes. Jack quietly waited for Meagan to return. Suddenly, without another word, she tipped her crystal glass into a mild collision with his own, downed the last of her wine, and set her glass on the table. Her precise delivery of body language left no doubt in Jack's mind that Meagan was finished with apologies. He knew from twenty years of observing spats between Susan and Meagan how difficult it was for her to admit error. He had always known that she was loathe to apologize to anyone for anything. Jack also knew there was more to this scenario, but opted not to press the matter. He was sure Meagan would enlighten him when, and only when, she was ready.

Henri materialized out of the melodies wafting from the Steinway. He artfully refilled both wine glasses, and then vanished.

"Now it's my turn," offered Jack. "It was wrong of me to deceive you about the reason for your invitation to join us at the Captain's Quarters this morning. I just didn't think you'd agree to help Will unless . . ."

"Unless Vermilion's movers and shakers put the strong arm on me?"

Jack took a tactical slug of wine. "Something like that I guess. Anyway, it was wrong and I'm sorry."

"Apology accepted," said Meagan as she raised her glass and took a small sip.

"We'll find some other way to deal with Mr. Delaney."

"No you won't," said Meagan. The unsettling darkness was back in her eyes.

"What do you mean?"

"You have no idea what kind of person Will has run afoul of." Meagan leaned forward with both elbows on the table to drive home her point. "He is in grave danger, and my uncle will not give up until someone dies."

Jack recoiled from Meagan's icy stare. He couldn't believe what he was hearing. This was a sinister side of Meagan he had never before observed. He wondered what demons Paddy Delaney had deposited into Meagan's soul—demons that Jack had unwittingly awakened.

He had heard Angie Mariano describe the death threat. He had uncovered Paddy's clandestine cargo. He had listened to Will recount his association with the Delaney Clan, and even his near death encounter atop the old Broadway Building. But Jack had remained an observer. He had not felt the threat until now. Meagan had unnerved him and now he knew he was in hopelessly over his head. "We should take this to the police," Jack finally offered.

"Paddy owns the police."

"The Sheriff then."

"Come on Jack."

"Are you suggesting that we're helpless?"

"Not at all."

"What then?"

"I'm going to help you."

"How?"

"I have an idea."

"Are you ready to order?" said Henri out of nowhere. Jack felt like he had been snatched from the deep dark abyss of his nightmares. He was relieved to be saved, but disheartened that he had been denied the final resolution. He looked at Meagan, almost pleading to return to the deep, when he saw her eyes brighten toward Henri.

"How's the Red Herring tonight? She asked softly.

*     *     *

*Chez François* was not the only restaurant that catered to a select crowd on Monday evenings. In a private dining room at the rear of the old Lorain Irish-American Club on Broadway, another faction of the Delaney family was mixing business with pleasure. Paddy Delaney was holding court around a large round table filled with traditional corned beef, cabbage, boiled potatoes, Irish soda bread and Harp's beer.

As usual, Paddy was flanked by two dark-suited lieutenants who ate as if they were refugees from the potato famine. The twin brothers had been entrusted to Paddy's sanctuary two years earlier by a grateful cousin in Belfast after a series of unsolved I.R.A. bombings. It was a patriotic accommodation that Paddy had provided several times during the conflict over British rule of his homeland. Paddy's patriotism, of course always had an ulterior motive. Such accommodations provided Paddy with useful and expendable human assets whose identities and origins were obscure enough not to be traceable.

These fugitives from the Crown also served as important personal couriers who plied the vital transatlantic link between the Irish Republican Army and its expatriate supporters in America. The young men were soon to be repatriated, however, with new resources to exploit, and new missions to pursue for the glory of mother Ireland.

Paddy gnawed steadily at a three inch mound of corned beef sandwiched between slabs of crusty soda bread. A slimy rivulet of grease and Stadium Mustard flowed out of the huge sandwich, between Paddy's thick hairy paws, and onto the huge white dinner napkin tucked into his collar.

Angelina Mariano couldn't have been more out of place, she thought, if she had been at the dinner table of a convent. She had become repulsed by these late Monday night feeding frenzies and merely picked at a small lean piece of corned beef on her plate. The small smoky room was quiet except for the munching, grinding and growling sounds of the Irishmen seated across the table, and the slow measured clink of stainless steel on china to her right.

A short slender man dressed in tweed and seated next to Angie seemed equally out of place at what had become a feeding trough. Red Riemer had the look of a small town college professor—the kind Angie and Will had avoided around the campuses of northwestern Ohio. With a full head of curly crimson hair, a meticulously trimmed beard flecked with gray, and hands full of freckles, Red Riemer had all the markings of membership in the Delaney Clan—all except one. The man was civilized.

Red quietly cut and consumed a nice London broil with oven baked quartered potatoes, and asparagus with Hollandaise sauce. In place of the Irish beer a full bottle of robust local Mon Ami Winery burgundy sat before him. Angie marveled at the near reverence displayed as the Irish gentleman washed down his fully masticated food with red wine. She entertained herself with conjectures about the identity of the curious little man with the gourmet meal at Paddy's traditional feast.

"Are you not hungry tonight Lassie?" Paddy asked as he wiped an accumulation of greasy mustard off his chin.

"I guess I've just lost my taste for corned beef," Angie said.

"That's not good Angie," said Paddy. "You know how much I like a girl with an appetite." The twins looked up like a couple of junk yard dogs in heat, licking their lips at the thought of Paddy's prurient remark.

"I'm on a special diet."

"Maybe the London broil is more to your liking?" Paddy quipped.

"No, strictly American."

"And here I thought you'd become more worldly," said Paddy. "Once you've experienced the best it's hard to go back."

"All it takes is willpower, Paddy."

"And you think you have what it takes? Is that it?" Paddy took a long pull on the Harp's bottle. "How much willpower do you have, Angie?"

"Enough to get my needs met."

"Let's try her out," spat one of the twins. "Let's see . . ."

"Shut up," said Paddy. The room fell quiet again. There was only the incessant sound of the flatware on china. Red Reimer had not missed a beat as he neared the end of his meal. "You've got guts Angie. I'll give you that," Paddy finally said. "That's why I've kept keep around so long. Courage is a rare quality. Most people think they have it—until they're tested." Paddy took another long drink of his beer. "That's when I like to watch them struggle—watch them fail."

Red Riemer carefully placed his knife and fork together in the center of his empty plate and pushed it to the middle of the table. He poured the last of the wine, being careful to avoid the inevitable sediment in the bottom of the bottle, and moved his wine glass directly in front of him. He still did not speak as he looked casually around the table.

"If you're talking about me, you can forget it because I'm not afraid to fail. It's too restricting," Angie said. "Am I going to be the only topic of discussion tonight?"

"That depends on you," said Paddy.

"Okay. Fine. Let's change the subject then."

"Fair enough," said Paddy. "Let's talk about your partner in crime, young Will Daysart."

Angie sensed that she had been marked as the evening's entertainment, a position she did not relish, so she raised her deflector shields. "He's not really that interesting."

"When did you see him last?"

"The day the last of your boxes was delivered."

"How much does he know?"

"He knows there's something more than air inside those boxes, than boat fenders," said Angie. "I told you that."

"Does he know what is inside?"

"I don't think so." Angie felt her temperature rise and her pulse quicken. "I mean, how should I know?"

"Because I pay you to know," yelled Paddy as he slammed his hand down on the table. "And I pay you to tell me what you know."

Angie tore her eyes away from Paddy's malevolent stare and looked around the table. The twins were panting and drooling like attack dogs on short leashes. The quiet man had turned his chair slightly toward Angie and was now sipping from his large wine goblet.

"You told me to make sure Will stored the fenders as you ordered. I did that. You told me to report any suspicions he might have. I did that. What else do you want from me?"

"Why is he packing to leave?" demanded Paddy.

"I don't know."

"Why has he sold the marina to Jack Grayson?"

"I don't know."

"Where is he going?"

"I don't know."

"When is he leaving?"

"I don't know."

"What have you told him about my plans?"

"Nothing," Angie spurted out. "I mean I don't know anything about your plans, Paddy."

"I always admired your gift for gift for deception, Angie. It was your most useful asset. But I knew that one day you would try turning it against me. I just thought that catching you would be better sport. You disappoint me, Angie. You've lost your touch," Paddy said as he looked across the table to the quiet man.

Red Riemer looked hypnotically into Angie's eyes and she felt a dread she had never known. The only words he spoke that evening crashed into Angie's brain like a bullet from Lee Harvey Oswald's rifle. "Dispose of her."

Red Reimer raised his wine glass in a ritualistic toast. The last image Angie had of the Irishman was of him smiling devilishly as he drank the rest of the blood red wine.

# CHAPTER 17

"Hold on Susan. I'm coming back for you. Hold on . . . just hold on."

Meagan Palmer wrenched up out of a deep sleep and fixed her eyes upon the luminescent digital clock. It was 3:15 a.m. and she had been asleep only two hours when the storm arose. Henri had expelled Meagan and Jack from *Chez François* at the stroke of midnight, after which she and Jack had sat up for another hour sipping B&B and listening to Meagan's collection of John Coltrane records.

"Night Train" Coltrane had been Meagan's favorite Jazz musician since her childhood. As her mother buried herself in drink and jazz, Meagan used the music to resurrect herself from the depravity of her worldly existence. The old vinyl records were one of the few mementos she retained after her mother's death. Meagan owned a digitally remastered compact disc collection of Coltrane's music given to her by a grateful client, but preferred the softer mellow tones of the old recordings. The scratched and marred black vinyl discs had become the shared property of two scratched and marred women, yet thirty years later Meagan still found tranquility in their music.

"The life ring," he yelled. "Grab the life ring Susan."

Meagan switched on the small Waterford crystal night stand lamp and looked over at Jack Grayson thrashing about on satin sheets beside her. He looked like a survivor from the Titanic laying there in his tuxedo trousers and socks. His hair and face were dripping and his starched white shirt was soaked through. Captain Jack Grayson could have just been plucked from the icy North Atlantic. But Meagan knew that Jack's shipwreck was mired in the tepid murky waters of Lake Erie.

She put her hand on his shoulder and shook him gently until he opened his eyes. "Good morning sailor," she said. "What's going on?"

Jack did not move and did not speak as Meagan wiped his face with a large tissue she plucked from a box on her nightstand. Her experience told her to wait for Jack to speak so she sat quietly beside him and reconstructed the unexpected events of the evening before.

\* \* \*

122

When Coltrane's A-Train had come and gone at about 1:00 a.m., Jack stood up, grabbed his white dinner jacket from the arm of the sofa and said, "We have a lot to do before the sun sets today, and I don't function well without a few hours of sleep."

Meagan had surprised herself with her response. "Why don't you crash here?" Meagan smiled as she remembered the bemused look on Jack's face when he finally spoke. "You make it sound like we're back in college." The Brandy and Benedictine blend had left Meagan with a little buzz that made her even bolder than usual.

"Jack, I've wanted to say that to you since 1966. So, what do you think?"

"I think we should take it nice and easy," he told her.

"I'll catch a few Z's right here on the sofa."

"I see you haven't forgotten the jargon either," Meagan said. "My queen-sized bed is much more comfortable though, and I'm willing to share." The rational side of Meagan's brain told her she was pushing things, but her creative hemisphere took control. "But you must promise to be good."

Meagan had not commented when Jack lay down with his clothes on. She simply slipped into the bathroom and changed into her customary long flannel pajamas. When she emerged, Jack was already sound asleep. She slid in beside him and cautiously laid an arm across his slowly heaving chest. It had been many years since Meagan had felt the warm security of a man beside her. Now her body stirred with sensations long ago pushed aside.

\* \* \*

"I was back in that storm again," Jack finally said, bringing Meagan back out of the euphoria of the events of last evening.

"The same nightmare as before?"

"In living color."

"Tell me about it."

"You've heard it all before," said Jack. "It's always the same. It never changes."

"Perhaps," Meagan said. "But this is the first time I've been able to get your impressions so soon after the dream."

"Why does that matter?"

"Almost immediately after we awaken we begin to forget the details of our dreams. The really good stuff recedes into our deep subconscious just as quickly as it surfaces in our dreams. You've heard motivation speakers tell audiences to keep a pencil and pad next to their beds to record dream recollections as soon as they wake up, haven't you?"

"Yes."

"Well, I'm your pencil and pad this morning. So let's start recording."

"Right now? In the middle of the night?"

"There's no better time," said Meagan. She reached into the nightstand drawer and pulled out her Dictaphone hand-held recorder. "And I *am* putting this on tape." She saw Jack recoil. "My note taking leaves a little to be desired before sunrise."

Meagan talked Jack through his nightmare two times. On the first pass she encouraged him to relate as much detail as he could remember, but did not interrupt his narrative except to remind him to include more detail. On the second attempt Meagan demonstrated a gift for cross examination that would have been the envy of F. Lee Bailey. She probed and tested and questioned every image conjured up by Jack's subconscious mind. Meagan became engrossed in the exercise, refining her technique with each series of questions. Although she had gathered a wealth of information that she would later use for a paper on "Debriefing the Dream," she soon realized that she had learned nothing helpful in Jack's treatment. Yet something continued to gnaw away at her—some elusive tidbit buried deep within her own subconscious.

Jack was clamoring for a shower and a cup of coffee. Meagan realized that she had put her guest through the wringer, but also understood the value of the momentum they had achieved in this unusual therapy session. It was only 4:15 a.m. and there was still time to make a breakthrough in purging Jack's demon, if she could just harness her own deep perceptions.

While Jack showered, shaved and made coffee, Meagan poured over her journal of six prior sessions with him. Meagan was sure the key that would unlock the demon's lair was nestled somewhere in her observations and notes. In time it would reveal itself to her. She looked up at the sound of clinking cups, and saw Jack walking through the bedroom door holding two mugs of steaming coffee in one hand and a plate of buttered bagels in the other.

"I'm sorry about the margarine, but the proprietor neglected to lay-in the cream cheese."

"*Au contraire*. In this establishment we serve not only the psyche but also the heart," said Meagan.

Jack handed Meagan her coffee and set the plate of bagels on the bed between them. Meagan was delighted that her feeble attempt at double entendre was not lost on her guest. She closed her journal and put it back inside the nightstand drawer.

"So what's the cure?"

"I'm still struggling with the diagnosis," said Meagan chomping through the boiled and baked dough.

"What do you mean?"

"There's something I'm missing in all this, and I just can't put my finger on it."

"Maybe you're searching for something that doesn't exist."

"Oh, it's in there all right," said Meagan pecking her forefinger at Jack's skull. "And I'm going to find it."

"Sounds enchanting."

"I've been accused of worse," said Meagan as she licked the oily crumbs from her fingers. "Now let's get back to work."

"What? Now?"

"I want you to start from the beginning and run through the whole dream again."

"Please to forgive dear lady. But I can't see what all this repetition is accomplishing."

"If at first you don't succeed," said Meagan. "What?"

"Abandon ship?"

"I thought the captain always went down with the ship? That he never gave up, no matter what the peril." Meagan could see a pained expression on Jack's face. Not something she cherished, but something that was necessary. At that moment she knew she had it. She had found the missing key. Now she wondered whether she had strength to use it. It was a question Dr. Meagan Palmer did not ponder for long.

"I want to take you into another regression," said Meagan.

"What? You mean now?"

"By sunrise you'll be a new man." Meagan saw Jack's shoulders slump and his head bow. She wondered how much deeper she would have to drag him before he could be saved. She took his hand in hers and lifted his chin until their eyes met. "I promise you. By sunrise it will all be over."

\* \* \*

Jack relaxed on the couch in the small office Meagan kept in her house. He watched the sparkling turning crystal, a duplicate of the one in her office, as it cast rays of colored light across his face. The routine was the same as always except for one new instruction. This time Meagan told him something she never before said: *When you come back you will remember everything you saw and heard. You will remember every detail of every thought and feeling.* Then he heard Meagan's parting words of encouragement—or were they Susan's? *Things always look better at sunrise.*

After several rhythmic blinks of his eyes he was back in the maelstrom. But now Jack sensed another presence on the yacht with him and Susan—a persistent prodding presence that made him uncomfortable. He watched Susan tying reefs into the small mizzen sail while he steered the boat into the storm.

Suddenly the presence ordered "Tell me about Susan going overboard." Jack yelled out as he saw Susan swept over the side by the gibe of the main boom. He felt the musty lake water on his face as he lay on deck looking into the scupper at the railing. He saw Susan in the water at arm's reach—yet out of reach. Jack grabbed the ring buoy to throw to her then he froze.

Susan was floating but not swimming. Her bloody head was tilted back and her eyes were closed. She was lifeless yet not dead, as the wind and waves pushed the floundering yacht slowly away.

*Go in for her*, the presence demanded.

"I have to stay with the boat," Jack yelled out. He threw the life ring into the water and saw it splash within inches of Susan's bobbing outstretched arms.

*She's unconscious*, the presence observed. *Tie yourself off and go into the water for her.*

"I can't do it," he screamed. "I can't go in the water."

*Why not, Jack?*

"It's against the rules."

*Whose rules?*

"It's not the drill. You have to stick to the drill."

*There is no drill for this*, the presence chided. *You have to go in and get her.*

"Help me. Please help me," Jack screamed. "I'm drowning. I can't swim. Please come back and help me."

*Where are you, Jack?*

Jack was coughing and choking as he screamed, "I'm in the quarry. Please come back for me."

*You're not in the quarry. You're on the boat*, the presence persisted. *What do you see?*

"Susan is in the lake, far away, bobbing far away, so far away."

*Why don't you save her?*

"I can't . . ."

*Why not?*

Jack began to sob. "I'm afraid."

*Afraid of what Jack?*

"I don't want to drown. I don't want to die."

\* \* \*

"Wake. Wake up now. It's over. Wake up Jack," Meagan continued. "It's all over now." Meagan took Jack's hand and looked deeply into his tearful red eyes as he snapped back to the present tense and sat up. "How do you feel?"

"Like I've just been on a voyage through the gates of hell."

"You have," said Meagan as she handed him the usual cup of steaming herbal tea. "But you survived it."

Meagan watched Jack quietly sip the hot brew and look out her bedroom window at the slowly emerging dawn. She knew he was processing bits of new information revealed during the traumatic regression through his past. Her emotional side wanted to hold him, console him, and talk him through his heartache. But Dr. Meagan Palmer, PhD, knew she had to let her patient sift and fashion his murky recollections into concrete conclusions. She assumed that those conclusions would, almost certainly, be wrong so she mentally prepared for her critical therapeutic role where she would reshape and resurface the concrete before it set.

Meagan was equally certain of her ability to guide Jack through the inevitable tidal wave of guilt and recrimination that would soon gush forth. So she waited and watched and prepared. This new dawning was not only changing Jack's life, but her own, Meagan thought as she sat cross-legged beside a man she had secretly loved for twenty years.

Thoughts of Paddy Delaney, Angelina Mariano, and Will Daysart were now as far away from her bedroom as Paris had been from Lorain thirty years earlier.

Meagan had been alone for almost fifteen years after her two rapid fire marriage encounters. As only Meagan Palmer could, she shrunk herself down after Scott Kennedy abandoned her in Virginia. She self-diagnosed a competitive and controlling nature that had destroyed her prior marriages, and she accepted those traits as an outgrowth of the physical and psychological bondage she had endured as a teenager. She would never again allow herself to be dominated or controlled by any situation or any person—certainly not by a man.

Whatever passions had since burned in Meagan's soul, surfaced not in the bedroom but in the offices, hospitals and universities that comprised the world of clinical psychology. She had established herself at the pinnacle of her profession, and that high totally sustained her—until now. But during this promising September dawn another deeply repressed passion stirred inside Meagan and she was titillated and challenged in a way she had never known.

Weeks earlier, when Jack first consulted her about his nightmares, Meagan had recognized the ethical conflict. But, she rationalized, she had laid the issue before Jack and he had blown it off. "You sound like you're producing a Sally Jessie Raphael show," he said. Men can be so naive, she thought as she watched him turn toward her with tears streaking down his face. The time to work the concrete had come.

"What's wrong, Jack?"

"I could have saved her."

"Why do you think so?"

"She was unconscious," Jack said.

"She needed me to go in after her."

"But you were alone on the boat. There was no way."

"I could have tied myself off on a long line."

"You're second guessing," Meagan said, testing and probing Jack's recollection. "It didn't occur to you at the time."

Jack sighed and finished off his tea. "That's just it, Meagan. It did occur to me."

"So why didn't you go for it?"

"I had this feeling that I would drown."

"But you're a strong swimmer; a scuba diver."

"That's what's so bizarre. My first instinct was to go into the lake. It looked like an easy swim. No more than ten yards, grab hold of her, and pull us both back to the boat. I had my hand on the ring buoy and line, ready to go over the side when something happened." Jack had broken into a profuse sweat and nervously ran his hands through his damp hair.

"What? Tell me what happened."

"I froze. I had this flashback to a day I thought was long forgotten."

"Tell me about it Jack."

"I was eight years old and was standing at the old limestone quarry throwing stones into the water. I used to go there every summer day with two of my friends. None of us could swim and it seemed exciting to be near that huge bottomless pool of water. My parents had warned me to stay away from the quarry, always telling me that kids who swam there drowned. And sure enough, every summer, someone did drown there. The newspaper always attributed the drownings to some sort of accidental injury or physical defect, but we knew better.

Every school kid in the county knew something evil lived in that quarry, something that snatched one victim every year, kind of like a sacrifice. It was all *Hardy Boys* type stuff. At least it seemed that way until the day some teenagers caught us.

We were at the edge of the quarry throwing stones into the water as usual. We always threw a stick into the water first, and then would see who could throw the farthest as the stick floated away. I had discovered that my chances were better if I used flat stones. They sailed a little and sometimes skipped across the water before sinking. The losers had to buy the winner a dill pickle and RC Cola from old man Duffy's store."

"That's all fascinating Jack," Meagan said impatiently. Obviously Jack missed having someone to reminisce his childhood exploits with, but Meagan was anxious to move the session along. She also sensed that his detailed digression was a subtle defense mechanism to avoid describing the traumatic event. "Now get on with the story."

"Well, like I said, we were minding our own business and were so deep into our little competition that we didn't notice the teenagers slip up behind us. They grabbed everyone, but somehow Carl and Dan managed to break away. I kicked and yelled and struggled but couldn't get loose. My heart sank as I saw my buddies running away. One of the kids had me in a hammer lock from behind. The other one stood in front of me and said, 'the quarry monster hasn't been fed this year.' Then he said to his pal, 'bring the victim to the edge of the pit.'"

"I told them I couldn't swim. I pleaded with them not to throw me into the quarry. I even tried to bribe them with pop and pickles from Duffy's Deli. The next thing I knew I was in the cold water, sinking like a rock. The drop from the edge of the quarry to the water was only ten feet, but I felt like I'd been thrown out of a flying plane. I remember how quiet and clear the water seemed. I felt this strange blend of peace and panic as I sank deeper into the quarry."

"All of a sudden I stopped sinking and began to rise. I thought maybe the quarry monster was going to spare me after all. I didn't know it then, but as I held my breath, the air in my lungs acted like a float that brought me up. But, of course, as soon as my head broke into the daylight and I exhaled, my head slipped back under the water. I kicked my legs and flailed my arms. I screamed out to the teenagers, 'I can't swim . . . please save me . . .' but no one came. I tried to swim, tried to float, tried to get to the side, but nothing worked. I was coughing and choking and exhausted when my head slipped under the water for the last time."

"I just couldn't fight it any more. I knew I was going to die, so I just gave up and let go. The next thing I saw was old man Duffy hunched over me. He looked like he had drowned himself, dripping water on my face from his hair and long beard."

"He saved you?" asked Meagan.

"That's what they told me," said Jack.

"I didn't remember anything that happened until today."

"Someone must have told you the story. It must have been the talk of the town for weeks," said Meagan. "I can't believe you didn't get every little detail."

"Apparently my mother freaked out and wouldn't allow anyone to talk to me about what happened. I guess she figured some forgotten tragedies are best left that way." Meagan felt a pang of empathy with that remark, but opted not to interrupt as Jack continued. "Old man Duffy died a few days later, and nobody wanted to talk about that either. The store closed, Danny and Carl moved away, and I never went back to the quarry again."

"Why not?"

I just didn't."

"When did you learn to swim?"

"Seventh grade gym class," said Jack. "Everybody was required to take swimming and swim a lap of the pool to pass the class."

"Did you have any problem with that?"

"Nothing more than any of the other non-swimmers."

"Except for the storm last year, have you had any other drowning flashbacks?"

"In the river the other day; when Maggie pulled me out."

"No, I mean before the storm and before the nightmares."

"Nothing I can recall," said Jack.

"Except for the book, but that was nothing really."

"Tell me about it."

"You remember how Susan liked to buy me books about the sea? Well, for my birthday she gave me *The Perfect Storm* by a journalist named Sebastian Junger. It's a non-fiction account of a New England fishing fleet caught in a huge storm off the Grand Banks. It's a gripping and tragic story, but Junger's description of the process of drowning made me so uncomfortable that I couldn't finish reading it."

"Anything else?"

"Nada. Nothing."

"I'll be damned," said Meagan, now scribbling notes in her journal.

"This is the most dramatic case of traumatic episode repression I've ever heard of. I've read several case studies and thought I understood the phenomenon, but never dreamed I'd see the day when . . ." Meagan paused and took Jack's hand. "You will permit me to write this up for publication won't you?"

"What do I get?"

Meagan smiled broadly and patted Jack on the forehead. "You already received your reward."

"And that would be?"

"A cure," said Meagan. "The demon that has haunted you all these months has finally been exposed for what it really is."

"And that would be?" Jack repeated.

"The Quarry Monster—a myth."

"I'm not following you, Meagan."

"It was your repressed fear of drowning that stopped you from jumping into the lake the day Susan died—not cowardice or inaction. It was a latent psychological switch that ironically turned itself on just at the right time."

"Why do you say that?" Jack asked through a growing appearance of anxiety and dejection. "That switch, as you call it, prevented me from saving Susan's life."

"Jack, she was already dead when she hit the water. Going into the lake in that storm probably would have killed you too."

Jack leaped off the bed and headed for the window, then stopped and spun around to face Meagan. "What are you saying? How could you possibly know that?"

"The autopsy report."

"What?"

"I got a copy of Susan's autopsy report from the Coroner's office and read it."

Jack's surprise suddenly turned to rage, but like a seasoned trial lawyer during cross-examination, Meagan pressed on, asking only questions she knew the answers to. "Didn't you get a copy?"

Jack turned to the window and Meagan watched the early morning rays of sun highlight his chiseled weary face. She had pulled out all the stops now, and there was no going back. She could see Jack taking himself back to the devastating days right after Susan's body had been recovered. Notations in the Coroner's files clearly indicated that the autopsy had been requested by Jimmy Grayson over the vehement objection of his father. Large red type on the cover of the file warned:

AUTOPSY REPORT NOT TO BE SENT TO CAPTAIN
JACK GRAYSON, PER HIS REQUEST.

After several agonizing moments of quiet, Meagan jumped back into Jack's head. "Do you want to read the report?"

Jack spun around and glared at Meagan. "How could you do that?" Meagan let him vent. "How could you pry into Susan's death without telling me?"

"I assumed, like you did yesterday, that you wouldn't mind allowing me to share the truth."

"Touché."

Meagan always marveled at the power of a single word to instantly alter the mood of any encounter. All it takes is a courageous and caring person to speak it. Meagan knew it was time to do what she did best—heal. She closed her journal, softened her tone, and carefully measured her next words. "Jack, there's no doubt from the autopsy. Susan did not drown. She died from a massive trauma to the head when the gibing boom hit her. There was no water in her lungs. She was dead before she hit the water. There is nothing you could have done."

"My God," said Jack softly. "I never knew."

"You never wanted to know. It would have been all the harder to punish yourself. I'm disappointed that Jimmy never told you the truth."

"I guess it would have been harder for him to punish me if I had known the truth."

Meagan got off the bed and walked to Jack. She took his hands into hers and looked deep into his hazel eyes. "Now we're beginning to get somewhere."

# CHAPTER 18

The first day of the month was for reflection and planning—at least it was so in the manager's suite at the Vermilion Yacht Club. Captain Ernie Beckett always arose at first light, long before any of the resident pleasure boaters, or their annoying spawn, were rattling around. It was the perfect day, and the perfect time for setting goals, making plans and assessing what was working, and what was not. It was a day when another page of the calendar was torn away to reveal another thirty days of opportunity, unburdened by the past. So it was at 6:15 a.m. on Tuesday, September 1, 1998—the morning after the night before.

The manager's suite occupied four compact rooms on the south end of the long one-story yacht club building. True to Percy Wheeler's lagoon development restrictions, the clubhouse was classic Cape Cod—white frame with black shutters and a black shingled roof. Access to the suite was obtained through the Manager's Office adjacent to the clubhouse Great Room. Ernie Beckett's office was decorated in the classic Spartan style of the Master's Quarters aboard a modern merchant ship.

To the chagrin of most club members, Ernie had painted the room in a light shade of battleship gray, accented with sea foam blue doors, window frames, wainscotings, and crown moldings. The furniture might have been salvaged from the *EXPORT TRADER*, Ernie's last command. There was a large steel desk, credenza and an array of file cabinets, all painted gun metal gray. A long gray metal table that jutted on the perpendicular from the front of his desk, surrounded by seven hard oak captain's chairs, allowed the office to serve as a military style Ward Room.

Ernie refused to meet with the membership anywhere but "on the Quarterdeck," an office description they resented and refused to allow him to formalize with a brass nameplate he had offered up. He selected the most uncomfortable chairs he could find so that no one would be likely to stay very long.

The walls held museum quality oils of all the ships Ernie had commanded during his "forty years at sea, man and boy." His only concession to an authentic sea going office was the large leather swivel executive chair on casters. Ernie's wife had given him the chair on the first day of his final command at the helm of the Vermilion Yacht Club, ten years earlier. She had only lived to see him in it for three months, succumbing quickly to an especially brutal case of cancer.

The weather-beaten old Captain emerged from the small bathroom in his skivvies, as he continued to call them, and passed into the compact Williamsburg style colonial bedroom where he donned his customary uniform of the day—khaki trousers, a navy blue knit polo shirt with embroidered VYC burgee, boat shoes, and a web belt trimmed in leather and cross-stitched sailing ships.

From the bedroom, Ernie passed through a large combination living room/dining room, also in classic Williamsburg decor, into a brightly shining stainless steel Pullman kitchen. As he stoked his coffee pot and large briarwood pipe, Ernie looked through white square window mullions down the easterly stretch of thirty piers that comprised the bulk of VYC's dockage—some of the finest on the entire Great Lakes. *All quiet*, he thought to himself happily, at least for another hour.

While the strong Hawaiian Kona coffee was percolating—"real coffee has to be cooked not drained," he often said—he ripped August off the wall, balled it up and flipped it into the trash can. By the time Ernie had enjoyed a few thoughtful puffs of cherry-rum tobacco from his pipe, the coffee was ready. He poured a large cup, took a sip, and headed for the Quarterdeck.

From the large mullioned picture window in his office, Captain Beckett scanned the Vermilion River flowing gently past the VYC north retaining wall into Lake Erie. Ernie could see the gray haze of another dog day in the slowly vanishing darkness of western Lake Erie. He tapped the barometer glass on the wall and noted that it was stuck again at 29.95 inches—almost no change in three days. There would be no sailing again today, he thought as he sat down at his desk and turned August's last day face down to reveal a new opportunity. The slate was clean. What was done was done. Time to look ahead and move ahead. There was important work to be done.

Ernie flipped on the radio for a quick dose of the early morning headlines from WEOL, "all news—all day." What he heard over the airwaves jolted him like his ship running aground in the quiet early dawn. He flipped nervously through his Rolodex card file, found a number he should have remembered, and quickly dialed.

*     *     *

Ednamae Bradley was elbow deep in a tub of rum raisin ice cream mixture. Her thoughts were miles away as she delighted in the Tuesday morning ritual of creating her most cherished confectionery delight. And yet she guessed this day would not be delightful. The neat orderly island she had worked so hard to maintain, amid an ever rising sea of chaos around her, was again threatened.

Too many things were changing, and Ednamae Bradley was feeling too old to continue the struggle. For nearly thirty as the President—some said "dictator" of the Harbour Town Preservation Society—Ednamae had fought more battles than General Douglas Macarthur. She had suffered her share of losses but always licked her wounds, made tactical adjustments, and sprung back to fight again. Perseverance was Ednamae's most powerful weapon and it had yielded important victories.

When a group of strip mall developers from Toledo swept into Vermilion in the sixties to demolish old houses in the northwest quadrant and build a "shopper's mall with a nautical motif," Ednamae went door-to-door, business-to-business, and head-to-head with the resident population. "It is time," she had told them, "to define who we are and what we stand for." It was indeed a defining moment for the historic north coast port-of-call.

A groundswell of publicans led by Captain Alva Bradley's only surviving descendant, bullied the City Council into protecting the northwest quadrant with strict zoning and development rules. At the end of the day, Harbour Town—1837 was established as a perpetual historic district. Ednamae chose the date in honor of the year her beloved Queen Victoria ascended to the throne of England.

In the seventies Ednamae Bradley again rallied her troops in a struggle to preserve the historic character of West Liberty Avenue. "Modernization plans" of a new bank holding company proposed to raze the decrepit old Vermilion Commerce Bank Building and replace it with a new steel and glass low-rise building. Once again, the elected city fathers caved in under intense public pressure to enact legislation that severely restricted building demolition and specified strict aesthetic guidelines for renovation.

Ednamae believed in leadership by example. In the heat of debate over the proposed legislation she was the first of Vermilion's citizens to renovate her own building to its original Victorian splendor. The effort, which depleted most of Ednamae's savings, proved that "seeing is believing." The Liberty Avenue Aesthetics Board was formed and given broad powers to oversee and approve building renovation on Vermilion's main thoroughfare from the bridge to the western city limits.

The eighties, however, were not so fruitful for the preservation group. A group of Cleveland condominium developers floated up the Vermilion

River one spring evening for dinner at *Chez François* and, after a few bottles of Château Neff du Pape, fixed their sights on the Firelands Fish Company. The docks, processing house and maintenance shed of the landmark fishery commanded six hundred feet of river frontage on the west side of the river between the French restaurant and the Vermilion Boat Club. Ednamae's preservation cadre was stunned to learn that the property had been sold to the Cleveland developers for the construction of eight townhouse condominiums. Ednamae felt both wounded and betrayed by Teddy Bear Parks who had signed the contract to sell the property that had descended from his great grandfather at the turn of the century. Even worse, in Ednamae's mind, was the sin of selling the property to "foreigners." A six month battle over zoning variances was eventually lost, the quaint old fish house was demolished, the condos erected and Teddy Bear's seat at the weekly Captain's Quarters breakfasts remained empty for a year.

But now, in the final years of the quiet enjoyable nineties, Ednamae's world was under assault once again. But this time it was not houses, building facades, and fish houses that were at risk. The stakes had been raised. Flesh and blood was in the mix. The life of young will Daysart had been threatened. Ednamae's adopted family tree was being hacked at by another foreigner, and now she knew she was faced with her greatest challenge.

But on this sultry September morn Ednamae didn't know what to do. For the first time in decades, a battle plan did not jump out at her. So she retreated to her rum raison ice cream mix. Somewhere in the familiar sweet goop there was an answer, and she knew it would emerge in time. If only the damned telephone would stop ringing.

Ednamae never answered her phone before eight o'clock. All of her friends knew that every morning between six and eight o'clock, Ednamae Bradley was elbow deep in the secret recipes that made her Victorian ice cream parlor a delight. She didn't believe in answering machines, often having said, *anyone who wants to talk to me that badly will call back or stop in.* The truth of the matter, according to Ernie Beckett, was that Ednamae could never figure out how to record her personal answering message, and wouldn't ask for help. She had no VCR, no electronic clocks, and no programmable appliances. Ednamae didn't do well with twentieth century contraptions, being very contently stuck in Harbour Town 1837.

But at the end of her reign, even Queen Victoria tolerated a telephone; Ednamae remembered between batches, so she washed her hands and arms at the deep porcelain sink and scurried into the foyer to put an end to the incessant ringing.

"Ednamae?" asked a familiar voice in the handset.

"Who else?" she replied.

"You, of all people, should know I don't answer the phone at this hour."

"Haven't you heard the news?"

"I've been working, Ernie."

"Turn on your radio—WEOL."

"What is it, Ernie. Just tell me."

Ednamae could not have been prepared for what she heard next. She dropped the phone and said softly into the shadows, "O My Lord. What's happening to us?"

After a few moments she heard Ernie's voice booming through the telephone receiver. "Ednamae . . . Ednamae? Are you there? Ednamae?"

She picked up the phone and whispered, "Yes, Ernie."

"Are you all right?"

"Yes. What should we do?"

"Get the crew together. We need to meet at your place," said Captain Beckett. "Let's try for nine thirty."

"Okay. I'll put on the coffee."

"Fine. You call Jack Grayson and Will. Make sure they know what's happened and be sure to get them to the meeting. I'll find Maggie and Teddy Bear.

\*   \*   \*

Teddy Bear Parks was at the helm of the *Cindy Jane* on a course for his favorite fishing grounds southeast of Pelee Island, a safe two miles south of the Canadian border that dissected Lake Erie from East to West. It was dead calm as *Cindy Jane* pushed northward at a respectable twelve knots. Teddy looked toward the east and smiled at the thought of how he once again defied the common wisdom of most Lake Erie fishermen which held that fish can't be found when the waters are still. Teddy's grandfather had discovered the Farmer's Almanac soon after entering the Lake Erie fishing business and the Parks family had relied on its fishing tables for over fifty years.

The mid-morning hours would be perfect—at least as perfect as the old lake would allow. A hundred years of indiscriminate over-fishing by over-zealous Canadians who encroached on American waters, and by Americans who encroached on Canadian waters, had depleted the Lake Erie perch population to a level that, in 1998, sustained only sport fishermen and a smattering of commercial boats.

By the time Teddy Bear took the helm of the Firelands Fish Company in the mid-seventies, after his father was lost in a dirty autumn storm off West Sister Island, the Firelands fleet had been trimmed to the three *Cindy* boats. The *Cindy Lou, Cindy Rose, and Cindy Jane* were named after Teddy's grandmother, mother, and wife. In the wake of his father's tragic death, Teddy was ready to take the money from the sale of the fish company property and move to South Carolina's Atlantic coast. In the brackish backwaters of the Carolina low country a man could fish with the sportsmen and forget the demise of a family tradition.

But at the last minute, Cindy Jane convinced her husband to keep one boat, one dock and continue to do what his father and grandfather before him had done, but only "as a retirement hobby." Teddy now fished three days, a week—Tuesday, Wednesday and Thursday—when the pleasure boat traffic on the lake was low. For nearly ten years his efforts had supplied coveted Lake Erie Perch to McGarvey's Nautical Restaurant and *Chez François* with enough left over for church and charity fish fry's in town.

*Cindy Jane* was a typical Lake Erie commercial fishing boat with a design that had been perfected over a hundred years of experience. She was a solid fifty feet long with a beam of eighteen feet. Heavy wood construction with a wooden deckhouse that ran from stem to stern, gave her the look of a European river excursion boat, with the utility and durability of an ocean-going tug. A large diesel engine and winch amidships allowed miles of fishing nets to be deployed and recovered by a crew of only two hard working men. Six foot square doors amidships on both sides allowed plenty of fair-weather ventilation and easy unloading at dockside. A helm and navigation station behind small windshields close to the bow, and a large opening near the stern allowed the boat to be worked in the lake's most violent and oppressive conditions. Captain Teddy Parks, and all Lake Erie fishermen before him, knew just how violent and oppressive their sustaining mistress could become.

The early November storm that claimed the lives of his father, a nephew and a cousin aboard their oldest fishing boat, the *Miss Penny*, although especially ferocious, was typical of the sudden storms that often sweep across Lake Erie without warning. The shallow basin that forms the lake, coupled with its long east-west fetch and geographical position southeast of the larger lakes makes it the most fickle and violent of all the Great Lakes; also one of the wildest storm regions in North America.

A typical Lake Erie storm rises when cold air from the northern reaches of Canada streaks south from Hudson Bay, across Canada and Lake Huron into the Erie basin. There it collides with warm subtropical air currents wafting northward from the Gulf of Mexico. The greater the temperature difference of these air masses, the greater is the relative atmospheric pressure gradient—the force that creates wind. High winds whipping across the surface of the lake from southwest to northeast, along the axis of Lake Erie, quickly build tremendous choppy seas that can break apart 1,000 foot ore boats and swallow up anything smaller. More than 500 shipwrecks littering the bottom of the lake testify to the often lethal combination of geography, meteorology, nature, foolhardiness, and fate.

On the November afternoon that a chunk of Teddy's family sank to the bottom, all of those elements carne together in the storm of the decade. A huge warm moist low pressure air mass churned its counterclockwise path from the south into Ohio. At the same time, an Alberta Clipper of dense cold air swirling clockwise rushed across the Michigan peninsula into Lake Erie. The two great weather machines collided in the western end of the lake where the *Miss Penny* was rounding up the last of a large catch of perch.

The old boat was loaded to her gunwales when a hurricane force wind of 65 mph overran her. The wind built from a brisk Beaufort Force 6 of 30 mph, to storm proportions in less than two hours. The air temperature dropped from 60 degrees to 30 degrees in a little over three hours. Seagulls and marsh birds were frozen to death in the torrent of blowing snow and ice. The waves reached a crushing 15 feet—each one breaking in rapid succession. As water was pushed across the lake, the water level in Maumee Bay, to the west, lowered ten feet and increased by the same amount in Buffalo, at the eastern end.

The wreck of the *Miss Penny* was never recovered, but when the massive storm blew itself out five days later, the bodies of the Parks family crew were recovered, washed ashore on South Bass Island. In the years following the great storm, NOAA weather forecasts for the Great Lakes became more frequent and more detailed. Though many a naive and foolhardy weekend mariner never carried or switched on his marine radio, Teddy Bear Parks had learned the benefits of constant radio vigilance the hard way.

Teddy Bear had lost the north coast behind him when the VHF marine radio over his head squawked to life.

"*Cindy Jane* . . . *Cindy Jane* . . . *Cindy Jane* . . . this is VYC calling on Channel 16."

Teddy pulled the microphone off the bulkhead, depressed the transmit button and said, "VYC . . . this is *Cindy Jane* . . . switching to Channel 52." Teddy turned the frequency dial to 52 and heard Ernie saying, "*Cindy Jane* . . . *Cindy Jane*."

"Ernie, I'm here. What's on your mind?"

"We have a little problem back here and I've called a meeting at Ednamae's for 9:30."

"Great. You can tell me what happened when I get back in this afternoon."

"Negative. You have to be there. It's important . . ."

"Do you want to give me a clue?"

"Not over the air," said Ernie. "We're locating everyone now. We're going to have young Will there too."

"That may not be so easy."

"Why's that?"

"He's here with me."

"Roger on that. Good news," said Ernie. "Now, turn around and get back in here. Park at the north wall of the club, and I'll be waiting for you."

Teddy hesitated for a microsecond to analyze the subtext of Ernie's command. He obviously didn't want the arrival of *Cindy Jane* noticed in town. But why? The old man had no problem barking out orders, and Teddy had come to know over the years that he never did so without compelling reasons.

"Aye, aye Captain," said Teddy. "*Cindy Jane* out."

Teddy looked at Will Daysart, who was standing at the helm and said, "You heard the man, Will. Turn her around and head for port."

"I was just starting to enjoy my going away cruise," said Will. "It seemed like every problem in the world vanished when the shoreline disappeared behind us."

"Don't be so sure," said Teddy. "Men have used the sea to run from their problems since the first boat was built. Look at Jonah in the Bible."

"Yeah. I guess it didn't work out too well for him though."

"And that's the message my boy. You can get lost out here for a while, but eventually you're going to get washed up on the beach."

"Can't we just hide out a little longer?"

"Nope. Something's happened back home and we best find out what it is," said Teddy. "He's only called me back from fishing once before."

"When was that?" asked Will.

"The day his wife died."

*       *       *

Maggie Wicks sat alone on the fantail of *Aphrodite* sipping her second cup of *English Breakfast Tea*. Maggie rarely had a second ration of tea in the morning, but the familiar aroma of the blend and the hefty shot of caffeine it carried worked to clear and sharpen her mind. It helped her not only to think, but to synthesize diverse bits of information. It was a tip she had picked up from her United States Coast Guard mentor, Commander Hugh Daley.

Hugh had been the forbidden fruit that young Ensign Wicks could not avoid. The Commander had seemed similarly smitten with his protégé, and like Adam and Eve, they betrayed themselves and the Uniform Code of Military Justice that forbade "sexual relationships between officers."

Maggie's year aboard the rugged rescue ship that patrolled the magnificent Aleutian Island chain, awakened her to the magnificence of her own sexuality. Long term exposure to pristine salt air has, for legions of sailors, proven to be a legendary aphrodisiac. Maggie unwittingly found it so.

Under the artful tutelage of master mariner Daley, Maggie discovered an appetite that had been maligned and repressed by her mother since her puberty. And Maggie's mother had been a world class repressor. Lest Maggie stray too far into a prurient world, her mother arranged her life as a music major at Heidelberg College, only 50 miles to the southwest of Vermilion. Hours of solitary practice in the musty music rooms of Heidelberg would keep her daughter chaste and pure, she had decided. But primal human instincts can only be suppressed so long, before they erupt.

No one, with the possible exceptions of Maggie and her mother, was surprised when the new college graduate chucked her cello and enlisted in the United States Coast Guard. Anyone in Vermilion could also have predicted the young officer's liaison with the virile and worldly mentor who had, at once, become Lt. Wick's teacher, protector, promoter and father figure. Anyone on board ship could also have predicted that Commander Hugh Daley would eventually champion Maggie's promotion to Executive Officer of the *Ticonderoga*, berthed 2,000 miles to the east. Anyone but Maggie, that is.

The sublime forces of first love infatuation have a curious power to simultaneously sharpen and dull the senses. She was not only crushed in body following her death defying accident in the North Atlantic, but was crushed in spirit when Commander Daley did not visit, did not write, and vanished from her life. Yet even twenty years later, as Maggie Wicks sipped her *English Breakfast Tea*, she often thought of her sailor fondly and without regret. But not this morning.

Maggie's deeply troubled thoughts this morning swirled around the early news radio reports of Angelina Mariano's murder. She had never been especially close to Angie and didn't particularly care for her brash flirtatious ways. But Angie had become a plot point in the strange drama unfolding with Jack, Will, and Meagan Palmer. Inevitable questions began to germinate in Maggie's hyper-organized mind.

How did Angie die?

What was the motive for her death?

Who was her executioner?

Was her death related to her knowledge of *SEAQUESTOR*'s mysterious cargo?

Of Paddy's plans?

Was Jack Grayson also in danger?

What could she do?

What should she do?

Maggie Wicks was in a deep psychic zone that nothing except her inner thoughts could invade. Nothing but the squawking of her VHF marine radio.

Whether at the dock or out on the lake, Maggie's marine radio was always switched on and always tuned to the international calling and distress channel 16. Now a familiar voice called through the remote radio speaker Maggie had installed in her private lounging area. She made her way forward to the communications console on the bridge, and temporarily stored the pesky questions in her substantial memory bank. "This is *Aphrodite* . . . Switching to channel 52," she answered. "Yes, on the early news . . . okay, but I think we should report it . . . all right . . . then to the FBI . . . no I won't . . . of course I'll be there . . . 9:30 then . . . *Aphrodite* out.

\*       \*       \*

Jack's first instinct, when Ednamae called and told him about Angie's murder, was to call the police. But then he remembered Meagan's warning about Paddy "owning them." Still, he knew that he and his little cadre of retirees were far outside their league. He had heard none of the details of Angie's death, but his gut told him that Paddy Delaney was responsible, and that both he and Will were in jeopardy. Then he thought about calling the FBI in Cleveland. Surely, he thought, they were equipped to handle such murky situations. But what would he tell them, he wondered? How about the fact that $24 million dollars of gambling and drug money was tucked away on his boat? That he had known about the cargo for weeks and elected not to report it? That he had told Will not to say anything to anyone? That he had sent Angie back to Lorain to gather more information? That he had unwittingly sent her to her death?

At least, Jack thought to himself, he would be spared the agony of writing another obituary—if not the insidious ache of ever-encroaching guilt.

He slumped in his desk chair and wondered how it was that Hell had again enveloped his village and his life. For a weekend shy of twenty years, Jack's life in Vermilion had been idyllic—the stuff of legend and lore, the stuff that people in the real world could not understand and seldom believed in. He remembered how often Susan chided him for living his life entirely within two fantasy worlds.

While Jack sailed with the Mobil Oil tanker fleet he spent ninety days on a floating village of machinery and electronics inhabited by forty men. Although sea and weather conditions changed outside, life on board Jack's ship was orderly and predictable. Vermilion had been that way for Jack on his quarterly month-long vacations from the sea. He liked the similar predictable tranquility of his home port, and seldom strayed from its boundaries. It was Susan's role to be the manager of diverse outside pressures of "real life" midway between the sprawling metropolitan spheres of Cleveland and Toledo.

Now the real world had descended upon Jack and his coastal sanctuary. Unlike the thousand foot supertanker, where he never doubted his ability to cope with any situation, for the last year he had found himself largely ill-equipped to deal with even his own existence.

He picked up his telephone and dialed.

"Jack, I'm so glad you called," said Meagan. "I've been going through my notes and tape recordings of our sessions. We're right on the cusp of a cure. I read through some of the latest literature on the Web, and I'm confident that I've got a bead on that little demon of yours. I'm mapping out a few therapeutic exercises for you to do on your own, before I give you your final exam."

When Dr. Meagan Palmer saw the solution to a puzzle, when she heard the final bell, and saw the finish line down the track she was unstoppable. She had the patient tenacity of an Amazon basin boa constrictor who hugs its quarry until its entire essence is extracted and the victor and victim become one. She had not moved from her desk for the two hours since Jack's early morning retreat, and was oblivious to everything outside the confines of her highly compressed psyche.

"I'm really excited about this breakthrough, Jack. I hope you can block out some time for me in the next few days."

"That may be difficult."

"And why is that?" Meagan shot back, a little miffed at Jack's apparent nonchalance.

"It's Angie Mariano."

"What does she have to do with . . ." Meagan fired, then immediately shifted gears. She knew, of course, what Angelina Mariano had to do with the other drama playing out in her life. "What's happened?"

"She's dead, Meagan."

"How?"

"Apparently murdered."

"Where?"

"They found her floating in the Black River."

"Was she clothed?

"Naked."

Meagan felt her pulse rise at the confirmation of an expected answer. "Do the others know?"

"Yes. They want to meet."

"Where"

"Ednamae's."

"When?"

"At 9:30. I think you should be there."

"Of course, Jack."

Meagan carefully put the phone down. She slowly closed her journal and tucked it back into her desk. She gathered the sheaf of notes and transcripts that littered her space and neatly placed them back into the file folder labeled "GRAYSON, Jack—August, 1998." The horrible way Angie Mariano had obviously died revealed the whole story to Meagan. History so often repeats itself, she had always known, and it's lessons must be absorbed if we are ever to advance ourselves . . . purge ourselves . . . cleanse ourselves.

The finish line that Meagan had so long awaited had been illuminated, paradoxically, by the dark crimson lanterns of Hades. A grotesquely familiar *modus operandii* had surfaced and shown the way. She was in the final turn.

For Meagan Palmer there could be no rest until the victor and victim where once again united.

# PART TWO

## The Turning of the Tide

*It is not only what we do, but what we do not do,
for which we are held accountable.*—Moliere

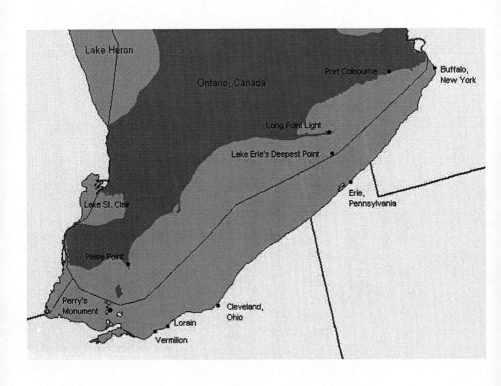

# CHAPTER 19

Ednamae's Ice Cream Parlor would normally be coming to life at 9:15 a.m. on a Tuesday morning. Even on the first day of the last month of the summer boating season there would be a throng of tourists, boaters and confection addicts on the front porch waiting for the usual 9:30 a.m. opening time to arrive. Ednamae enjoyed a brisk demand for her secret recipe ice creams by the pint, quart and half-gallon. With the Labor Day weekend just around the-corner, early store traffic would be substantial as folks stocked up for their holiday outings. But not today.

The first thing Jack Grayson noticed as he walked through the small wrought iron gate was the unusual hand-painted sign hanging next to the gate.

### SORRY! CLOSED UNTIL NOON!

From the abundance of parking spaces alongside and behind Ednamae's Jack sensed that he was the first of the Captain's Quarters group to arrive. Jack felt a paradoxically happy dread at being able to spend a few quiet moments with the gran-dame of Harbour Towne 1837. He could not recall any time in the past twenty years when Ednamae sounded so distraught and fragile

Before Jack reached the porch he heard the old wooden parlor door open and glimpsed the specter of Ednamae in the doorway. Dressed in a long flowing white smock, with her wispy white hair uncharacteristically tousled and her normally pinkish cheeks flushed pale she looked to Jack like a defeated angel. Without speaking a word Jack wrapped his arms around the fragile woman and smothered her in a warm embrace. Even angels need a hug every once in a while.

After a few quiet moments Ednamae seemed to gather some strength. She eased away from Jack, took him by the hand and closed the door. "What is happening to us, Jack?"

"Hopefully we'll be able to figure that out when the others arrive." They walked together into the dining room where Ednamae had the large table set in the usual configuration for a meeting of the Captain's Quarters. Even the cut crystal ship's decanter of rum surrounded by seven matching shot glasses was in place at Captain Ernie's place.

"This doesn't seem quite the occasion to play out our hokey little ritual," said Jack.

"What do you mean?" The look of anguish on Ednamae' s face was as unmistakable as the angst in her voice.

"The shot glasses, the rum, the seating arrangement. It just seems so trivial under the circumstances."

Ednamae pulled out a chair and gestured to Jack. "Let's sit and talk for a few minutes. I want to tell you a little story."

Jack was delighted to see the frail old lady coming back to life, but was uncomfortable at the thought of enduring another matronly tongue-lashing. Nevertheless, he resigned himself to the ordeal, knowing it would end as soon as another one of the group arrived—within a few moments he prayed. He sipped the strong cup of black coffee Ednamae had placed before him as he focused his attention on the storyteller.

"How long have you been coming to our little weekly meetings?"

"About five years," Jack answered.

"Hmmm. And how long do you think the Captain's Quarters have been meeting here?"

"I don't know," said Jack. "From what Susan told me, I'd guess about ten years."

"Pretty close. It's been twelve years actually." Ednamae took a sip of her own herbal tea. "Did Susan tell you how it was that we got started?"

"Not that I recall." Jack glanced at the ship's clock and wished its hands would move a little faster.

"Well then it's time you heard the story," said Ednamae with such intensity and drama that Jack regretted his earlier impatience. Among Ednamae's abundant gifts was the art of transforming life's triumphs and tragedies into parables.

"Proceed, Madame."

"Up until twelve years ago this past July we were all going our separate ways, living our private lives, pursuing our businesses and enjoying our families. Then we got a wake up call—the first of many to come. Ernie Beckett tried to commit suicide."

"What?" Jack was flabbergasted. "That's not possible."

"I recall saying the same thing when the hospital called me. It was about three months after his wife, Eleanor died. She had battled cancer for over a year. Ernie refused to check her into a nursing home or hospital, and stayed by her side at home through the whole ordeal. It was the most beautiful act of love that I have ever seen. Ernie often told me that those months when he cared for her every need, like a parent nurtures a baby, were the most intimate and bonding days of their entire married life. When Eleanor died, quietly in Ernie's arms, he was devastated. To Ernie, she had not just died but had abandoned him. He told me soon afterward that he felt like a dead ship that had slipped its anchor."

As Ednamae's parable unfolded, Jack found himself looking back into his own last year of helpless drifting. Suddenly, for Jack, time stood still as he heard the angel's voice continue.

"We all thought that Ernie would snap out of his morose depression after a period of grieving. But he just sank deeper and deeper into his own despair. He rarely came out of that yacht club, and when he did, the members wished he had stayed inside. He became so crotchety and sullen that the board began to talk about retiring him. When he called me to the lawyer's office to announce that he had named me as his power of attorney and estate executor, something in my gut told me it was more than just routine estate planning."

"I don't know why Susan never told me any of this," Jack said as he poured himself another cup of coffee.

"She never knew the story," said Ednamae. "No one but me ever knew how bad it really was with Ernie. I thought I could handle it alone until I found him one morning unconscious in a pool of his own blood. Ernie and I go way back, and I knew that if anyone could haul him out of his despair it would be me. Of course I was wrong, but I never really admitted that to anyone either. Sometimes our frailties are best left locked up in a closet with a big lock."

Jack would normally have taken the bait offered by Ednamae's last comment, but was so shocked by what he was hearing that he dared not interrupt.

Ednamae took another sip of tea, inhaled deeply and seemed to quickly rearrange her thoughts. "As I sat by Ernie's bedside in the hospital we made three solemn promises to each other. First, we would never tell anyone about the suicide attempt. Next, we agreed that we would always be available for each other and that no matter how muddled or hopeless a situation might seem, we would not act without consulting the other. Finally, we agreed to have a weekly Monday morning coffee klatch. Not long after we started our little gossip sessions, Teddy's family was lost in that storm out on the lake, and Maggie came home from the Coast Guard. The Captain's Quarters were born with three wounded hungry souls and a pretty fair pancake cook. Not a bad match, huh?"

"Made in heaven," Jack replied. "What about Will Daysart and Susan? When did they come on board?"

"Soon after Eleanor died we lured Will into the group, and Susan followed him. She had a lot of time on her hands while you were at sea, and I think she wanted to watch over her business partner."

Jack looked up just as the old Chelsea clock sounded the bells for 9:30 a.m.

"So this became the port of last resort for Vermilion's lost souls, I gather?"

"Isn't that what brought you into our little cove, Jack?"

"Ouch! You don't pull any punches do you?"

"That was another promise Ernie and I made to each other years ago—that we would never deceive each other."

Jack raised his coffee cup in a mock toast and said, "I'll drink to that."

"Which brings us back to your original question about our customary rum—how did you say it—hokey ritual?"

Jack was on the ropes now, but still marveled at Ednamae's prowess as a counter-puncher.

"Susan brought the ritual to us. It was something Commodore Perry used to bond his officers together. It wasn't long before we all realized the anointing power of that solemn moment. Jack was now humbled before the angel. "So yes, it is necessary that we begin each session with a libation. Anything less would separate us from those no longer at the table."

Jack was in awe of the saga he had just heard. He had always taken great stock in a familiar line from the Old Testament book of Ecclesiastes: "There is nothing new under the sun" He had found this especially, and comfortably, true in Vermilion—until now.

What other secrets lie buried under shelves of nautical artifacts, beneath coats of uniformly weathered white paint, and smothered under mounds of rum-raisin ice cream and twenty-inch pizzas? He suddenly felt the naiveté of a teenager. A loud creak of the old oaken door jarred Jack out of his reflective trance.

"Sorry we're running a little late," said Maggie Wicks as she strode into the dining room with her entourage trailing behind. "I figured we would be less conspicuous if I just picked up everyone in McGarvey's van."

"A great ploy," Ednamae offered. "They drive over here about this time twice a week to pick up ice cream for their dessert menu."

"I still don't understand what all this secrecy is about," said Teddy Bear as he took his usual seat at the table.

"You will," grumbled Ernie. "Now, let's all sit down an' get started."

Without a further gesture or comment, the crew moved into their customary spots. "Will, you take your father's seat over here next to me. Dr. Palmer, you will be seated there between Jack and Maggie. When everyone was seated, Ernie nodded to Ednamae. "The libation Madame, if you please."

Ednamae stood up and ceremoniously filled all the shot glasses from the decanter, then passed the tray to Teddy Bear on her right. She watched as the tray moved around the small circle to Maggie, Jack, Meagan, Will and Captain Beckett. When she had taken the last glass from the silver tray, Ernie rose from his chair, shot glass—in hand. "As the unceasing tide of life ebbs and floods in our lives, it purges and renews with each cycle. I dedicate this toast, and this meeting of the Captain's Quarters, to young Will Daysart who joins us today in his dear father's seat. Now that the tide has turned in your life, may we work together to purge your troubles and renew your spirit and hope for the future."

Everyone paused for a moment, obviously mesmerized by Ernie's unusual eloquence.

"Here, here!" said Teddy Bear, and everyone downed their shots.

"Will, is there anything you want to say before we get underway?" asked the aged captain.

"Nothing much," said Will. "Except that I'm scared as hell and have nowhere to turn. My dad always told me that you guys would help me out of any problem. I guess I just didn't have the sense to believe him until now."

Jack glimpsed a veil of disbelief that had descended over Meagan Palmer's face, so an instant before she erupted, he jumped in. "Don't become a believer yet, Will. We're in an awful mess here and only hope we can find some practical solution."

"Well then," grumbled Ernie. "Let's have a damage report. Maggie, what have you found out?"

"According to a friend of mine on the City Desk of the *Journal*, a couple of kids who were going fishing, found Angie Mariano's body floating face down in the Black River early this morning. She was naked and had been strangled. She had multiple broken bones and bruises that looked as though she had fallen from a great height to the ground. There was no water in her lungs, leading them to the conclusion that she did not drown. There were no signs of sexual assault."

"Thank God," said Ednamae softly.

Will, however, seemed to physically express the feelings of the table guests as he wretched and gagged mildly. Ernie poured him another shot of rum, which he quickly upended. "Sorry," he said shamefully.

"The police believe that Angie was abducted and robbed," Maggie continued. "Her car, clothes, jewelry, phone and purse are all missing. They believe she was trying to escape her abductors when she fell off the Bascule Bridge to the river bank. They believe her attackers then stripped her and rolled her body into the river to cover their trail."

"Jesus Christ," bellowed Ernie. "What the hell did that little girl do to anyone to deserve this?"

No one spoke a word, but as Jack looked around the table at the masks on six other faces he sensed that they all had some opinion, based upon their unique experiences with the complex Angelina.

Ednamae broke the silence. "Has anyone spoken to Joey?"

"Not directly, but the police located him with some friends in Cleveland. According to my reporter friend, when the police told him what had happened he had some kind of seizure and is now in the University Hospital down the hill from Little Italy."

"This is just dreadful," said Ednamae. "Of course I must go and see him."

"Yeah . . . well I guess that's a good idea, and Angie's death is a terrible thing, but I don't understand why you called all of us over here to talk about it," said Teddy.

Once again, Meagan was on the edge of her seat, ready to pounce on Teddy, whom she had often referred to as being a few perch short of a full catch. And once again, Jack intervened.

"Don't you see? He's sending a message to Will that he's next," said Jack as though he was trying to imprint the thought on Teddy's brain.

"He who?"

"Paddy Delaney."

"How do you know that?"

"Will's story."

"What story?"

Now Jack found himself looking at Meagan and seeing the mirror image of his own frustration.

"Come on Teddy . . . you remember. Will told us all how Paddy had his goons haul him up on the roof of the Broadway Building with orders to throw him off, then strip him naked and dump his body into the river . . ." Another sideways glance at Meagan. "You do remember that, don't you?"

"Sure I do," said Teddy. "But he didn't."

"Didn't what?"

"Didn't kill him."

"Kill who?"

"Paddy didn't kill Will," said Teddy looking at the young man. "Did he Will?"

Before Will could even muster a response Ernie jumped in. "What the hell? You two sound like Abbott & Costello, and it's not gettin' us anywhere."

"Wait a minute Ernie," said Ednamae. "Maybe Teddy has a point. How do we know that Paddy was responsible for Angie's death?" A breath . . . "And how do we know that he really means to murder Will?"

"We don't," said Maggie.

"We do," said Meagan.

Maggie shot back, "The police seem to have a handle on this tragedy, and they haven't implicated Paddy Delaney in any way. We just don't know, and the truth of the matter is that when it comes to Paddy's death threat against Will . . . we really don't know."

"Yes we do," repeated Meagan softly yet with such intensity that all eyes fixed on her.

"Can you explain?"

"He killed my father the very same way forty years ago."

"You mean that your uncle murdered his own brother?"

"That's right."

"But why?"

Jack grasped Meagan's hand under the table and gave it a reassuring squeeze. "It doesn't matter why he did it," said Meagan. "What does matter is that my uncle Paddy is a treacherous and ruthless man who will do anything to have his way." Another reassuring squeeze . . . "That girl didn't fall off the Bascule Bridge running from some mugger, and the police know it. Despite Will's reprieve from the roof of the Broadway Building, I can assure you that Paddy does not make idle threats."

"My lord," said Maggie. "I think we're in way over our heads here. We need to go to the police."

"He owns them," said Will.

"Then to the County Sheriff."

"He owns them too."

"Well he sure doesn't own the federal government, so we need to go to the F.B.I."

"With what?" asked Jack.

"With this story. With this murder. With the death threat against Will."

"They have no reason to believe us," said Jack.

"Why not?"

"Because the only witness to the threat against Will is dead. Angie risked her life to give us that information, to try to save Will." Jack paused to run his hand through his hair. "And she lost the wager."

"That's the way Paddy operates," said Meagan. "And that's why we have no choice but to beat him at his own dirty tricks."

"How are we going to do that?" asked Teddy.

"I have a plan."

"So why are you all of a sudden so willing to help me out?" asked Will in a tone that shot like a bolt of lightning across the table, quieting everyone for a moment. "I mean, you've made it pretty clear that you don't like me, and that you didn't want us digging into your family history. So what's up?"

"What's up, you insignificant sniveling little shit is that I have my own reasons for taking down Paddy Delaney, and none of it has anything to do with you."

Will looked as though he had stepped into a rattlesnake's nest as he retreated to the lee of Ernie's still robust frame. He recognized the fires of hell burning in Meagan's eyes and could almost feel the sting of the venom dripping from her fangs. He wanted no more of Meagan Palmer.

"Meagan, I'm sure that Will didn't mean that quite the way it came out," said Ednamae. "I'm sure he's delighted to have your help and is sorry for . . ."

"I'm not interested in Willy Daysart's delight or his sorrow," said Meagan in a steadily calming tone. "We have a mutual problem here in the form of Paddy Delaney, and I have a plan that should get him out of our lives once and for all." Meagan felt another long warm squeeze of her hand. "But I can't do this alone. I'm going to need everyone's total commitment to make it work."

Meagan looked around the table, deep into the eyes of each member of the council. One by one they nodded their assent, until her eyes fixed again on Will.

"Yes Will, I need your help in this too."

Ernie put his arm around the young lad and nudged him back up to the table edge. "Well?" he asked.

"Okay . . . sure. Whatever it takes." Again Ernie nudged him. "And I didn't mean what I said before."

"Fair enough," said Meagan now fully back in control. "Well then, I guess we have a deal."

"I think we can all stand another drink to that," said Ernie as he glanced at Ednamae. "The libation once again Madame, if you please."

# CHAPTER 20

Jack hadn't been on board Teddy's boat in over a year, since before Susan's death. As much as he missed Susan, he couldn't say the same for the *Cindy Jane*. Even though the old work boat had been retired from the daily rigors of the Lake Erie fishing trade for over a decade, Teddy's mid-week restaurant perch excursions kept the aroma alive.

*   *   *

The rancid stench of fish oil had offended Jack since the days of his first sea year shipboard assignment as a midshipman at the U.S. Merchant Marine Academy. Just as no man or woman ever forgets their first lover, no mariner ever forgets his first ship. For midshipman second class Jack Grayson, that ship was the American Export-Isbrandtsen Lines *SS Exporter*, known, less-than-affectionately to her crew, as the *Fish Oil Maru*.

Jack often recalled bounding out of the taxi at Hoboken, New Jersey's pier 34 and feeling like Joseph Conrad's *Lord Jim* looking up at the forsaken *Patmos*. As he stood alongside, the twenty year old tramp steamer he could not fathom why the entire vessel, save a few upper decks of superstructure, was painted black. Neither could the young midshipman identify the pungent odor wafting over his sensitive Long Island nostrils. It wouldn't be long before both questions were answered, most dramatically.

After a short overnight passage from Hoboken to Norfolk, Virginia followed by a quick turnaround after loading one cargo hold full of Post Exchange merchandise for the U.S. Naval base at Rota, Spain. Young Jack Grayson finally realized his dream of going to sea—but not comfortably.

The *Exporter* was only an hour beyond the outer buoy marking the approach to Norfolk harbor when it happened. The ship began pitching rhythmically to the rise and fall of typical North Atlantic rollers. These incessant long and low rolling waves, the remnants of some distant storm, lifted the big ship up and down . . . up and down . . . up and down . . .

Jack was hanging his head over the leeward side of the ship, puking his guts out when he first heard the unfamiliar voice that would change his life. "*Heads up dere gadget. Ain't no more vomit in dem guts fo' you to lose.*"

Jack turned slowly to face a sailor as black as the deck the stood upon. Even through the paint and oil-stained dungarees and thick crew-neck oiled wool sweater, Jack immediately realized this short stocky man was absent any noticeable body fat. He quickly raised one of his huge black paws to the dingy seasoned khaki officer's cap he wore at a cocky angle and issued a half-hearted salute to the young midshipman.

"*Dat de last salute you gonna receive from me gadget. Fo' de res' o dis here voyage your young ass belong to me—Bosun Cooney. Now hustle up for'ard to number one hatch an' slush down dem runnin' gere wit' a bucket o' fish aisle and lamp black.*"

As Jack struggled to the heaving, stammering bow of the ship, which was rising and falling ten feet every thirty seconds, he heard the burly Caribbean boatswain remark to one of his crew with a sinister laugh, "Dat should cure da keed of his seasick."

Cure him indeed. For the next six hours Jack Grayson *slushed* rags full of a molasses-like fish oil and lamp black mixture over what seemed like miles of wire rope that rove through the winches, blocks, sheaves and guides of the cargo handling booms of the forward-most cargo hold. For the next six hours Jack Grayson puked, and retched, and gagged, and dry-heaved his innards out.

In those next six hours, however, Jack would become immunized. For the rest of his seagoing career—through storms and gales and hurricanes and typhoons—Jack Grayson never again felt the agony of seasickness. For that gift, and for six weeks of practical on-deck seamanship experience as the bosun's "gadget," he would never forget old Bosun Cooney.

He would also never forget the awful smell of fish oil.

*     *     *

"Teddy," said Jack. "Isn't there something you can do to get rid of this stinking fish oil odor?"

"I'll second that suggestion," chimed in young Will Daysart.

"Smells like honey and money to me boys," said Teddy Bear Parks with a flippant edge on his voice.

"Well, I guess one man's skunk is another man's fur coat," said Jack as he followed Teddy's lead forward to the boat's control center and steering station.

Teddy jumped up into the Captain's chair behind the wheel of the *Cindy Jane*, and motioned for Will and Jack to climb up on the small bench seat beside him. "This is what I want you to see." Jack took the two small plastic boxes that Teddy handed him and passed one to Will. The yellow boxes were rounded on all corners and obviously water sealed with rubber gaskets. Each one had a short rubber-sheathed flexible antenna and a covered "ON-OFF" switch.

"They look a lot like the emergency life raft distress beacons we carried on the big ships," said Jack never missing the chance to distinguish himself as a "blue water" ocean sailor.

"That's right," said Teddy. "But these babies are in a different league."

"G.P.S.?" asked Will.

"I'm impressed," said Teddy. "This stuff is pretty new and in very limited use."

"Hey, don't forget that I'm in the marine supply business. I know I don't sell much, but I do read the catalogs."

"So what are you doing with these things Teddy?" asked Jack.

"Sometimes I layout nets in different locations then go back and pick them up. In the old days we attached a buoy with a flag and charted the drop position using old dead-reckoning and RDF."

"Those were the days," mused Jack. "When we were navigators rather than computer operators."

"Yeah, well times have changed for the better," said Teddy. "Now these G.P.S. beacons send a signal to an orbiting satellite system which beams the information back down to this here receiver and voila, I can read the exact longitude and latitude right off the screen."

"What's the accuracy?"

"About three feet," interjected Will.

"Right on the money," said Teddy.

"So what are we going to do with them?"

"I figure we'll attach one to the top of *SEAQUESTOR*'s mast, so we'll be able to track her exact location while Paddy's captain has her. You never know, we might just have to run her down."

"Why would we have to do that?" asked Will.

"Call it a little insurance, that's all."

"Fair enough," said Jack.

"And what about the second one?"

"Well, since Maggie, Ernie and Meagan will be alone on *Aphrodite* with Paddy Delaney, I thought we just might want to be able to trail them . . . out of sight, of course."

Jack sat back on the bench for several moments trying to comprehend how Teddy had so quickly embraced and refined Meagan's daring plan. He was pleased to feel that he might have underestimated the aging fisherman. On his boat and in his element, at least, he was undeniably a master mariner. And Teddy's G.P.S. beacons were a master stroke, Jack quickly realized. For all the cunning and bravado of Meagan's scheme, there was a serious drawback—the lack of any safety valve or escape route.

It was so typically Meagan, Jack thought. She had made it clear that she was committed to taking down her Uncle Paddy at any cost. In planning to do so she had, unwittingly put two of Jack's dearest old friends in harm's way. Teddy had realized it too, and without any comment or recrimination had simply inserted some of his own "insurance" into the scheme.

"I have to hand it to you Teddy. This system is pretty spiffy."

"Thanks Jack, but you haven't seen the best part yet." Jack and Will looked at each other with mutual expressions of astonishment. The man who just a few hours earlier could not seem to comprehend why he had been called to an emergency meeting, had suddenly become the electronic wizard "Q" made famous in the James Bond "007" movies. They were in awe of the foam-padded suitcase full of electronic paraphernalia Teddy displayed before them.

"What is all this stuff?" asked Jack.

"Sub miniaturized self-contained VHF radio transmitters with concealed microphones—three of them."

"Awesome," said Will.

"Incredible," said Jack.

"I had no idea you were into this sort of thing."

"That's the only way it works Jack," said Teddy with a mischievous smile. "Stealth, surprise, cloak & dagger. This was just a hobby until now. I never really thought I'd be able to use this stuff in a real operation."

"Operation? Did you say operation?" asked Will. "You two sound like you're playing out some kind of board game or something. Shit, that mick sonofabitch wants to kill me!"

"Sorry Will," said Jack. "Of course you're right. We just can't afford to take any more chances than we absolutely have to." Jack gave Will a fatherly nudge, then turned again to Teddy. "Just how *do* you plan to use these little radios?"

"Okay. This whole *red herring* that Meagan has cooked up by getting her uncle Paddy alone on Maggie's boat only works if . . ."

"If she can get him on the boat," said Will. "Which I seriously doubt. He's not that dumb."

Teddy continued, ". . . only works if she can document what he says and then protect the evidence. That's where the radios come in. Meagan, Maggie and Ernie will all be wearing these radios when Paddy arrives. They will transmit everything that is said to this VHF receiver over here, all the while . . ."

"Hold up a minute," said Will. "Assuming he gets on the boat, who's going to get a microphone on Paddy? And how?"

"Not necessary. The mics will pick up any conversation within six feet."

"And if they can't get that close to him?"

"We all die, and Paddy flees to Canada with his ten million bucks."

"I get the picture," said Will. "Go on."

"Like I was saying . . . all the conversation on *Aphrodite* will be picked up over here and recorded on this machine. When Meagan gets Paddy to admit that his captain has millions of dollars of illegal gambling money on a sailboat on the way to Canada, we'll have it all on tape."

"But Meagan planned to make a secret tape of her own," said Jack.

"With what?" shot Will. "Her office palmcorder? Get real!" Jack shot back a vicious look at the kid, but before Jack acted on his dismay, Will continued. "That's not all. If Paddy thought that tape was on *Aphrodite* somewhere, he'd hold them all hostage, torture them, and tear the boat apart to the waterline to find it. Then he'd kill them all," said Will. "I still don't think you know what that creep is capable of."

"Okay Will," said Jack. "Point taken, but you might cut Meagan a little slack. She's putting her neck on the chopping block for you, remember."

"I have a feeling that's not the whole story," said Will with an accusing look.

"I don't think it really matters what Dr. Palmer's motivation is here Will," said Jack. "She's going to be saving your ungrateful ass in the process."

"Not ungrateful, Jack. I'm just getting a little worried about what we don't know about the mysterious Dr. Palmer."

"I suggest you forget worrying about Meagan and concentrate on Paddy Delaney." Jack dismissed Will with another harsh glance and turned back to Teddy.

"Now, how will Meagan be able to threaten Paddy with the tape recording if she can't prove she has it?"

"We'll be happy to play it back for him over the air . . . from a safe distance."

"Teddy, you're making a believer out of me," said Jack. "What is the range of these things?"

"Over open water . . . probably eight miles. No problem. We can't miss on this one."

"It's too bad we can't take that sleazy bastard's money too," said Will.

"The money doesn't matter," said Jack. "It's the same dirty gambling money that got us all into this mess, and thank God it will be far across Lake Erie by the time we cut our deal with Paddy—the deal that is going to save your life." Jack put his arm around Will and looked him squarely in the eyes. "That is the only point of this 'operation' isn't it?"

"Okay Jack, you're right. I guess I'm just a little paranoid or something," said Will. "Just one more question." Jack braced himself. "This G.P.S. beacon, the one that's going on *SEAQUESTOR*, what's the point of that?" Jack turned and looked at the Teddy Bear, realizing he too didn't have a clue as to where that fit into the plan. "What was all that about possibly having to 'run down' the yacht?"

"I'm not really sure yet," said Teddy. "But I do know that knowledge is power, and it won't hurt for us to know where those $24 million dollars is at all times . . . and be able to prove it to Paddy." He tossed the small yellow beacon to Will.

"Is that it?" persisted Jack.

"What else could it be?" said Teddy with, Jack sensed, a hint of mischief in his voice.

*       *       *

Meagan Palmer was uncommonly uneasy as, she listened to the ringing tone through the handset of her office phone. She had rehearsed her spiel for two hours, had even made note cards, and yet as the telephone rang . . . rang . . . rang on the other end of the line her hands felt cold and clammy.

"Yeah," said a voice through the phone.

"I would like to speak with Mr. Delaney," she said. "Is he available?"

"Dunno. I'll check."

Now, an immense wave of doubt washed over Meagan. Why was she digging up the dead? Many years ago she had, she thought, wisely buried her uncle only to reach down now, into the cesspool that harbored his dark soul, and give him a hand; her hand. That was the emotional side of her mind. But the professional side knew that her old predator was not dead. Though long buried, like in some cheap "B" rated horror film, the predator would one day return. Meagan's *Friday the 13th*, her *Halloween* was now. Her irrational panic was overtaking her reason as she waited, it seemed like forever, for the demon to make a connection with her.

There was still time to bailout, to lock the door, to slam the top down on his coffin. There was still time to . . .

"Talk to me." His chilling voice froze Meagan's vocal chords for an instant. "Talk to me," he repeated calmly.

"Paddy, it's Dr. Pal . . . It's Meagan."

"I know that."

"But I didn't . . ."

"Caller I.D. It's a great time to be alive, wouldn't you agree, princess?" Meagan was frozen again as she detected a sinister chuckle at the other end. "So, what can I do for you, my little queen?" Meagan struggled to pull herself together as she tried to shuck off the faux regal mantel Paddy had so deftly reapplied. "Are you still there sweetie?"

"Yes, sorry Paddy."

"What do you want?"

"I'd like to buy you brunch."

"Why?"

"I need to talk to you."

"About what?"

"I have a proposition for you." Paddy's chuckle unnerved her again for a moment but she inhaled deeply and pressed on. "A business proposition."

"What kind of business?"

"I can't discuss it on the phone."

"Why me?"

"It's a unique situation requiring a unique person with a unique solution."

"So that's what I am these days? Unique?"

"Paddy," said Meagan gathering courage. "You always have been unique."

"So when do we eat?"

"Saturday, the 5th." This time it was Paddy who seemed quietly lost. Meagan savored the moment before she turned the table. "Are you still there Paddy?"

"Bad day. How about Sunday?"

"Afraid not."

"Monday, then."

"Sorry."

"What are you up to, princess?"

"Paddy, I have a very narrow time frame on this deal. It's Saturday brunch or nothing." A dramatic pause. "Of course if you can't accommodate me, I'll just have to go elsewhere."

"So maybe I'm not so unique anymore?"

"Unique, yes. Indispensable, no."

"Hold on a minute." Meagan was beginning to enjoy herself and, for the first time in thirty years, sensed an advantage over her wily uncle. "Okay, you've got it," said Paddy abruptly. "But it'll have to be here at the hotel."

"When I pay, I choose the location," said Meagan.

"I'll buy the meal then, damnit."

Now it was Meagan who allowed herself a slight laugh. "That's not the point Paddy."

"So what is the point?"

"The point is that I have a unique situation that you have to see to fully appreciate."

"Meaning what?"

"I've chartered a boat for a short private cruise with brunch served on board."

"Where?"

"Vermilion," said Meagan.

"We need to be on board at 9:00 a.m."

"What the hell . . ." Another long pause punctuated by labored breathing wafted through the line.

"I promise that this is a trip you really don't want to miss."

"Okay. You win," said Paddy. "Where in Vermilion?"

"McGarvey's Restaurant. Meet me on board the *Aphrodite* at nine o'clock sharp."

"I got it."

"Don't be late."

"It'll be just like old times again, my little queen." Meagan heard another muffled snicker the phone line died.

Paddy Delaney sat back in his leather swivel chair and lit a huge Cuban cigar. As the acrid black smoke filled the room, he pondered the events of the last ten minutes. Something about Meagan's increasingly flippant tone warned him that this was more than just a phone conversation with an estranged niece; more than a simple invitation to a family business brunch. He stabbed the buzzer beside his knee on the inside of his desk knee hole. Almost instantly his two black-clad Irish lieutenants slithered through the door and came to a cocky attention in front of him.

"Either of you lads ever heard of some charter boat in Vermilion called the *Aphrodite*?"

The lads looked at each other, shrugged their shoulders and said in unison, "Nay."

"I wouldn't expect so," he expired through a filthy cloud of smoke. "I want you to find out who owns that boat, who runs it, where it goes, and who its passengers are." Then Paddy dismissed them with a cloudy wave of his hand. "And have Derry get me a picture of the boat and the crew."

*     *     *

Meagan's phone was still warm from the last call when she poked the speed-dialer with her pencil then tapped out a playfully pensive rhythm.

"GrayDays Marine."

"Jack. I'm glad I caught you."

"I'm just up here in the office sifting through some file cabinets, drawers and closets. For some reason this afternoon I got the urge to get things in order. It's been a long time."

"Is Will there?"

"No, I left him with Teddy. They're tinkering with all their electronic gear—running tests I suppose."

"Well then, you can tell him the news." Meagan hesitated an instant and took a deep breath. "Jack, I did it. I hooked him. Paddy agreed to have brunch with me on board *Aphrodite* on Saturday."

"Well done, Meagan. How did it go?"

"Difficult at first. When I heard his voice, with that overdone Irish brogue, a lot of bad memories began to swell. Then I reminded myself that I was controlling this encounter."

"Are you all right?"

"Yes, I'm fine. In fact I haven't felt this free in years. I had no idea a simple phone call could be so liberating."

"Not so simple I think," said Jack. "What you did took a lot of courage. I'm very proud of you, Meagan."

"Thank you Captain."

"Do you think he suspected anything?"

"Not really, though he was reluctant about the day."

"Not surprising," said Jack. "That he would want to stay close to home while his cargo is in transit across the lake."

"Right, but then he pecked and nibbled at the bait and never saw the hook."

"Let's just hope he swallows the whole hook, Meagan. He's a pretty big fish."

"Oh, he will Jack . . . until he chokes."

"Meagan, are you sure you're going to be okay with all of this?"

"Yes, yes. I'm sure," she answered. "Hey, I have to run. Don't forget our date."

"I'll pick you up at eight bells sharp."

# CHAPTER 21

Jack felt the exhilaration of a school1boy on his first date as he wheeled the sparkling green, freshly detailed, Range Rover into Meagan's driveway at 8:00 a.m. sharp. It was a refreshing, stormy, blustery, autumn-like Wednesday, a day that left no doubt that the dog-days of summer had ended. Jack felt frisky and alert in the chilly morning air.

Before he could turn off the engine, Meagan bounded down the driveway. She was dressed in baggy white canvas slacks, a yellow crew-neck cotton sweater, blue-windbreaker, and her ever-present Topsider boat shoes. She was a picture of the young girl he first met thirty years ago at a Kent State University sailing regatta on Twin Lakes.

Jack switched off the engine then climbed out and met Meagan just in time to relieve her of an immense, heavy-laden, lacquered cane picnic basket. "Good morning Doc," he beamed.

"Mornin' sailor. Lookin' for a good time?"

Jack laughed at the image of the very proper Dr. Meagan Palmer playing the part of a Piraeus, Greece hooker. "Sure, what do you have in mind?"

"Food, wine and indescribable merriment."

"Not the best day for a picnic though."

"Oh, but it's perfect for the spot I've chosen," said Meagan.

"And where might that be?"

"Just start driving west on old Route 2 and I promise to light up your life."

As Jack piloted the Range Rover along the old Lake Road westward out of Vermilion he didn't have a clue where he was going and didn't really care. He never tired of Meagan's chatty company and could never get enough of the familiar path through miles of historical landmarks, vacation towns, and quaint tourist villages that took names like Ruggles Beach, Huron, Beulah Beach, Sandusky and Rye Beach. Some took the names of ancient Indian tribes that had once populated America's north coast, while others adopted the names of the "Sufferers" who, though burned out of their eastern roots, quickly evicted their indigenous predecessors from the Great Western Reserve's Firelands.

Jack and Meagan talked about how every inlet, creek and estuary along the way had become a haven for tiny powerboat communities and fishing camps. Weather beaten signs in front of small cabin settlements advertised "Sandy Beaches and Heated Family Cabins." These icons of a more tranquil era struggled to survive amid the lure of more glitzy vacation spots that advertised on the internet.

Meagan urged Jack across the modern four-lane divided highway that rose above and transited Sandusky Bay. A slight speeding hump over the Bay Bridge and Meagan directed Jack to turn off at the Marblehead exit. A few more miles and several turns past the "World Famous Cheese House," the "African Safari," and a miniature golf course, and Jack began to sense the end of the line.

The Marblehead peninsula juts into Lake Erie to form the north shore of Sandusky Bay. At the end of the peninsula, atop a picturesque promontory, facing the islands to the north and the Cedar Point Amusement Park to the east, towers one of the Great Lakes' grandest and most historic sites—The Marblehead Lighthouse. Jack wheeled into the driveway and quickly pressed into a crunchy sliding stop.

"It looks like we're out of luck. The sign says 'Closed on Wednesday.'"

"Closed to the public," Meagan said with a flirtatious smile.

"Go ahead and pull into the lot. I've made special arrangements for us."

Even before the engine stopped turning Meagan leaped out of the car and began jogging toward the immense black and white striped limestone light tower. She gave a quick friendly wave to the old man rock . . . rock . . . rocking on the porch of the light-keeper's house. Meagan tugged at the old black metal door and found it open. Then she turned and beckoned, "Hurry up Jack. I'll meet you at the top."

Although he had visited the old beacon with Susan and Jimmy a dozen times before he quickly realized that this visit would be something different, something adventurous. As he maneuvered the gourmet's picnic basket through the tiny door he prayed silently that this day would never end.

Jack tried to conceal his deeply heaving chest as he reached the lamp prism platform over 90 feet above the squeaky old door he had squeezed through only minutes earlier. As he maneuvered around the beautifully symmetrical, precision cut magnifying prism, he marveled that the tiny 60 watt bulb inside could be seen over twenty miles out into the lake. In the old days, before reliable light bulbs and electricity, it was the resident light keeper who tended a tiny oil lamp inside the prism from dusk to dawn.

"Come outside and look at this Jack," Meagan bellowed from the railing overlooking Lake Erie.

What Jack saw as he inched up alongside Meagan was dazzling and surreal. The surface of the great lake was covered in clouds, or so it seemed. The phenomenon called "sea smoke," was actually a wispy cloud of condensed water vapor that formed when cold moist air rushed across the surface of the 70 degree summer-warmed lake. The sea smoke rolled and bubbled and swirled like the surface of a witch's cauldron.

"Spectacularly eerie isn't it?" said Meagan as she wrapped her arm around Jack's waist and gave him a little squeeze.

"From up here, yes," said Jack. "But I wouldn't relish being in a boat down there right now."

"Which is precisely why this light has been here since 1821."

"I had no idea you were a lighthouse historian."

"Just a little hobby of mine," she said with *faux* nonchalance. "Actually, I've visited all the lighthouses on Lake Erie—all except one."

"Let me guess," said Jack.

"Take your best shot Captain."

"Long Point, Ontario."

"How'd you guess?"

"Because it's so hard to get to," said Jack. "It's just sitting out there at the end of that long skinny finger of sand and rocks about 150 miles northeast of here. It's the only natural obstacle between the islands and the Welland Canal. Dozens of ships ran aground there until the Canadians erected that light there 75 years ago."

"Well, it's just a candlestick compared to this light," said Meagan. "Still, I'd like to find an excuse to visit it one day."

Jack had found an opportunity to return Meagan's squeeze. "Maybe when his thing with Paddy and Will is over we'll celebrate with a little trip to the Long Point light." A searching pause . . . "Just to complete your education you understand."

"Maybe we shouldn't plan the celebration just yet."

"A few doubts beginning to creep in?" asked Jack.

"No, it's more like firing line jitters at the nationals."

Meagan looked out over the smoky lake and seemed suddenly lost in the past. "You know the feeling I'm talking about. You're in the right place, at the right time, doing the right thing. It's the national pistol championships and you're there with the best team facing the toughest competition in the country. You've trained, practiced, waited, and anticipated. You know you're ready and equal to the task. But when the line judge shouts out 'Ready on the right. Ready on the left. Ready on the firing line,' and you sight down range over your pistol barrel, and the adrenalin begins to pump . . . well, you know, you've been there."

Jack took hold of Meagan's shoulders and turned her to face him squarely. "Yes I have. I've been on the firing line and I've been on the starting line with fifty yachts tacking and gibing for position as the clock counts down. But they were all games. I was there by choice, with nothing much to lose but a little chunk of ego. But this is different, Meagan. It's no game. You have a lot to lose if you go out there with Paddy."

"I have a lot more to lose if I don't." Meagan's moist eyes betrayed the depth of her emotion and fear. "And I'm not going to lose anything to him ever again."

"Or to anyone else, I suppose?"

"I guess it's just not in my nature to lose," she whimpered. "I can't bear coming in second to anyone." Very suddenly, Meagan snapped out of it, and jabbed Jack in the ribs playfully. "Most people accept that about me."

"And then there were Gus and Scott."

Meagan wrenched away and pulled herself up close to the old wrought iron railing. "They were weak."

"You knew that when you married them, Meagan."

"That's why I surrendered myself. That's why I tried to fit in, to live my life for them. But they betrayed me."

"No, Meagan," said Jack pulling her to him again. "You betrayed yourself, just like you betrayed yourself to your uncle Paddy." Jack could have slapped himself as he saw tears well up in Meagan's eyes. He had no idea how their discussion had gone to this grotesque level, but he was committed now and couldn't step back. Even so, something inside told him this engagement was necessary. "And you still haven't forgiven yourself . . . well, not totally anyway."

"What do you mean?"

"Going after Paddy like this takes an enormous measure of courage. I can't imagine you summoning up that determination without first forgiving yourself for being the weak little girl who was victimized so horribly by that bastard." Jack braced himself for the inevitable barrage he had invited.

"Go on," Meagan whispered.

"Okay . . . and I think that until you forgive yourself for failing in your marriages to Gus and Scott, you'll never have a chance at a loving relationship with a man."

"So what am I to do? I can't go to a *shrink* as you call them . . . I *am* the shrink."

"Meagan, you're one of the most intuitively caring people I've ever known. It oozes out of you like honey from a honeycomb. I suppose that's why you're so good at your work."

"It's been enough for me," said Meagan.

"It is not enough, Meagan. Can't you see it? You're able to shrink down everyone but yourself, and if you're ever going to be fulfilled and happy you have to reconcile your feelings with your life."

"How?"

"Let me in, Meagan. I want to be more than just your date. I want to help you."

"Making *you* the psychologist?"

"No, Meagan. I don't want to compete with you."

"What do you want? Jack."

"I want to love you."

"That would be impossibly complicated."

"No more than we make it."

"That's exactly the point Jack," Meagan said.

"We've already made it impossible."

"How?"

"I'm your psychologist, your therapist. I've gone too far. It's not ethical, and it's not right. It goes against all of my training."

"Didn't we have this discussion a few weeks ago when I came back to you with my nightmares?"

"Yes we did," said Meagan. "And I told you then that if I got too close I'd want out."

"Okay then, fair enough. You're fired."

"What are you saying Jack? You can't just . . ."

"Sure I can. You're fired." Jack forced a huge smile on his face and did his best to overact his next line. "Now milady, let's get on with our lives."

"What about your therapy? What about your nightmares?"

"I haven't had one since Will and I cleaned out *SEAQUESTOR* for delivery to Paddy's mysterious captain on Saturday. I think that whatever demon was in my soul is going away with the sale of the boat. Once I let go of Susan's boat, the demon will let go of me. And in three days, when she's no longer floating in the middle of my world behind GrayDays, I know I'll be free again."

Meagan was back at the wrought iron railing, and Jack sensed that she was working to sort out the unexpected turn of the day's events. He hadn't quite figured out how he and Meagan had reached this nebulous milestone. Maybe it was destiny, Jack thought. Maybe it was just an accident. Whatever the cause, for the first time in a year Jack felt fully alive and free; driven to unshackle himself from his painful past, and help Meagan do the same.

"It's possible," said Meagan with a tense look on her face. "It's possible that I was wrong about you needing to get back on Susan's boat. Maybe you just had to get it out of your sight and out of your life."

"I don't think I could ever bear to sail that boat again. Whenever I get near her or go on board a choking sense of foreboding overtakes me. I now know that as long as that boat is docked behind the store I'll carry around my subconscious fear that someday, somehow, she'll trap me back on board. You brought that fear to the surface for me Meagan, and now that the boat is sold I'm sure I'll be fine."

"Just like the old book title proclaims, *You're Okay, I'm Okay*," said Meagan.

"I think it's the other way around."

"Yes, well I need food to get my brain back into gear. The smoke is clearing off the lake, and the sun is breaking through so why don't we have our lunch out here on the deck?"

"I left the picnic basket downstairs."

"A round trip on the original Stairmaster won't hurt you." Meagan's mood seemed to have brightened with the emerging sunshine. "I'll move that small table and chairs outside while you're gone."

"Sounds like a plan."

Meagan watched Jack descend the metal spiral of steps for a moment before turning back to the lake. She knew she had deluded herself, and in doing so had also deluded her patient. All of her training had warned her that this was going to happen, yet she had allowed her normally infallible instincts to lessen the proper professional distance that ethics, and common sense, demanded. But there was something more primal operating here on several different levels.

Meagan realized that she wanted Jack Grayson in her life, and that she wanted him content and healed. But Dr. Palmer understood that Jack's demon was no more going to vanish with Susan's yacht than her own demon would disappear by estranging herself from Paddy Delaney for thirty years. All demons, she knew, have two common traits going for them: persistence and patience.

The murky, smoky, swirling question that haunted Meagan this day was whether she truly had it within her to beat the demons at their own game.

# CHAPTER 22

Jack was still delighted with himself for his performance at the Marblehead Light as he parked his Range Rover at the east gate of the Historic *All Souls Cemetery*. He was even more delighted at Meagan Palmer's response to his impromptu overture.

Jack had long ago realized that the circumstances make the man, and not the other way around. A year on the desolate rivers of Vietnam followed by a quarter century at sea had made him a fatalist. It is not the incessant planning and attempted manipulation of our lives that defines us, but our reaction to unexpected tragedies and opportunities. Jack treated both as the challenges that make life memorable and valuable. And now he was pleased at his adroit handling of the opportunity that sprung out of his confrontation with Meagan yesterday.

But this was a new day—a special and sacred day, and Jack had to shift gears. It was Thursday, September 3, Susan's birthday, and like all the deceased Wheelers before her, she was about to have her birthday visit at graveside.

Jack grabbed the two essential packages off the front seat and suddenly felt horribly alone. It's only fair, he thought as he stepped onto the neatly trimmed gravel path that flowed into the cemetery. He was merely following Susan's footsteps on all those occasions when she was obliged to follow the Wheeler family ritual alone while he was at sea.

Twenty-two years earlier Jack had been introduced to what he first thought of as a bizarre and eerie family event. He had been visiting Susan during spring break, and was commanded by Susan's grandmother to "kindly accompany" them to Grandpa Wheeler's birthday party. Jack's initial elation at the prospect of going to a party turned into queasiness as he helped Susan carry a bouquet of spring daisies and a picnic basket into the haunting old cemetery.

The family patriarch, Percy Wheeler, was devoutly Christian and had been the architect, general contractor, and primary financier of the Vermilion Methodist Church that stood beside the ancient cemetery. "Nanny" Wheeler took young midshipman Jack Grayson to her husband's grave, put her hand on Percy's tombstone and told Jack, "We believe very strongly that death is not an end, but another beautiful beginning. That's why we visit our family members here on their birthdays, and never on the date of their passing. I know that Susan and her children will keep our family tradition alive."

Jack watched Nanny lay the daisies on her husband's grave while Susan carefully unpacked the picnic basket and laid out lunch. He remembered thinking that this was pretty spooky stuff, but deferred to the heart-rending love he saw in the old woman's eyes.

Susan Wheeler Grayson did carry on the tradition, and with the passing of years Jack marveled that he himself looked forward to these unique Wheeler birthday celebrations. There was a profoundly spiritual connection with the past that was undeniable, and Jack and Susan always came away from the "birthday parties" feeling strengthened and inspired.

No one knows for sure how old the *All Souls Cemetery* is. Nanny Wheeler once showed Jack an unmarked grave she claims held the remains of a sailor drowned in Perry's great Battle of Lake Erie in 1813. There were a dozen or so graves dating to the Civil War. Union soldiers of the 103rd O.V.I. lay beneath a dozen markers with a common date, July 2, 1863—Gettysburg.

Jack carried his small bouquet of Aster, the traditional bloom for those born in September, and his brown bagged lunch through the compact old graveyard. The Wheeler family plot was not difficult to find since Percy had predictably placed it at the very center, next to the historic Civil War graves.

The towering Firelands limestone obelisk, with the name WHEELER chiseled into all four sides, dominated the four acre fenced enclosure, a size limitation resulting from one of Percy's last master strokes. In fact, only two designated graves remained to be filled in the entire cemetery, and Jack felt a chill as he stood upon them. He wondered when, and how, his time would come. Then he wondered whether the last of the Wheeler bloodline, Jimmy Wheeler Grayson, would ever come home for his parents' birthday parties.

Jack carefully placed his two parcels on the Grecian style stone bench facing Susan's grave, and reached into his back pocket for the pair of hand trimmers he always brought along at the behest of Nanny Wheeler who, until the day she died, was at war with the groundskeepers at the cemetery. Jack meticulously clipped blades of grass that crept up the face of the headstone. He removed an old bouquet from the pot at the base of Susan's highly polished marble monument, and cautiously trimmed the grass around the opening in the sacred ground. Satisfied with the results of his manicuring, Jack retrieved one of the packages from the bench and carefully withdrew the large bunch of Aster which he shook gently then placed into the pot. He emptied the contents of a small container of fertilized water into the pot, and then placed a framed 8x10 inch photograph of Susan against the headstone.

Susan and Nanny Wheeler would have been proud of him, he thought as he wrapped the wilted old flowers and grass clippings into the empty paper bag and sat down on the bench to ponder the fruits of his efforts. Jack had, years ago, come to enjoy these tranquil interludes in the memorial gardens of the Wheeler family legend. It had become, for him, a place of idyllic peace—a place not often visited except by occasional rainy-day tourists looking for a bit of history in place of their water sports.

But today the weather was fair, the wind was blowing gently off shore, most of Vermilion's population was on the lake or the river, and Jack Grayson was enjoying a birthday luncheon date with his wife. Jack unwrapped his usual birthday sandwich—sliced smoked turkey breast, baby Swiss cheese, lettuce, tomato and real mayonnaise on crusty Italian bread. During twenty two years of marriage Jack could never bring himself to ask how anyone could enjoy such a dull concoction. But this was Susan's sandwich of choice, one she had unabashedly fed her husband and son on every "lunch meat occasion," and Jack felt obligated to bring it to her birthday celebration.

However, he also felt privileged to bring with him the "antidote"—an ice cold, dark amber bottle of *Killian's Irish Red Ale*. It was, he thought, a small act of defiance to tradition that even Percy Wheeler would have enjoyed.

Halfway through his sandwich, and bottle of beer, Jack finally sucked it up and cast his attention to the inscription on Susan's headstone:

> *The bitterest tears shed over graves are for words left unsaid,*
> *and deeds left undone.*—Harriet Beecher Stowe

It was, Jack remembered, the mere carving of that inscription on Susan's memorial that precipitated the "bitterest tears" that had yet fallen on the relationship between Jack Grayson and his son Jimmy.

How could he have known? Jack asked himself as he sat there and choked back his own bitter tears. Susan had included the inscription in a codicil to her Last Will and Testament, signed only six months before her death. Jack had not even known that the codicil existed until family lawyer, Joe Ryan opened Susan's safe deposit box at Vermilion's Central Trust Bank. Jack had carefully and silently read the document before he exploded. "What's this all about?" he recalled yelling at the lawyer.

Joe Ryan's response still stuck in Jack's craw, and even the bitter Irish ale could not wash it down. "Susan told me it was the most important legacy she had to leave."

Jack had immediately declared, "No way. I'm not going to put that on her grave. I'm her husband and executor. It's my call, and I'm not going to look at that for the rest of my life."

Then James Wheeler Grayson came home from California.

A year after the fact, Jack had to give the kid credit. He had always thought Jimmy too weak and timid to buck him, or anyone else for that matter. But when Jimmy demanded that his mother's wishes be honored, and Jack resisted, an unlikely war was on. Jack recalled overhearing Ernie Beckett comment at the funeral, "Those two are fightin' the Battle of Lake Erie all over again."

Jimmy Grayson played all his cards in an attempt to gain his father's cooperation. He gathered the Captain's Quarters together, *sans* Captain Jack Grayson, and pled his case. Ednamae Bradley, in her unique role as guardian of the Harbour Towne 1837 heritage, assured Jimmy that Jack would "do the right thing."

Jack would never forget, and always lament, the final interment ceremony at *All Souls Cemetery*. The day Susan Arthur Wheeler Grayson was laid to rest was an unusually cool, damp and blustery afternoon. The kind of day boaters hated and funeral directors had grown accustomed to. It was the kind of day that no amount of prayer could lift you out of; the kind of day that brought with it not only a dismal spirit, but also a foreboding of doom.

The memorial service inside the stately Methodist Church had tested the occupancy limits of the sanctuary, balcony, and narthex. To the horror of the church's "old guard" the basement multi purpose room was, at the last minute, rigged with closed-circuit television for another 150 people. If it was true that the funeral of Princess Diana was viewed by the world, it is equally true that the funeral of Lady Susan was seen by her world.

The brief service at grave side, although officially listed in the newspaper as "family only," drew a large crowd of mourners, passersby, and curiosity seekers. Perhaps miraculously, the cadre of Auxiliary Police, VFW volunteers and AMVETS Color Guard were able to keep most of the crowd outside the low fenced perimeter of the cemetery. Even so, the onlookers had a nearly unobstructed view of the slightly raised knoll crowned by the Wheeler family plot, no more than fifty yards away.

Reverend Harland Hubler recited the customary Methodist burial litany to a small group comprised of Jack and Jimmy Grayson, Jimmy's "friend" Raul Delacourt, Ednamae Bradley, Ernie Beckett, Maggie Wicks, Teddy Parks, the omnipresent lawyer Joe Ryan, the omniscient psychologist Meagan Palmer, and Will Daysart who barely missed the memorial service but slipped in at the grave side amid a few raised eyebrows. At the end of the commitment litany,

Rev. Hubler recognized Captain Jack Grayson to dedicate Susan's memorial headstone for consecration.

As Jack sat on the Grecian bench assessing the past he couldn't quite fathom his stupidity, when he unveiled the headstone and read the inscription:

*0 hear us when we cry to Thee,*
*for those in peril on the sea.*

What happened next, Jack lamented, had become a legend in the folklore of Vermilion.

Jimmy Grayson looked up suddenly and turned to his father with fire in his eyes and vengeance in his voice. "I don't believe it! How could you do this to her?" Raul put his arm around Jimmy's shoulder and tried to calm him down, but Jimmy would not be silenced. This was to be one of those defining moments in a family's history. No one spoke a word as all eyes turned to Jack to "do the right thing."

Silence.

"I'll bet mom cried out to you when she was in peril didn't she?" Jimmy yelled out with uncommon violence. "Did you hear her then? Where were all your great ideas a year ago when mom needed you to save her life?"

No one, not even Jack, could have seen the next move coming. Jimmy charged toward his father as the stunned gatherers reached out too late to restrain him. Jack remembered standing his ground, ready to take whatever his wounded son had to offer. Jimmy quickly side-stepped his father and with a tremendous Tai Kwan Do kick, knocked the headstone off its make-shift pedestal. Reverend Hubler was horrified as he reached out feebly to steady the falling stone, only to see it crash on the side of a wooden platform and break in two. It was, Jack thought, a sight rivaling Moses' hurling of the stone tablets upon the idol-worshipping and unrepentant Israelites. Jack had always understood that the Israelites deserved Moses' rage. Now he also understood that he was equally deserving of Jimmy's wrath. But, like most parents whose judgment is challenged, Jack overreacted in the heat of the moment.

"Leave this place, Jimmy! Get out of here right now! You have defiled your mother's memory and I never want to see your face again."

"And you . . . ," screamed Jimmy. "Have defiled my mother, and I will always hate you for it."

At that moment there was a hush that was uncommon, even for a cemetery. Jimmy left the grounds with Raul hot on his trail. Yet even in his rage, Jack knew that Susan had left her son a most important legacy—honesty. And for the last year that legacy had kept father and son apart, but not out of conflict.

A week after the funeral, Jack received a phone call from Cleveland's most eminent probate lawyer. Richard W. Schwartz, Esquire laid down the law for Jack Grayson, and before the first leaves of autumn dropped upon Susan's grave her newly engraved *bitterest tears* headstone was in place. Ironically, the epitaph that was bequeathed to Jack by a wife who somehow sensed that she had run out of time, then shoved down his throat by a son whose patience had been crushed by fate, was now carved into his heart as indelibly as it had been carved into stone.

Jack vowed that when his "operation" for Will Daysart and the Captain's Quarters was complete, he would make peace with Jimmy. He owed that much to Susan's memory, and he owed that to his future, whatever that might be, with Meagan.

As long as they were in the business of purging demons, Jack thought, they might as well be rid of them all. Today, he said to himself, would be the last time he would shed bitter tears over this grave.

Jack gathered up the ritual remains of the afternoon and put a warm loving hand on Susan's stone. Despite his best efforts, a single tear seeped through the steely curtain of determination he had assumed. As he began to walk back down the narrow white gravel path, he suddenly turned and took a small camera from his pocket. "Sorry Susan, I almost forgot." Jack put the viewfinder to his eye and raised his finger to the shutter release . . .

\*       \*       \*

The noisy focal plane shutter behind the long Nikkor telephoto lens streaked a final exposure across the high speed film just as Maggie Wicks and Ernie Beckett looked up from the deck to see what had splashed in the Vermilion River. What they saw were only the tell tale concentric circles of muddy water that approached *Aphrodite* like a sonar's warning "ping." Even more elusive was Derry "Red" Reimer lurking in the shadows of a stack of boat cradles in Parson's Boat Yard across the river.

Satisfied with his final shot, Red Reimer snapped on the lens cap and slung the camera strap over the shoulder of his elbow-patched Irish tweed jacket. To any casual observer he was just another tourist capturing images of Vermilion's historic past.

But the quiet precise epicurean that Angie Mariano had run afoul of a week earlier was no casual observer. Red took his missions seriously and studiously. And since he had no confidence in the ability of Paddy's black-clad lieutenants to uncover anything meaningful about the charter boat crew he had just photographed for Paddy, he decided to have a late luncheon at McGarvey's and book a short afternoon cruise.

# CHAPTER 23

On board *Aphrodite*, Ernie jumped at the splash of water just below where he was working. "What the hell . . ."

"A little jumpy today?" quipped Maggie Wicks.

"Did you see that guy over in the boat yard taking our picture?"

"Not just a picture you paranoid old coot," said Maggie looking across the river to the jumble of empty boat cradles. "A picture of *my* boat. It happens all the time."

"So why did he throw a stone into the water?"

"A fish jumped."

"No, no. He wanted us to look up."

"Who, the fish?"

"No damnit," the old man spat. "The guy in the boat yard."

"He's just another tourist. Forget about him and help me get this awning lashed on." Maggie turned back to the awning frame and continued her work. "I want everything ship-shape and Bristol-fashion, as you always say."

"I still think you should cancel your trips this afternoon and tomorrow so we can get ready for Meagan's charter on Saturday."

"We can do whatever we need to while we keep our normal schedule," said Maggie. "It's less obvious that way. Besides, Jack Grayson just called and said he wants to ride along with us this afternoon."

"Why in the hell would he want to do that? He's been around these lagoons a thousand times."

"But not lately," said Maggie. "Anyway, he said he needs my advice about something."

"Did he say what?"

"No. I think it's just a ruse to come on board and give the ship a once-over. You know he's worried about that jury-rigged stuffing box."

"She'll hold just fine," said Ernie. "I laid on a good solid patch. Hell, all we have to do is follow behind that stinkin' old fishin' boat of Teddy's."

"I'm sure you're right Ernie. But you know how persnickety Jack is about nailing down every detail. Just like someone else I know." Maggie leaned over and patted the old sailing master on the head. "It won't hurt to humor him for an afternoon."

"You're the captain down here. An' I think you better see to your passengers." Ernie aimed his grimy paw toward the dock. "They're gatherin' at the gangway."

"Okay Ernie. You finish tying that off, and then go single-up the dock lines for me." Maggie checked her watch. "We leave in ten minutes."

"Aye, aye skipper."

\*      \*      \*

Jack was running a little late as he rounded the corner of McGarvey's riverside patio with a little too much wind in his sails. He collided with the slight red-haired man and nearly knocked him off his feet. Jack was surprised at the lean, hard body of this scholarly looking little man as he grabbed him in a lurching bear hug to stop his fall.

"Thank you there mate," said the Irishman as he broke Jack's hold and gathered himself together.

"I'm sorry," said Jack. "I should have sounded a couple of short blasts on the whistle before I tacked around that corner."

"Ah, a fellow seaman," beamed Red with large misshapen tea-stained teeth. "No harm done."

"Are you sure you're okay? Can I do anything for you?"

"No, no. I'm fine." Red checked his Nikon quickly then moved it around to his side. "There is one thing," he said with a serious grin. "Where might I be buyin' a passage on that yacht?" pointing to *Aphrodite*.

"Did you have lunch at McGarvey's?"

"Aye, I did indeed. A fine plate of Lake Erie perch with a glass of North Bass Island Chardonnay."

"A fine choice of a meal, and a fine choice for a cruise," said Jack. "The lagoons cruise is included with lunch. Just go back inside and they'll give you a ticket."

"Thanks mate." Jack escorted the feisty leprechaun through the rear patio door then looked down the dock at *Aphrodite*. Jack always delighted in the beautifully classic lines of Maggie's vintage yacht. *Aphrodite*, named by Maggie after the ancient Greek goddess of love and beauty, received one and exuded the other. Maggie and Ernie had maintained her with all the dedicated love and money of any antique collector. Although she was now nearly a half-century old she showed none of the usual telltale signs of aging. Long after her contemporaries had fallen prey to the scrap yards, *Aphrodite* radiated refined and mature beauty. As Jack admired the little ship from stem to stern, beholding a machine that had become an exotic mixture of history and function, he recalled Maggie's fanciful "birth" story of a vessel that had become Maggie Wick's anthropomorphized baby.

\*   \*   \*

*Aphrodite* had been commissioned by a wealthy Wall Street tycoon in the early fifties as his opulent floating refuge and transport from Manhattan to his "cottage" a few miles down the river from the U.S. Military Academy at West Point. He had spared no expense in retaining the famed Door County, Wisconsin naval architects Sparkman & Stevens to draft a unique design for his weekly Hudson River passages.

The Bath Boat Works, legendary for its craftsmanship, built the yacht in its *down east* boatyard on Maine's rocky shore. At christening she glistened as the miniature of an ocean liner with two decks of white superstructure above a sleek black rakish-bowed steel hull. A mahogany sheathed wheel house atop the promenade deck, with a faux smoke stack just aft completed the steamship image.

Maggie had discovered the yacht rusting away beside a bankrupt nautical restaurant in Annapolis, Maryland during one of her annual pilgrimages to the famed Annapolis National Boat Show. After a week of negotiations with a relieved federal bankruptcy trustee, she purchased the yacht for "a smidgen" over her scrap metal value. For the next two years, Maggie's retired engineering chum from the Coast Guard painstakingly overhauled the entire mechanical plant. At the same time, Maggie and her navy of midshipmen from Annapolis chipped, scraped, painted and recreated the ship that awestruck New Yorkers had so admired at three decades earlier.

When the newly anointed Captain Maggie Wicks, who had spent most of her inheritance and savings, steamed northward toward the Saint Lawrence Seaway for a passage through the Welland Canal and into Lake Erie in 1985 she reveled in the joy of motherhood. She had "birthed her baby," received command of a beautiful ship, and begun a new log book, not only for her vessel, but for her life.

\*   \*   \*

"Ahoy there Jack," yelled Ernie from the bow of the ship. "Cast those lines off them cleats. We're singlin' up for departure."

Jack stepped up to the heavy cast iron cleat fastened to the dock and slipped the loosened line over the edge. He watched as the sprightly old man heaved the thick polyester line aboard with the nimbleness of a middle-aged able seaman. "Now slip off that spring line and meet me back aft. We're pullin' out in ten minutes."

"Aye, aye, Captain." Jack paced down the dock, past the queue of waiting tourists, eighty-five feet to *Aphrodite*'s classic counter stern. He hustled a few more strides farther to the stern line that Ernie had eased from the deck. Just after he threw off the last line and turned to head for the gangway he noted that his Irish collision victim had joined the end of the passenger line.

*     *     *

Halfway through the hour-long lagoons cruise, narrated by Maggie Wicks as she piloted the ship through myriad shallow and twisty turns, she spoke again into the P.A. microphone mounted directly in front of the ship's wheel. "This afternoon I have a very special treat for you. Captain Ernie Beckett, the last living sailing master of full-rigged ships and Port Captain of our own Vermilion Yacht Club, will be taking the helm and narrating the remainder of our cruise."

Maggie relinquished the wheel to Ernie with a slight bow, then turned to Jack and said, "Let's have a cup of tea in my sea cabin."

"Sounds great," said Jack as he followed Maggie through a glossy mahogany door at the rear of the wheelhouse. Jack was no stranger to the room he and Maggie entered. All large ships, even miniaturized ones, had a Captain's sea cabin. When weather conditions were foul and Captains wanted to stay near the bridge, or just needed a change of scenery, they would often retreat to the rugged simplicity of the sea cabin.

The small cabin that Jack and Maggie now occupied was simply elegant. A small single ship's bunk with heavy-weather side boards was recessed into the rear cabin bulkhead. At the foot of the bed was a small enclosed lavatory with a highly varnished and louvered door. There was an angled, lighted chart table, resembling a drafting table, on the starboard wall near the doorway with a high swivel chair bolted to the deck in front of it. On the port side of the room beneath a shiny brass round port light stood an oriental motif teak and brass rectangular table with three matching chairs. On the forward bulkhead, beside the cabin door, stood a beautifully crafted brass-hinged cabinet that contained a small refrigerator, wet bar, two burner electric stove and lighted shelf space, above and below. Jack noticed immediately that the small table was set with a bone china and silver coffee and pastry service salvaged off the *H.M.S. Queen Mary* before her exile to Long Beach, California. The tea kettle was whistling its invitation as Jack and Maggie entered the cabin.

"Please Jack, have a seat," Maggie said. "I'll pour."

"As you wish, my captain."

Jack delighted in Maggie's charming fussiness as she tinkered with the tea, sugar, lemon slices and aromatic glazed pound cake set out before him. It was a fitting presentation on board the vintage vessel.

"Now then," said Maggie after a long deliberate sip of English breakfast tea. "I presume you've not come here to inspect the ship and chastise me about the stuffing box patch."

"Is that what Ernie thinks?"

"That's what I encouraged him to think," said Maggie with a mischievous smile. "I assume that you can do without his incessant snooping."

"He means well," said Jack. "But yes, you're right. You created the perfect diversion."

"So, what is on the agenda this afternoon?"

"Meagan Palmer."

"I thought as much," Maggie said as she adored a small piece of the sweet cake. "I take it that you two are, shall we say, involved?

"Yes we are."

"That's marvelous, Jack." Maggie swallowed a healthy bite of pound cake and quickly washed it down with the warm spicy tea. "You know that Ednamae and I have been conniving for months to find you a suitable lady."

"You hit on just the right adjective, the one that's causing me concern. Suitable."

"Why Jack? Meagan's a lovely girl, and you two have so much in common."

"That's just it," said Jack as he carefully placed his empty cup on the gold-rimmed saucer and watched Maggie quickly refill it. "Maybe we have too much in common."

"How so?"

"Well, being Susan's roommate and confidant. Will and Jimmy both despise her. And then there's Ernie. Not only did he idolize Susan, he believes in mating once for life."

"Pretty weird for a sailor, wouldn't you say?"

"Yes, he's brusque and opinionated, but I can live with that," said Jack. "I'm just not sure I can live with Meagan's view of our past."

"Okay, but before you can begin to think about living with someone else, you have to learn to live with yourself."

"I've been trying to do that since Susan died," Jack sighed through a long sip of tea. "And I wasn't doing very well . . ."

"Until?"

"Until I went to Meagan for help."

"Okay, that's a start," said Maggie. "But now you're wondering whether it's really love you're feeling or just the warmth and safety of a kinky fantasy with your therapist. Right?"

Jack could tell from the reflection of his face in Maggie's eyes that he had come to the right place. The complex woman across from him had not only lived it all, but was willing to share it all. "I guess that about sums it up."

"Give it some time, Jack. Only time and shared experiences will sort out your true feelings. If it's a fantasy, it will pass like an early autumn storm on the lake."

*She's good*, Jack thought as he plowed ahead. "And what about Jimmy and Will? Both my son and my godson hate her."

"Let them go, Jack." Maggie reached across and took Jack's hand. "Those boys are grown. You can't control them any more and you certainly don't have to account to them. They will love or they will hate; they will succeed or they will fail; they will be happy or miserable . . . all on their own. Cut them some slack and let them do whatever they're going to do. When they're finished, praise them when they win and console them when they lose. Just don't presume to tell them how to live, where to live and with whom to live. And don't allow them to do it to you."

"So this thing with Meagan sounds okay to you?"

"You sound okay to me," Maggie said as she released Jack's hand and finished off the last of the pound cake. "And that's the only opinion I'm entitled to."

"Ain't you two finished with your break yet?" Ernie's raspy voice boomed through the speaker above the chart table and broke a moment of intense quietude. "We're gettin' close to the east lagoon and I think you outta be up here and start doin' your job."

As Maggie stood up Jack put his arm around her shoulders and whispered, "Thank you dear."

Back in the wheelhouse Ernie had just throttled back the two big Cummins marine diesels when Maggie and Jack eased up on either side of him. "Well folks," he spat into the microphone. "My watch is over so, I'll give you back to the Master of the vessel for the rest of the tour. I hope you've enjoyed these ramblings of an old man." Ernie stepped aside and gave Maggie the wheel.

"... the ramblings of an old man who's in love with this river, this town and these lagoons," finished Maggie through the public address system. Maggie switched off the P.A. system and turned to Ernie and Jack. "Will you boys each take the bow and stern lookout for me? I don't need any close scrapes today."

The two former ship captains snapped to attention and offered up snappy salutes. "Aye, aye."

The turn at the dead end of the East Lagoon was a tricky one because of the narrow 105 foot available turning width. *Aphrodite's* 85 foot length left only ten feet of maneuvering room ahead and astern of the big excursion boat. Maggie literally had to "turn on a dime." This unique cruise requirement spawned the only major mechanical alteration Maggie had made to the carefully restored yacht. When she fully understood the important history at the end of the East Lagoon she resolved to find a way to make a successful round trip passage into the long tiny inlet.

A trip to dry dock in Detroit, a three-week haul-out, and a major modification to *Aphrodite's* underwater bow section provided the solution. The unique transverse "bow thruster," in concert with either the port or starboard engine allowed Maggie to pivot the ship in an almost perfect circle with no assistance from shore lines or a padded pivot point on the bow.

The tricky maneuver made use of the paddle wheel effect generated by the large stern propellers when turning at slow speeds. Each stern propeller turned outboard to provide the greatest hydrodynamic cavitations and thrust along the centerline of the ship. Viewing from the stern, the starboard prop turned to the right, while the port prop turned to the left. By using the paddle wheel effect of the starboard engine alone, the prop would grab the water and pull the stern to the right. The opposite effect was achieved when using the port engine alone. But the turning moment of the stern props alone was not enough to turn the vessel in close quarters. Maggie's addition of another two-direction propeller low in the bow section gave *Aphrodite* mystical maneuverability.

Still, the margin of error was slim, and when the wind was blowing across the lagoon in the wrong direction even the most precise helmsmanship was not good enough. Aided by ten-foot long boat hook poles, Maggie's crewmen on the bow and stern could fend off a crunching episode.

Jack unsnapped the long aluminum and plastic composite boat hook off the bow bulwark as *Aphrodite* swung gracefully into the East Lagoon. He waved to a carload of McGarvey's waitresses who had parked at the lagoon end of the restaurant parking lot on their way to work for the evening shift.

On the west side of the narrow lagoon, off the port side, Jack noticed friends, customers, and acquaintances preening their gardens, polishing their boats, and painting their pristine and sterile little habitats, as Will often referred to them. When an image of Susan, pruning her "American Beauty" roses in her trellised garden near the Victorian-style gazebo behind their lakeside house, invaded Jack's thoughts he blinked twice then quickly turned to starboard.

Bennie's Bait Bazaar and small boat launching ramp was abuzz with boaters backing all sorts of watercraft into the lagoon for early evening fishing trips. Bennie looked to Jack like a big dusty kid caricature from *Peanuts* with his greasy work shirt, cut-off khaki work pants, hiking boots, and Australian "Tilly Hat" complete with a plastic night crawler wrapped around a large sparkling "Erie-Deerie" fishing lure.

"Hey Jack," Bennie yelled then spat out a nasty brown glob from his ever present *Red Man* chaw. "Do you need some fresh bait for that *big* hook you're holdin'?"

"I'm hoping I won't catch anything with this one today," Jack yelled back with a laugh. It was an old joke, but it amused *Aphrodite*'s passengers and Bennie's fishermen. Jack felt Maggie swing the bow gently to starboard around the final East Lagoon dogleg. A hundred yards ahead he could see the end of the lagoon, the quiet docks of GrayDays Marine and Susan's *SEAQUESTOR* resting sedately at the end of pier No.1.

As the collision distance closed to fifty yards, Jack felt the telltale vibration of Maggie backing the engines down slowly to stop *Aphrodite*'s progress. Maggie would stop her ship just twenty-five yards in front of GrayDays docks, in the wide little basin that formed the end of the lagoon, and there commence her paddle-wheeling-bow-thrusting pivot. The thrice daily maneuver gave the passengers a panoramic view of the GrayDays Marina as well as . . .

". . . the historic Wheeler mansion built by Vermilion city father and lagoon developer Percy Wheeler," Jack heard Maggie announce over the public address system. "This historical site is now the home of GrayDays Marine, Vermilion's oldest and finest boat broker and chandler."

"Bonnie advertising for the lad who owns that place," said a distinctively familiar voice.

Jack turned to see the tea-stained smile of the tweed-clad Irishman he had run into on McGarvey's dock. "She tries to spread it around," said Jack. "Most of the business owners on the river are friends of hers and they can all use the business." Jack felt the low building vibration of the bow thruster beneath his feet and directed his attention to the steel shore retainer that was his responsibility.

"I wondered how she was going to get us out of this dead end," said the Irishman.

"What sometimes seems hopeless often turns out to be miraculous," said Jack with a sly wink.

"So, it's a spiritual journey we've been takin' then."

"With a little technology to keep the screws turning," said Jack as he tapped the retaining wall with his boat hook.

"Then I best be makin' a picture of this moment," said Red Reimer as he put his eye to the viewfinder of his Nikon. From the whine of the motor driven film advance and the slow swing of the camera, Jack sensed that the scholarly little man had "mapped" the whole marina in a blazing twenty-shot sequence.

"You must go through miles of film with that thing," said Jack. "Or is there something special over there you want to study?"

"I just want to make sure I don't miss anything on this trip." The Irishman's eyes bore into Jack's, and for the first time since their collision he felt something foreboding in this complex man's mien. Jack looked away and was relieved to see that Maggie's pivot was nearly completed and that the bow was nearly headed back toward the river. "Well then," said Jack as he snapped his boat hook back into its cradle. "My job is complete. Hope you enjoyed the cruise."

"Very informative," Jack heard the tweed whisper with words that seemed to cling to his back as he headed toward the wheelhouse.

By the time Jack reached the wheelhouse, Maggie had just nosed the yacht back out into the river and come to a stop to allow some small boat traffic to clear. When the river traffic was clear from the bridge at the south end of McGarvey's dock to about fifty yards north of Maggie's present position, she would turn back down river then back *Aphrodite* into her slip, starboard side to the McGarvey's dock.

Ernie Beckett entered the wheelhouse just as the VHF marine radio squawked, "*Aphrodite, Aphrodite, Aphrodite . . .* this is U.S. Coast Guard, Lorain calling *Aphrodite.*"

Maggie grabbed the radio microphone off the bulkhead. "Lorain Coast Guard, this is *Aphrodite*, switching to channel six."

"Roger that *Aphrodite.*"

"I wonder what this is all about," Maggie said to Ernie as he switched the radio channel selector.

"Go ahead and handle the call Maggie," said Jack now nudging her aside. "I'll hold our position here in the river until you're finished."

"Lorain Coast Guard, this is *Aphrodite* on Channel six. What can I do for you?"

"Maggie, Lieutenant Baldwin here. I thought you might want to know that some men were down here asking questions about your boat and your crew."

"Probably just future customers."

"I don't think so."

"Well then, maybe journalists or travel agents getting background information."

"Not these guys."

"Why not?"

"They look and talk like a couple of Irish gangsters," reported the young lieutenant. "They were dressed in black and always looking over their shoulders."

"Okay lieutenant. I think I get the picture now," Maggie said casting a concerned glance at Jack. "*Semper paratis.*"

"*Semper P*, Captain. Always happy to assist one of the club. United States Coast Guard, Lorain out."

"What was that all about?" asked Ernie.

"Just my boys looking out for me. *Semper paratis.*"

"What the hell does that mean?"

"It's the Coast Guard motto Ernie," she said. "Always prepared."

"Prepared for what?"

Maggie nudged Jack aside and took the ship's wheel again. "The guy with the camera . . ."

"Yes?"

"He isn't Irish by any chance, is he?"

# CHAPTER 24

Paddy Delaney's table looked like a photograph from a glitzy magazine on Irish country cooking, as the small catering crew from the Irish-American Club backed out the doorway like servants dismissed by the King of Siam.

It was Friday night and the nefarious "King" of Lorain circled the heavy round table setting for four people. The old Regulator clock on the wall displayed the time—6:47—and Paddy knew that in precisely thirteen minutes he would have the final pieces to the puzzle that his niece had thrown down before him.

When Paddy Delaney commanded his council to dinner no one dared be a minute early or late. He uncovered the heated serving tray full of sliced corned beef, garnished with a decorative array of julienne carrots, celery and sprigs of fresh parsley, and inhaled deeply of the spicy aroma that billowed forth. He uncovered a crock of steamed cabbage with caraway seeds, and then proceeded to savor the subtle aroma of a large heated serving tray of new Irish potatoes resting expectantly in a light garlic butter sauce. There were two heaping baskets of soda bread beneath coarse green muslin napkins. A dozen bottles of Harp's beer were sweating onto coasters, and would be at a reasonable drinking temperature when Paddy's guests arrived.

The wily old gangster knew that nothing loosened tongues like a hearty meal.

\*　　\*　　\*

The old Chelsea clock on the mantle dinged out its six-bell announcement to the landlubbing world that it was 7:00 p.m. just as Will Daysart charged in the door, out of breath. "Sorry I'm late," he puffed. "But the traffic is murder."

The Captain's Quarters members, plus Meagan Palmer, who were seated around Ednamae's huge oaken table, chuckled at Will's obviously lame excuse.

187

"Murder's the only thing that would cause a traffic jam in this town," quipped Meagan to looks of dread silence. "Sorry . . . bad joke."

"Well, now that you're here," said Ernie. "Maybe we can serve up our dinner and get down to business."

"Ednamae, can I give you a hand?" asked Maggie Wicks from her usual seat.

"No Deerie, you just sit there and enjoy yourself. I have everything waiting on a serving cart just inside the kitchen. I won't be a minute."

True to her word, Ednamae reappeared in a flash that would have made David Copperfield envious and began unloading enormous platters on to the table. Teddy Bear and Jack Grayson used their strong long arms to redistribute the evening fare around the table. There was fresh batter-fried Lake Erie perch, complimented by two huge platters of crispy brown shoestring potatoes and hushpuppies. A nice crystal bowl full of homemade Harbor Towne 1837 coleslaw completed the traditional Friday night repast—one that those assembled had not enjoyed together since Susan Grayson's death.

Two large pitchers of sun-brewed iced tea followed the placement of Diet Cokes in front of young Will and Meagan Palmer. Just as Ednamae set the cans and ice-filled glasses in front of them their eyes met as if to say, *I didn't know we had anything in common.*

When it appeared that everything was in place and Ednamae had taken her seat, Ernie Beckett tapped on his iced tea glass with a spoon and said, "Let's dispense with the usual formalities tonight and dig in." He reached for the platter of fish. "Maybe a good meal will help us all find a clearing in our minds."

*     *     *

"Maybe the two of you could let go of that corned beef long enough to tell me what you found out," said Paddy to the dark clad clansmen with grease running down their chins.

One of them reached into his jacket pocket as he hastily swallowed a partially chewed chunk of meat, and pulled out a small notebook with a rubber band marking a page. "The boat is eighty-five feet long, diesel-powered, twin-screw, custom designed, twenty-ton displacement, documented vessel . . ."

"What are you telling me?" spat Paddy.

"What we found out."

"Who owns the boat?"

"Aphrodite Corporation."

"Who owns the corporation?"

"I don't know." The kid wiped his chin nervously and looked at his brother across the table. "I mean how are we supposed to find that out?"

"Who operates the boat?"

Page flip . . . flip . . . flipping. "Uh, Aphrodite Corporation."

"Who is the Captain?"

"I don't know."

"Why don't you know?" yelled Paddy.

The brother across the table answered the panicked plea in the youngster's eyes. "Those bastards at the Coast Guard wouldn't tell us anything."

"Did you think to try anywhere else?" asked Paddy with uncommon calm.

"Yeah. We drove out to Vermilion but the boat was just leaving the dock."

"Then what?"

"Well uh," grabbing for his greasy soda bread stuffed sandwich. "Then we went down to the club and shot some pool."

"I'll be a sonofabitch," yelled Paddy. "I sent you two dummies out to get me a little information and what do you bring back to me?" Paddy threw his napkin on the table and stood over the two young men. "Ignorance, stupidity . . ."

"Calm down Paddy," said an amused Derry "Red" Reimer after washing down the last of his precisely cut-up and masticated dinner with a healthy drink of Harp's. "That excursion boat you're goin' on tomorrow is owned and operated by a woman named Maggie Wicks."

"Well, well," said Paddy collapsing into his chair. "Derry, tell the lads how you discovered that?"

"Remember the boat you said you just missed?" Red took a measured drink from his beer glass as his rhetorical question hung in the air. "I was on board."

"Hey," Paddy yelled as he threw a chunk of soda bread at one of the boys who was already consuming another huge sandwich. "Pay attention, you might learn somethin'. It's no wonder they had to get you out of Dublin."

The kid stopped chewing for a moment, looked at his brother with a bewildered look on his greasy face, then shrugged and went back into his sandwich.

"And while you were enjoin' your cruise did you find time to bring back any other souvenirs?" asked Paddy to the still amused Red Reimer.

Red reached into his inside jacket pocket and withdrew a small stack of photographs which he slid across the table to Paddy. "The old gal at the awning wearing the white slacks and striped top is the owner and captain of the boat."

"Looks like more of a ship to me," said Paddy. "Who's the old man working with her?"

"He goes by the name of Ernie Beckett. She introduced him during the cruise as a retired sailing master who now looks after the yacht club down at the end of the lagoons."

"And what about the rest of the crew?"

"That's it. Just as you see in the photo."

"You mean those two old folks manage that ship by themselves?"

"Yes," answered Derry. "It's really quite fascinating to see how easily they handle their little ship." Derry took another sip of Harp's as he pondered his next revelation. "There was another man on board today helpin' out a bit. I ran into him on the dock earlier, but I think he's just one of the locals who tag along from time to time."

"What's his name? What was he doing?"

"I heard someone call him Jack, and all he did was fend off the bow with a long boathook while we were turning around near the end of the trip. He's not significant."

Paddy shuffled through a few more photos then paused at one and held it up to Red's view. "What's this here?"

"It's a picture of your new sailboat sitting down at that little marina owned by Will Daysart."

"What do you think of her?"

"Seems seaworthy enough. She'll do for this crossing."

*   *   *

"Okay Jack," said Ernie sliding his plate toward the center of the table. "Why don't you run down this plan for all of us?"

"My pleasure Ernie. If anybody has any questions along the way, now is the time to get on the same page." Jack looked around the table and into the eyes of his expectant team. "We're about fourteen hours from launch. After *Aphrodite* leaves the dock with Paddy and Meagan on board, there's no turning back. We'll be committed to finish what we've started." Jack continued to search for doubting faces. "Does everyone understand?" Jack made hard eye contact with each member and paused until he received a silent affirmative nod.

"Okay, let's take it from the top," Jack said as he leaned up on the table with his elbows. "Paddy's captain is scheduled to arrive at the marina at 6:00 a.m." He looked over at Will. "Are all the tanks topped off on the boat?"

"Yep. Diesel, fresh water, and propane; and the holding tanks are pumped."

"Teddy," said Jack. "What about the GPS beacon?"

"Up, tested, and running," boasted Teddy Bear. "He'll never know it's there and we'll be able to track him all the way across the lake."

"Good work guys," said Jack.

"And the GPS beacon on *Aphrodite?*"

"A.O.K."

"What about your super-sleuth microphones?"

"We tested the system on Maggie's last cruise," said Teddy with a sly grin. "I'll bet you didn't even know it. We recorded the whole Coast Guard radio call, and got you and Ernie talking in the background."

"It's the damnest thing I've ever heard," said Ernie.

"Will I need to test mine?" asked Meagan.

"We tested all three units and they're working fine," said Maggie. "I'll help you get it into a discreet nest when you come on board in the morning. It won't take but a minute."

"Okay then," said Ernie. "It sounds like the sailboat and all the spy stuff are ready. What comes next?"

"The way I see it," said Jack. "I'll be at GrayDays with Will for the delivery . . ."

"Maybe that's not such a good idea," said Teddy. "From what Will described, it sounds like Paddy expects him to handle this alone."

"But I don't want to be there alone with that guy," whined Will. "Okay then," said Jack. "I'll stay out of sight, but I think I should be there for Will . . . Just in case."

"How long will it take you to send off the boat and the captain, Will?" asked Ednamae.

"I figure maybe an hour, by the time I get the delivery papers signed, show him around the boat, and point him toward the lake."

"That's perfect," said Teddy. "I was planning to get down to the *Cindy Jane* at 7:00 a.m. to get everything ready and do a final check of my gear. You two can meet there . . . the earlier the better."

"Right," said Jack. "The fewer people who see us coming and going, the better."

"Jack, I don't normally start setting up *Aphrodite* until about eight-thirty . . ."

"Hellfire Maggie," said Ernie. "Don't you think you could reset your alarm for tomorrow?"

"No Ernie," said Jack. "Everything should be just like any other day. If you're accustomed to arriving at 8:30, then follow through with that tomorrow morning."

"What about me?" asked Meagan.

"What time did you tell Paddy to be on board?" asked Maggie.

"Nine o'clock sharp."

"Okay, that doesn't leave us much time, but we can make it work." Maggie shot a glance to her salty second-in-command. "Ernie can single-up the lines and get the engines started while we get our microphones on. Then we'll wire-up Ernie by 8:45 a.m. and finish everything else afterward." Maggie looked at Teddy and said, "We should be passing you in the river at 9:15, so stay low and be ready to follow us."

"I'll turn on my running lights if we're tracking and hearing you as you pass by."

"And if not?" asked Meagan.

"Plan B," said Jack.

"And what exactly is Plan B," asked Meagan.

"Brunch . . . Just enjoy your little reunion, give him some imaginative investment scheme and get back to port." Jack shrugged in response to Meagan's obvious chagrin, and then continued. "Hey, we'll figure out what to do afterward. Let's not take any more risks than we have to."

"Meagan dear," said Ednamae. "Are you sure you're ready to go through with all of this?"

"I've never been so ready to do anything in my life," she replied with a look that froze Ednamae in her seat.

"We'll be listening all the time Meagan," said Jack. "When the time is right we'll call you on the VHF radio and tighten the noose around his neck."

*     *     *

"Has anyone heard anything about this investment deal my niece is inviting me to participate in?" Asked Paddy too long into a meal that he wished had ended.

"Nobody's talkin' about anything new down on the street," said one of the lieutenants.

"No, I wouldn't expect you to hear much about this kind of deal down in the pool hall," spat Paddy.

"What about you?"

"I've been playin' the part of an investor with money for somethin' special for the last week," said Derry. "There's nothin' going on that anyone wants to talk about." The tweed Irishman finished the last of his Harp's and stood up to leave. "Maybe she's got something of her own that she doesn't want out in public."

"And maybe she's running some kind of game on me," said Paddy. "So, we're going to give ourselves a little insurance."

"How boss?" said one of the lads. "You'll both be coming with me on Meagan's little cruise tomorrow. Have my car running out front at eight o'clock."

"It only takes half an hour to drive out there," belched one of the lads.

"Yeah," said Paddy. "But I have a stop to make on the way, and then we're going to swing by Will's marina and make sure everything got delivered." Paddy fixed his malevolent eyes on Derry "Red" Reimer. "I'm moving up the schedule to 4:00 a.m. I want you, the boat, and the kid's body out of Vermilion before the sun comes up."

The wiry Irishman bowed deeply and whispered only, "As you wish."

# CHAPTER 25

Saturday, September 5, 1998 rang itself in at 12:01 a.m. through the incessant ringing of Will's telephone. As he reluctantly tossed and rolled into a hazy consciousness he could still smell the pungent sweet aroma of the last of his marijuana, inhaled only two hours earlier.

After Will left the final planning session with the Captain's Quarters he drove home slowly reflecting on all he had just witnessed among his unlikely group of new friends and protectors. He tried to sort out the unsortable paradox of feeling welcomed and rejected, loved and despised, saved and forever shackled. He had seen these forces at work with his father.

Vermilion was like a giant dying star that sucked its disparate elements back into its core; and at the vortex of the dense black hole sat the Captain's Quarters. Even Dr. Meagan Palmer, whose disdain for the stodgy group of old cronies was as well known as his own, had been pulled inside. As Will pondered the events of the last month he realized that the macabre attraction of the group was in its ability to meet whatever crises its members encountered, and to nurture the group amid a world that was changing faster than any of them wanted to endure alone.

After Angie died, Will sat alone for hours in his loft; adrift in the comfortable embrace of rock music and weed. But now they seemed unable to comfort him, even teased and taunted him to cast them out of his life. So it was that on eve of Dr. Palmer's grand scheme to purge her uncle from their midst, he packed away his heavy metal and burned the last of his leafy drugs. But as he stirred himself to life, the hanging scent and ringing phone reminded him that our past is not always so easily blown out the open window of our refuges.

Will snatched the phone off its cradle like a handler behind a coiled snake. "Hello . . ."

"I didn't wake you up did I kid?"

"No . . . uh . . . well, I must have just dozed off." Will scratched at his still scraggly and matted hair. "Who is this?"

"Just listen to me."

"Okay."

"There's been a change of plans. I want my boat ready for delivery at 4:00 a.m."

"What are you going to . . ."

"Shut up and listen to me."

"Sorry."

"My captain will arrive in exactly four hours. Make sure everything is in order." The callers tone sent a chill coursing through Will's body and he was speechless. "Do you understand me?" Paddy barked.

"Yeah."

"In four hours," Paddy whispered. "I'll be out of your life."

"What?"

"Four o'clock, kid. Don't fail me."

Before he could respond, Will heard the click and dial tone in his ear. He looked around the empty room and already felt like it was a place he used to live. It was almost as though he were viewing it from some remote location. He laid his head back on the soft warm pillow and tried to sort out what was happening—what he had just heard. The day had only begun moments ago and already the timetable had changed. Paddy's whispered words echoed in his ears—everything in order . . . out of your life . . . out of your life . . . out . . .

Will picked up his telephone and punched out 32 on the speed dialer. A voice booming through the line on the first ring gave him a start. "Jack Grayson here."

"It's Will."

"What? You couldn't sleep either?"

"No. I was doing fine until Paddy Delaney called."

"When?"

"Five minutes ago."

"What did he say?"

"It's more like what he didn't say that freaked me out."

"What are you talking about Will?"

"He said his captain will be here for the boat at 4:00 a.m."

"Old Paddy's just building in a little safety factor I imagine."

"How so?"

"At best he's looking at a 32 hour crossing to Port Colborne," said Jack in the most nonchalant tone he could muster. "This change will get the boat up there by noon on Sunday if he averages six knots."

"Yeah, that makes sense," said Will. "I guess it's just the midnight call and the way he whispered that I'd be out of his life soon . . . no, that he'd be out of my life soon and that I should have everything in order."

"Don't worry about it Will," Jack said, trying to conceal his concern. "It's just his style. Try to get some sleep and I'll see you there at 3:30."

"Okay Jack. Thanks."

"One more thing. Are those big floodlights on the back of the building still working?"

"Yeah, I think so."

"Let's remember to turn them on just before four." Jack put down the telephone and went straight to the hall closet. He pulled out the hard black suitcase that held his video camera, then reached deeper inside for the tripod. Just before he closed the door, he reached back inside to the top shelf and took down a highly lacquered rosewood box. He slowly lifted the top and, in the dim light, admired the quietly deadly beauty of the .45 Colt semi-automatic pistol cradled between two loaded clips of copper-jacketed ammunition.

Images of Navy swift boats, jungles, Napalm and the insidious fear of what dangers lurked around the next river bend, flashed into Jack's mind. He closed the case, tucked it under his arm and snatched up the camera equipment.

Soon it would be dawn. Time to lock and load.

*       *       *

Captain Riemer sat alone on a hard-backed side chair he had placed in the center of his small, but beautifully appointed, room in the Renaissance Hotel. His tweed jackets, wool slacks, custom-made Irish linen shirts, and Dubliner Club cravats were hanging neatly in a long, sleek, zippered hanging bag. Now the quiet gentleman gourmand had morphed into a present day buccaneer, dressed in cotton twill sailing slacks, white-soled boat shoes, and top layers built up from the skin—a snug silk undershirt, cotton short-sleeved polo shirt, tightly knit bulky cotton crew neck sweater and a brilliant international orange foul-weather jacket to complete the ensemble.

A small bulge at his ankle betrayed a .32 semiautomatic pistol. The sinister protrusion was complemented by the outline of a Philippine butterfly knife Derry placed in his right rear pants pocket as he stood.

"Captain Blood," a swashbuckling code name given him by his comrades in the I.R.A., was armed to the teeth and dressed to kill.

The Captain checked his Tag-Heuer mariner's watch and noted that it was 3:25 a.m. He picked up his canvass sailing bag, the keys to his borrowed car that Paddy's lads would recover later in the day, and his hanging bag. Without looking back he left his room, rode the elevator to the lobby and stopped at the front desk.

"Mr. O'Rourke," smiled the night clerk. "Your bill has already been taken care of. I hope you've enjoyed your stay."

"It's been quite entertaining," said the Captain as he turned to leave.

"Oh . . . Mr. O'Rourke," called the clerk as he reached down beneath the counter. "I almost forgot the picnic basket you ordered last night." The clerk used both hands to heave the large brown woven basket to the counter top.

"How could I have forgotten," said Captain Blood as he returned. "Any problem filling my order?"

"We had all of the breads, meats and cheeses you wanted in stock. Our baker made up six small loaves of the French bread you ordered," said the wide-eyed youngster. "We did have to send a driver into Cleveland for the '79 St. Emilion Grand Cru you specified. We were able to come up with three bottles." The young man pulled a bottle from the basket and turned the label toward the Captain. "A special occasion, I presume?"

"I hope so," he said as he took the basket from the counter and vanished through the front door.

*     *     *

Jack Grayson parked his Range Rover behind Romp's Dairy Isle, across the street from GrayDays Marine. The large clock inside the quiet ice cream stand read exactly 3: 30 as he crossed the deserted road to the historic Wheeler house. He noted a single lighted window in Will's loft as he crunched down the gently sloping side driveway that descended alongside the building to the lagoon marina below. He rounded the corner to the back door and set down his bag of camera equipment as he fumbled for his door key. Just as he inserted the key into the lock he was startled by a harsh blast of light from inside and the silhouette of a man on the other side of the glass door panel.

"Why don't you kill the light Will?" Jack whispered as the door swung open. "Let's not wake the neighbors just yet."

"Right," said Will from the sudden reassuring darkness.

"Is the boat ready to go?"

"She's been ready for a week."

"How about the paperwork?"

"It's all right here," Will said pointing to a file folder on the drafting table next to the door.

"What about Teddy's G.P.S. beacon?"

"I turned it on just after dark," said Will. "Teddy told me the battery should last for ten days."

"Okay then. How are you feeling?"

"I just want this over with. I want that boat outta here, and I want Paddy Delaney stuck in the middle of the lake with no option but to leave us alone."

Jack could see the tension in the young man's eyes and could hear the distress in his voice. "Don't worry, it won't be long now." Jack put his hand on will's shoulder and felt him recoil slightly. "Calm down now, and let's finish up here. Fetch that camera bag and let's go up to your room."

"Why?"

"We're going to film a little documentary," said Jack. Jack trudged up the narrow stairway into Will's loft, and then paused for a moment at the top of the stairs. For a few moments, Jack practiced some deep breathing as he scanned what now looked to him like unfamiliar territory. In years past the loft had been used as a storeroom, junk room, and, most recently, Will's room. Regardless of the use, the room always had that cluttered look of purpose and activity. Now Jack felt a certain sterility in the space. The room's life seemed to have been sucked out of it.

"I don't ever recall seeing this loft so tidy."

"I sent all my stuff out on a truck yesterday," said Will.

"So you're really going through with it."

"Yeah."

"I was hoping," Jack paused again and took another deep breath. "We were *all* hoping that you'd reconsider your move."

"Why would I do that?"

"Maybe because you had rediscovered your family?"

"Jack, you've all been really nice to help me out with this nightmare with Mr. Delaney; and I do feel much better about all of you." Will said into Jack's expectant eyes. "Yeah, even Dr. Palmer." Jack smiled. "I guess she's not as evil as I always thought. But that doesn't change anything."

"Why not?"

"Because there's still nothing left for me here." Will walked to the corner and sat down at his mother's old desk. "Nothing but bad memories."

"Come on Will. You've had good times too. We all have."

"Yeah, but lately all the bad stuff is piled so high I can't see anything good anymore."

"I know how you feel Will. I've been there for a year myself." Jack walked over to the desk. "But I didn't run off to California."

"No, you just locked yourself up in your house and shut the world out."

"Touché," said Jack.

"I just feel like I have to put some distance between me and all this drama."

"Do you expect to see Jimmy while you're out there?"

"Yeah, he's going to put me up at his place for a while."

"When did you speak to him?"

"Yesterday, when the truck left," Will said uncomfortably. "I needed to warn him that my stuff was on the way."

"Did he ask about me?"

"No."

"Did you tell him anything about what's happening today?"

"Of course not."

"Okay," said Jack trying to rise above his heartache. "When you get out there will you try to talk to him about . . ." Jack hesitated and looked away as if he were searching for the right word. ". . . well, about me?"

"Sure Jack. You've got that coming. "Will stood up and jabbed Jack in the midsection. "You're not all that bad either."

"Thanks for the glowing endorsement." Jack gave Will a quick but intense fatherly hug. "Now, let's set up this equipment. Paddy's captain should be here soon."

Jack unloaded the large camera bag and mounted the video camera on the tripod. He snapped on a new two-hour battery and switched on the camera to make sure he had power. He set up the taping station at the window overlooking the small lot between the building and the docks where SEAQUESTOR bobbed slowly in the gentle breeze that wafted across the lagoons. He peered through the viewfinder and adjusted the ZOOM so that the camera framed the entire area from the lot to the waiting sailboat. An amber LOW LIGHT signal blinked in the viewfinder.

"Okay Will," said Jack consulting his Rolex Submariner. "It's 3:55 and I expect our visitor will be here any moment. Go on down and turn on the flood lights and all the lights you have on the docks. I'll stay up here while you complete the delivery of the boat."

"Okay," said Will. "I feel a lot better with you up here."

"Good. Now, remember to take the transfer papers outside to that picnic table in front of the dock, and be sure to turn on the lights before you go outside."

"Gotcha." Will turned to head downstairs.

"And Will . . . don't let this guy inside the building." Jack couldn't miss the instant look of panic on Will's face as he stopped for an instant and looked back.

"Right."

*      *      *

Red Reimer drove slowly past GrayDays Marine and was miffed at the bright aura of light emanating from behind the quaint old house. *I'll have to do the kid inside the house*, he said to himself harshly. He had planned to take him outside in the dark, where he had the advantage. He would kill him quickly, stuff his body into a sail bag, and then put it on board for a later drop into the lake. The small boat anchor he would stuff into the bottom of the bag would ensure that Will's body would never again see the light of day.

But now he knew he'd have to do the kid inside, in unfamiliar surroundings, where things could become messy, where evidence could be discovered. Captain Blood drove a hundred yards past the house and turned into the dark deserted parking lot of McGarvey's Nautical Restaurant, where Paddy's lads could easily recover his car later in the day. He parked near the building, slid the keys over the driver's visor, popped the trunk lid, and slid out. From the trunk he grabbed his sailing bag and slung it over his shoulder, then hauled out the heavy-laden picnic basket and folded garment bag for his hundred yard return hike to the marina.

On the way up the slippery gravel driveway, Red lost traction and fell to his knees. The weight of his load pulled him down the slope until he rolled over and clutched his bloody knees protruding through ragged cotton twill.

"Mother Mary and Jesus!" he yelled out loud then laid back for a moment to gather his thoughts. "So, you've drawn the first blood," he whispered to the starry night. "It won't be the last though." In another moment he was back up on his feet like a stubborn pack mule struggling to the summit.

*      *      *

As Will waited on the brilliantly lit picnic table he felt like he was on stage, yet as he looked away from the light and across the docks and lagoon he discerned no audience. The few lagoon houses visible to him were still dark and quiet. He wished he had been able to sleep so soundly. He looked upward to his loft window hoping to catch a glimpse of reassurance, but was blinded by the stage lights.

Then he heard it. The telltale crunching sound of footsteps descending his driveway.

He turned into the light again in time to see what he had not expected to see. A foul-weather-clad hiker emerged from the eerie early morning mist like an image from a page of *The Rime of the Ancient Mariner*. Visibly worn out, bloody at both knees, and fully laden with a sea bag, garment bag and—*Is that a picnic basket?* Will thought to himself. This certainly was not the image that Will had conjured of Paddy Delaney's captain. He jumped off the table and hurried up to the old man. *I'll be damned! It is a picnic basket,* Will realized as he grabbed the deceptively heavy container out of the captain's right hand.

"Hi, I'm Will Daysart," he said extending a handshake. "I guess you're Mr. Delaney's boat captain?"

"Danny O'Rourke," said Red dropping his two bags onto the pavement.

"Did you walk all the way from Lorain?" Will asked as he surveyed the damage.

"No laddy. Had a bit of a mishap though. My rented car stopped a few miles back, so I pushed it into a closed gas station, left a note for the agency, and hiked over here."

"When did the dogs attack you?"

Red cracked a smile at the kid's quick wit. "Just a little loose gravel that took advantage of me."

"Here," said Will. "Let's get your stuff over to the table and take a look at your knees."

Will snatched the other two bags off the ground while the ancient mariner limped over to the table and sat down. He plopped all three bags onto the table top and turned to his visitor. With both pant legs pulled up the old man's wounds were illuminated like he was in a hospital operating room.

"Can you turn off those lights?" Red asked.

"No . . . sorry . . . uh . . . they're on a photoelectric switch," stammered Will, finally satisfied with his response. "When it's dark, they're light . . . and vice versa." Will knelt down for a closer look.

"Maybe I should call EMS."

"What's that?"

"The Emergency Medical Service truck from the Fire Department. They'll clean that up a little and take you over to the hospital."

"No, that won't be necessary. It's just a couple of wee scrapes," said Red looking into the youngster's naively compassionate eyes. "All I need is a little soap and water."

"Okay, I'll bring some right out, along with the first aid kit." Will's tone betrayed his uneasiness, but he felt some comfort in following Jack's earlier instructions. "There's some gauze and tape in the kit."

"Forget the first aid kit, laddy. I'll just follow you inside and clean up in tile bathroom." When Will turned around and locked eye contact with the captain it was clear that they both knew what was at stake. But only one of them knew how to play his hand. "You do have a bathroom now," said the captain with a chill. "Don't you laddy?"

Will was feeling trapped but couldn't concoct an escape plan in the heat of the moment. Like a moth drawn toward a hot killing light he finally said, "Of course I have a bathroom. I guess I just wasn't thinking. You can leave your gear on the table," Will said, deciding quickly that this would be safer. "There's never anybody out this early in the morning."

Jack Grayson couldn't believe what he was seeing through the viewfinder. Why would Will deliberately ignore his last direction? And what was with the rolled up pants legs? Something must have gone wrong.

Jack left the camera running and eased quietly to the top of the stairs. He heard the back door slam shut and strained to make some sense of the muffled conversation down below.

Then all hell broke loose.

Jack cringed at the unmistakable sounds of a struggle. In a reflexive action he lunged at his camera bag, withdrew his .45 semi-automatic, rammed home a loaded clip of hardball, and snapped the heavy barrel slide back to chamber a round of ammunition. He bounded two flights down the narrow stairway without a sound. He was only half way down the final leg of the open stairway leading into a room full of rigging, ropes, fittings, and fixtures resting quietly in large Formica display cases, when he saw the back of an attacker, shrouded in international orange, holding Will upright in a half-nelson.

Will seemed to have stopped struggling as though he had submitted to his fate. Jack was frozen on the steps for a moment, pistol at the ready, as he realized he had no clear shot that would not endanger Will. Suddenly he saw the attacker's right hand reach into his back pocket. The flash of reflected stainless steel and telltale clanging of metal-on-metal alerted Jack to a butterfly knife being readied for a silent kill.

It was crunch time.

Before the knife was fully engaged, Jack stomped on the staircase and yelled out, "Freeze!"

The attacker dropped his grip on Will and tried to turn to face Jack. Will immediately came to life, as Red slashed his knife wildly. In the frenzy, Red tried to put some distance between himself and Jack. In the process of jerking away from the staircase, Red banged one of his scraped knees against the corner of a cabinet, let out a wild screech, then lost his balance and fell sideways to the floor. On the way down his temple caught the corner of another display case and he dropped to the floor.

Will retreated quickly to the bottom of the stairs just as Jack reached the floor. "I was praying you would come in time."

"Damned straight," said Jack. "But it didn't look like you were doing much to save yourself."

"He was too strong for me," said Will. "So I decided to turn his back to the stairs and play possum."

"Nice move, Will, but I think you played it a little close for comfort." Jack turned Will toward him and eyed him up and down. "Are you sure you're okay?"

"Better than him," Will said as he looked down toward the cabinet. "He's awfully quiet over there."

"Do you know how to use this?" Jack asked as he handed his pistol to Will.

"Aim and squeeze?"

"That's about it. Now, cover me while I go over and check him out." Jack eased over to the attacker and immediately saw blood pooling on the floor from beneath the side of the Irishman's head. Without disturbing his position, Jack applied two fingers to Red's jugular vein and, as he suspected, felt no pulse.

"He's dead."

"Holy shit," yelled Will. "What the fuck are we going to do now?"

"I don't know," said Jack as he stood upright and stepped away from Red's body. "Give me a minute to think this through."

Will didn't have a minute to spare. "Shit, shit, shit," he yelled with clenched teeth and arms hanging limply at his sides. "I killed the guy. Damnit Jack, I killed him right here in my store. Shit, shit, shit."

"Give me the gun Will."

Will backed away with his eyes glazed. He started pacing and brandishing the pistol in a way that Jack had seen with young sailors who had snapped under the agony of their first killing.

"Will . . . give me the gun. NOW!"

Will spun around to face Jack. He looked at the loaded pistol and looked again into Jack's pleading eyes. Jack held his ground and prayed. After a few moments Will slumped his shoulders, looked into the barrel of the pistol. Finally and predictably, Will hung his head down and handed the pistol to Jack.

Jack put the pistol on the counter top and embraced his godson as he wept like a small child.

"I'm so scared Jack. I'm so scared."

Jack led Will into the back office room and sat him down in his father's old desk chair next to the softly lit drafting table. He went to the small refrigerator and opened two cans of Pepsi, one of which he put into Will's hand. Then he pulled up another chair directly in front of the quiet vulnerable kid.

"Okay," said Jack after a sip. "We have to get hold of this situation and decide what to do." Will did not answer him, but he did take a long drink of the cold Pepsi and looked up at Jack. "For starters," Jack said. "You did not kill that man. He tripped and fell on his own. You never laid a hand on him." Jack leaned into Will's space. "Even if you had it would be a simple matter of self-defense."

"Okay," whispered Will. "But we have to call the police, and when we run the whole thing down for them, Dr. Palmer's plan, the money, Mr. Delaney . . . everything is going to be out in the open."

"Maybe not." Jack slowly sipped the Pepsi while he organized his thoughts. "Nothing here, including the money on that sailboat can be linked to Paddy Delaney, and don't forget that he's our problem."

"But if the police have the money, and it's not my fault, he'll leave me alone. Right?"

"Don't kid yourself Will. You know too much and no matter what we tell the police about the man who died here tonight, Paddy will blame you. And don't forget what you told me about Paddy's relationship with the police."

Will slumped down in his chair and began to sob. "Oh God, what am I going to do?"

"Listen Will, we can still manage this situation as we planned." Will refused to look up, but Jack forged on. "What happened here tonight looks like nothing but a burglary gone bad. It'll be obvious to any investigator that this guy just slipped and fell in the dark while trying to rob the store."

"And where was I when all this happened?"

"With me," smiled Jack. "I'm your alibi. You spent the night at my house."

A twinkle of light sparked out of Will's swollen eyes. "Okay, but what is Paddy going to do when he finds out that his $24 million dollars is still sitting at the dock?"

"It won't be."

"What do you mean? Like where's it going to . . ." Will was suddenly alert and upright in his seat. "Oh no, not me Jack. I can't single-hand that boat across the lake."

"But I can."

# CHAPTER 26

It was nearly five o'clock when Jack walked down the narrow wooden pier behind GrayDays Marine. The sun would not peek above the horizon for almost two hours, yet there was already a sense of expectation in the cool still air.

Jack always enjoyed the eerie, almost erotic, pleasure of walking toward a ship lying ready for departure in the early hours before first light. Captain Jack Grayson had a sensual relationship with ships and with the sea. Every nerve ending in his body sensed the intrigue that hung like fog in the stillness of night surrounding a ship ready to be born again . . . and again.

The act of breathing life into a leviathan of steel, machinery, oil and gadgetry excited Jack beyond words and kept him coming back to his supertankers for twenty-three years of pre-dawn departures.

He felt the same excitement rising as he squeaked down the pier toward Susan's *SEAQUESTOR* lying in wait under the early September moon and stars. Jack moved toward the silent brooding yacht with the same sense of wonder that had always ignited his seafaring instincts. At the same time there was an enveloping feeling of unpredictable dread, as he eyed the ship he was now compelled to sail into the great inland sea called Lake Erie. Was this, Jack wondered, to be a rewrite of Jim's voyage upon the ill-fated *Patmos?* Should he call Meagan? Should he consult with the rest of his crew? No, Jack quickly realized that this was another of those fateful situations that had defined him in the past.

Plans, Jack knew, would invariably go awry. What mattered was how the Captain reacted—whether he did his duty or failed.

Jack had left Will with a specific game plan for the remainder of the day:

Tidy up the room and display cases around O'Rourke's body.

Was that really his name?

Leave the back door ajar.

Hang the "SORRY, GONE FISHIN'" sign in the front door. Jack figured that one of the resident marina boat owners would discover the open door and find the body. It would look to them like the tragic accidental end to a burglary.

Will would drive to Jack's house and try to get a few hours sleep, and establish his alibi, before meeting Teddy on the river. He would tell Teddy only that Paddy's captain didn't show up and that Jack was delivering the boat to Port Colbourne.

Ednamae, Maggie, Ernie and Meagan would get the same information before Paddy arrives for the cruise.

No one is to know what really happened.

It was a simple plan that would immunize the group, leaving Will and Jack to deal with the inevitable police investigation together.

Jack heaved his weathered academy sea bag onto the deck of the yacht, and unclipped the pelican hook that secured a lifeline across the access opening to the main deck. He loaded "O'Rourke's garment bag, sea bag and picnic basket onto the deck and climbed aboard. Whatever the former captain had packed for the voyage would have to do.

Although he hadn't sailed for a year, Jack quickly recalled Susan's methodical departure routine. Seamen, like aviators, know that during the crucial pre-flight check nothing can be assumed—nothing taken for granted.

Jack removed the hatch boards from the cabin companionway.

Carried his gear down below.

Opened tIle side port lights and overhead cabin hatches.

Started the cold reluctant diesel engine.

Checked the refrigerator for cold air.

Packed perishable foods inside.

Flipped on the chart table light.

Turned the radar unit switch to STANDBY.

Switched on the VHF marine radio.

Tuned the marine radio to WEATHER 1.

Listened to a weather report from NOAA Weather Radio.

Tapped his finger on the barometer glass.

Opened Susan's log book and started a new page. September 5, 1998—Vermilion to Port Colborne, Ontario. 0500—Barometer 30.05 steady—Fair weather.

On the way up the ladder to the cockpit, Jack flipped on the night running lights and instrument lights. He noted with a smile that the Perkins diesel had settled down to a healthy subtle rumble.

Jack stood on deck and, like a kid on his first cruise, and felt the urge to cast off, but quickly realized that only half his work had been completed. He stood motionless for a moment as if searching the foredeck for a glimpse of Susan's familiar form moving aft to meet him. It had always been Susan's preference to attend to the duties on deck. They were, she often chided, "the Captain's responsibilities."

First, the burgundy sail covers on the main and mizzen booms came off, revealing the neatly flaked white Dacron sails which had become the tenuous abode for hundreds of spiders. Two white shock cords, firmly affixed by Susan's hands, would secure the sails until Jack was ready to sail. A quick glance at the jib sheets satisfied him that they were running clear, and outside the stainless steel shrouds and onto the big self-tailing winches on the cockpit combing.

Jack cast off the spring lines and extra bow and stern lines, leaving the yacht loosely secured with only a single line at each end. In the dead calm of the early morning, Jack felt comfortable in pulling up and untying the large white plastic fenders that cushioned the hull from bumps and bruises.

Jack unlocked the lazarette hatch, pulled Susan's long emergency trailing line out and then casually tossed the fenders and dock lines over the mass of neatly stacked and "heavy laden" new fenders delivered by Malta Marine over the last several weeks. Jack lowered the hatch, snapped the padlock, stood up, and inhaled deeply of nature as he remembered an ancient Gaelic blessing Susan often recited:

> *Deep peace on the running wave to you.*
> *Deep peace on the flowing air to you.*
> *Deep peace on the quiet earth to you.*
> *Deep peace on the shining stars to you.*
> *Deep peace on the gentle night to you.*
> *Moon and stars pour out their healing light on you.*
> *Deep peace to you.*

\*     \*     \*

But there was no peace for Will Daysart inside the tomblike Wheeler house. He had done exactly as Jack directed and quickly satisfied himself that everything was back in place around the grotesquely out-of-place corpse of Paddy Delaney's killer captain. By the time he finished his ghoulish task in the shadowy darkness of the showroom, and darted upstairs to the safety of his loft he had come unglued.

Now Will was sweating as he paced the floor trying to make some sense of this new twist of fate. He stopped at his window and saw Jack on the after-deck of the yacht peering upward toward the stars as if he were praying. Will wished he knew someone to pray to, someone who could give him the peace he saw in Jack Grayson. But for young Will Daysart, God died years ago with his mother and father. The God he wanted to pray to would not have taken his parents from him would not have made him the target of an assassin.

The sharp press of Jack's car keys against his thigh reminded him that he had to move ahead with the plan. He looked nervously around the room, as if he expected to find something he had left behind, but the loft was almost bare. By now, he figured, his few pieces of furniture and boxes of clothing wrapped trinkets of bygone days were already in St. Louis and heading west. Will grabbed the large leather overnight bag he had packed with his few remaining possessions. He had enough fresh underwear, socks and clothes to see him through the day of tracking *Aphrodite* from Teddy Bear's fishing boat, and to get him on board the jetliner from Cleveland to Chicago to San Francisco the next day.

Now he eased down the staircase to the main floor where he carefully skirted the corpse on his way to the back door which he would leave slightly ajar on his way out. It looked like Jack had gone back down into *SEAQUESTOR*'s saloon as Will looked out the back door toward the boat docks. Godfather and son had said their farewells, yet Will felt the urge to say something that was left unsaid . . .

He shucked off the thought and pressed his cold clammy hand around the door knob and pushed his way outside. He felt like the proverbial "thief in the night" as he quickly crunched his way up the driveway toward the deserted parking lot at the Dairy Isle, where Jack had left his Range Rover. Still jumpy, he broke into a trot across the dimly lit misty highway, and then dashed past the ice cream stand to the back lot where the British green machine lay in wait.

Once inside, Will started the engine and heard the telltale recycling of Jack's old cellular phone. The electronic tone seemed to transfix and distress Will all at the same time, as he lightly tapped his forehead against the thick leather-padded steering wheel. A few moments later he picked up the phone and dialed for directory assistance.

"I need the number for American Airlines at Cleveland Hopkins."

"Hold one moment please."

Again, Will tapped his forehead against the steering wheel.

"That number is 555-4545."

Beep . . . tone . . . dial . . . send . . .

"American Airlines. How may I help you?"

"I have a confirmed reservation on Flight 702 to San Francisco tomorrow evening." Will paused and tapped his head again.

"Yes."

"Do you have a flight going out there sometime this morning?"

"Yes. We have seating available on an 8:30 a.m. flight through Dallas-Ft. Worth."

Will glanced at the digital dashboard clock and noted that it was still only 5:45 a.m. The airport was an hour's drive to the east, and Teddy's fishing boat was a five minute drive to the west.

"Okay, book me on that earlier flight," Will said as he turned Jack's car toward the brightening vermilion sky.

*       *       *

Jack lounged in the cozy sanctuary of *SEAQUESTOR*'s spacious cushioned cockpit. He was mesmerized by the sound of Susan's yacht slicing through the violet gelatin ripples of the quiet great lake. His eyes were entranced by the ever-brightening eastern sky, as his deep subconscious mind registered a faintly rung six bells on the ship's clock. Sunrise was only a quarter of an hour below the horizon.

For the last idyllic hour the powerful ketch had sailed on a warm steady southerly breeze with all three sails eased outboard to take full advantage of the efficient broad reach. The yacht was heeled a comfortable ten degrees to port and had nearly reached her maximum hull speed of 8.5 knots. Jack was floating through a cruising sailor's dream, oblivious to the storm thundering down behind him.

What Jack could not have seen was the viper that had leapt forth from the dark northwestern sky. The weather pattern was viciously familiar in the early autumn latitude of Lake Erie. A large slow moving low to the south whose counterclockwise vortex swept warm moist air from the Gulf of Mexico in the form of pleasant southerly offshore breezes, suddenly ran afoul of a steep and wild cold air mass that plummeted southward from Canada on the clockwise churning wheels of a freight train loaded with destruction. The two opposing forces had, only an hour ago, converged over the western end of Lake Erie and had spawned thirty thousand foot high thunderheads in a squall line that would cross Lake Erie's axis in only five hours.

Jack would have heard the emergency weather broadcast but for the fact that he had switched off his VHF radio half an hour after his departure from Vermilion. A group of, what Jack had assumed were, drunken weekend boaters were conversing loudly on VHF Channel 16, against warnings from the U.S. Coast Guard to get off the emergency broadcast channel. Normally such banter entertained lonely solo sailors, but this morning Jack was not in the mood. He silenced them with an ill-timed flip of a switch that now left him vulnerable.

A sound like the low rumble of a distant freight train nudged Jack out of his trance.

A loud crack of lighting jarred him upright.

A sudden drop in temperature chilled him into a glance back into the darkness. A violent wind shift jibed the sails to starboard and nearly killed him.

Jack ducked from the onslaught of the swinging main boom, just as another bolt of lightning electrified the ship and called forth a barrage of ice cold stinging rain.

Jack cussed himself for his lack of attention as the ketch lurched heavily to starboard. Then he fought to survive.

In a fluid action that consumed less than ten seconds, Jack cast off the jib sheet, main sheet and mizzen sheet. He watched hopefully as the braided Dacron lines reeled out through the blocks, sheaves and pulleys that tamed the huge white sails. Now he was in a torrent of rain as he looked astern at the ten foot waves bearing down on him. Captain Grayson broadened his stance and braced himself against the helm with both hands tightly gripped around the huge stainless steel steering wheel. As he felt the stern rising quickly like a surfboard catching a wave, he fixed his eyes upon the dimly illuminated compass. It would be important to hold his course as the huge wave snatched up the now insignificant sailboat. If the boat broached sideways to these ten foot crests, even his thirty ton yacht could be knocked-down on her side and swamped.

At the crest of the first wave *SEAQUESTOR* yawed wildly to starboard and Jack had to duck again to avoid the slashing aluminum boom that whipped past his head on another uncontrolled jibe. Jack fought the helm back to port as the yacht slid down the backside of the wave and jibed again to the correct starboard tack.

Jack knew the rigging would not take much more abuse. The giant mainsail had to come down, and to do it he would have to make a quick and daring jaunt forward to the main halyard cleat attached to the mast 25 feet forward of the cockpit. He fought off two more giant waves that overtook him and this time was barely able to avoid another jibe.

Jack estimated the interval between the largest breakers to be just under thirty seconds. It would have to be enough time for a mad dash to the mainmast and back. The self-steering vane would hold the yacht's course through the howling wind-driven whitecaps and spray, but not the menacing ten foot breaking waves. In the next interval, Jack opened the large cutting blade of his mariner's knife and attached it's lanyard to his belt. He screwed in as much tension on the steering vane as he dared and still keep it functional. He flipped on the two bright white main spreader lights high above the deck.

Now, in the early dawn the deck of the ketch was fully lit, but Jack was blinded to the lake around him save the horizon's red hue to the east. *You predicted this one Susan*, he thought as he readied himself for his forward lunge.

Now Jack reached forward to the long tethered safety harness cradled beside the companionway hatch. He fastened the harness over his shoulders and chest then played out a few yards of the carefully coiled thirty-foot line, to ensure that it was running clear. The annoying little harness line had prevented many a sailor from being swept overboard in heavy seas—a lesson that had been painfully beaten into young Lieutenant Maggie Wicks years earlier. *If only Susan had harnessed up*, Jack thought as he cinched the harness tightly around him.

Jack now had little difficulty avoiding a violent jibe as rollers that had risen to twelve feet swept beneath him. Timing was everything, he knew. And now it was time to go. As quickly as the ketch slipped over the crest of a passing wave, Jack slipped around the steering pedestal and hopped onto the cabin roof. His foot caught on the taut wire that controlled the fully deployed eight foot steel centerboard, and he crashed face down on the hard wet deck. When the yacht lurched to port under a strong gust of wind, Jack grabbed the low teak handrails and barely avoided rolling off the cabin roof to the deck that was now fully awash in an angry lake. Jack fought through the rage of his own clumsiness and quickly found his feet. Four steps to the mast and he threw the soggy main halyard off the cleat, then unwound five turns from the small stainless steel winch head. Jack was relieved to see the sail slide down toward him.

Fifteen seconds to go, and he could already see the next big roller roaring down on him. He grabbed hands full of Dacron sail and pulled them into the big mesh turtle that was secured at the base of the mast. The turtle was like a giant laundry bag. Once the massive sail was stuffed into the bag and the drawstring cinched up, there was no danger of the sail dragging over the side. It was another innovation that Jack thanked Susan for.

Jack had just secured the drawstring on the turtle when the next wave hit the stern. The yacht started another jibe.

With the main sail doused and the main halyard run all the way out, the big main boom swung easily across the deck toward the starboard side. He was only three steps from the cockpit when the jibing boom caught him in the gut. The momentum of the swinging boom carried Jack out over the starboard railing and held him, like a trapeze artist, precariously above the boiling cauldron of the great lake. He clutched the slippery metal boom with failing strength, but mounting determination. Then as quickly as he had seen oblivion, the yacht swung back to port and Jack dropped onto the glistening wet cabin top and into the cockpit. For the next forty-five minutes, Captain Jack Grayson sparred with his favorite opponent. Then as quickly as the storm had come upon him it passed, and with its passing came the sunrise.

By the time *SEAQUESTOR's* clock rang out eight bells, the wind had shifted back to its sedate southern aspect, the lake had calmed down to an ocean of ripples, and an exhausted Jack Grayson retired to the Master's cabin for a quick comfortable, and well-deserved, nap.

*     *     *

Teddy "Bear Parks' watch read 8:20 a.m. as he stood at the dockside telephone a few yards upriver from the *Cindy Jane.* He couldn't fathom why Jack and will were already twenty minutes late, and couldn't understand why he couldn't raise anyone at GrayDays or at Jack's house. A dozen scenarios slogged through his mind as he listened to the steady ringing of the telephone.

Maybe they were involved in an accident on their way to the dock.

Were they coming together?

Maybe Will overslept, as usual, and Jack had to shake him up.

Perhaps they had an early errand to run.

Maybe the plans had changed.

Maybe they were injured.

Could Paddy have had them killed in the night?

They ran out of gas.

Had car trouble.

Stopped for breakfast somewhere.

They're just leaving the bakery with a box of my favorite Svenson's chocolate cream-filled doughnuts.

They probably stopped at Ednamae's and got lost in another one of her long-winded stories. Teddy hung up the handset and pushed another quarter into the worn grime-ringed slot, then dialed Ednamae's.

"Top of the morning to you. This is Ednamae Bradley."

"Are Jack and Will with you?"

"Who is this?"

"I'm sorry Ednamae. It's Ted."

"No, they were supposed to be on board the *Cindy Jane* with you at eight o'clock if memory serves me."

"It does indeed," said Teddy Bear. "But it's almost eight thirty and I haven't seen either one of them."

"Very curious. You know how punctual Jack is. This is not like him at all." Ednamae paused for a moment. "Have you tried to call them?"

"Yes, both at the marina and Jack's place. No answer for the last fifteen minutes."

"Okay," said Ednamae. "I'll drive out to Jack's house and see if I can find them."

"That's great Ednamae. If you don't find them there, swing on down to GrayDays, and tell them to hurry. They have to be on board with me when Maggie and Ernie pass by."

"Don't give it another thought. You just stay put and I'll find them."

Teddy stepped away from the phone booth and squinted upriver toward McGarvey's dock. Although he couldn't see any movement on *Aphrodite*, the wheelhouse window covers were off and the afterdeck side curtains were rolled up. He stepped back into the booth, inserted another quarter and dialed up *Aphrodite*. "History cruises aboard *Aphrodite*," Ernie Beckett growled.

Teddy cracked a smile at the thought of how much the old sea captain hated answering the phone that way. But, as he always said while on board the cruise ship, *Maggie's the captain here.*

"Ernie, it's Ted. Are Jack and Will down there?"

"They're supposed to be with you."

"Well they're not."

"Where the hell are they then?"

"That's what I'm trying to find out."

"Well I haven't seen them."

A long thinking silence.

"Did you call Ednamae?" asked Ernie. "She seems to know everything."

"Yeah, but this time she came up dry. She's driving over to Jack's place now."

"Why not the marina?" he growled again. "When I drove past there this morning I noticed that *SEAQUESTOR* was gone."

"What time was that?"

"Half an hour ago."

"Okay then," said Teddy. "Everything must be on track."

"Ednamae 'ill find 'em."

"And if she doesn't?"

"Teddy, the ship never waits for the crew. When it's time to cast off you better do it," barked Captain Beckett in his most officious tone. "We need you behind us."

*     *     *

Dr. Meagan Palmer sped down River Road toward the Liberty Avenue bridge at 8:50 a.m. feeling unusually frisky for a usually sedate and peaceful Saturday morning. She glimpsed the wet pavement strewn with fallen branches and leaves, the remnants of an early morning squall that, to Meagan, seemed paradoxically to cleanse everything it touched. The adrenalin was already pumping, she realized, and she felt positively euphoric.

Although she was already a tad late, she wanted to stop by the office for her good luck charm. Susan Wheeler's old foul weather gear had always brought her luck, and she sensed she needed a bit of the *Old Blarney* on her business cruise today.

She wheeled her SL380 coupe to a sliding stop in the loose gravel lot at the foot of her office stairs, and was surprised at how sprightly she bounded up the long outside staircase and through her office door. She hustled over to one of her trophy walls and snatched Susan's white cracked KSU slicker from its repose upon the Thistle tiller. As she pivoted to speed back out the door, her peripheral vision caught the silent flashing of a tiny green light.

She had a score of patients in myriad stages of therapy, and she had given each of them leave to call her at home or office twenty-four hours a day. Meagan's knee-jerk reaction was to keep moving and to handle the call later in the day. Her morning was already spoken for, and there was no time for counseling. *Right, but I have a couple of minutes for listening*, she quickly told herself as she returned to her desk and pushed PLAYBACK MESSAGES on her answering machine.

As a voice cried out through the speaker, she wished she hadn't pushed the button.

"Meagan . . . uh, Dr. Wheeler, this is Will. We have a terrible problem. Everything is going wrong. That captain, the one Mr. Delaney sent . . . was supposed to send . . . well he's uh . . . he didn't show up this morning so Jack decided to sail Aunt Susan's boat to Canada with the . . . you know . . . with the cargo. I couldn't stop him, and I'm scared and just can't stand this shit anymore. I'm sorry I let you all down but, well . . . it's just that . . . well, I'll call Jack when I get to California . . . to Jimmy's place. Good luck."

"You neurotic whining little shitheel!" Meagan yelled out as she rushed to her window and looked out over the great lake toward the east. Intellectually she knew that Jack's boat was already far out of sight, but an emotional spark sent her to the window anyway. As much as her therapist side had wanted Jack to sail his demons away on that boat, this was not the right circumstance. He wasn't ready. The purpose of the voyage was all wrong. Just like at the quarry, he was being forced to sink or swim.

Meagan pounded her fist against the window frame, and then focused her eyes upon *Aphrodite* laying in wait below her. It was almost as though providence had drawn her to the window at that instant, just in time to see her uncle Paddy Delaney and two black-clad-hoodlum-looking young men walking down the dock to *Aphrodite*'s gangway.

*I haven't even come face-to-face with Paddy yet*, Meagan thought to herself, and our plan is already faltering. Jack has Paddy's cash out in the middle of Lake Erie; Will has fled to the West coast; two uninvited goons have joined Paddy on the cruise; and "I'm late," she finally said aloud. She went back to her trophy wall, grabbed the pistol and a loaded clip of ammunition, stuffed them in her bag and rushed out the door.

# CHAPTER 27

"Welcome aboard *Aphrodite*, Mr. Delaney. I'm Maggie Wicks and this is my boat."

"Hardly a boat miss . . . or should I say, captain," Paddy beamed as he warmly shook Maggie's outstretched hand. "How exactly shall I address you?"

"Maggie will be just fine."

"Then Maggie it shall be," said Paddy with a huge grin. "I hope you won't be mindin' the intrusion, but my lads here haven't yet been out on the lake. I hope my dear niece will understand."

"I'm sure that will be just fine," Maggie said as the two handsome young men stumbled up the gangway to the deck. "It will be a pleasure to have such fine looking young men with us this morning," she said, then turned to Paddy. "You must be very proud of them."

"Oh yes," he said putting his arms around their broad shoulders. "Very proud indeed. Now then where might my dear Meagan be hidin'?"

"Oh I'm sure she won't be a minute. Just some last minute checking on the brunch they've prepared for us in the restaurant."

Maggie saw Ernie coming down the ladder from the wheelhouse and gestured to him. "Ernie, I think Meagan must be ready for that serving cart she wanted. Why don't you take it to her, while I serve some refreshments to Mr. Delaney and his sons?" Maggie ushered the three men towards the stern then turned to Ernie with a wink. "And don't forget that *heating wire*."

"Aye, aye my captain," Ernie snorted.

"Isn't he a little old to workin' on a ship?" asked Paddy.

"Oh, I keep him around mostly for show," said Maggie. "It's a little retirement job for him."

Ernie gathered his equipment, shuffled down the gangway, then paddled into McGarvey's back door and through the restaurant to the front entrance just in time to flag down Meagan Palmer who was easing her glitzy little Benz down the sloping driveway.

"Where the hell have you been?" huffed the old captain as he charged Meagan's open window. "You shoulda been here half an hour ago."

"I had a telephone call."

"We have a schedule," growled Ernie. "Paddy and his boys are already aboard and lookin' for you."

"Let me park the car then," said Meagan.

"But we have to talk before we go on board."

"Just leave the car here and I'll have one of the cooks move it for you later." Ernie pulled the wire out of his pocket and thrust it through the window into Meagan's hand.

"Okay, but first you need to go into the ladies' room and put on this microphone."

By the time Meagan Palmer carne out of the ladies' room tucking her long-sleeved blue cotton blouse into her white cotton slacks, Ernie was already waiting at the door with a small rolling serving cart with three covered stainless steel hotel pans in place. A friendly aroma filled the air as Meagan stepped up to the cart and lifted lids.

"Eggs Benedict, Swedish pan-fried shredded potatoes, peach waffles." She opened the lower cabinet door and discovered a chilled pan of fresh fruit and a complete china and silver service for six. "Where's the coffee and tea?"

"Maggie has it brewed already," said Ernie.

"And who are these extra plates for?" Meagan asked.

"Paddy invited his two sons to come along on the cruise."

"And you agreed?" barked Meagan.

"Maggie didn't seem to have any choice. What's the difference anyway?"

"The difference," Meagan spat. "Is that Paddy doesn't have any sons."

"What the hell . . ."

"So now we have his gunmen to deal with."

"This isn't a battle Meagan," Ernie said. "Just convince your uncle of the threat, get him on tape, and have some chow. Nothin's changed."

"Really? How about the fact that Jack is sailing Susan's boat across the lake with Paddy's cash, and Will has run off to California?"

"What are you talkin' about?"

"The phone call . . . the reason I'm late," said Meagan. "Will left a message on my office machine."

"What happened to Paddy's captain?"

"Will said only that the captain didn't show up, that he got scared, and that Jack is sailing the boat to Canada."

"None of this makes any sense," said Ernie. "Do you think Paddy knows?"

"I can't imagine how. But he did come here this morning with backup . . . and that concerns me."

They both turned quickly at the loud sound of *Aphrodite*'s whistle blaring a familiar imminent departure signal.

"What are we going to do now?" said Ernie. For an instant, Meagan sensed that the old salt was showing his age.

"We're going on board and following through with the plan," said Meagan as she put her arm around Ernie's shoulder. "I don't see that we have any other choice. If Jack wanted to abort the plan he wouldn't be out on the lake right now, or he would have contacted us somehow."

"Okay then, let's get this over with."

"What about Teddy?" asked Meagan. "Shouldn't he know what's going on, and that Will won't be with him?"

"Teddy's job hasn't changed. He can take care of it by himself," replied Ernie as he started pushing the cart toward the dockside door of the restaurant. "Anyway, he has Ednamae out looking for Will and Jack. They probably left a message at the marina, and Ednamae will tell Teddy before he leaves."

"You're a good liar Ernie. But I have to believe you."

*     *     *

Ednamae Bradley spied the "GONE FISHIN" sign in the front door of GrayDays Marine as she wheeled her white Saturn sedan through the small front parking lot and down the sloping gravel drive beside the Wheeler house. The first thing she noticed that brought her both delight and chagrin was that *SEAQUESTOR* was gone.

She was delighted that the often demonized yacht had been delivered and cast-off, but was chagrined to think that through some nefarious plot of Paddy Delaney's, Jack and Will might be hostages on a voyage destined for . . . where? Ednamae switched off the ignition, got out of the car and immediately saw that the back door of the marina was cracked open. She pushed the door open and peered into the eerie shadows of grayish ambient light.

"Will . . . Jack? Anybody home?"

Silence.

Ednamae had rushed through the open door into the rear of the Wheeler house a thousand times, but now seemed frozen in her place. "Hello in there. Is anybody about?"

Apprehension.

She stepped inside and easily found the light switch on the wall near the large drafting table. She flipped on the overhead lights and immediately saw there was no message on the table, so she turned to face the large bulletin board on the adjacent wall. She scanned the potpourri of pinned and stapled notices, warnings, advertisements and work orders—all of it months old. Ednamae glanced quickly at the telephone answering machine and was relieved to see that the MESSAGES light was dark.

Now another dark portal into another shadowy room beckoned her. She inched inside and slid her hand across the rough painted plaster in search of a light switch that today would remain elusive. She squinted toward the open staircase leading toward Will's loft. "Will? Are you up there?"

Dread.

She steadied herself with her hands and skimmed along the sides of the heavy display cases as she walked cautiously in the dim light toward the stairs. When her foot bumped against the familiar resilience of a person on the floor, she quickly backed off a step and looked down—afraid of what she already knew she was going to see.

Ednamae looked down upon the lifeless prone form in the heavy grayness of the morning and then everything turned dark as night . . .

*       *       *

"Ah, my pretty little queen."

The words scraped across Meagan's ear drums like fingernails on a blackboard. "Not so little anymore, uncle Paddy."

"But just as pretty," he said as he extended his bearish arms. "Come over here and give me a hug."

"I don't think so. I'm not really fond of displaying my feelings in public." Meagan looked toward the two men seated beside Maggie Wicks in deck chairs. "I had hoped we could discuss this deal privately."

"And so we shall my queen. So we shall."

Paddy motioned his lads to stand up. "Why don't you boys see if you can be of some assistance to Captain . . . eh, Maggie."

"That's a marvelous idea," said Maggie noticing Meagan's distress. "You can help get the gangway stowed and the lines cast off while Ernie stays here and gets the brunch set up." Maggie gave Meagan a sly wink as she ushered the two young men toward the bow. "We leave in five minutes."

"Now you two just sit down here and have a little drink," Ernie said. "While I make sure everything is ship shape and Bristol fashion." He pulled the serving cart toward the bulkhead where a set of restraining clamps and an electrical outlet were affixed for the purpose. "I'm sure you have a lot to talk about."

Meagan and Paddy eyed each other for several moments, neither seeming to have a suitable opening line. Meagan was shocked at how old and tired her once virile and intimidating uncle had become. His weight, posture, thin gray hair and wrinkled mask betrayed the stressful life of a man of seventy, who had aged badly. And yet there remained a cold steel sharpness in the old man's eyes that revealed a clinical, calculating mind—one that harbored the shrewdness of Satan himself.

Meagan broke off her examination, shuffled in her chair and pretended to watch Ernie tinkering with the table and seating arrangements for brunch.

"How long has it been princess?"

"Please don't call me that."

"How long?"

"Since what?"

"How long has it been since we've seen each other?"

"Since the day my father was . . . the day he died," said Meagan. "Surely you remember the day your brother died."

"And a tragedy it was too, comin' up oh . . . oh about 37 . . . 38 years, I'd guess."

"Forty years," said Meagan with a jade laser shot into Paddy's eyes. "Forty years ago today."

"A pity too, that they were never able to solve the crime."

"Never willing might be more accurate."

""Well princess," Paddy grinned widely. Excuse me. Meagan. You know back in those days another drunken Irishman washed up on the riverbank after a drownin' wasn't exactly a federal case."

"Just a family matter, right Paddy?"

"Somethin' like that," whispered Paddy. "But you kids with your fancy educations, and your money and marryin' into the establishment wouldn't understand any of that."

"Don't be so sure. I understand kissing my dead father goodbye. I understand a grainy black and white news photo of my father's naked body in the mud. I understand being uprooted from my home, and exiled to a foreign country. I understand the pain of a mother who never learned to forgive herself. And I certainly understand the abuse of power and trust." Meagan looked deeply into the quiet river then turned back to her uncle. "Don't presume to lecture me about understanding."

"So that's what this little cruise is all about?" Paddy leaned forward in his chair. "It's to be a day of reckoning then is it?"

"Is that what you think?"

"I try not to think too much princess; I just observe what's going on around me and react."

"And just what do you see around you today uncle Paddy?"

Paddy took a long sip of his Glenlivet single-malt scotch, and then sat back into his deck chair. "I'm still just takin' it all in princess. Still takin' it all in."

Two long blasts of *Aphrodite*'s whistle broke through the tension on the afterdeck as Meagan felt the vibration of the propellers against the river and saw the dock slipping away to starboard.

"Okay, Paddy. I'm sorry this conversation took the direction it did," said Meagan. "I really didn't bring you out here to dredge up old wounds. I need you to solve a problem for me."

"What kind of problem?"

"For now let's call it an investment in the future."

"Whose?"

"Patience, uncle Paddy. Everything will be revealed to you in due course."

Meagan stood up and walked to the railing where she could see Teddy's fishing boat with the engine running and navigation lights fully illuminated. Meagan felt a certain comfort in the confirmation that Teddy was listening. "Just sit back and enjoy the cruise, the brunch, and our little family reunion."

As *Aphrodite* churned past the smelly old fishing boat and pointed toward Lake Erie, Paddy's two lads came bounding around the corner.

"When do we eat?"

*     *     *

Teddy shoved the final bite of a granola bar into his mouth, looked down the dock for any sign of Ednamae, Jack or Will then quickly cast off the bow and stern lines holding the *Cindy Jane* against the dock as *Aphrodite*'s passing wake gently shook her awake. The signal having been passed, he switched off his running lights and once again pushed the RECORD button on the tape recorder next to his specially tuned VHF secret microphone receiver. All three microphones were picking up beautifully and the tiny recorder was preserving every word.

Teddy watched the digital readout on the two illuminated G.P.S. receivers adjust as *Aphrodite* passed by, and as the yacht *SEAQUESTOR* headed east toward the Welland Canal. Teddy took a moment to log the latitude and longitude coordinates of *SEAQUESTOR* and noted that she had traveled almost twenty-five miles. *Either Mr. Delaney's captain got an early start, or he's the fastest damned sailor on the lake,* Teddy thought to himself as he turned his attention away from the chart and back to the river.

Teddy planned to stay about five miles behind *Aphrodite,* just out of sight, as she headed toward the open lake between Vermilion and South Bass Island. Cruising at a comfortable fifteen knots, he would have to give them a twenty minute head start. In a pinch he could crank up his powerful diesel engine and close the distance in twelve to fifteen minutes, a contingency he preferred not to dwell upon.

*    *    *

Inside GrayDays Marine, Ednamae could see nothing but a bright light off in the distance, and someone waving as if calling her toward the light. She felt no pain or discomfort as she seemed to be floating helplessly in a billowy cloud. She had no idea where she was, and didn't really care, as she floated nearer and nearer to the light and the beckoning hand . . .

Now she heard something beyond the light.

Whispers.

No, voices.

Conversation.

Footsteps.

Clicking and whirring.

Bright flashing lights.

A pungent chemical odor.

Awful. Overpowering.

"Ednamae. Ednamae. Come on dear. It's alright now. You're safe. Ednamae. Ednamae."

Now she could see them clearly. Faces, uniforms, cameras, flash guns, a hand waving a plastic vial under her nose.

"That's right dear. Come on now. Everything is okay."

She tried to sit up, get her bearings, to clear her head but could not.

"Just lie still for a moment. You'll be just fine."

Suddenly her eyes widened and focused on the familiar faces of two kids she had known for twenty five years. Scott Williams and Jason Roberts, Vermilion's premier paramedics were on their knees beside her, flanking each side. Scott was plugged into a gleaming stethoscope pressed against Ednamae's arm just below gray Velcro that squeezed her flesh. Jason had discarded the plastic vial and now held a single finger in front of her face.

"How many fingers do I have?" Jason asked.

*Is this a trick question?* Ednamae wondered. "Ten, but I can only see one of them right now."

"She's fine Scott," he said as he rocked back and gave her a firm but gentle tug on her upper arm in unison with his partner on the other side.

As quickly as she reached the sitting position she saw it. The telltale white sheet that formed a bas relief of a corpse lay perpendicular to her feet. "Who is it?" she asked warily, not really wanting the answer.

"We were hoping you could tell us," said the suit who stepped forward. Ednamae immediately recognized Jay Richards, Vermilion's Chief of Police.

Jay was another favorite son of Vermilion who had found fame and a nickname as an all-American middle line backer for the Ohio State University Buckeyes in the eighties. Then a bruising Wolverine tight end found Jay's already vulnerable knee in the Rose Bowl and ended his dreams of an NFL career. Thanks to respectable grades in criminology, Jay had no problem finding a job with the detective bureau of the Cleveland Police Department—a job he loved, in a city and police department he hated. But Jay Richards hung in there, learned his trade, earned his stripes and bided his time.

When the Mayor of Lorain recruited Jay to run the city's revamped Detective Squad, he saw an opportunity to get closer to home and to the roots he cherished. Three years ago he was again recruited, this time by the Mayor of Vermilion, "to come home and keep our city safe."

Jay lived up to his assignment. Violent crime in Vermilion was unheard of. Burglaries and arsons were few and far between, save the occasional bogus insurance scam. And the gambling? Well, the gambling was there but it wasn't. Hidden beneath strata of society, it just didn't seem to be hurting anyone . . . as Jay Richards was occasionally and bountifully reminded.

"Help me up please," said Ednamae offering her hands to the boys. "I'm sorry Jay Bird," she said delighting in the offense he so obviously took to her usual characterization. "It was dark and I didn't see who was lying there. I just knew somehow that the person was dead. Then I guess I fainted."

"Are you up to taking a look?" the Chief asked.

"It's not Will Daysart is it?"

"Why would it be?"

"Because he lives here?"

"Is that the only reason?"

"Of course Jay," Ednamae lashed back. "Who else would be here in the middle of the night?"

"That's what I mean to find out," Jay said as he whipped the sheet off Red Reimer's contorted body.

Ednamae gasped. She had seen the death mask many times before but never in its final agony. "No, I've never seen him before." She turned away. "What is his name?"

"We don't know that either. He has no identification, no criminal tools, no bags, no vehicle . . . nothing." The Chief reached for two plastic bags beside him on a display case and held them up to eye level. "Nothing but this interesting butterfly knife and this small caliber pistol he had concealed in an ankle holster."

"Why interesting?" asked the ever-curious meddler.

"Not exactly standard issue for your run-of-the-mill second-story artist or mugger." He handed the evidence bags to a uniformed officer. "Top of the line stuff, just like his watch, clothes and shoes." The Chief pulled the sheet back over the corpse and motioned the Coroner's crew to come forward. "No, this guy wasn't here to steal."

"Why then?"

"Good question Ednamae." The Chief took Vermilion's gran-dame by the arm and led her toward the back room. "Now, let's talk for a few minutes about why you were here."

# CHAPTER 28

Jack braced himself against the port side cockpit combing and sighted across the azimuth ring that rotated around *SEAQUESTOR*'s compass. He had set the azimuth 45 degrees off his magnetic course of 068 degrees. When Cleveland's Society Center came into the cross-hairs at a bearing of 113 degrees magnetic, Jack would note the exact time.

"Mark," he said aloud to himself. "9:10 a.m."

On his way down the companionway ladder into the cabin, he glimpsed the speed log and made a mental note of the yacht's speed. Now at the chart table where he had laid out his Lake Erie sailing chart, he measured a line with his parallel rulers across the chart's compass rose at 113 degrees. With a sharp pencil in hand, he walked the parallel ruler down from the compass rose to the circled dot on the chart that represented the Society Center office building. He struck a pencil line from the landmark south westerly to intersect with the course line he had earlier drawn on the chart. At the intersection point he made a small notation: 0910—4.7 mph.

Jack could have easily established his distance off-shore with his radar unit, but he loved the ancient art of dead-reckoning navigation he learned as a Midshipman at Kings Point. The calculation he had begun—double the angle on the bow—was the simple solution to a right triangle. When the Society Center that at first had a relative bearing of 45 degrees, moved to a bearing of 90 degrees, Jack would again note the exact time and speed. A simple computation of elapsed time and average speed would allow Jack to compute the distance the, yacht had traveled between the two relative bearings. Geometry proved that the distance traveled across the water was the same as the distance from the landmark. This essential tool of coastal navigation had been used by mariners for a thousand years. Jack had learned to make this computation, and a dozen others, in his head. It was a gift that dazzled the young ship's officers who had grown up with satellites, LORAN, and radar.

When Jack deferred to his practice of the old ways, Susan would often chide him for being such a "crusty old salt." But he would just smile and reply, "When all your fancy electronic gadgets go haywire, you can get old pretty fast." Twenty-five years at sea had taught Jack that despite all the technology

and gadgetry that had invaded the bridge in recent years, at the end of the
day the contest was still between the man and the sea. And only the man
whose instincts were fueled by the many facets of nature had any chance of
surviving to sail another day.

Jack peered across the starboard side at the distant skyline of Cleveland.
He could see only the tallest buildings through the early morning haze—the
Terminal Tower, the BP Building, Erieview Plaza, and his navigation landmark,
the Society Center building. He could not see the shoreline, the new Cleveland
Browns stadium under construction, or the old Lakeside Courthouse since
they had dipped below his apparent horizon. He guessed he was ten miles
offshore, right on course, and well away from the crunch of hectic weekend
boat traffic. As he sailed diagonally across Lake Erie he would, by nightfall,
slip into Canadian waters near the center of the Great Lake, and there find
the tranquil solitude most sailors yearned for.

Except for a chance encounter with a "salty" rounding Long Point from
the Welland Canal en route to Cleveland or Toledo, he would be alone with
his past and his future. Jack had not had much time to ponder his situation
up to this point in the voyage. He had cleared the Vermilion break wall at
0510, just as an ominous red twilight began to emerge. Then came the early
morning storm. Every voyage seemed to have its own special challenge, a test
that keeps sailors honest, and keeps them coming back. Jack had met the
challenge of this voyage. The rest would be a piece of cake.

Now with about 90 minutes to kill, before his 90 degree beam bearing, Jack
poured himself a cup of hot tea from the cockpit Thermos jug, and kicked
back for a few minutes of reflection and planning. He figured that by now,
Meagan's brunch cruise was well underway, and that Teddy and Will would
be trailing along in the spy ship, well out of sight. By the time he was ready
to sight again on the Society Center, *Aphrodite* would be on station a few
miles east of Perry's Monument on South Bass Island and Meagan would be
drawing Paddy Delaney into a sticky web from which he could not escape.

In retrospect, although the incriminating tape being recorded by Teddy
aboard the *Cindy Jane* would have been enough to cinch the deal, the
serendipitous, if ugly, twist of fate that put Jack in control of Paddy's $24
million dollars were the sprinkles on top of Ednamae's rum raisin ice cream.

Jack imagined that, by now, the body of Paddy's dead captain had been
discovered and that Ednamae had unfortunately been drawn into the ever-
thickening plot. With the advance warning Will had given her, Jack was
confident that the conniving matriarch of Harbor Towne 1837 would be able
to conjure up a story to keep the investigation at bay until *Aphrodite* returned

to port with Teddy and Will close behind. After all, the Irishman's death was an accident and Will did have an implacable alibi.

Regardless of any early misgivings, Jack now knew for certain that he and the Captain's Quarters were on a righteous mission. Paddy Delaney really had decreed Will's death, and Angie Mariano gave her life to bring advance warning of the fatal edict to her friend.

There was something mystical, Jack thought, about how so many dynamic elements came together like a thunderstorm to wreak havoc upon, and then cleanse so many people, and clarify so many issues. Meagan would have her day of reckoning, if, not atonement, from Paddy Delaney. Jack would have his final demon-purging voyage aboard the yacht that embodied so many joys as it fueled endless nightmares. His godson's life would be saved and, in the process, a lifelong bond forged among the diverse group of surrogate guardians who had risen to the threat.

Even Maggie, Ernie and Teddy Bear Parks would enjoy a brief interlude of excitement and purpose, while Ednamae would forever proclaim that she managed the entire scheme.

Jack had, more often than not, seen goodness emerge from foulness, and had experienced the sweet triumphs snatched from circumstances that spelled certain defeat. It is the raging fires and icy waters of our lives that make us better, not the lukewarm treacle that so easily lulls us into an illusion of comfort and well-being.

Jack downed the last of his tea then stood up and took a deep breath of the fresh moist lake air. For the first time since Susan's death—actually the second time he reminded himself—he felt alive and full of purpose and promise; the way he felt as he and Meagan Palmer gazed toward Long Point from atop the Marblehead light.

Just as the Society Center was coming abeam, Jack glanced at his watch, amazed that the time had passed so quickly. He scanned the horizon full-circle around the yacht and saw nothing but the white plastic bottle skipping across the water two hundred feet astern, at the end of Susan's old emergency trailing line.

The landmark building passed slowly through the azimuth ring and Jack checked his Rolex quickly: 11:56 a.m. He looked over his shoulder at the speed log then made a quick mental computation: *9.7 miles offshore*, he said to himself. *Damn, I'm good.*

# CHAPTER 29

"Damn, I'm good!" Teddy Bear yelled out as the corroded old ship's clock rang out its eight bells marking high noon. He pushed the STOP button on his tape recorder and flipped over the tape cassette with his thick and clumsy fisherman's hand. The G.P.S. receiver confirmed that he was exactly five miles south east of *Aphrodite*, and he delighted in knowing that he had successfully overheard and recorded Meagan's threat and Paddy's cocky admission.

It all seemed so easy now that he had the incriminating evidence they would use as an insurance policy. Teddy had expected a much longer recording session, and was surprised when Paddy so quickly admitted his scheme to bilk Ohio's college kids out of millions of dollars that he would use to fuel the Irish Republican Army struggle in his homeland. But then he also understood how quickly the crafty Dr. Meagan Palmer could get under your skin. She had been under his a time or two, and he wasn't anxious to repeat the experience.

With the new cassette in place, Teddy pushed the RECORD button and once again turned his attention to the conversation taking place on Maggie's boat. The first few sentences seemed benign at first, and then another squall erupted.

"You're gettin' in over your head princess." Dark wet cigar juice dribbled through Paddy's quivering lips and down his chin. He didn't seem to notice.

"I've been over my head all my life Paddy," said Meagan. "Thanks in part to you, I've developed a few survival skills."

"And what makes you so sure you can survive this?"

"Well Paddy, you're a businessman—a businessman who stands to lose $24 million dollars if I go to the F.B.I."

Paddy pulled a cell phone from his pocket and shook it at Meagan like a weapon. "With one phone call that money disappears."

Meagan now seized upon the good fortune that had put Jack on board *SEAQUESTOR*. "What makes *you* so sure, Paddy?"

Her uncle stepped back slowly, wiped his chin with a handkerchief he pulled carefully from his back pocket, and looked across the lake to the east. It seemed as though he were searching for a piece of a puzzle he had earlier thought was complete.

"Go ahead Paddy," said Meagan. "Make the call."

He stood his ground and bore into the eyes of the two snakes that had slithered in beside Meagan. The boys looked at each other, then at their boss and finally just shrugged. Paddy carefully refolded his handkerchief and slid it back into his hip pocket. He turned again to gaze across the lake. Several quiet and tense moments passed as Meagan wondered whether her wily uncle could hear the rapid pounding of her heart.

"All right princess. I'll call your little bluff." He flipped the phone over to one of the lads and nodded subtly.

The lad pushed only two digits on the keypad and put the phone to his ear. "He's not answerin'"

"You mean he's out of service?"

"Nay. It's ringin' but he's not answerin'"

Paddy lunged forward like a coiled snake and snatched the phone from the side of the lad's face. "Give me that!" He listened for a moment then pushed the END button and redialed.

Meagan could see the muscles tightening in her uncle's neck and shoulders, could see the increased heaving of his chest, could see the increasing rage burning in his eyes—could feel her own heart beating itself to death.

"This is a hellish thing you've done here princess," Paddy whispered as he closed the phone abruptly with a harsh snap. Then he looked at his lads and said, "Bring the old man down here and throw him into the lake."

"Wait a minute Paddy," screamed Meagan. "Ernie has nothing to do with this."

Paddy dismissed her comment as though she had not even spoken, and then nodded again to the boys and they scurried off to find Captain Beckett.

"Okay Meagan . . ." Paddy was so close that she could feel his fetid breath on her skin. "Now that we're alone maybe you can explain to me what's going on here."

The new form of address gave Meagan a shot of confidence as she struck out viciously with both hands and pushed him backward into the ship's railing. Like a linebacker in a fifty yard line brawl, she was back into Paddy's space and in his face.

"You want to know what this is all about. Okay, I'll run it down for you! This is about the fact that you murdered my father! This is about the fact that you murdered Angie Mariano! This is about the fact that you stole $24 million dollars from a bunch of naive college kids! This is about the fact that you put out a contract on Will Daysart!" Meagan had her finger in Paddy's face as she paused a microsecond for a breath. "And this is about the fact that you raped me!"

"That's right princess, and I'd do it all again to get what I want." Paddy clamped his big paw down on Meagan's shoulder and squeezed like a vise grip. "All that information is useless to you where you're going."

In one of the worst moments of her life, Meagan found herself grinning broadly—a smile that seemed to unnerve her uncle. At the sound of footsteps Paddy stepped back and Meagan saw Ernie Beckett round the corner under full sail with both of Paddy's-lads in tow.

"So, you've had your little chat?" asked Ernie as he eased up beside Meagan and put a fatherly arm around her shoulders.

Meagan could see that she had gained a brief psychological advantage so she inched in for the kill. "Ernie, will you have Maggie play back the tape?"

"What tape?" Paddy yelled.

Meagan reached inside her sweater and pulled out the tiny microphone and transmitter she had donned earlier at McGarvey's. Now she dangled it in front of Paddy's face like a piece of bait in front of a shark. With a wild swing of his arm, Paddy slapped the microphone set out of Meagan's hand and they all watched it fly overboard.

"Where's the recording machine?"

"A place where you'll never find it," said Meagan.

"Wrong again, princess," Paddy whispered as he turned his gaze back upon his young lads. "Throw the old man into the lake then tear this ship apart until you find that tape recorder."

\*    \*    \*

Teddy Bear Parks couldn't believe what was happening on board *Aphrodite*, but became a believer when he heard the unmistakable bellow of Ernie Beckett followed by a loud splash of water. There was no doubt in his mind now that things had gone really bad, and that his old friend was somewhere in Lake Erie.

"No, not somewhere," Teddy yelled. "You know exactly where he is." Teddy pushed the HOLD button on the G.P.S. receiver assigned to *Aphrodite* so that the exact latitude and longitude coordinates where Ernie hit the water were saved. If Ernie could stay afloat for fifteen minutes he would find him.

The heavy wooden bow of the *Cindy Jane* lifted slightly out of the water as Teddy pushed the throttles forward into what had now become a life or death race. A quick flip of a switch near the steering wheel set the autopilot to hold a course directly to the spot Ernie had gone into the lake. Teddy quickly started the digital timer on his wristwatch so that he would know when the fifteen minutes he had calculated elapsed. He was now free to make some preparations for a lifesaving pickup.

Teddy Bear walked aft and opened the large sliding amidships doors that were customarily used for hauling in nets and offloading the day's catch. As he looked out on the mercifully calm lake, Teddy knew that Ernie would never survive fifteen minutes in any kind of wind and waves. He thought for a moment about calling the Coast Guard with a "man overboard" distress call, but knew that the nearest Coast Guard station was thirty miles away at Marblehead, and the odds of a patrol boat being in the area were slim. Besides, Teddy wasn't sure that he wanted the Coast Guard involved in the drama at this point. If they were needed, Maggie Wicks surely knew how to get a message to them.

Teddy walked further aft to a large wooden storage box, which he opened. He stood for a moment contemplating the gear inside, then stooped down and withdrew a large international orange life saving ring with the name *Cindy Jane* stenciled around the perimeter. There was a neat coil of a hundred foot poly propylene line attached for throwing and retrieval. Next he pulled out a ten-foot long aluminum telescoping boat hook, a couple of blankets, and a small portable oxygen bottle with mask attached. He turned the nozzle on the tank, put the mask over his face and was relieved to feel the rush of oxygen as he inhaled. He turned to carry the emergency gear over to the doors when, in his peripheral vision, he glimpsed the old flare-gun case. Then he got an inspiration.

*       *       *

Captain Ernie Beckett coughed up some tepid lake water as his head broke the surface, and then wiped the water from his eyes in time to see *Aphrodite* churning away toward the north. In forty years at sea he had never been overboard. Now Ernie wondered, in a paradoxically frivolous moment, if this was how Captain Bligh felt as the *Bounty* sailed away from him in the South Pacific.

Everything had happened so quickly that Ernie couldn't figure out why he had been tossed overboard and what purpose was being served. What he did understand, though, was that they had all badly underestimated Paddy Delaney. Did Paddy really want him dead? And if so, why? Hell, he didn't even know the man, except by reputation, and hadn't even met him until three hours earlier. What was to become of Meagan and Maggie? Where was *Aphrodite* headed now?

It seemed that Ernie was thinking about everything but his own predicament. After his head dipped under the surface again and he gulped another mouthful of lake water, he realized he'd better take stock of his own situation. *Aphrodite* was already nearly out of sight as he turned himself in a circle to scan the horizon. He was alone.

Ernie had always been a strong swimmer, and had kept up his thrice-a-week trips to the YMCA swimming pool for a half-hour of laps, but this was different. There were no spectators, no ladders, and no shallow end to stop for a quick breather. When *Aphrodite* finally disappeared from sight and it was clear that she was not just going to circle and return, he knew he was in one hell of a mess.

And maybe not a mess. Perhaps this was the way it was supposed to end. No hospitals, no life-support systems, no nursing homes full of strangers who don't care whether you live or die. No, maybe old Neptune had smiled on him once again, and given him a shot at an honorable death—a seaman's death.

Ernie was just getting comfortable with his own mortality, a subject he had not seriously pondered before, when he saw it. A white smoke trail behind a bright green flare rose into the pale blue sky to the south of him. "Sonofabitch," he growled. "Teddy and Will are comin' for me."

Teddy's watch told him that he was coming into the vicinity of Ernie's splash into the lake, so he throttled back the *Cindy Jane* and started scanning the water in front of him. Locating a small floating object in a vast expanse of open water is extraordinarily difficult. Lake Erie fishermen had long ago replaced their old colorful floating net buoys with fifteen foot floating flagpoles. Even with bright orange flags atop the poles, the targets became elusive against the backdrop of clouds, wave caps and the ever-present sea gulls.

The advent of portable watertight G.P.S. beacons, like he had placed on *Aphrodite* and *SEAQUESTOR*, had finally spared many a fisherman's eyesight and saved more than a few full catches of famous Lake Erie perch. Although Ernie did not have a beacon attached to him, Teddy had the advantage of an instant position fix obtained with the secret beacon on board Maggie's boat. The audio feed of Paddy's command, and the sound of Ernie's splash, gave Teddy an exact time to work with. All he needed now was a floating object, Ernie's big head would do, and he would make the rescue.

He hoped that Ernie had seen the warning flare he fired earlier, and would be sustained by the knowledge that help was on the way. After a few minutes of staring at nothing but water, Teddy decided he needed a better vantage point than the confined field of view offered from the steering station inside the boat. He eased the throttles back to idle, lashed the helm amidships, and climbed out onto the small convex foredeck. Since the footing there was not good, he pivoted 180 degrees and then climbed atop the cabin roof, which was firm and flat. He now had a perfect platform from which to do a full unimpeded 360 degree binocular search of the area.

"There you are you old coot," Teddy said softly to himself as he focused the Nikon 7x35 glasses on the unmistakable form of a man in the water. Ernie had wisely aided the speedy identification by removing his yellow windbreaker and waving it above his head.

In less than three minutes the *Cindy Jane* had glided within ten feet of the old captain. Teddy threw the orange life ring to Ernie and waited a short moment to satisfy himself that Ernie had enough strength left to hold on. A few short polypropylene pulls later and Ernie was crawling over the gunwale and into the old fishing boat—albeit with a hefty tug from the younger man.

"Welcome aboard captain," said Teddy. "You must have really pissed off your crew."

"An' I'm not finished with 'em yet," the old man growled.

"Let's hope not." Teddy helped Ernie to his feet. "Where do you think they're headed?"

"As you probably heard over the radio, they didn't include me in their travel plans." Ernie started to shiver as the lake water evaporated from his waterlogged frame.

"Let's get a blanket around you," said Teddy. "And then we'll track down Maggie and Meagan."

"You mean that fancy satellite beacon of yours really works?"

"It's what led me to you."

"Damn lucky thing for me," said Ernie. "Back in the old days I wouldn't have stood a chance. Hell, you wouldn't even have known I was in the water, much less where to find me." Ernie put a big hug on the Teddy Bear. "I owe you one old friend."

"Yeah, well let's not celebrate just yet. It seems to me like we're still in a hell of a mess here."

"And the kid who put us all here didn't even have the guts to stick around."

"What are you talking about?" asked Teddy.

"You mean you don't know?"

"I know that Will and Jack didn't show up this morning," said Teddy. "I assumed there was some last minute change of plan."

"Oh there's a change all right." Ernie pulled the blanket off and threw it on a bench. "The kid's run off to California and Jack's sailing that cursed, damned yacht across the lake by himself."

"The hell you say?" Teddy ran his hand through his hair. "What happened to Paddy's captain?"

"According to Meagan, the man didn't show up, Will panicked and Jack decided to take the boat across himself."

"There's something real fishy about all this," said Teddy. "Gotta be something we don't know. From the talk on *Aphrodite*, Paddy thinks that his cash is floating towards Canada as planned. The only thing is that his captain wouldn't answer the phone."

"Well that's it then," 'said Ernie. "Paddy's not takin' any chances. They're goin' after the sailboat. Only thing is, they don't know where it is."

"But we do," said Teddy pointing to the G.P.S. beacon receivers, both of which were slowly changing their position readouts.

"Okay then," said Ernie. "Let's plot their positions and follow along. Can we contact Jack?"

"He's way out of radio range, and you know he doesn't carry a cell phone. When he gets out near Conneaut this evening he'll probably catch a land line through the marine radio telephone operator. I'm guessing he'll call Ednamae."

"Damn," said Ernie. "By then they'll have run him down."

"So what are we waiting for? Let's start heading east."

"You're the captain."

*    *    *

"Mr. Delaney," said Maggie Wicks. "I can't run the engines at this speed for very long. They're too old and patched up to take this kind of pounding."

"Thank you for your input captain, but we'll continue at this speed until we find my boat."

"But you don't even know where she is right now, and we don't have any way to find her."

"Don't be so sure," said Paddy with a calm smile. "I studied some navigation back when I had a little cabin cruiser docked in Lorain, and I have a plan."

"Which would be to blow up my boat and swim after yours?"

"No, no. Nothing that extreme. We'll just head due east until we intersect my captain's course line at Cleveland, then swing in on the same Vermilion to

Port Colbourne heading that he's on. From there we can follow along until we run him down."

"Interesting."

The discussion was interesting to Meagan Palmer as well. It had become clear that Paddy still didn't know that it was Jack Grayson, rather than his captain, aboard *SEAQUESTOR* with his $24 million dollars. His instant rage had denied him the obvious inference of Meagan's taunt to "make the call." He still didn't know about the existence of Teddy Bear Parks trailing behind them in their "surveillance" ship. *You are trailing behind us, aren't you Teddy?* Meagan thought to herself. She was sure, actually she had to believe, that he had rescued Ernie shortly after his dive into the Lake. *Please God, let Teddy save him.*

Meagan also realized there were a few other things her uncle didn't know. He couldn't know that Teddy knew exactly where *SEAQUESTOR* was located, knew exactly where *Aphrodite* was located, and could hear, and record, everything that was being said on board—at least everything that was being said in Maggie Wick's presence, assuming that her secret microphone system was still transmitting. And knowledge, Meagan had always known, is power.

She reckoned that it would take at least five hours to intercept Jack in the sailboat, so there was no rush to play whatever cards she still had available. She would keep her little secrets secret until she decided how to use them to maximum advantage. More than ever now, Meagan was determined to rid the world of her menacing uncle.

Now that his temper had subsided, and until he secured his cash, he would not harm her or Maggie. They were still needed. So she patiently waited, watched and schemed.

\*     \*     \*

Jack had spent the last half-hour ravaging the gourmand's feast. Whoever the little Irishman was, he sure knew how to pack a picnic lunch, Jack decided. A half-loaf of crusty French bread, slathered with Grey-Poupon, piled high with thinly sliced smoked Bavarian ham, cracker barrel cheese, crisp lettuce, and a fresh tomato allowed Jack a moment of tragic respect for the mysterious seaman whose charter he had usurped.

Although Jack was not prone to drinking anything alcoholic while underway, he couldn't resist one of the half-dozen half-bottles of delicious red wine. Now, in the sunny cool late summer breeze, Jack was feeling a bit drowsy.

He stood up, scanned the empty horizon once again and opted to slip below to the Master's Cabin for a short nap. On his way past the radar unit he paused to flip the ON switch and set the ALARM switch to 2 MILES. He turned the alarm VOLUME to HIGH and walked into the aft stateroom knowing that if anything floated into his space he would know it.

As he lay on top of Susan's quilted sea-gull bedspread, in Susan's Master Cabin, he watched Susan's shiny brass inclinometer pendulum swing almost imperceptibly back and forth through the five degree starboard heel that *SEAQUESTOR* was comfortably sailing upon toward Canada.

Back and forth . . . back and forth . . . back and forth . . .

# CHAPTER 30

An hour had passed on the bridge of *Aphrodite* since Paddy had directed the due east course change and speed increase that put them in hot pursuit of his elusive treasure. Not a word had been spoken since Paddy blew-off Maggie's warning about overworking the old engines.

Paddy had taken up a position in the Captain's chair behind the steering wheel, where he could see both Maggie and Meagan whom he had directed into seats on opposite sides of the wheelhouse. Paddy's two lads reported that they had "tossed" the entire two upper decks of the ship and were now headed below into the storage and machinery spaces. Paddy was now convinced that the tape recorder was concealed somewhere below decks amid complicated and unfamiliar electrical or mechanical gear, so that it could not be easily located.

In his last outburst, Paddy had admonished them to *not even think about coming up without that machine.*

"So what's the money for?" Meagan finally asked into the aggravating silence.

"You wouldn't understand."

"Oh come on Paddy, humor me. You always fancied yourself a teacher."

"That was different."

"Not really," Meagan said.

"Something beautiful and good turned into something ugly and evil. It's what you do best."

Finally, Paddy turned his brooding quiet stare toward his niece and she could see the fury in his tired eyes. "I'll give you this much princess, you have learned how to push buttons, but you can stuff your damned psycho-babble, because it won't work on me."

"What? You don't have enough gambling dens and whorehouses in Ohio? Now you have to spread your filth to Canada?"

"You're still just a naive little girl who's too caught up in herself and her own safe little world to see the big picture."

*Not a bad counterpunch*, Meagan thought as she quickly recovered. "So why don't you tell me about what I'm missing out there?" She saw the growing terror on Maggie's face, but couldn't help herself from pressing on. It was family. It was personal. It always had been. And now she had a chance to end it all. "Dirty deeds are no fun if no one knows about them? Come on; tell us a wicked ten million dollar tale."

"Okay then princess," Paddy whispered as he swiveled around his chair. "Even though you'll have no use for the information after I get my money, I might as well give you a history lesson."

"I've read Dante's Inferno so you can spare me all the graphic details," said Meagan. "Just get to the grand scheme."

"The grand scheme, princess is religious freedom. It's national independence. It's self determination."

"Big concepts for a gangster."

"We are what the English have made of us."

"The Irish Republican Army? The I.R.A.? You've got to be joking."

"Even you must finally know that things seldom are as they first appear."

Suddenly, Maggie walked into the wheel house to again confront her hijacker. She had felt the vibration a few minutes earlier, but dismissed it to some lake debris they had run over. Now it was back, and becoming ever more pronounced. "Mr. Delaney," she interrupted. "We have to talk about our . . ."

"Shut your mouth before I shut it for you!"

"But if we don't . . ."

"If you say another word about those damned engines I'll have the lads dispose of you like they did the old man." Paddy swung back around to face Meagan. "I'm educating my niece and I don't want to be disturbed."

Meagan had no idea why Maggie had suddenly become so agitated but felt helpless to come to her aid, so she pressed on with her uncle. "Isn't it a lot faster to send your terrorist buddies a check than deliver cash to them by sailboat?"

"That's what I'm talking about princess. So bright and yet so naive to the ways of the world."

Now Paddy felt a shudder himself and quickly scanned the panel of instruments. Engine temperature and oil pressure were both normal, and the old boat was still churning out 3000 r.p.m.'s from both engines as it had for the last hour, so he looked again at Meagan and continued.

"Once the cash is laundered a bit in a Canadian casino, it can be *donated* by wire-transfer to the right people in Ireland. All very legal and proper in Canada, but not possible in the U.S."

"And no one will think to search the sailboat at Canadian customs?"

"And find what?" Paddy smiled. "A few extra boat fenders?"

*    *    *

"We're not gonna find anything down here they *dun* want us to find," said one of the tired and sweaty lads. "And I'm bloody tired of opening and closing doors."

"Right you are," said the other. "Maybe that bitch is bull shitting ole Paddy. Maybe there's no tape recorder at all. Maybe this whole fuckin' thing is a bluff."

"Or maybe they're beamin' the messages back to shore . . ."

"Or to another boat around here somewhere . . ."

"Let's go back up and tell Paddy what we figured out."

"Yeah, okay.

But we better check through that last door back there, or he'll have our bloody heads."

"There's nothin' back there but the engines. And they're makin' a terrible racket. Let's forget it."

"And end up in the bloody lake like that old man? Not me."

That final door the young Irishman opened was the last door he would ever open. In a horrific explosion of metal, oil, steam and water the entire stern of the ship seemed to blow through the steel door. The lads never knew what hit them.

*    *    *

"What the hell?" yelled Paddy.

"Damnit! I warned you!" Maggie was now on her feet and hovering over the control panel. All the gauges had zeroed out and the ignition warning buzzer was humming loudly. Maggie turned the key to silence the buzzer then reached for the VHF radio microphone.

"What do you think you're doing?" said Paddy.

"Get out of my way," Maggie shouted as she body checked Paddy Delaney against the bulkhead. "Mayday . . . Mayday . . . Mayday," she spoke calmly into the radio microphone. "This is the motor vessel *Aphrodite* on Channel 16. Mayday . . . Mayday . . . Mayday."

"What's happening, Maggie?" Meagan was now on her feet and had nudged in between Paddy and the woman who had resumed command of her ship.

"Get some life jackets out of that cabinet behind you."

"What the hell are you sayin'?" yelled Paddy.

"Shut up," she barked back.

"*Aphrodite* . . . this is the fishing boat *Cindy Jane* . . . switching to channel 68."

"Meagan," Maggie said as she took her life jacket. "Put on your vest and then help Mr. Delaney get his on securely."

"*Aphrodite* . . . *Cindy Jane* on channel 68. Are you there Maggie?"

"Roger that Teddy, but not for long I'm afraid."

"What's your status?"

"Both engines are out. I'm transmitting on batteries and . . ." Another alarm buzzer erupted from the control console and Maggie quickly silenced its menacing shriek. ". . . and the bilge alarm just went off, so it looks like we're taking on water."

"What happened? Did you hit something?"

"Negative," said Maggie, a little aggravated at the old insinuation. "Same problem as before I think. Probably the stuffing box blew apart and the lake's running in through the shaft bearings. But I don't know for sure."

"I'm going to find out what's going down there," said Paddy as he headed for the wheelhouse door. "My lads must be down there somewhere."

"Okay then," said Maggie. "But take your life jacket and put it on."

"I'm not ready to buy into your little scheme just yet."

"Suit yourself then," Maggie said as he opened the door to the aft passageway.

"Meagan, I want you to stay right here with me."

"Okay. Right," said Meagan feeling a tad out of her element.

Maggie turned back to the VHF radio. "Did you hear all that Ted?"

"No, Maggie. We're too far behind you to pick up your small transmitter. What happened?"

"Paddy thinks this is all some kind of ruse to trick him."

"Where is he now?" asked Teddy.

"He went below to look for his two goons." Maggie glanced quickly at the trim gage located on the bulkhead beside her. "Teddy, just how far behind are you?"

"From the readout on the G.P.S. it looks like almost thirty miles."

"What do you think, maybe 90 minutes?"

"A little more."

"Is Ernie there?

"A little wet, but still ornery. I'll put him on."

"How you doin' out there captain?" Ernie's voice was calm and reassuring.

"We're already down by the stern almost ten degrees," Maggie said softly. "Please hurry."

"Maggie, we're runnin' all out. Just stay tuned to this channel as long as you can and remember the drill."

"Okay Ernie. Thanks. *Aphrodite* out."

"What did all that mean'?" Meagan asked.

"It means we're taking on a lot of water through the stern. The bilge pumps can't handle it. We're going to sink." Maggie stared out over the calm lake and ruffled her hair with both hands. "When the bilge pumps stop running, she'll go fast."

"Maggie, I'm so sorry."

"There's no time for regrets now dear. We have work to do." Maggie Wicks zipped up her brilliantly colored life vest and took Meagan by the hand. "Let's go out on deck and get our lifeboat ready."

Captain Maggie Wicks was a safety fanatic and had overstocked her ship with the latest lifesaving gear. Her six twenty-person inflatable life rafts ensured that there would be no Titanic scenario where the women and children left everyone else behind. Two of the rafts were stowed on each side of the ship up near the bridge, with two more amidships near the gangway openings, and two more near the stern. They were stowed in large fiberglass cocoons that rested in specially fabricated cradles on the deck. Stainless steel straps with "EZ Release" locking mechanisms had pressure release gauges built in that would deploy the raft automatically if submerged more than twenty feet under water.

"Let's get this raft off the cradle and into the water," said Maggie. She banged the release with her hand and winced in pain as her hand gave, but the lock did not. A couple of rapid-fire kicks offered no release either. Her sky blue boat shoes were no match for the lock that had not been opened for years.

"Maggie, step back out of the way please." Maggie turned around to see Meagan Palmer holding a fire axe she had pulled off the bulkhead. "I don't think we'll be needing this for a fire," she said as she swung the butt end of the metal head at the locking mechanism. The lock snapped open and the whole assembly sprung apart like the spring from a watch.

"Okay, let's lift this whole canister over the railing." Maggie commanded.

The shipmates bent down to lift the raft canister but soon found that they couldn't even budge it off its cradle. "Maybe, I should go find Paddy for some help," said Meagan.

"I don't think that . . ." All of a sudden Maggie felt like she was in a roller coaster clearing the top of the first drop. The deck was moving under her feet and was now past thirty degrees.

"What should I do?" yelled Meagan.

"Get into the water and swim away from the boat."

"What about uncle Paddy?"

"It's too late to worry about him," barked Maggie. "I'm going back to the radio for one last report. See you in the pond." Maggie could see Meagan jump over the side as she wedged through the wheelhouse door and struggled to the radio.

"Teddy . . . it's over. She's going down and we're in the water. Out."

The deck was now slipping over the forty-five degree mark as Maggie pulled herself along the chart table toward the starboard side wheelhouse door. She paused for a moment at the sight of her U.S. Coast Guard Captain's License hanging in its frame on the aft bulkhead. She reached up impulsively, to retrieve it from the frame then stopped abruptly and jerked her back as though she had been singed by a fire. Maybe, she thought, it was better for the captain to go down with the ship—at least symbolically.

When she felt the deck rise again under her feet, she darted for the open door, lunged for the starboard bridge railing, and threw herself over the side.

The lake water felt surprisingly warm as Maggie calmly allowed the buoyancy of her vest to lift her through the turquoise realm of water, bubbles and foam. Rather than the panic associated with abandoning ship, she felt the tranquility of floating blissfully in her mother's placenta . . . quiet, calm, peaceful, serene. Suddenly she was reborn.

"Maggie, Maggie," she heard as her head broke the surface of the lake. Then she heard the frantic splashing of a swimmer approaching. A moment later, Meagan Palmer took hold of her hand and was bobbing next to her like an orange cork.

"Did you see uncle Paddy? Did he get off the ship?"

Maggie swung around to clear her head and get her bearings. As the lake water cleared from her eyes she gasped at the sight of *Aphrodite*'s stern sticking straight up out of the lake like a fishing bobber. She felt like she was watching her child being bound and hooded on an executioner's gallows. Helpless agony. "I don't see him Meagan. He must not have made it out of the engine room."

"Good riddance then," said Meagan without a hint of remorse in her voice. "Finally that old bastard got what was coming to him."

Then the gallows trap door opened and Maggie's child slid into the abyss. The moisture that only moments ago had covered Maggie's eyes from outside now welled up from within and consumed her.

Then, like the specter of Freddie Kruger emerging from a swamp, Paddy Delaney stepped off the fantail of the sinking ship and into the bubbling hissing torrent of lake water. Maggie and Meagan watched in quiet disbelief as he seemed, for a moment to walk on water only to disappear again beneath the surface.

"Did you see that?" shouted Maggie. "He's alive!"

"Not for long," said Meagan. "He wasn't wearing a life vest."

"I'm going after him," said Maggie.

"Forget it. Let him die. It's already too late."

"You know it doesn't work like that out here. I have an obligation to my passengers, no matter who they are."

Meagan watched Maggie swim away clumsily under the constraint of the bulky life vest. She did not move, except to tread water lightly, and felt herself hoping that he would not resurface. Halfway to the still boiling entry point, Maggie stopped swimming, and curled over quickly as if trying to fend off something that had grabbed her leg. As she thrashed and bobbed, it became obvious to Meagan that she was in some kind of distress. "What's the problem Maggie?"

Meagan had easily covered the fifty yards of lake, and now clutched her captain's life vest. "Leg cramps," Maggie moaned. "Can't go on. You have to save him."

"Not on your life," spat Meagan over the ripples in the water. "You have your code and I have mine."

"And I thought a part of that code involved being a doctor obligated to help people in distress." Maggie reached down again quickly to massage her calf muscle.

"Patients, not scumbag predators."

"That's a pretty fine line you've drawn there Dr. Palmer. Do you think you can live with it?"

"I've lived with it all my life," said Meagan.

"You've lived with what *he* did to you. "You were the victim and he was the villain," coughed Maggie. "Are you sure you want to reverse those roles now?"

Just then Meagan saw Paddy's head break the surface of the water twenty-five yards away. He was coughing, choking and retching as he flapped his arms frantically like all non-swimmers. "You know lady," yelled Meagan. "You should have been a shrink." Meagan pushed away and swam over to her nearly defeated uncle. She kept a two-arms-length distance. "Paddy! Paddy! Listen to me!" He stopped for a nanosecond and shook the water from his face. Then he lunged toward Meagan, and again slipped under the surface. Once again his bloated-red head broke free. "Paddy, listen to me! Don't grab me. Just stop fighting and I'll help you." She watched his head dip under the surface again and then reemerge. "Paddy! Do you understand?"

Meagan thought she saw a nod from her uncle just before he stopped swinging his arms and slipped again beneath the surface. She kicked toward him, reached down and grabbed the shoulders of his shirt. Before pulling him to the surface she quickly spun him around so that his back was to her. As she pulled his motionless body to the surface she slipped one hand into his belt and the other around the back collar of his shirt. Now she held him at half-arm's length with both of their heads barely breaking the surface as she kicked furiously to aid the buoyancy provided by the life vest she wore.

"What am I doing?" she yelled as she realized she couldn't keep both of them afloat for much more than another ten minutes, far less than the ninety minutes until the *Cindy Jane* would arrive.

"Need a little help?" asked Maggie from behind.

"Yeah, I don't think I can do this much longer."

Maggie eased in behind Meagan and attached herself to Paddy's backside much the same as Meagan had wisely done. "He's awfully quiet," Maggie said. "Is he alive?"

Meagan was now treading water more comfortably and had caught her breath. "I don't know, but I definitely like him better this way." Meagan looked into Maggie's tired bloodshot eyes. "Can we do this until Teddy and Ernie arrive?"

"We won't have to," said Maggie with a huge smile. The life raft they had cut loose on the bridge deck popped up a few yards from them. "Just hold on to your patient there, and I'll go get the raft."

"I can do that."

Within five minutes, Maggie had paddled the inflated raft over to Meagan's position, helped her into the raft, and then the two of them hauled Paddy aboard in a maneuver reminiscent of a harpooned whale being dragged aboard old whaling ships.

For the first few minutes everyone just sat quietly in their rubber nest apparently pondering their arrogance, their near destruction, and their resurrection. Maggie stood up and scanned the horizon for any sign of help, but as she looked at her watch she knew it was too early. "I figure we have about an hour to wait."

"Better here than in the water," said Meagan. "I never really understood what those torpedoed sailors in the Pacific went through until today. "I don't think I could have lasted an hour and a half, even with my life vest."

"Oh, you would have made it," said Maggie. "The key is the water temperature. The lake must be about seventy-five degrees right now, pretty much the same as the Pacific. Some of those sailors you talked about lasted for days in the water before being rescued. It was a much different story in the Atlantic Ocean where hypothermia gets you pretty quickly. A lot of people who boat up here on this lake don't realize how quickly they can die if they go overboard during the spring and fall when the water is in the fifties."

Almost as if she had forgotten they were not alone, Maggie finally looked over at Paddy. "Is he all right?"

Meagan kicked Paddy's leg with her bare foot, realizing for the first time that she had lost her boat shoes in the water. "How are you doing Paddy?" He seemed like he was in a trance just staring blankly out into the lake. He did not move or speak at Meagan's first approach. She tried again. "Paddy, are you okay?"

"Yeah."

"Can I get you something?" asked Maggie reaching for the small emergency supply bag. "Some water maybe?"

Finally he moved his head toward her. "No, I've had enough water for one day."

"Exactly what happened back there in the engine room?" asked Meagan.

"I saw him."

"You mean one of the boys?"

"No."

"Who then?"

"My brother."

"What are you talking about?" said Meagan.

"I saw my brother." Both of the ladies were now leaning forward and focused on Paddy's face. "Are you talking about my father?" asked Meagan.

"Aye."

"Tell me about it," said Meagan. "Try to remember."

"The ship was sinking," said Paddy. "I found the lads below, near the engine room. They were dead. Blown apart by some explosion. Then I panicked and tried to get out, but everything turned upside down and got very dark. Then the water started rushing in all around me. I saw a light above so I started climbing toward it. When I got outside I could see you in the water so I jumped." Paddy's eyes filled with tears. "I never learned how to swim, and so I figured it was over, and that I was a dead man." He wiped his cheek in a gesture that Meagan never would have believed possible. "All of a sudden, you were there and I tried to reach you but couldn't. Then I gave up and slipped under the water. That's when I saw him."

"Did he speak to you?" Asked Meagan.

"No, but he smiled and held out his hand like he wanted help me. I didn't understand what was happening."

"Why not?"

"Why would my brother want to help me after what I did?"

"What did you do?"

"I don't . . ." Paddy wiped his eyes. "No, I don't want . . ."

"Come on Paddy, say it!" said Meagan. "Tell me what you did."

"I killed him damnit! I killed my brother." Paddy was bawling now and reaching out toward Meagan who did not budge. "I killed him but he just stood there and smiled at me. He wanted to save me, but I couldn't reach him."

"Then what?"

"Then you were there," he said suddenly aware and intense. "You reached down and pulled me out of my grave."

"That's right."

"Why? Why would you save me after everything I've done?"

"Because I didn't want to be like you." Meagan pushed her self deep against the side of the life raft. "I didn't want to be a murderer."

*     *     *

Captain Ernie Beckett looked up from the chart table he had been hunched over for the last several minutes. He put down his pencil and dividers, and then squinted at the red flashing numbers on the G.P.S. receiver. "We should be able to see them any minute now."

"Okay, I'll throttle back a bit," said Teddy. "Come on up and grab these binoculars. They may be hard to find out here."

"Hard my ass," growled Ernie. "There they are, dead ahead."

"Leave it to Maggie Wicks to get everybody nice and comfortable in a life raft."

"Yeah, she's a damned fine skipper, that one," said Ernie. "But don't tell her I said so."

"So what's next?" asked Teddy.

"Pick 'em up and call the Coast Guard."

"What about the money? What about Jack?"

"Jack's fine," said Ernie. "And the money's safe; at least until he puts in at Port Colborne. We need to start playin' by the rules and buy ourselves some time to figure out where we go from here."

"And what are we going to tell the Coast Guard?"

"Exactly what happened," said Ernie. "Maggie took Meagan and her uncle out for a cruise, the old stuffing box cracked loose and the ship sank. They don't need to know anything else."

"What if Mr. Delaney won't go along?"

"He won't have a choice," said Ernie reaching for the VHF radio microphone. "Lorain Coast Guard, Lorain Coast Guard . . ."

# CHAPTER 31

"Hang on Susan. I'm coming back for you!" Jack yelled through the howling wind and flapping canvas. He could see her red hair atop the familiar white foul weather gear. Susan Grayson bobbed in the waves and whitecaps of Lake Erie like a fisherman's float that had cut its line. Jack ticked off the drill in his mind:

Throw out a life ring.

Start the engine.

Douse the sails.

Call the Coast Guard.

Remembering the drill was easy, executing it was not.

"Susan . . . Susan," he screamed into the maelstrom. "Keep swimming."

Jack tossed a yellow horseshoe buoy into the water. He tried to start the big Perkins diesel engine. Nothing. The force of the storm against the sails pushed the boat's starboard rail into the great lake. Foaming water rushed into the engine compartment. The sails had to come down. He had to get the engine going. He had to turn the boat around, to get back to his wife bobbing in the angry lake.

Jack struggled against a conundrum of tangled sheets and halyards. He couldn't free himself. Couldn't react. Couldn't move. He looked across the canted gyrating stern and saw the yellow horseshoe in the distance but lost sight of the red and white bobber.

"Susan . . . Susan . . . Susan," he screamed.

\* \* \*

Jack's scream woke him and he sat up with a start and looked around as if lost in time. His hands felt the soaking wet comforter beneath him. He worked to slow his labored breathing as he swiped at the sweat on his face, and licked the musty salty flavor from his still trembling lips.

"My God!" he moaned, and then banged his wet fists on the berth where Susan once slept. "What's happening to me?"

As his head cleared he felt the motion of a yacht slogging heavily through wind and waves. He checked the brass inclinometer that had earlier mesmerized him to sleep. The old brass pendulum was now swinging purposefully through a ten degree arc on either side of a twenty degree starboard midpoint. His angle of heel had increased dramatically, a sure sign that the breeze had freshened while he slept.

Jack checked his Rolex and was shocked to see that it was 6:30 p.m. Almost six hours had passed since he had decided upon a quick nap. "I wonder what was in that bottle of wine," he said to the empty cabin, then jackknifed himself out of the bunk and onto the cabin sole. It took a few steps down the passageway to the main salon to get his sea legs back.

Jack was amazed at how "landlocked" he had become in only a year off the water. He walked unsteadily a few more paces to the navigation station and chart table. He quickly checked the radar screen and saw no targets in his vicinity; then glanced at the barometer and noted that it had fallen to 29.8 inches. He made a hasty log book entry then pulled himself up the companionway ladder to the cockpit.

The sun was shining, the wind from the north had freshened to twenty knots, and the lake was covered with whitecaps. *SEAQUESTOR* was in her glory, pounding away toward Canada at a respectable 7.4 miles per hour.

Jack stepped out of the cockpit and on to the leeward deck where he could sight down the waterline to the yacht's bow and gauge the draw of the gigantic white Dacron sails. Lake Erie splashed over the starboard rail and nipped at his Topsiders.

Jack had always felt a unique exhilaration from the lee rail of a yacht beating to windward. In his yacht racing days at Kings Point, he always stationed himself on the leeward side, down near the water, where he could see the rigging and feel nature's impact on the sailing machine. Jack had always had a connection to wind, water and waves that bordered on arrogance, and now he was back in the "slot" as racing captains were so fond of saying. It felt good. It also felt good to have his feet wet again, but wet on deck was not good.

Jack could see the yacht's bow digging into the lake and beginning to take water over her bow chock. *SEAQUESTOR* was overpowered and needed a sail change up forward.

The operation was simple and Jack ticked off the routine in his head . . .

Pull the new smaller jib up through the forward cabin hatch.

Cast off the jib sheet wound around the starboard side self-tailing Barient winch.

Release the jib halyard from the main mast block leading into the cockpit.

Retrim the main and mizzen.

Check the auto-pilot.

Finally, go forward to change the jib from the bow pulpit.

He was about halfway through the drill, just about to trim the main and mizzen so that the sails would luff lightly, spilling enough wind to keep the yacht moving ahead but more upright, when Jack paused for a moment to catch his breath. Single-handing a yacht this size is no joke, he thought to himself. It was something you did when you were young and brazen with something still to prove.

Jack thought about the twisted and lifeless corpse of the wiry little Irishman who might have been in his place right now, had fate not intervened. He guessed that the Irishman had nothing more to prove either, and yet each time a man goes to sea he is tested—and by his actions, either proven or mocked. But the Irishman would never again have the chance to prove anything, never again the chance to test himself, to triumph or to fail. Never again.

Now, back in the cockpit, Jack smartly trimmed the main and mizzen, and noted that *SEAQUESTOR* was now carrying no more than a five degree starboard heel as she regained speed. He adjusted the auto-pilot a tad and stepped back to admire his work. On board a sailing vessel however, there is always another task waiting. As he started forward to begin the jib sail change, Jack eyed the lifeline harness stowed near the cabin hatch. He knew the drill, had lived by it all his life, but this was a piece of cake.

The yacht was moving along nicely on her bottom, the deck was stable and, with the jib sheet thrown off the winch, the big No.1 jib was luffing softly in the breeze. No problem.

Jack was only two steps from the bow when his nightmare returned.

He heard a dull thud, and then felt the thirty ton yacht shudder as it stopped dead in the water. He careened head first over the bow, as though he had been launched from a medieval catapult. Jack instinctively reached out for the head stay, then grimaced as the stainless steel wire tore into the flesh of his right hand.

In a slow motion moment his body pivoted over the tubular steel bow pulpit just as the boat lurched to starboard, under the press of wind in her sails, and gained speed. Jack's chest crashed into the stubby teak bowsprit and knocked the wind out of him. In another flash of agonizing pain he lost his grip and was in the lake. The port side of the boat, now high out of the water, brushed past Jack as he searched for some illusive handhold he knew very well was not there.

In the lonely wake of Susan's ketch, Jack read words painted on the transom, from a vantage point all sailors dread:

*SEAQUESTOR*
Vermilion.

Now he grasped the irony of it all. *SEAQUESTOR*—the "sea searcher." He thought about the "disaster" plan he had set into motion and wondered if anyone would search for him. Then he remembered how Susan always delighted in the name of their home port. Vermilion was a French word meaning "brilliant red," and the early French trappers had so named the river for its abundant supply of red clay found up stream from the present lagoons. Red clay . . . red hair . . . red sky. He could still hear Susan reciting the old mariner's rhyme:

*Red sky in the morning, sailor take warning;*
*Red sky at night, sailor's delight.*

Jack had sailed into the early red dawn, and had failed to heed its warning. Now he would have to atone. Images flashed through Jack's mind. These were grainy snapshots of life, followed by sharper images of death. Now there was a new crystal-clear photograph to add to his macabre collection—a self portrait. As he floated helpless and alone in the great lake he thought it somehow fitting that he would now die a seaman's death—a fate his arrogance had again made inevitable.

His arrogance, he suddenly knew, had killed Susan, forced his son into exile, and put his friends in peril. He had even allowed a woman he was growing to love, engage an enemy she was no match for. Jack's once flawless life had become a litany of failure. It was time to die, he thought.

Then something brushed across his leg.

*A feeding frenzy?* He mused, conjuring images of circling sharks. Another brush—longer this time. He kicked frantically. Contact.

A familiar texture shimmered up his leg. Not alive, yet moving and gyrating wildly. Jack took a deep breath and plunged his upper body into the murky lake. Through the green sunlit water Jack could see the long eel-like form rushing through the water at his fingertips. He grabbed the slimy pulsating line with both hands and was abruptly jerked through the water. He had found the long emergency trailing line that Susan always insisted on towing astern as part of her usual man overboard routine.

He had always wondered whether a crew member unfortunate enough to find himself alone in the drink could actually grab hold of the theoretical lifeline. Now, Jack Grayson was at the end of the line. The only question remaining was how long he could hold on.

*     *     *

Once Teddy Bear Parks had the three survivors safely aboard the *Cindy Jane*, and had learned about the demise of Paddy's two young men, he headed his fishing boat due north and ran at full speed for ten minutes. Now, at the suggestion of the wily old Ernie Beckett, he again throttled back the engines.

"Okay," said Ernie. "Call those boys from the Coast Guard and tell them we're on station with the survivors from *Aphrodite*." When Teddy had placed his earlier call to Lorain Coast Guard, he merely informed them that he had received a distress call and was going to the assistance of a sinking ship. He told them he would search for survivors and radio back an exact position when he was on the site of the sinking. He knew that even with their high speed crash boat, it would take them nearly two hours to reach the area where *Aphrodite* went down.

Paddy Delaney had suggested that there was no reason for the Coast Guard to find the wreckage and its two dark secrets. *Some things are best left buried deeply out of sight*, he had warned them. Coming, as it had, from an expert in such matters, they quickly decided to heed the gangster's advice. The ten-minute full speed run had *Aphrodite* safely tucked away for later handling. Now that they were safely out of the area and the Coast Guard still an hour away, it was time to have a strategy meeting.

Teddy reached the Coast Guard crash boat en route to the sinking site, and he read off to them the exact G.P.S. coordinates now showing on his receiver.

"What if they decide to search for my ship?" asked Maggie.

"They surely will," said Ernie. "But they'll never find her."

"Oh, they'll find her all right," said Maggie. "If they put their minds to it and bring in some special equipment."

"They won't," said Paddy Delaney quietly.

"How can you be sure?" asked Maggie.

"Because it's a waste of money and time."

"He's right," said Ernie. "We're going to report that all passengers are accounted for, and that the sinking was caused by mechanical failures."

"But what about those boys?" asked Meagan. "Won't their families come looking for them?"

"No." The cold stare of Paddy's eyes left no room for a follow-up question.

"I have a very bad feeling about this whole thing," said Maggie Wicks stepping up into the center of the reluctant co-conspirators. "But I want this over and done with. Let me see if I have the story right. Ernie and I were out on a routine charter for Meagan and her uncle." She looked into Ernie's eyes. "Did anyone see those two boys come on board?"

"I don't see how," said Ernie.

"What about the cooks and waitresses inside McGarvey's?"

"Negative. The boys never went into the restaurant."

"Okay," Maggie continued. "I assume the patched-up old stuffing box gave way and . . ." Maggie shook her head. ". . . and what?"

"The damned thing must have split apart then threw the shaft out of alignment. The vibration and heat must have torn the stern out and sparked an explosion. Hell, I don't know," said Ernie with a tired look in his eyes. "Does it really matter? Those kids from *your* Coast Guard will believe anything you tell them."

"I guess you're right," said a retreating Maggie. "I just want to make sure we're all telling the same pack of lies."

The instant pall of dead silence left no mistake about what everyone was thinking. Everyone except . . .

"Don't get pious now," said Paddy Delaney. "You all set me up with a pack of lies to hustle and extort me. "You can save your guilt and confessions for Sunday morning."

"Yes . . . well . . . and what about me?" asked Teddy. "We were just out fishing and heard the distress call?"

"It works for me," said Paddy. "You'll probably get your name in the paper for a heroic rescue." Paddy erupted into a macabre and hideous laugh.

"And that's it?" yelled Meagan. "Just the end of another one of your games, uncle Paddy?"

"No princess, this was your game."

"I don't recall killing Angie Mariano. I don't recall putting out a contract on Will Daysart. And I damn sure didn't send those two young boys to their death."

"Oh but you did, princess." Paddy dug into her eyes. "Your invitation. Your brunch. Your charter. Your responsibility."

"And your stupid decision to throw this man overboard and destroy Maggie's ship."

"You should have known when you decided to take me on with your little crew and your pathetic pack of lies that it wasn't going to be easy. Revenge never is."

"I can't believe I saved your wretched life," she said. "Ah, but save it you did princess. And for that I'm willing to forget this whole thing; forget that any of it happened." Paddy looked around at the group. "All I want is my money, and then we'll live and let live."

Now there was silence again as everyone looked to Meagan to drop the next bombshell on her uncle. "I'm afraid it's not quite that simple."

"You're always complicating things princess. What's the problem now?"

"When your captain didn't show up . . ."

"What are you talking about?" Paddy screamed.

"Before I came down to the boat this morning I got a phone call from Will Daysart who said that your captain didn't show up and that Jack Grayson took the yacht and is sailing it across the lake."

"Across the lake?" Paddy bellowed. "Across the lake to where?"

"Port Colborne, the Welland Canal."

"And who the hell is Jack Grayson? That name is familiar."

"His wife owned the boat you bought."

"Yeah right. And where's the kid?"

"It's not important."

"Maybe . . . maybe not," he grinned. "But I'll let you keep your little secret for now." Paddy had another mystery yet to solve. Captain Derry "Red" Riemer had never failed him before. He was a solid professional who would never just fail to show up for a job. Not unless . . . . Paddy sensed there was more to this scenario than Meagan was willing to tell him, and he had come, in a strange way, to admire the way his niece was playing the few cards she might have left. Maybe she had a little more spunk than he expected. He began to realize that things had changed dramatically and there was too much that he didn't know at the moment. He would have to slow down the pace a bit, he decided, until he knew exactly what to do. What he did know, however, was that he now owed his life to Dr. Meagan Palmer and in his world, that debt was sacred.

*     *     *

"*Cindy Jane . . . Cindy Jane . . .* this is Coast Guard rescue on channel 16."

"This is *Cindy Jane,*" said Teddy into the VHF microphone. "Go ahead Coast Guard rescue."

"Captain, we're five minutes from your approximate location. Can you give us an updated position?"

"Roger that Coast Guard . . ."

As Teddy Bear Parks read the new G.P.S. coordinates over the radio, Paddy huddled again with the group. "Are we all on the same page now?"

"We know what we're supposed to say," said Ernie. "But we're not quite ready to offer you membership in the yacht club."

"All I want is my money," said Paddy. "You can keep your club and all your sheltered old friends."

"Not so sheltered any more, uncle Paddy," said Meagan.

"I suppose not. And what about this Jack Grayson? Will he cooperate?"

"He'll do what's right," said Meagan.

"How can we contact him? asked Paddy.

"Why?" asked Maggie Wicks.

"I want him to turn that boat around and bring my money back to me."

"Why don't you just let him deliver it to Canada for you?" asked Meagan. "I thought this was all about some grand patriotic mission for the mother land."

"She's waited a hundred and fifty years, a few more weeks won't matter," said Paddy. "I have some other priorities right now. Besides, I don't let people I don't know into my business affairs."

"Well, there's no way to reach him now," said Ernie. "He's far out of our radio range, and he never carries a cell phone with him. "We're expecting that he'll call us tonight."

"You better hope he does," said Paddy. "I want my boat back in Vermilion tomorrow morning."

"Tomorrow will bring what tomorrow brings," said Meagan.

# CHAPTER 32

Tomorrow couldn't come soon enough for Jack Grayson. He didn't know what the new day would bring, but knew that, at least, there would be closure. He would miraculously live or, more certainly, die.

At one end of the line *SEAQUESTOR* sailed herself toward Canada. At the other end, electric shocks of pain coursed through Jack's side from his slashed right hand to his smashed ribs. His hands were hard up against the handle of the plastic bleach bottle that served as a buoy to keep the trailing line afloat. When he fought the impulse to let go, another jolt of agony ripped upward from his ribs and exploded in his right hand. Jack could feel the hollow white plastic handle giving way to the dragging resistance of his body. He wouldn't have the bottle much longer and knew that he couldn't hold on to the slimy Dacron tether.

Jack repeated the riddle in his mind, searching for the simple yet elusive answer. What does the drowning man do when he can't hold on and won't let go? Ever so slowly the riddle answered itself. Jack had to tie himself off before his strength, or his willpower, gave out.

Susan had known how to tie every knot in the book—something that, even as an Eagle Scout and a master mariner, Jack had never mastered. As he sliced and bounced through the water he could see her looping the end of the trailing line through the plastic bottle handle at the end of the trailing line as she recited, *the bunny comes out of the hole, runs around the tree, and goes back down the hole.*" A bowline. A knot with a loop the size of a man's hand. A knot designed never to slip.

*Did I retie it?* Jack couldn't remember.

"What the hell," he yelled.

Jack reached between his legs and grabbed the knot. The force of the rushing water threw him into a somersault and he felt the plastic bottle tear away. It was now or never, he knew. For an instant the line went slack as he vaulted head-over-heels through the lake. He plunged his right hand through the perfect loop that Susan had fashioned months ago.

The strain of Jack's body weight was now on his wrist, rather than the deeply slashed fingers of his otherwise useless right hand. He was able to turn on to his back and look upward at the sun, now low toward the western horizon behind him. He checked the Rolex Submariner strapped to his good left arm and noted that it was 7:15 p.m.—about an hour before sunset. *Red sky at night, sailor's delight*, he heard himself pray. Perhaps God would take pity on him and grant him a quiet and hopeful vermilion sunset.

For the first time in half-an-hour that felt like a week Jack could lay back and assess the damage. He cussed himself for choosing to change the sail underway. He could have put the ketch into the wind, let her drift, and play it safe. He cussed himself for failing to clip on the safety harness that beckoned him on his way forward. Jack knew that Lake Erie was treacherous—that nature itself was unforgiving. He had always known that it was the shortcuts that came back to haunt a man—like the errant jibe that had swept Susan into the lake when Jack insisted on holding course rather than heading up to a safer and slower line. The ghost that haunted Jack's dreams replayed that jibe a hundred times, and on each instant replay Jack felt the boom crack himself in the head.

*Focus*, he told himself. *Get your head out of the past or die.*

Jack reviewed the scenario. At his current speed, which he judged to be about three knots without the jib, more than twenty hours of remote open lake lay ahead. Even if another boat or ship passed nearby, he wouldn't be seen trailing so far astern. To add to his problems, it would soon be dark. An hour or so of slowly dimming twilight would dissolve into a morbid nine hours of darkness.

Jack had always relished the special feeling of nighttime on the water. There was something about the unknown and unseen that challenged and exhilarated him. But now he was not on the water, but in the water, and the change of perspective chilled him to the bone.

"I'm in one hell of a mess here, Susan."

*So get back on the boat dummy*, he heard her say.

It would be easy for Jack to grab the stainless steel swim ladder affixed to the transom of the yacht, if only he could get back there. Two hundred feet from the end of the line to the transom—that's all, he told himself. Less than seventy yards pull along the trailing line and Jack would live.

Jack remembered that that salmon fight their way upstream many times more than that to spawn. *Then they die.*

"Focus," he yelled until a wave swelled over his head and he retched up musty lake water and bile. Jack caught his breath, looked again at the transom that didn't seem all that far away, and mapped out a self-rescue plan.

On his back, eight hand-over-hand tugs against the trailing line should move him ahead twenty feet, he reasoned. At the end of each cycle, to secure his position, he would tie a knot then rest fifteen minutes. Jack figured it would require ten tugging cycles to get to the swim ladder. *I'll be back on board in four hours*, well after dark, but he was already getting tired and had to manage his dwindling energy reserves.

"Okay, let's do it!" he yelled out loud as if to psyche himself into victory.

Jack reached over his head and grabbed the slimy trailing line with his good left hand. When he couldn't get a firm grip he scraped the algae free with his injured right hand. A lightning bolt of pain ripped up his arm, but rather than recoil he clamped down and used the pain for motivation. Now he was able to pull himself forward until his pulling left hand reached the top of his head, but no further.

"What now, damnit?"

*So try something else*, he heard Susan say.

Jack took a deep breath and rolled over to his stomach. The water rushing past his face made it harder to breathe. In this new position he would need more energy and more time, both of them precious quantities in short supply. But his leverage was now better and he delighted in his progress.

Five tugs and a breath . . . five tugs and a breath.

Each cycle was a new experiment in agony.

After five full cycles of pulling, tugging, tying-off, flopping over and resting, success was within his grasp. All Jack needed was a big second half.

Five tugs and a breath . . . five tugs and a breath . . . He felt a bump. The trailing line jerked. Another bump and another jerk. Then the line went slack. Jack's heart raced as he slipped down the slippery line. Now his pain was gone, but was replaced with panic. He felt the next knot run up against his hand and he clamped down as hard as he could. In an instant that knot disappeared from his grasp.

Another slippery slide.

Another knot undone.

Another loss.

Jack groped for some hold on the elusive slimy lifeline. Hand-over-hand, grasp-after-grasp, Jack slid farther astern with each slipping knot. He screamed aloud until he could scream no more. Jack had finally failed his final exam in knot tying. Now he was back at the end of the line, secured only by Susan's reliable bowline still looped around his wrist.

Jack turned over to skim along on his back and noticed the yellow sun sinking toward the horizon. He smelled the heavy evening air. He heard the woeful sound of his limp body surfing through the water. He felt the melancholy of failure.

Panic had passed. Now, Jack Grayson was euphoric in his distress, as he became one with the line and the lake.

\* \* \*

The *Cindy Jane* glided up against her berth in the Vermilion River just as the sun nipped at the western horizon. The tumultuous events of the day had left the passengers and crew of the old fishing boat weary and looking for asylum.

In spite of Maggie's carefully crafted report to the young Lt(jg) in command of the Coast Guard vessel, she had nevertheless been asked a hundred questions right out of the book. Beginning with Maggie Wicks and Ernie Beckett, everyone had been examined and cross-examined by the seriously intense young officer. She made penciled notes and tape recorded every fact, every exaggeration, and every lie.

Maggie had admired the brash confidence of the young woman in whom she saw a reflection of herself—an old reflection that now had been tarnished by the fabrication and painful falsification of an official accident report. At the end of an hour of thorough report-taking on board the gleaming white Coast Guard ship, the *Cindy Jane* and her eclectic company had been released for a twilight cruise back home.

As the two duty-tested women parted company, the zealous young officer assured Maggie that she would find her sunken ship by nightfall. Maggie could not bring herself to offer any encouragement for, what she knew would be, a futile search.

\* \* \*

It was not surprising that the group was exasperated at the sight of Ednamae Bradley standing on the dock alongside Chief Jay Richards. From the looks of things on the dock, it would be a long night of representations and misrepresentations. Maggie was the first to reach the dock and the waiting Ednamae. Their tearful embrace told a greater tale of tragedy than an hour of tape recorded creative non-fiction.

"What happened out there?" asked Ednamae as Ernie Beckett and Meagan Palmer approached.

"It's a long story," said Ernie guardedly. "Everything that could go wrong . . . did."

Paddy Delaney and Teddy were the last to leave the fishing boat. As Teddy turned back to snap a lock on the boat's large sliding door, Chief Richards gestured to Paddy with a look of dread that was not lost on Meagan Palmer. Neither was Paddy's subtly negative nod lost.

"I thought Jack and Will were out with you," declared Ednamae as she craned her neck around the dockside area.

"Nope," said Teddy. "Haven't seen them."

"Mr. Parks," said the Chief. "Do you know where I might find either of them?"

"Why?"

"There's been a bit of a situation over at GrayDays I'm afraid."

"Situation?" growled Ernie. "Stop talkin' like a cop, Jay Bird, and tell us what the hell's goin' on here."

The young chief was accustomed to this kind of dismissal from Vermilion's old guard, so he politely and casually sloughed it off. "There was a B&E . . . sorry . . . a burglary over at the store. A man is dead."

"The hell you say? Who is it?"

"No one seems to know him," said Jay.

"We're running his prints now, but I was hoping that Jack Grayson or Will Daysart might be able to shed some light on what happened over there and who the DOA . . . who the dead man is."

"When did this happen?" asked Meagan.

"The Coroner put the time of death at somewhere between 3:00 a.m. and 6:00 this morning."

"After Will and Jack were gone," said Meagan quickly, as all heads turned.

"How do you know that?" asked the Chief.

"Because Will and I saw Jack off on a yacht delivery at midnight, then I drove Will to the airport."

"You folks keep some pretty strange hours," said the Chief with unmistakable sarcasm. "Can anyone verify what you've just told me?"

"Sure. Jack and Will."

"Well, that's the problem then isn't it?" Before Meagan could utter a response her uncle sidled up beside her. "Good evening Chief. I'm Paddy Delaney, Dr. Palmer's uncle. I'm sure my niece's statement needs no further verification now does it?"

Everyone's eyes were now fixed solidly on Paddy and the young policeman.

"I'm sorry. Of course you're right," said the Chief. "Where can I reach the two of them?"

"Will Daysart is in California," said Meagan. "I don't know with whom." She sensed that her eyes had betrayed her, but she pushed on. "When he calls me later tonight I'll have him get in touch with you."

"And what about Mr. Grayson?"

"He's delivering a sailing yacht to Canada. He should be arriving there late tomorrow afternoon and I expect him to phone me," said Meagan. "I'll ask him to call you as well."

"I think you're going to have to do better than that," said Jay, unable to contain his substantial instincts.

"I don't think so chief," interjected Paddy. "She's told you what she knows. Now, do you have a photograph of this burglar?" Chief Richards reached into the inside breast pocket of his navy blue blazer and pulled out a small Polaroid photo.

Paddy snatched the picture from his beefy hand and studied it quietly for a few moments. "I know this man," Paddy said.

"Where from?"

"He came into my office a few weeks ago. Said he needed work."

"What kind of work?"

"Nothing I would be interested in. Turns out he was some small-time second-story man from Baltimore."

"Did he give you a name?"

"Shamus something." Paddy scratched his head theatrically. "Ah yes. I have it. Shamus O'Reilly, he said. "Probably bogus."

"You think?" said Jay finding it difficult to contain his, distress at being made a fool of. But he knew Paddy Delaney's ways all too well, and knew that as the little dockside drama was winding down, he would get nothing more. For whatever reason and to whatever purpose, Paddy Delaney had decreed the death of the little Irishman to be of no interest. He had been summarily consigned to the *unsolved* drawer of the small homicide cabinet, and Chief of Police Jay Richards was sure that no one would ever find a reason to open it again.

"Now, if that's about it," said Paddy. "I think we could all use something to eat."

The spellbound remnant of the Captain's Quarters now broke out of their collective trance, no longer able to separate fact from fiction.

"Good idea," said Ednamae. "I'll cook. Would you like to join us Jay?" After another subtle nod from Paddy, and the young Chief declined. "Okay then," said Ednamae. "Let's all adjourn to the parlor. You can freshen up there while I rustle up a survivor's feast."

Meagan Palmer joined the soaked, matted and wrinkled crowd that trekked up the hill toward West Liberty Avenue and, from her position at the end of the pack, came to a sullen realization. Even though a little soap and water would wash the musty lake from their bodies, it would take something more severe to purge their souls of this day's grievous losses and multitude sins

*     *     *

"You can't be serious," shouted Jimmy Grayson across the small elevated table in the little San Francisco International Airport bar.

"I'm just telling you what happened," said Will, quietly trying to dampen the attention they were getting from the other customers.

"That my father killed a man?" Jimmy's attempt at whispering seemed frustrated by his bulging eyes and pulsating neck arteries.

"It all happened so fast. It was dark, and I was in the showroom, and Paddy's captain grabbed me and then your father came down the stairs and yelled something and there was some kind of loud noise and the guy spun around and then he fell down and Jack came running up and the next thing I know the guy was dead." Will took a deep breath and a long drink of his beer. "I didn't lay a hand on the guy. Your dad must have done something to him."

"It sounds like he saved your ass Will." Jimmy leaned across the small table and grabbed Will's arm. "I can't believe you ran out on him. What the hell were you thinking?"

"I didn't run out, Jimmy. Jack told me what to do, then said he was going to sail Aunt Susan's ketch across the lake to Canada."

"Are you sure this guy, Paddy's captain or whoever he was . . . are you sure he was dead?"

"I know he didn't move the whole time I was there." Will was shaking badly again. "After your dad left with the boat, and I was alone with that body I just freaked out. I knew I was next, that Paddy Delaney was going to get me." He finished off his beer and held up the empty to signal for a refill. "I thought you would understand. I didn't know what else to do." Now Will was sobbing and the bar patrons were straining to hear their conversation.

"Forget the beer," said Jimmy. "Let's get out of here." Jimmy grabbed Will's overnight bag and ushered him out of the bar. Instead of turning toward the front entrance however, Jimmy guided Will back toward the ticket counters.

"Where are we going?" asked Will through his tears.

"Home."

"Where?"

"We're going home to Vermilion."

"But why? It's too dangerous there."

"Yeah, and it sounds like my dad is the one who's got his neck stuck out the farthest."

"I thought you two were on the outs," said Will. "That you weren't speaking."

"But we have been crying," said Jimmy. "I think it's time for me to heed the message on my mother's tombstone that I fought so hard to keep in front of my father's face."

At that moment Jimmy Grayson felt like his mother was speaking to him from her grave. *Bitterest tears . . . deeds undone . . . words left unsaid.*

# CHAPTER 33

"This is the Conneaut Marine Operator calling the sailing yacht *SEAQUESTOR*." Familiar words, Jack realized, but distant and faint. "This is the Conneaut Marine Operator calling the sailing yacht *SEAQUESTOR* on VHF channel 16." Jack reached out for the radio, but something held him back. He was tangled in lines . . . standing. No, he was floating . . . bobbing like a cork in a wash tub. *Did I fall asleep again?* He shook his head and wiped his eyes.

Slowly things began to emerge in the eerie calm twilight—familiar things, depressing things, horrid things. He looked ahead and saw the ketch creeping through the water, its giant white sails flapping lazily and expectantly. Ahead of him the sky was already a dark blue black shade that lightened progressively above his head until it turned a shade of light blue behind him to the west. Lake Erie had the glassy sheen of a tray of Jell-O, and there was not a sound except for the slow rhythmic flap . . . flap . . . flapping of the sails.

Although he was wearing no lifejacket, Jack bobbed effortlessly in the calm water. Air bubbles trapped in his pants and windbreaker buoyed his body, if not his spirits. Now he focused on the radio message. Someone was trying to call him through the Great Lakes radio telephone network, he realized. Who?

Jack glanced at his watch and saw that it was a few minutes past nine o'clock. He had been in the water for nearly two and a half hours of a voyage that already had consumed more than sixteen hours. Maggie and Ernie would have charted his progress and would certainly have expected him to check in by now through the nearest radio telephone operator.

"*SEAQUESTOR . . . SEAQUESTOR . . . SEAQUESTOR . . .* Conneaut Marine Operator on Channel 16." The radio speaker mounted near the cockpit steering pedestal was beckoning him, yet he felt helpless to answer its call. Then it hit him.

He was barely moving through the water. The sails were flapping. The lake was calm. Ahead of him the long trailing line was serpentine as it lay near the surface. There was the barest hint of light reflecting off the folded swim ladder on the transom of the yacht—the ladder that had been so elusive. The Jell-O-like glassiness of the lake was a certain harbinger of a weather change, he knew. It was the proverbial "calm before the storm." It was also serendipity—a providential chance of survival.

"Pull, damnit!" he yelled out as he seized the slimy line that held his past at one end, and his future at the other. One hopeful handful of Dacron after another brought Jack closer to the swim ladder that would be his escape, if not his salvation. Forget the knots. *Forget the drill,* he thought. *Just get back on the boat.*

With each tug at the line Jack felt his energy surge, his pain subside, and his spirits rise. Seventy marathon yards of trailing line had now evolved into a short fifty-yard dash. Jack counted out the scant yards of line as he fought off the ominous p6unding of his heart and heaving of his chest. "39 . . . 40 . . . 41 . . . halfway home . . ."

The words on the nearly obscure transom loomed larger with each tug. Slower now, "63 . . . 64 . . . 65 . . ."

He swallowed a mouthful of musty water.

He paused, retched and caught his breath.

He choked and coughed and rubbed his eyes.

He wondered if this was all some kind of cruel joke played on him by nature, as the home-port "Vermilion" seemed more distant now than ever. *It's the darkness,* he told himself. Now he pulled more desperately.

"78 . . . 79 . . . 80."

He felt energized and empowered as the lake water rushed past his forehead and foamed down his outstretched legs.

Pulling, slipping, tugging, sliding.

*One final burst,* he told himself as he counted "98 . . . 99 . . . 100."

Jack closed his eyes, gritted his teeth and with the final number called out, he instinctively reached ahead for the swim ladder, like a swimmer reaches out for the pool wall at the end of a racing lap.

Nothing but water.

He paused . . . actually he tried to pause . . . to stop the rush of adrenalin . . . to get his bearings. But he could not.

Jack sped through the water again as the slimy trailing line came to a stop at the bowline around his wrist. He watched *Vermilion* dissolve into the darkness ahead of him. Now he was defeated. Now he lay motionless against the surge of water again pulling him eastward at the end of his line. Above him in the star-studded sky, Orion, the hunter, looked down on him—poised for one final shot from his bow.

*        *        *

"So why isn't he answering his radio telephone?" asked Paddy impatiently.

"I don't know," said Meagan. "I suppose there are lots of reasons."

"Let me hear a few."

Meagan looked across the table to the experts, hoping they would come to her rescue and assuage her uncle's mounting doubt.

"The most logical reason is that he's simply out of range," offered Maggie. "Even though he can certainly hear the call from just about anywhere in the eastern lake, his own radio may not have the power for him to transmit a response."

"I thought your fishing boat captain just told us, from checking his G.P.S. receiver, that he was right on the usual course line from Vermilion to Port Colborne." He took a long sip of Ednamae's famous blend coffee. "Even if he is going a little slower than you expected."

Teddy jumped in. "You're right, Mr. Delaney. He's about twenty miles offshore from the Conneaut radio station. Over water that should be a long, but decent connection." He could tell he wasn't helping as he looked around the table. "Of course local conditions vary so much that sometimes you can't transmit more than five miles."

"Maybe you're all lying to me about him and what he's doing, huh?" Paddy searched the eyes around the table for some clue, some sign of fear or weakness. "Maybe he's already put into port somewhere with my money. Maybe he's going to run."

"He said he was going to make the delivery," said Meagan. "Jack Grayson's word is better than yours."

"Really princess?" Paddy leaned back in his chair and crossed his arms over his barrel-like chest. "How do you know he agreed to deliver my boat and cash to Canada?"

"Will told me when he called and left his message on my machine."

"Little piss ant," said Paddy. "He's weak and can't be trusted. It's his fault that you're all involved in this little humanitarian mission of mine."

"It's not his fault that your captain didn't show up," said Meagan leaning over the table.

"Oh, he showed up all right princess."

"What do you mean?"

"The man in the picture," smiled Paddy.

"The corpse laid out on the floor of GrayDays Marine . . ."

"No . . . No . . . It can't be," said Ednamae.

"That man was my captain," said Paddy leaning forward in his chair. "And from the looks of things one of your two missing friends killed him."

Paddy was obviously enjoying this little game, a fact that was alternatively annoying and frightening Meagan Palmer. "Now we know that young Will Daysart isn't capable of rolling his own joint, so that leaves us with your Jack Grayson." Now Paddy zeroed in on his niece. "So princess, how much faith are you ready to put in the word of a fugitive killer with a cool 10 million in his pocket?"

"You've got it all wrong," said Meagan. "Jack wouldn't do such a thing and Will couldn't."

"Look at the facts," said Paddy. "Will lives in the house and had made arrangements with me to deliver the boat to my captain. Jack Grayson owns part of the marina, and used to own the boat I bought, so we know he was there too. Now, according to you, he's sailing my boat across the lake." Paddy paused a moment to let his story gel. "So, Jack present. Will present. Captain present. Captain dead. Will missing. Jack missing." Paddy shuffled forward in his seat and folded his hands in front of him. "You don't have to be Sherlock Holmes to connect the dots."

"Which leaves us where? Mr. Delaney?" asked Ednamae.

"I don't care about another dead sea captain. All I want is my money returned to me so I can make some other arrangements."

"As soon as we can contact Jack, I'm sure he'll agree," said Ednamae.

"You better make damned sure he does," said Paddy as he stood up from the table.

"Right now he has my money, but I'm holding the trump card." He turned toward the front doorway. "You have until 8:00 a.m. tomorrow morning to make me a believer. After that I can assure you that the police investigation into my captain's death will take another turn."

The Captain's Quarters were speechless as Paddy ambled through the door and disappeared. They were so focused on him that no one noticed the whispered conversation between Teddy Bear and Ernie Beckett. Nor did they see the small package Ernie slipped into his pocket.

*     *     *

Captain Ernie Beckett stood on the old Victorian front porch of Ednamae's house like he had stood on the quarterdeck of his full-rigged sailing ships—the master of all he surveyed. He had followed Paddy Delaney out the door and reached the head of the wooden steps just as Paddy walked through the wrought-iron gate to the quiet dark sidewalk.

"Paddy Delaney," the old captain bellowed. He watched the old gangster stop dead in his tracks and turn back to the house. "Do you think I might have a word with you?"

"You're not still mad about that little dunking are you?"

"I don't get mad," said Ernie.

"You understand then that it was only business."

"I understand that you're an evil murderin' sonofabitch that answers to nothin' but intimidation."

"I haven't met the person yet who can back me off," said Paddy returning to the foot of the porch stairs.

"You mean until tonight?"

"What? You want a piece of me?"

"I've already carved off a chunk," said Ernie as he reached into his pocket and flipped a small package down to the Walleye Pike he had just snared in his net.

"So what's this?" Paddy asked holding the small plastic case up to the distant dim streetlight.

"Your confession."

"How the hell did you manage this?" scowled Paddy.

"That's not important. But since we're playin' cards I thought I might as well give you a hint of what's in my hand." Ernie opened his stance as though he were bracing against the roll of a ship's deck, then crossed his burly arms across his chest.

"You'll get your money back when it suits us, so you can save your threats for the college kids you exploit."

"Just don't push me too far," said Paddy. "I cut you all a little slack because of my niece. Don't take it as a sign that I'm weak or soft." Paddy tucked the small tape cassette into his shirt pocket. "I'll wait for your call."

Ernie started toward the door, but after two steps he stopped and turned back to Paddy, who was still standing at the foot of the steps.

"And as for the 'dunking' as you called it," Ernie pointed his knurled finger at Paddy and sighted down through it like a gun sight. "I haven't forgotten that you left me for dead."

Meagan Palmer met Ernie at the doorway and put an arm around his shoulder. "What happened out there?"

"I cashed in one of our chips and bought us a little time."

"Don't underestimate him, Ernie," said Meagan softly. "He's a heartless and devious killer."

"You don't have to remind me," said Ernie with a smile on his sunburned face. "My skivvies are still wet."

"You sailor's are a strange lot."

"That's why all the girls love us," chuckled Ernie.

"Which brings us to the big question of the night. Where *is* Jack?"

\*     \*     \*

Jack was drowning, ever so slowly, at the end of a lifeline meant to save his life.

The process of drowning terrified him far more than the fact of death itself. Soon after Susan's death he had become obsessed with death by drowning. At a time when he should have been rejoicing his wife's life he instead immersed himself in the macabre task of trying to define the details of her death.

With each new medical book he studied, and with every account he read of seamen who had witnessed the drowning of their shipmates he choked more, gasped more, and blamed himself more for Susan's tragic end.

For Jack, by far the most chilling account of the drowning process came, paradoxically, from Sebastian Junger's *Perfect Storm* that Susan had given him. What he learned from that book bothered him then, and horrified him now.

A drowning victim lives every excruciating detail of his death: the deep painful resolve not to inhale followed by the unbearable urge to breathe as the level of carbon dioxide grows in the bloodstream. Next there is the agony of that first gulp of water that so often precipitates diaphragm spasms and lungs that burn and convulse against the unnatural onslaught of alien water. Then the larynx constricts so painfully that the brain screams out "BREATHE, GASP, COUGH, LIVE!"

The victim's entire body, his circulatory system, respiratory system, muscle system, and all of his five senses are in turmoil and extreme distress. The entire organism searches desperately for some means of survival. Finally, a dose of adrenalin is released and in a matter of seconds all of the agony subsides. All of the victim's bodily functions shut down—except the brain. And that is the final insult. In the last euphoric moments the victim becomes a spectator at his own demise.

After Susan's death Jack again read Junger's account of drowning, and became more depressed and reclusive with each recollection of the journalist's words. Depression grew into fear, and that fear had kept him off the lake for a year. The depression of his life coupled with his deep immersion into death, seemed to spawn the nightmares from which he could find no respite. Captain Grayson had unwittingly, or not, created for himself a world where he was drowning every minute of his life, without ever being near the water.

Now, as Jack floated in the water behind Susan's ketch, he recounted every detail he had read and studied about drowning. He hoped that Susan had not been conscious in her final moments. He strained to believe that the autopsy report Meagan revealed to him had been correct—that his shipmate had been knocked out by the crush of the steel boom against her head—that she had been somehow spared a front row seat to the grotesque spectacle of her own death.

Jack knew he would not be so fortunate. His luck had long since run out. There would be no fatal blow to his head; no quick killing arrow from Orion's bow. These would not be Jack's denouement. After being dragged through a hundred miles of open water, his death would be a textbook classic.

Now, Jack studied the bright luminescent dial of his Rolex Submariner. It was a quarter past midnight. He had spent almost six hours at the end of the line.

It was Sunday, and Jack Grayson said his prayers.

# CHAPTER 34

Meagan could hardly believe her eyes as; she squinted at the glowing red 4:12 A.M. on her bedside clock radio. She had slept the *rest of the dead* for more than five hours since retiring with the notion that she would toss and turn until dawn. But the heady events of the day had taken their toll, and her worn-out body, if not her mind, had seized the opportunity to rejuvenate itself.

When she realized she had been awakened by the soft electronic ringing of her cordless phone, she abruptly swung her feet out of bed and was at once fully alert and standing. Now she was back in the game, as if she had not missed a minute of action. "Dr. Meagan Palmer here."

"Dr. Palmer, I'm sorry to be calling you at this hour but I wanted to give you a few minutes warning."

"Warning?" she asked as she strained to put a face and name to the vaguely familiar voice on the other end of the line. "What kind of warning?"

"No . . . no . . . bad choice of words I guess. It's Jimmy Grayson."

"Jimmy? My God . . . Jimmy . . . where are you?"

"I'm at Cleveland-Hopkins Airport."

"Okay . . . yes. Jimmy, just wait at the lower deck baggage claim area and I'll come in to pick you up."

"That won't be necessary Dr. Palmer . . ."

"Please Jimmy, call me Meagan."

"Yeah, well . . . I just flew in from San Francisco with Will."

"Thank God he's with you. Is he all right?"

"Yeah, he's okay. Anyway we're coming back to Vermilion and I need to talk to you as soon as possible."

"Well, how are you going to get here?"

"Will left my dad's Range Rover in long-term parking so we'll drive ourselves out. We should be there by five . . . if that's okay?"

"Yes, of course, Jimmy. I'll make some breakfast and get you up to speed on what has happened."

"Great. Then we'll see you later. Oh, wait a minute. Have you heard anything from my dad?"

"Not yet, but I'm expecting a call any time now."

"Okay, thanks. Bye."

As the phone clicked and restarted its dial tone, Meagan stood still for a moment pondering the little lie that had so easily slipped out. Although she had hoped, with all her heart, for a phone call from Jack, something deep within her portended otherwise. Something, Meagan's muse told her, was dreadfully and fearfully wrong.

The unexpected return of Jack's long lost son from California convinced her even more that this would be a day of drastic and painful change. Meagan's toes and fingers tingled as her heart rate began to build. *Ready on the right, ready on the left, ready on the firing line*, she thought. *It's show time.*

*     *     *

Jack was wandering through the old Vermilion cemetery he had visited dozens of times and yet he was somehow lost. He was searching for something or someone but could not put a name to it.

The setting was familiar and yet there was a morbid unfamiliarity with the names and dates he saw as he swirled from the outer fringes of the cemetery toward some vortex that pulled him ever so slowly inward. Names and dates. Mothers and fathers. Dear sisters and brothers. Beloved aunts and uncles. Grandmother. Grandpa. Ever so slowly, swirling inward. Daughter, son, infant child. Swirling, drifting, sinking. Dearest husband . . . beloved wife.

Swirling faster now.

Bitterest tears.

Deeds undone

You killed her.

Swirl, swirl.

Words unsaid.

Teardrops shed.

I'll never forgive you.

Whirl, sink, swirl . . . beloved wife . . .

Jack's head broke the surface of the rushing water and he coughed and retched to expel the fluid from his throat and lungs. There was nothingness—a void.

No . . . sound, the sound of a waterfall, the rush of a brook. Now, out of the darkness, a pinpoint of light . . . stars . . . planets . . . the universe unfolding above his head. As his breathing steadied and his eyes cleared, he could see clearly above him written on the great black board of the heavens . . .

*The bitterest tears shed over graves are for deeds*
*left undone and words left unsaid.*

Susan's epitaph was staring down at him, taunting and provoking him to . . . what?

"What do you want from me Susan?" Jack yelled into the darkness that enveloped him like a shroud. Then as quickly as the words were lost into the night he knew the answer. He had always known the answer. But instinct and expectation are powerful forces, driven by some deep primal force that defies and obscures reason and decency.

Susan had always known that Jack's instinctive images of what a son was supposed to be and do would destroy even their natural biological bond. She knew this just as surely as his faulty expectations would exile his son to a more embracing and encouraging place. And for what? Jack thought as he looked upwards. Ten hours in the water had shown him how trivial such issues were in the larger scheme of life.

*Live and let live,* was a concept Jack could never fathom, but definitely now tried to comprehend. Jack began to weep as he thought how, even Susan's final message to him—her most desperate plea—had become just another grotesque battleground between father and son.

*Why didn't I listen? Why didn't I take the challenge? Why couldn't I bring myself to accept my son, even at his mother's grave?* These thoughts and recriminations swirled around Jack's mind like the water that rushed past his weary soaked body.

Now he wished upon a billion stars that he had taken his young son in his arms and shared the love of a father; the irrational and unconditional love that makes the world a garden rather than a garage, a place of nourishment and growth rather than stagnation and decay. Why, Jack asked himself, is it that we come to these epiphanies so late in life and so often in dire and hopeless straights? Jack still had no answers but he did have a mounting and well-defined package of regrets as he was dragged slowly through his own purgatory. It was time to end it all, Jack realized, and yet the horrid fear of death by drowning now limited his options.

He reached for the bowline knot at his numb chafed wrist. If I can get this line around my neck, he told himself, it will end quickly. The thought of suicide had always repulsed Jack, but now asphyxiation seemed better than drowning. He reached forward and grabbed an arms-length of line, then another and another—enough for a noose. Jack paused for a gallows moment to catch his breath before proceeding to choke himself to death. The irony of it all brought the hint of a smile to his tortured face.

He decided that a quick death by strangulation is quick, isn't it? It would forever chase away the demons that had haunted him for a year, wouldn't it? Susan's beckoning ghost will finally be vanquished, wouldn't she? There would be no more broken promises, no more failed attempts. Jack's circle of failure would be complete.

With his free left hand Jack tied a long slip knot, the only knot that he had finally perfected, then tested it quickly to ensure that once placed around his neck it would actually slip, and quickly cinch up around his throat to snuff out his life. His tired left arm was shaking badly as he dropped the knotted loop over his head and down to his protruding collar bone. He took a final and long deep breath of the cool night air and relished its sweet mystery, as he always had during this hour at sea. A star twinkled brightly . . . a comet streaked through the heavens on its way to . . . "where?" Jack asked himself.

Now he had the answer: Nowhere, anywhere, somewhere. It didn't matter.

The comet just kept on going.

"No damnit!" Jack bellowed out into the night sky. "I'm not going out like this! I still have deeds to do and words to say!" Then he thought back to a musing of the wise old Bosun Cooney from his first sea-year voyage as a cadet. "Gadget," he said in his thick Rastafarian accent . . .

*Wheen ure powrless and driftin' out to sea, jus hold on like hail and wet fo da tide to turn.*

Jack slipped the noose from his neck, clamped down on the slimy knot with both hands, and held on like hell.

*       *       *

Meagan stood in her foyer and put an unexpected bear hug on Will Daysart. "Will, you look like crap, but I'm glad to see you anyway."

"I've just made two cross-country flights in twenty-four hours," he said wondering where Dr. Palmer's public display of affection had come from. "In non-smoking, to boot."

"You're still in non-smoking sport," she shot back with the mien of a D.E.A. agent. "Nice tan Jimmy," Meagan said as she held out her hand, astonished at the thin gaunt look the young man presented.

"Can't an old, old friend get a hug too?" he asked as he opened his arms.

"Like father, like son," she smiled as she reeled him in and planted Greek-style kisses on each cheek.

"You may be the only person in Vermilion who ever said that."

"Well then," she said as she ushered the boys into her ample country kitchen. "Let's hope it catches on."

Meagan sent the travelers off to freshen up while she laid on the breakfast buffet. While she worked with the fluffy vegetable omelets, shredded fried potatoes, Canadian bacon and fresh fruit bowl, she pondered the unlikely encounter that had just begun. She was not surprised at Will's skid row appearance—she had seen it before. He obviously had not had much sleep, was noticeably grubby from long term confinement with the masses, had obviously been considerably drunk, and was now in some uncomfortable state of transition to sobriety.

As Meagan reached for the Tabasco sauce she would add to the pitcher of Virgin Mary's headed in Will's direction, she lamented the pathetic vulnerability and insecurity that had continued to grow in this young man who, even now, was so easily led. Given the horrendous events of the last few days, Meagan was at a loss to understand why Will had returned, just as she had been surprised to learn that Will would be staying in San Francisco with Jimmy Grayson, so too was she now confounded by Jimmy's apparent power to bring him back into the conflict. She had no idea that the two childhood friends were still so close.

But Meagan's biggest surprise was the sudden return of Jimmy Grayson. She still had a vivid recollection, as most of Vermilion did, of Jimmy's outburst at Susan's graveside and his angry vow never to return. What forces drew him home now, she wondered? He could not have known how badly the group's master plan for Paddy Delaney had gone. Not even Will knew the swath of drama, agony, intrigue, near-death, and nagging uncertainty he had left behind only twenty-four hours earlier.

Jimmy's smile and beaming bright eyes had always been his greatest assets, ones that immediately endeared him to everyone he encountered. Well, almost everyone, she recalled as she tried to expel the ugly thought. Meagan was pleased that his infectious friendliness had survived his nearly three-year exile in California. She was concerned, though, about his significant weight loss and, what seemed to her to be, thinning of his formerly lush hair—at least from what she could quickly discern as she took in his new close cropped hairstyle. All little things, she told herself.

The big news was that she now had an opportunity to help with the emotional reunification of an estranged father and son. Although she now had a vested interest in this case study she believed that, just like the regression therapy she had practiced on Jack, she was the best person in the world to handle the mission.

By 5:30 a.m. the boys had ravaged the breakfast buffet while Meagan nibbled at the fruit bowl, sipped coffee, and recounted the saga of the previous day on the lake. Meagan and Jimmy had endured a fractured and confused story from Will about what happened to Paddy's captain. After intense cross-examination from Jimmy, it became clear to Will, at least as clear as anything became to him, that Jack had not killed the slight Irishman, unless he was to be charged with scaring him to death with a tactical shout from the stairway.

"So where's my father?" asked Jimmy. "I mean, I know he's out on the lake in mom's boat, but has anyone spoken to him since he left port?"

"Not that I know of," said Meagan pushing away her third cup of coffee. "We tried late last night through the radio telephone system, but he was not answering."

"Which means what exactly?"

Meagan cast a pleading look toward Will.

"It could be lots of things," said Will. "His VHF radio doesn't have much range. He's probably just too far out in the lake."

"Is that it?"

"Well, he could have blown a fuse, his batteries could have died."

"He could be unconscious or dead," said Jimmy.

"Let's not jump to conclusions," said Meagan quickly. "It may just be that he doesn't want to talk to anyone. He's made that crossing a dozen times, and you know how he is when he gets on the water."

"Oh yes Meagan," said Jimmy mischievously. "I know *how* he is. What I want to know now is *where* he is."

"Did Teddy's G.P.S. beacons work?" asked Will.

"What's a G.P.S.?" asked Jimmy.

"That's what saved us when *Aphrodite* sank," said Meagan.

"Okay then," said Will suddenly showing some signs of life. "Let's call him and get a G.P.S. fix on Jack's progress."

"If Jack is still heading for Port Colborne at least we'll know that he's all right," said Meagan. "Why don't you go into my study and give Teddy a wake-up call, Will? Jimmy can help me clean up this mess."

Will's sweaty odor had not even followed him out of the room when Meagan pounced on Jimmy. "How long have you known?"

"Almost two years," Jimmy replied coolly.

"Does your father know?"

"Of course not."

"Why haven't you told him?"

"It would have killed him," said Jimmy.

"What's killing him Jimmy . . . ," said Meagan as she reached for the young man's clammy hand. ". . . is being alone. You probably can't even imagine the torment your father has endured since you left home and your mother died."

"Oh, I think I could tell you a thing or two about torment, Dr. Palmer,"

The tears began to well up in his pale eyes. "Our family has always thrived on it. It's a house specialty."

"So when are you going to change the menu?"

"Why me?" he cried out. "Why does it have to be me?'"

"It's the nature of things Jimmy. We always look to the young to renew us, inspire us, and yes, even scold us once in a while." Meagan squeezed his hand again and poured herself into his misty eyes. "If you go and talk to him, he'll listen."

"That's what mother always said."

"You mean Susan knew that you had contracted AIDS?"

"I called her from the doctor's office, when I got the diagnosis."

"How did she take it?"

"She begged me to come home, to get treatment at the Cleveland Clinic, and to get things straight with my dad."

"And?"

"And I couldn't face it," said Jimmy. I couldn't face my disease. I couldn't face the reality that Raul ran out on me when I told him, and I couldn't face admitting to my father that I had ended up just as he had predicted—a failure."

"Is that why Susan flew out to San Francisco last summer?"

"Yeah, she tried to bring me back." Jimmy's eyes were now gushing and his hand was quivering. "It was an awful scene. You know the last image I have of my mother alive was her crying? That's what the whole tombstone thing was about. When I read it in her will, I knew she had written it for me. She wanted to remind me that I had some unfinished family business before I . . ." Jimmy choked a little. "Before I die."

"And that's why you came home?"

"When Will told me what was happening, something told me it was the right time."

"How bad is your condition?"

"The cocktails don't seem to be doing much."

"Night sweats?"

"Yes."

"How much weight have you lost?"

"Thirty pounds in the last six months."

"Lesions? Discoloration? Coughing?"

"Not yet," said Jimmy. "But my physician warned that it's on the way."

"Oh Jimmy," Meagan said as she leaned over to hug him.

"For some reason it doesn't look like you two are having that much fun said Will as he bounded back into the room.

"Just talking about the old days," said Meagan.

"And the new I'll bet." Will sat down at the table and plunked down a note pad he had scribbled upon.

"You told her, didn't you old buddy?" Jimmy did not answer as he dabbed the tears from his eyes with a paper napkin.

"So you knew?" asked Meagan.

"Yep."

"For how long?"

"About three months," said Will. "That's when this whole thing started."

"What do you mean?"

"Jimmy made me an offer. He said if I would come out to San Francisco and help him out until he died, he would give me his condo, a job, and a new life.

"That's when he started skimming cash from Paddy Delaney," said Jimmy. "He thought I needed money for doctors and drugs."

Meagan was incredulous as she spun around to look at Will, who just shrugged his shoulders and smiled. She slumped down in her seat and thought about the irony of it all. "Son of a gun," she said. "So this has all been about Jimmy from the start?"

"He's a real inspiration isn't he?"

"No one will believe this," said Meagan joining in the communal laughter that freed them at last from their self-pity. "It's like one of these pot-boilers you read during a day at the beach."

"I didn't come back home to write my life's story," said Jimmy. "Nobody needs to hear any of this. Now, did you find out where my father is?"

"Okay," said Will as he stared down at the notepad. "I'll spare you the navigation coordinates. According to Teddy Bear, Jack is about twenty-two miles west south west of Long Point. He's above his normal course line a few miles, but it still looks like he's sailing toward Port Colborne."

"How long will it take him to get there?" asked Jimmy.

"That's what we don't know," said Will.

"It seems like he should have been past Long Point by now and we have no idea how fast he's going, or whether he's under power or sail."

"What's the earliest he can make port?"

Jimmy doodled a few moments on the pad then looked up. "I think he's looking at a good ten hours—maybe four o'clock this afternoon."

"Let's go meet him then," said Meagan.

"That's a long ass drive," said Will.

"We'd better get on the road."

"Or into the air," said Meagan.

"What? How?"

"I have my plane out at the airstrip." Meagan saw the look of shock in the young men's eyes. "What can I say? Business has been good."

"In this town," said Will. "That doesn't surprise me."

# CHAPTER 35

Now Jack Grayson was ready to live. He just wasn't sure how to make it happen. He had faced down his darkest moments and in doing so found a new vitality that had been absent for many months. He had no idea what his destiny would be, but he was now certain that he had one—somewhere other than as another hapless victim of Lake Erie.

Jack's instincts told him his luck had to change. Murphy's Law had played itself out hours ago and now he found himself humming one of his favorite tunes from West Side Story:

> *Could it be? Yes it could.*
> *Something's comin', something good.*
> *If I can wait . . . .*
> *I don't know what it is . . . but it is . . .*
> *Gonna be great!*

Jack's mind was again on Meagan Palmer. He missed her, and the cocky self-assurance she wore like perfume. He wondered how the "great master plan" had gone and how they had all reacted to his final voyage decision. He thought about the radio telephone call he had heard during the brief calm. He imagined Maggie and Ernie mounting a grand rescue effort; and then realized they had no reason to think he was in trouble.

The boat was making steady progress toward Port Colborne, a fact they would know if Teddy's G.P.S. beacon was still working on the mast head. For a loony surreal moment he envisioned himself being dragged into Port Colborne harbor, where *SEAQUESTOR* would finally crash herself up against the pier and he would swim the last few strokes to dry land.

Then he got real. Even if his navigation and course setting had been so precise as to run the yacht into port, he would not be alive to see it happen. There was no way he could survive another ten hours, or more, at the end of the line.

Something had to give, he thought. There had to be some way out of this mess that he wasn't seeing. A passing ship with a good lookout.

Another calm that would allow him to dog paddle back on board, with the little strength that remained in his body. *Aphrodite* running up out of the western horizon with a *bone in her teeth*, homing in on his beacon. "Come on," he yelled out loud. "Cut me a little slack here!"

Jack dozed off for a few more moments then opened his eyes again to see the faint yellow dawn emerging ahead of him in the east. Nice color change, he thought. Now he changed his position—rolled over to his right so that he could body surf along and see the shadowy silhouette of his boat ahead of him.

*What's that?*

He wiped the water from his eyes with his free hand and squinted ahead to the left of the slowly sailing yacht. A flicker? A twinkling star? Certainly not a star on the dim horizon. Another flicker . . . now another . . . and another.

Someone or something is signaling he realized. Jack checked his Rolex. Its large luminescent dial cast a familiar and reassuring glow. 6:05 a.m.

The navigator in Jack's mind came back to life and began to plot his position. It was a dead-reckoning nightmare, he knew, like one of those awful and unlikely scenarios that so often showed up on the Coast Guard license exams for Merchant Marine officers.

The yacht's average speed over the last eleven hours was unknown, and from Jack's position in the water the yacht seemed to be going faster than she actually was. He would make an allowance for his unique perspective then *guesstimate* an average speed—maybe 4.5 knots, he thought. The computer in his waterlogged head was turning, albeit very slowly. Jack labored over the equation, then turned again and searched out the rhythmically flashing light. He sighted up the lifeline and took an estimated bearing—maybe sixty degrees off the port bow, he guessed.

Jack turned over to his back again and stared upward into the slowly brightening sky. *Let's see . . . 4.5 knots . . . eleven hours . . . sixty degrees off to port . . . fifty miles . . . maybe a little slip to the north . . .*

Then it sunk in.

The Long Point, Ontario lighthouse.

Jack Grayson had held on.

The tide had turned.

*   *   *

"I've never seen the sun rise over the lake from this angle," yelled Jimmy Grayson over the surprisingly loud engine noise of the small airplane. "I wish I could paint it."

"Some things are better left in their natural state, "shouted Meagan Palmer from the left seat of her fast little Piper Comanche. "Sometimes the things we can't easily define, we treasure all the more."

"Touché," said Jimmy.

"I think we must be getting close to his position," said Will from the back seat of the four-place aircraft.

"Can you call Teddy for a good position fix on him?"

"I can try," said the pilot. Meagan had pushed her gleaming blue and white Comanche along the same course line Jack would have steered from Vermilion to Port Colborne. At its top speed of 165 m.p.h. they would easily overtake the yacht in an hour's flying time, and hope to make a visual confirmation that everything was all right, if not actually speak to Jack on the radio.

"*Cindy Jane* . . . *Cindy Jane* . . . *Cindy Jane* . . . this is Piper aircraft Tango Echo one four zero niner Whiskey . . . do you read me?"

"Meagan, I have you five by five," said Teddy.

"Roger that Teddy. Can you give me your latest fix on Jack's boat? We're coming into his area right now."

As Will heard the longitude and latitude coordinates crackle through his radio headset, he jotted them down and then plotted the position on one of Meagan's aircraft navigation charts.

"Thank you Teddy, we should have a visual in the next few minutes."

"Give him a wave for all of us back here."

"We can do that," said Meagan. "Tango Echo 1 4 9 0 Whiskey, out."

\*       \*       \*

Sunrise couldn't have come soon enough for Jack. The long cool night had taken its toll on his body after being fully immersed at more than twenty degrees below his normal temperature for over twelve hours. When he lifted his arm out of the water for a quick time check—6:55 a.m.—and felt the cold nip of early morning air that had shifted to the north, he began quivering.

For the first time in half a day, Jack was feeling cold to the bone—the kind of cold you feel when you step out of a heated pool into a chilly autumn day. Now, even the water seemed cooler than before, something Jack correctly attributed to his relative proximity to the Canadian shore that had cooled over night.

The quivers turned to shivers, which turned to quakes and then uncontrollable agonizing shakes. *Not now*, Jack thought to himself. *Not after all I've been through! Not this close to land!*

Jack couldn't see any land from his vantage point low in the water, but he knew it was nearby—the Long Point light house was ample evidence of that. Jack was urging the yellow sun upward with its warm life-giving rays, when the leg cramps set in.

First one calf, then the other.

Now down into the arch of his left foot.

He tried desperately to massage the knotted muscles with his one free hand, but each time he bent his knee to bring the calf into range, the pain intensified until it finally brought tears to his eyes.

Now the cramp rose into Jack's thigh muscle.

Next, into his abdomen.

His guts felt like they were being twisted out, when he lost consciousness. *Not now for chrissakes! Not now . . .*

\*     \*     \*

"There she is!" yelled Jimmy over the drone of the engine. "Just off to the left a little."

"Okay . . . right," said Meagan. "I have her."

Meagan eased the wheel slightly to port and pushed the Comanche into a slow descent. The plane flashed across *SEAQUESTOR* from the stern and Jimmy lost sight of her for a moment—his sight blocked by the low white wing. "She looks like she's sailing okay, but I didn't see dad up on deck."

"I'll make another pass from the bow this time," said Meagan enthusiastically. "I'm sure he heard our engine and will be back up on deck for our next pass." Meagan adjusted her flaps for additional lift as she slowed her airspeed to 80 m.p.h.—just short of a stall.

"Here she comes," said Jimmy like a kid at a circus parade.

"I don't like the sight of that big jib loose and luffing," said Meagan. "It's not like Jack."

"I didn't see him, did you?" asked Jimmy as the Comanche lumbered over the yacht.

"No," said Meagan. "I'm going to fly past him from the north this time. We'll have him in sight a little longer." As Meagan dipped the port side wing of the Comanche down toward the brightening lake and began her slow banked turn to the north, Jimmy turned to Will in the back seat of the compact four-place cabin.

"Hand me those binoculars." By the time Meagan had finished her turn and began her low run on a course perpendicular to that of' the yacht, Jimmy already had this eyes locked into the binocular eyepieces.

Meagan steadied her course, eased her airspeed back to 65 m.p.h.—almost gliding, rather than flying—and adjusted her trim tabs slightly to maintain a low and slow level surveillance run. Now she pointed the Comanche right on the yacht's bow. "Are you focused on her, Jimmy?"

"Yeah, I don't see any movement at all."

"Does anything look out of place?"

"Everything looks normal," said Jimmy. "The self-steering vane is engaged, the cabin hatchway is open, and the deck is clear. It looks like the jib halyard and sheet are both loose."

"That's weird," said Will from the back seat. "Maybe he's down below sleeping. It's still pretty early and he might have stayed up all night."

"Are you sure there's nothing else?" Meagan yelled as she throttled up and passed directly over the mainmast, watching the giant white sail flutter in the prop wash.

"Not a thing that I can . . ."

"Wait a minute," yelled Will with his neck craning out the starboard side window toward the west. It looks like he's towing something a couple hundred feet astern."

"That's just mom's old emergency trailing line," Jimmy said dismissively.

"Maybe not," said Meagan as she pulled the throttle out, eased back on the steering yoke and put the Piper into a steep right climbing bank. "Let's take a closer look." As Meagan settled the plane back on another north-south run, now astern of *SEAQUESTOR*, she glanced over at Jimmy. "See if you can make out what's at the end of that trailing line."

Meagan ratcheted in full flaps, readjusted her trim tabs, and throttled back until it felt like the Comanche had stopped in mid-air. The noise level inside the cabin lessened as the tension rose. Jimmy seemed to crawl into the glasses. He squinted and focused, then squinted and focused, and squinted again . . .

"My God! Oh, my God!"

"What is it?" yelled Will.

"Dad's at the end of that line."

"Is he . . . is he moving?" asked Meagan.

Squint and focus . . . inhale and exhale . . . refocus . . . lower . . . closer . . . "Oh my God . . . no . . . no," panted Jimmy as the small plane strafed Jack. "He's not moving. I think he's dead. My God . . ." Jimmy was sobbing. "We're too late."

"Drop me in," yelled Will as Meagan pushed the plane into another climbing bank to the right.

"What did you say?" yelled Meagan twisting her head to the rear."

"Get as low as you can and drop me in," he screamed. "I can get him out. Come on Meagan just do it."

"You're out of your mind," she shouted. "The drop would kill you."

"I don't think so . . ."

"And what would you do if you survived the fall," Meagan interrupted. "I have no life jackets in here and you have no way of getting on the boat."

"Just turn around and drop me you bitch," Will yelled.

"I'm going to pretend you didn't say that to me," said Meagan forcefully. "Now just sit there and shut up."

"Do something Meagan," sobbed Jimmy. "Please do something."

"I have an idea," Meagan told him as she pushed the steering yoke forward.

The Comanche arced in the sky like it had just crossed over some unseen hump in the road. Meagan banked again to the right and pushed the small plane so low over the Long Point lighthouse that she could see the reflection of the plane in the glass. She banked low to the left and studied the small dirt and gravel road leading to the remote point. Now she banked back to the right, cranked in full flaps and dropped her landing gear.

"Cinch up your seat belts real tight," she said. "We're going to land."

"What?" said Will.

"Where?"

"On that small access road."

"Then what?"

"If we don't crash, I'll let you in on it," she said. "Now put your head down to your knees and say a little prayer." As Meagan eased the little plane down toward the road, she was reminded of the controlled crash experience that Navy aircraft carrier pilots describe. Her stomach now felt queasy as she sighted down her north to south glide path. A small wooden bridge over a sand bar precluded a long slow descent just like the tall lighthouse made an approach from the north impossible. The access road, which was no more than a hundred yards long from the bridge to the lighthouse, was no more than twenty feet wide and was built up so that the sides sloped off at a gentle but lethal angle.

A flag flying from a high pole near the lighthouse reassured Meagan that the light northerly wind, which would make her speed over the ground faster than she would have preferred, at least would not blow her off course. Meagan dropped in quickly over the little bridge and as soon as she lost sight of it over the propeller made her decision. It's now or never, she thought as she immediately cut her power then reversed the pitch on her prop.

"Hold on boys," she yelled out. "This is it."

The air-braking power of the reverse pitched propeller seemed to stop the Comanche in dead air as it plummeted to the ground. At the moment of impact, Meagan pulled out the throttle to full power and struggled to ease, rather than jam, the brake pressure onto the tiny aircraft wheels. An immense cloud of dust and sand occluded the windshield for a moment that seemed to consume a lifetime.

When the dust settled, Meagan's eyes opened widely at the sight of the lighthouse looming up much too quickly. The controlled crash was perfectly aligned but too fast. They were nearing the end of the road.

Will screamed from the backseat, "We're gonna hit it!"

Jimmy threw his hands up over his face.

Meagan jerked the steering yoke to the right and jammed her foot into the right rudder pedal, as she rammed the power throttle into the instrument panel to stop the engine. A swirl of sand and dust leaped up from the access road and all of a sudden Meagan felt like Dorothy trapped inside the tornado that swept her over the rainbow.

Then there was silence.

"Is everyone okay;" said Meagan.

"You play rough," said Will from the rear.

"I thought you knew," whispered Meagan.

"I'm sorry about what I said up there," said Will. "I just lost my head I guess. I didn't mean it. I hope you know that."

"I've been called worse." Meagan touched Jimmy's still shaking arm. "Are you okay old sport?"

"I don't know. That was the worst experience of my life."

"Well shake it off," said Meagan as she opened the cabin door. "Because no matter how bad you feel, I'd guess your Dad is feeling worse."

"Look," said Will. "There's the boat."

Meagan looked past the lighthouse and saw *SEAQUESTOR* sailing easily toward the east as if she had a mind of her own and not a care in the world.

"She looks like she's only about a half mile out," said Jimmy. Can we swim out to her and get on board?"

"We don't have to," said Meagan as she climbed out the door.

*     *     *

The three aviators splashed, pulled, panted and . . . panted, as they plunged the bright yellow plastic paddles over the side of the Avon inflatable dingy.

"I can't believe it," said Will. "You don't carry life jackets but you have an inflatable boat on board?"

"If I go in the water," said Meagan pausing to catch her breath. "I want to be comfortable."

The rescue crew was already less than three hundred yards from *SEAQUESTOR*. The same northerly breeze that had plagued the Piper's descent now helped to push the Avon raft toward its target.

"We have to keep pointing ahead of her," said Will. "Or she's going to sail past us."

"Good point," said Meagan. "We're only going to get one shot at this."

"Okay, what's the plan?" asked a very winded Jimmy Grayson.

"Captain . . ." said Will. "You make the call."

Will's attempted deference pleased Meagan as she quickly assessed the situation. "Okay, here's how we'll do it." Meagan stopped paddling long enough to layout the plan. "Jimmy, since you're the tallest you have to get our bow line attached to the yacht. Without a connection, she'll leave us behind."

"I can do that."

"I'll get on board and throw off all the sheets," said Meagan. "That will stop her progress. While I'm doing that you boys need to attach this raft to the trailing line and start easing your way back to Jack. You need to be sure you get to him before the yacht stops, or he'll sink."

Meagan looked ahead and noted that they were only about fifty yards from *SEAQUESTOR*. She was surprised at how large she seemed from the low vantage point in the water. "Do either of you know C.P.R.?"

"I do," said Jimmy.

"Good. When you reach your dad, get him into the raft right away. I'll start winching you back so you can concentrate on Jack." She grabbed Jimmy by the arm. "Time is very important. Every second counts, so as soon as he's in the raft, if he's not conscious I want you to shake him and slap his face. I want you to talk to him even if you think he can't hear you." Meagan could see that she was scaring the young man, but she too was frightened so she pressed on. "If your dad is not breathing . . . do you know how to check for his vital signs?"

"Yes, yes. I remember."

"Okay, if he's breathing just elevate his feet, throw some clothes over him and continue to try to awaken him." She paused. "Have you got that?"

"Yes . . . but what if . . ."

"If he's not breathing, make sure his airway is clear and start C.P.R. Just keep it going until I get you back on board the ketch."

"It's time to rock and roll," yelled Will.

Meagan looked up and gasped at the sight of the slightly heeled ketch bearing down on them. Just as it seemed they were going to be crushed under the bow, Jimmy leaped to his feet, stepped up on the side of the raft with the thin bow line in hand and jabbed . . . jabbed . . . jabbed . . . clipped the line to one of the ketch's lifeline stanchions.

"Hold on!" yelled Will as the immense hull streamed past them. "We're in for a rough . . ."

The momentum of the large yacht moving through the water, against the tiny rubber raft, jerked the raft ahead violently and slammed the passengers back into the stern of the little craft. "Radical!" Will bellowed. "Anybody up for a game of Twister?"

"Maybe later," said Megan as she pried herself away from the kids. "Let's ease this thing back to the swim ladder."

In another thirty seconds the crew had secured the little raft astern of the large yacht and Meagan had climbed on board. Will had looped a small line around the trailing line and back to a large metal mooring ring on the side of the raft. "Say when."

Meagan quickly surveyed the cockpit, oriented herself to the configuration of sheets, halyards and winches, and then checked to see that the key was in the ignition for the Perkins diesel. It was. "Okay," she yelled over the stern. "Go!"

Will quickly produced the Swiss army knife his father had given him years ago, and handed it forward to Jimmy. A nod later and Jimmy had cut the bow line away. With a swoosh . . . the little raft slid down the trailing line toward Jack Grayson.

Meagan Palmer quickly threw off the mainsheet from the starboard main winch and watched the large boom swing alee causing the huge sail to spill its powering wind and begin to luff in the diminishing morning breeze. Now she cast off the mizzen sheet and glanced astern to satisfy herself that it was paying out smoothly. Without wind power, the drag of small life raft with the three men inside had nearly stopped the yacht dead in the water. Meagan switched on the engine ignition and heard the big diesel engine grumble to life, and turned her attention to the activity in the life raft. Jack was now inside the raft with his head inside and both feet propped up on the side. Will covered him with the shirts and windbreakers the boys had just stripped off, while Jimmy hunched over his father's face.

"Come on dad, wake up," Jimmy pleaded as he shook Jack's limp shoulders. "Dad . . . Dad . . . it's Jimmy, Dad . . ." A light open handed slap on his face. "Come on Dad, you're okay now . . . you're safe . . ." Another slap, harder this time.

"Is he breathing?" asked Will.

"I think so," said Jimmy. "But I'm not sure."

Will dipped his hand into the water and shook off the excess, then put the back of his hand against Jack's lips. "I can feel his breath . . . but it's really slight."

"Are you sure?"

"Yeah . . . I 'm sure . . . he's alive, Jimmy." Will rocked back on his knees and ran his hands through his wet hair. "Can you feel a pulse?"

Jimmy slipped two fingers against Jack's jugular vein and waited . . . and waited . . . and . . . "Yes . . . yes. I can feel it, but it's really weak and fast."

Will stood up and turned back toward *SEAQUESTOR*. He saw Meagan at the stern rail and yelled out, "He's alive . . . he's alive! Pull us in," as he waved his right hand above his head in a rapid circular pattern.

The small raft jerked in the water as Meagan cranked the slack out of the trailing line with the big stainless steel self tailing winch. Will lost his balance and fell heavily across Jack's body length. He was now whisker to whisker with the man who had nearly given up his life for his god son. Rather than pull himself up immediately he collapsed on Jack and cuddled him like a child clutches a torn rag doll. Will's tears dropped on Jack's cheeks and ran in tiny streams to his wrinkled neck.

"If this is what death is like, please bring me back to life," Jack muttered softly.

The large barreled chest under his was now heaving mightily as Will pushed himself upward and looked down into Jack's blood shot weary eyes. "Welcome back," said Will. "We were beginning to worry about you."

"It took you long enough," said Jack while he blinked his eyes and moved his head from side to side.

"Yeah, well it's a hellava long trip from California to Long Point."

"What?"

"It's a long story," said Will. "I brought someone to see you."

Jack now craned his neck and lifted his shoulders. A shadow fell over his eyes and they opened widely. "Jimmy? My God, Jimmy . . . what are you . . . how did you get out here?"

"Dad, are you all right?"

"I've felt better," Jack said as he struggled to sit up in the wet floppy bottom of the raft. "No, I take that back. I've never felt better in my life." He reached out for Jimmy and they embraced. "You came for me . . . my God, you came back for me." His tears seemed to wring all of the musty lake water out of his soaked body.

"Somehow I imagined that our reunion would be different," said Jimmy. "But this works for me."

Jack felt the familiar thud of the rubber raft bumping up against the side of a boat. He released Jimmy and looked ahead at the gleaming steel swim ladder that had been so elusive for the last twelve hours.

"Hey, do you think a girl can get a hand up here?" yelled Meagan from the deck. "This is an awfully big boat for one person."

"Tell me about it," said Jack as his eyes melted into hers. Suddenly Jack felt not only saved but redeemed. As he looked around the miraculous assembly he knew that he had indeed come home. His faith had been tested and he had endured. Through God's providence and his will he had been reunited with his family, one he would never again take for granted.

*What God has joined together* . . . , he thought with a smile.

# CHAPTER 36

The old Chelsea mantle clock had just rung out the last of its eight bells when Ednamae Bradley strolled into the parlor with a huge grin on her face. "They found him," she announced. "And they're on their way back to Vermilion right now."

"Who did you talk to?" asked Maggie Wicks.

"It was Meagan. She called me on her cell phone."

"From where?" asked Teddy Bear Parks, obviously astounded. "My last G.P.S. fix had SEAQUESTOR abeam of Long Point." He scanned the room and fixed his eyes on Ernie Beckett. "There's nothing out there except a sand bar and a light house. No docks, no airstrip . . . nothing but water and sand."

"Well I don't know anything about all of that," said the gran-dame. "All she said was that they had to fish Jack out of the lake and that she was bringing him home in her airplane."

"The hell you say," grumbled Ernie. "Fished him outta the lake?" The old man shook his head. "You must have got somethin' wrong there dear."

"Maybe so," she bubbled. "The main thing is that Meagan and Jack are flying home, and the boys are bringing Susan's boat back to Vermilion."

"What boys?" said Maggie.

"Jimmy Grayson and Will Daysart."

"I thought they were in California?" said Maggie.

"Not anymore I guess," said Ednamae now questioning her own recollection.

"Could anything else possibly happen that we're not expecting?" asked Maggie with a facetious tone in her voice.

"I think we've had our share of surprises for this mission," said Teddy. "Shouldn't we call Mr. Delaney and let him know that his cash is on the way?"

"Let him stew a little longer," spat Ernie. "They won't have the boat back here until early tomorrow mornin' anyway."

"There's something going on here that I can't quite get a fix on," said Maggie.

"Like what?" growled Ernie.

"I just have a feeling," said Maggie. "There's something in the wind."

*     *     *

The wind had shifted around to the south and with the centerboard raised, *SEAQUESTOR* had drifted into the shallow five feet of water just fifty yards north of the lighthouse point. Jack was already in the rubber raft, rested and ready to get off the lake after drying out, taking some nourishment and telling the saga of his ordeal for nearly an hour.

Meagan turned to Jimmy Grayson and handed him her portable cell phone. "We'll be back in Vermilion in ninety minutes," she said. "By 10:00 a.m. we'll be at my house. I want you to keep in touch. Just press #1 on the speed dialer."

"I promise," said Jimmy. "We owe you Meagan."

"Yes you do," she said. "And I fully intend to collect."

"Anything . . . anything at all," he said almost tearfully.

Meagan took him by the shoulders and stared deep into his sky blue eyes. "I want you to consider getting rid of it."

"What? Get rid of what?"

"You know what I'm talking about," she insisted. "Just do the right thing, Jimmy."

Will Daysart bounded up beside the pair. "The wind is stiffening a little," he said. "If we don't get out of here soon we're going to end up on the beach."

"Right . . . okay," said Meagan as she climbed over the stern rail to the swim ladder. "Bon voyage."

"I'll call you later dad," Jimmy yelled as the little raft drifted downwind toward the sandy beach.

"Just take your time," Jack hollered. "And be careful!"

Jimmy heard the loud rumble of the yacht's diesel engine as Will backed away from the beach and into the safety and security of deep water. It was a strange paradox, Jimmy thought as they backed into the lake, that the same deep water that had so threatened his father's life would now become their haven. And what of the mysterious Meagan Palmer, he thought? As he watched Meagan beach the rubber raft, Jimmy wondered again about the meaning of her intriguing vague request. *Get rid of what?* He asked himself. *My Dad's problems? The money on the boat? The boat itself?* Once again there seemed to be a ton of issues needing resolution, and he struggled to understand why they had come home to roost with him. After all, he already had gotten what he had come back for—reconciliation with his dad.

The reunion had been understandably stressful and shorter than he had hoped, yet he could never have orchestrated a scenario that would have put him in the unique position he found himself today. He had always before looked to his father to rescue him from his difficulties. Now the tables had turned, and the timing could not have been better. So much of what he had planned to say had been left unsaid in the hysteria of the last few hours, but Jimmy knew there would be time to work out the details as his mother's yacht tacked to starboard toward Vermilion.

*   *   *

"When we were on our little picnic out at Marblehead and I suggested that one day I would take you on a trip to the Long Point lighthouse," said Jack weakly. "This isn't quite what I had in mind."

"Somehow I think this little junket will be far more memorable than just driving out here in a rented Jeep with a couple of boxed lunches in the back seat," said Meagan. "So just lay back and enjoy the view."

Meagan was thigh-deep in lake water as she fought to pull the raft over the sandy shoals so that Jack would be able to step out onto dry land. He had already spent enough time in Lake Erie, she figured, and was still weak enough that she didn't want to risk him slogging up the soft shelf to the beach.

"That is undoubtedly the ugliest lighthouse I've ever seen," said Meagan as she finally beached the heavy laden raft and then paused for a moment to catch her breath and fix her wet wind blown hair.

"I'll grant you that it's not much to look at from here," said Jack. "But from my vantage point early this morning it was absolutely spectacular."

The Long Point light was one of the modern automated low maintenance metal frame light towers that began to populate the reefs, shoals, points, harbors and promontories around the Great Lakes since the budget crisis days of the mid-seventies. What these lights lacked in charisma, they made up for in utility and economy. And this new technology was there for Jack when he needed it, just as countless lighthouses had led scores of seamen to safety in the past.

"I'm sure you're right Jack. Still, it's a shame that we've lost so many of the great old lighthouses to these grotesque little things," Meagan sighed as she looked up at the erector set style structure. "That's why I want to visit them all before it's too late."

"I hope you'll bring me along," said Jack. "I'm definitely more interested than before."

"We'll see," she said with a coquettish wink. "But first we have to get out of here alive."

Meagan and Jack made their way up the beach and dragged the raft behind them. After they reached the plane, then deflated and stowed the life raft, Jack leaned against the tail section of the Piper Comanche and watched Meagan poke, prod, smooth, and shake the undercarriage of her plane. There was a rough, almost tomboyish demeanor about this delightfully complex woman; one that stood now in stark contrast to the elegant enchantress he had dined with at *Chez Francois* only a few weeks ago. He wondered if he would ever fully comprehend the magnificence of this creature. He hoped not.

Now Jack looked to the north and saw the tiny bridge just a hundred yards up the rough dirt road. "I can't imagine how you landed this thing here in one piece."

"And I'm happy to report that she *is* in one piece," said Meagan standing up alongside the low wing. "It *was* a little hairy coming in over that bridge. You should have seen the look on Jimmy's face. I guess I'm not surprised that the boys jumped at the change to sail back rather than fly."

"And that from two kids who claim to hate sailing. You must have put a pretty good scare into them."

"Now it's your turn."

"Actually, I was hoping that maybe we could call a cab."

Meagan looked up at the Canadian maple leaf flag standing out in the ever-stiffening north wind, and then sighted down the road toward the bridge. "Somebody will have to fly this plane out of here," said Meagan as she tossed some dry grass into the air and studied its fall. "It's my plane. I put her here, and I'll get her out." She turned to Jack and looked hard into his tired eyes. "Of course I'll understand if don't want to come. I'm sure the Canadian Mounties will be happy to ride in and pick you up."

"You're not leaving me much of a choice," said Jack. "But since I don't ride very well and just discovered that this is *not* my day to die, I guess I'll ride with you."

"Jack, I wouldn't try this without that north wind blowing down on us, but it will give me an extra twenty knots of air speed right away."

"Let's do it then. We have people to see and things to do back home."

"Really?

What do *we* have in mind?"

"Patience. I want it to be a surprise."

\*     \*     \*

Meagan and Jack sat in the cramped cockpit of the Comanche and stared down the narrow road at the tiny wooden bridge. The engine was idling smoothly and neither of them attempted to speak above its rumbling anticipation. Jack glanced over at Meagan, in the pilot's seat, and felt like he was watching daredevil Robbie Knieval on his motorcycle searching for the proverbial *moment of truth.*

Jack knew that when that moment arrived and the brakes were released, there would be no turning back, no second chance, and no second guessing. Now Meagan checked her wheel brakes and reached forward to the red throttle knob. She studied her instrument panel gauges as she eased the throttle out and watched the r.p.m.'s rise slowly.

Jack suddenly found the vibration and noise unsettling as the small plane sat coiled in the starting blocks. When he looked again at Meagan, however, and realized that she was fully one with her flying machine, he was reassured.

The tone and level of the engine noise changed as Meagan adjusted her variable pitch propeller so that it would grab the air in front of it hungrily. The Comanche was now in a frenzied dance and Jack felt on the brink of internal combustion. Meagan released the brakes and Jack felt an amusement park ride exhilaration as he was pushed back into his seat. The thrill grew exponentially with the approach of the bridge.

The throttle was now at full thrust and the rough engine vibration had been replaced with the bumping, scraping, jarring passage of airplane tires crunching across the rough little access road. Jack reflexively pulled his seat belt tighter while, at the same time, resigning himself to his captivity by the smooth powerful well-tuned roar of the engine. It was indeed a glorious machine, Jack thought. Now the road vibration lessened as the plane gathered speed and began to generate lift over its sleek and shimmering airfoils. Roaring . . . thumping . . . humming . . . acceleration. Jack was gaining more confidence as he admired Meagan's rapt attention to duty, despite the sight of her white knuckles glued to the steering wheel.

"Brace yourself, Jack!"

"I'm bracing, I'm bracing!"

Meagan eased the steering yoke back and Jack felt the nose of the airplane rise hopefully. A sputter . . . a misfire . . . "We're in trouble!"

*No shit*, Jack thought. He couldn't see the bridge ahead, and then suddenly it was back in the windshield. He turned to Meagan and watched her calmly pull back on the steering yoke, while quickly pumping the red throttle knob. Nose up . . . bridge gone . . . nose down . . . a bump . . . a thud . . . a deep pitched roar now turning higher and stronger . . . a cloud of dust and sand . . . blue sky.

"Oh . . . oh . . . oh," panted Jack. "What happened back there?" As soon as he spoke he knew that he had asked a stupid question, yet somehow it seemed just the right occasion for stupidity.

"I think I just invented a new aeronautical maneuver," Meagan said trying to catch her own breath as the plane soared into the northern Canadian sky.

"What?"

"I leap-frogged that bridge back there," she said with a smile. "I thought we were going in until the nose popped up and I felt us bump down on the other side."

"You can write an article. Call it the Palmer Plunger. Up . . . down . . . and back up again." Jack laughed. "You'll be famous like Amelia Earhardt."

"I'd rather just be obscure and alive."

# CHAPTER 37

"I never imagined—not in my wildest hallucinations—that I would be sitting out on this lake, on this boat, ever again in my life," said Jimmy from the cushioned comfort of the long and low cockpit seat as *SEAQUESTOR* sailed easily toward the west.

"That's a good one," said Will from the seat on the other side. "I'm the one with the hallucinations. I'll bet you never had a hit of weed in your life."

"I never thought I needed it. Life was weird enough as it was . . . as it is." Jimmy sat upright and looked over at Will. "Look at all the crap that's happened in the last two days. I think even you would have to classify it as a bad trip."

"True enough," said Will. "But some good did finally come out of it all."

"I assume you're not talking about three dead people, Ernie nearly being drowned, my father being dragged like live bait across the lake, or the sinking of Maggie's boat?"

"No. I'm talking about the fact that you and your father are speaking to each other again."

"We haven't said much yet," said Jimmy. "And I still don't know where it will all lead."

"At least you have him back in your life, and you have the time to make something happen." Will looked out over the lake and seemed lost. "I don't have that option."

"It seems like my options ate getting a little short too."

"Bullshit.

You're going to beat this thing."

"Really?

Then why did you agree to come out to California to live with me?"

"I didn't really come to San Francisco as much as I ran to it," said Jimmy. "I needed you to help me more than the other way around."

"Fair enough," said Jimmy.

"But where do we go from here?"

"What do you mean?"

"Well, you're suddenly back in the middle of your problems with Paddy Delaney, and I've got a new set of issues with my father and my AIDS treatment."

"I don't have a clue, and I don't really want to think about it. I think we should just kick back and enjoy the cruise. I have this feeling that everything will work itself out if we stop trying so hard to manipulate everyone."

"That's pretty deep thinking for a dope head," Jimmy said with a sarcastic smile on his face.

"Yeah, I guess I lost my head there for a minute." Will grabbed an empty wine bottle off the steering pedestal table and pitched it into the lake. "Let's have another bottle of the Irishman's wine and see what else pops into our heads."

"I think you're on to something there. While you're down below I'm going to call Ednamae and update her.

*     *     *

Ednamae Bradley was relieved to hear the phone ring. It was already a quarter past ten and, with no news since the early morning call from Meagan, the little group had fallen into a malaise that she didn't enjoy being around.

"It must be one of the boys," she said as she approached the ringing telephone. "Meagan said they would check in with us."

"Tell them to do whatever they have to do to get that boat back here before sunrise tomorrow," said Ernie. "If they have to run the engine all day and night, that's okay."

"What's the point?" asked Maggie as Ednamae picked up the telephone handset. "We still don't know what we're up against do we?"

"Yes we do," said Maggie, now clearly tired of the intrigue. "We give Paddy his cash and his boat, and go on with our lives."

"Do you really think it's goin' to be that easy?" asked Ernie.

"What else does he have to gain?"

"Victory . . . control . . . one-upsmanship . . . evil . . ."

"My God Ernie," said Maggie. "When did you become so paranoid and suspicious?"

"Probably when I was floatin' around in the lake, not knowin' whether I'd live to see another sunrise. Besides, you remember Meagan Palmer tellin' us we couldn't trust him."

"Okay . . . okay. I get your drift."

Ednamae Bradley walked up between the two squabblers and looked down at Ernie. "He wants to talk to you."

"Who wants to talk to me?

"Paddy Delaney."

The old captain stood up from his chair and looked around the room, finally resting his sharp clear eyes on Maggie. "Looks like our trustin' Irish friend is gettin' a little impatient."

"Just take the call Ernie," said Maggie. "And try not to aggravate him."

Ernie made his way across the parlor and picked up the phone. "Ernie Beckett here. What can I do for you?"

"I want my money," whispered Paddy.

"An' we all want you to have it."

"Where is it?"

"It ain't "here.""

"Do you know where it is?"

"Not exactly."

"See if you can make an educated guess."

"Somewhere out in the lake."

"What?" growled Paddy. "What did you say?"

"I said it's somewhere out on the lake. We found the boat this mornin' and got it turned around, headed back to Vermilion."

"Where is she now?"

"Who? Meagan?"

"No, the boat."

"We don't know," said Ernie. "We still haven't been able to talk to them."

"Them who?" said Paddy. "I thought you said Jack Grayson was alone on my boat with my money."

"Slip o' the tongue, I guess."

"God Damnit Beckett, don't play games with me. I want my money, and I want it now!"

"Listen to me Paddy," said Ernie in his most brusque sea captain's tone. "You're the one who put the money on a sailboat. You're the one who sent it off to Canada. You're the one who decided it should come back to Vermilion, so the game is of your own makin'." Ernie paused for a reaction that did not come. "When the boat arrives back here I'll let you know."

"And when will that be exactly?"

"No way of knowin' exactly. 'Bout this time tomorrow if the wind's blowin' right."

"All right then. I'll be on the door step of that ice cream parlor at 10:30 a.m. Don't disappoint me." Deep exhale of toxic smoke. "Just because my niece saved her old uncle doesn't mean that I owe any of the rest of you anything. Do you understand me?"

"Yeah Paddy. I think I got that."

Captain Beckett had just put the handset back on the telephone when it rang again. He picked it up before the second ring pulsed through. "What? Did you forget somethin'?" said Ernie.

"Yeah. I guess I forgot how much I dislike sailboats."

"What the hell? Who is this?

"Will Daysart. Captain Will Daysart.

Who were you expecting? The devil?"

"Somethin' like that," said Ernie.

"Where are you boys?"

"Fifteen miles west southwest of the Long Point light on a course of 246 degrees magnetic."

"Okay," said Ernie.

"How fast are you going?"

"We're making about six knots on a nice broad reach."

"Are you carrying that gennaker up for'd?"

"No," said Will. "I don't even remember if it's on board. But it doesn't really matter, since I don't think Jimmy and I can handle it."

"Okay. You're right. So's the number one jenny up?"

"Yeah, I think so," said Will. "It's the same jib that Jack was trying to change when he went into the water."

"Listen to me now Will," said the old man. "You boys have to have that boat back here before sunrise—that means before five o'clock so you can slip in before it gets too light."

"Why?

What's going on now?"

"That's not important. Just work on increasing your speed. You're going to have to make about seven and a half knots all the way in. If the wind picks up or shifts more to the west and you're able to make speed under sail then do it. Otherwise run the engine," Ernie said then hesitated. "Just make sure you get in here and get docked before anyone can see you."

"It's Paddy again isn't it?"

"Yes, but don't worry about that now. Just get in here."

"Don't worry?" shot back Will. "He tried to kill you and wants to kill me and I'm not supposed to worry?"

"He's going to be here at 10:30 tomorrow morning to pick up his cash."

"So give it to him and get him out of our lives," said Will.

"I don't trust him. He's got something up his sleeve and I don't think the money is going to satisfy him."

"What about the tape recordings?"

"We have them," said Ernie. "I even gave him a copy to try to back him off."

"And?"

"And he didn't back off," said Ernie. "Now he's back on the phone threatening again. I don't know what he's plannin' but I get the feeling it ain't gonna be pretty."

"So what are we going to do?" asked Will.

"We're gonna buy ourselves a little time. Maybe when we're all back together again we can figure somethin' out."

"Jack and Meagan should be back soon; maybe they'll know what to do."

"Don't worry Will," said Ernie. "We'll come up with something by the time you get here."

"Yeah, right. That's what we told Angie Mariano."

Ernie could feel the blood drain from his face at the sting of Will's, frightfully accurate, remark. He strained to find the right words for the young man—words that would comfort and encourage him—but today the words were not there. "Just make your speed and get in here before first light."

"Okay. I'll call you around supper time." Will pushed the END button on the small phone and turned back to Jimmy who was basking in the morning sun, and seemed to be oblivious to the quagmire they were sailing into.

"What's wrong with you sport?" said Jimmy. "You look like you've just had a bout with the devil."

"Been there and done that," said Will. "And I'm not going to give a repeat performance."

"What in God's name are you talking about? What did they tell you on the phone?"

"We have to do something," said Will shaking off the questions. "We have to find a way to get out of this. There's got to be something we can do to end this nightmare."

*   *   *

Paddy Delaney sat motionless and brooding in his dark smoke-filled office for half an hour after slamming the phone into its cradle. The gritty millstone of evil was turning and grinding ever so slowly in his head. The shear humiliation of being upbraided by that salty old bastard, first outside Ednamae's last night with the flipping of the feeble little tape cassette and then on the telephone this morning, was pushing his psyche toward critical mass. Paddy was not in the mood for head games this morning; not after the calls he had been obliged to make late last night. He could just imagine what they were saying about him back in Dublin.

The common bond that held Paddy close to his mates in the I.R.A. was that they did not countenance defeat. Now, with the two boys and Red Reimer dead, not to mention the delay in shipping the $24 million dollars, Paddy was surely being tried and convicted *in absentia*. He would have to make this right. Someone would have to make a blood sacrifice. But first things first, he reminded himself in his rage. He had to get his hands on the money. First, the mission had to be completed, and then the retribution could rain down from the victor. It was the natural order of war.

He grabbed the phone off the desk and hastily dialed a number recovered from his personal directory. "I need the fastest boat you have . . . a sailboat out on the lake . . . on a course line from Port Colborne to Vermilion . . . I don't know, maybe around Long Point . . . find it, stop it and call me—now!"'"

\*     \*     \*

As Ernie Beckett had predicted, the wind had indeed shifted to the northwest and had increased to about twenty-five knots. *SEAQUESTOR* was now on a close reach, her fastest point of sail, and Jimmy noted that she was moving along at almost eight knots, under the big jib, main and mizzen. Even at this point of sail, a few degrees off the wind, the number one jib was at its limit. If the wind shifted farther to the west or increased very much the sail would have to be replaced with the smaller number two or storm jib—a task Jimmy did not relish in the wake of Jack's horrendous tale.

And now the horror was again residing within Will. Despite Jack's rescue. Despite the recovery of the money. Despite the apparent offer of compromise from Paddy Delaney. Despite the so-called insurance afforded by the tape recordings, and despite the idyllic surroundings, Will was again consumed by a shroud of dread.

"What's come over you?" asked Jimmy.

"Meagan was right. She warned us to stay away from Paddy Delaney. She knew we couldn't beat him, but we thought we were smarter than him." Will slumped back against the cockpit combing and stared blankly at his friend. "Now he's right back out there, madder than hell, and bent on having revenge."

"What are you talking about? How do you know that?"

"It's just a feeling you get when you're up to your ass in alligators," said Will. "I've been there before, up in Paddy's office, when they threatened to pitch me off the roof of the Broadway Building. You just know when the shit's about to hit the fan."

"What did Ernie tell you to do?"

"He wants us to maintain our speed and get this boat and the money back into port before first light."

"Why the rush?"

"I think Paddy's pressing them for the money, and they're trying to buy some time."

"Time for what?"

"I suppose to keep him from killing me, or maybe all of us." Will ran his hand through his scraggly dark hair. "Ernie was trying to be cool, but he sounded like he was in a real panic with no way out."

"Okay . . . then let's find our own way out," said Jimmy.

"Yeah, right. The last few days proved to me that it's not that easy."

"You know," Jimmy said leaning toward Will. "Meagan said something strange to me just before she got into the raft this morning."

"Yeah," Will said dismissively, still lost in his dread.

"Listen to me now," Jimmy said as he grabbed Will's arm. "She said 'I want you to consider getting rid of it.' When I asked her what "It" is, she just said 'Do the right thing.'"

"So what do you think she was talking about?"

"I don't know," said Jimmy. "But it's been on my mind since she got off the boat."

"She must be talking about your problems with your dad. You know, like let it go . . . make peace . . . life is too short, that kind of bullshit."

"That's what I thought at first, but my dad was already in the raft and she knew I wouldn't see him again until we get back to Vermilion."

"So?"

"So I think she wants us to solve this problem with Mr. Delaney ourselves."

"How are we supposed to do that?" asked Will. "We're about as far from the problem as you can get right now."

"Come on Will, think about it." Jimmy was standing now in the slanted cockpit. "We're right on top of the problem. We have the money, and we have the perfect way to get rid of it."

"No you don't," said Will now fully into the discussion. "You're out of your mind if you think I'm going to throw Paddy's money into the lake.

When that happens, I can guarantee you that I'll be next . . . and you won't be far behind."

"Not if it's an accident. Not if we report it to the Coast Guard. Not if we tell them that Paddy Delaney owns the boat, and especially if nobody knows where the money is but us."

"You're crazy, and you're going to get us killed."

"No, my friend. I'm going to set you free," said Jimmy with a broad smile. "And while I'm at it I'm going to set my father free too."

"I'm starting to get interested."

"I think the 'it' Meagan was talking about was this boat. She knows it's the curse that my father cannot seem to let go of. She also knows that the money is the curse that got us all into this mess."

"I'll be damned," said Will. "She is the great manipulator and sooner or later she gets her way. I have to hand it to her. She may be onto something. I suggested to your father a long time ago that he ought to just take this damned boat out on the lake and open the seacock."

"What did he say?"

"He said he'd still know where it was."

"Not this time," said Jimmy. "And neither will Paddy."

"So we sink his boat and his money, then call the Coast Guard and report an accident . . . and . . . what?"

"We fix the location, sink the boat, paddle and drift off in the dingy for a couple of hours, call the Coast Guard on the cell phone and get picked up. The point they pick us up will look like the sinking site and no one but us will ever know where the money is buried."

"And Paddy won't dare touch any of us for fear of the Coast Guard getting involved."

"Well, I don't know about that," said Jimmy. "But at least we can figure out some way to cut a deal with him down the road."

"Once we do this we can't go back," said Will.

"Don't want to," said Jimmy holding out his hand for a handshake. "Now where can we scuttle this thing?"

"There's only one spot."

"And that would be?"

"The deepest hole in the lake," said Will pulling a plastic Lake Erie chart from a cabinet in the steering pedestal. "It's only a few miles north of us, and it's 210 feet deep."

"Let's do it then."

In less than thirty minutes Will had maneuvered the yacht into position and had secured the sails and started the engine. The depth meter bounced between 200 and 220 feet within a quarter mile circle.

Jimmy had busied himself with the preparation of the wooden Dyer dinghy and small British Seagull engine. He had earlier stowed and locked down everything he could find inside the cabin so as to minimize any debris flotsam that might betray the wreck's location. He repacked the Irishman's picnic basket and made sure that the food, water and cell phone were in the dinghy. "I'm ready to go when you are," Jimmy said to Will.

"It's time then," he said as he shut down the engine. In the quiet drifting just north of the deep hole, the boys slipped the loaded dinghy into the water.

Will went below and opened the two sea cocks that allowed water from the lake to rush into the bilges. Will was startled by the ringing of the alarm bell beside the electric power panel. The BILGE ALARM was sounding a loud warning that the ship was in peril as the water level raised above the floor boards of the cabin sole. Will leaned over the counter to the panel and slowly silenced the alarm. A quick look around and he headed for the companionway ladder. Will hesitated, and then retreated to the chart table. Now he was knee deep in water as he pulled the ship's Log Book from the cabinet.

"Let's get off this thing," Jimmy yelled from the deck. Will popped out of the cabin and leaped across the cockpit to the lazarette hatch just forward of the swim ladder leading to the waiting dinghy.

"How about loading on a couple of these new fenders for the trip?"

"It's your life."

Will stood frozen on the lazarette hatch cover fighting with his instincts. Then the lake napped at his feet and freed him from his self-defeating thoughts. Will slipped through the stern railing, climbed down the swim ladder, and stepped into the lightly-bobbing dinghy. He cast off the little stern line and pushed the small boat away from the sinking yacht. Jimmy began rowing from the bench seat in the center of the dinghy as Will sat in the stern seat watching as a page of his autobiography was torn out and thrown into a swirling whirlpool.

When the dinghy had pulled fifty yards away from the yacht, Jimmy stopped rowing and shipped the small wooden oars. Will looked at him and forced a comment, when silence might have been better.

"What's with the tears?"

Jimmy made no attempt to conceal his emotion as he looked through Will to the sight of the mainmast slowly plunging downward. The water was almost at the main spreader and Jimmy watched the Vermilion Yacht Club burgee flutter and flap in the wind like a wounded butterfly. "I feel like I just buried my mother again."

"Yeah, I know what you mean," said Will wiping a tear from his cheek. "Aunt Susan didn't just own that boat, she *was* that boat."

"That's why Meagan knew it had to go," said Jimmy. "For my dad, as long as that symbol lived my mother lived too."

"That should have been a great thing."

"Except for his feeling that he was responsible for her death," said Jimmy as the masthead light and radio antenna refused to drop below the surface. "For him that boat became the haunting ghost of failure, rather than the enduring angel of love."

"For me it was the last thing in my life that represented goodness," said Will. "When I looked out my window and saw her floating at the dock, I remembered all the good times we had. I remembered feeling like I was part of something larger than myself. I remembered what it felt like to be part of a family."

"I kept of picture of all of us in the cockpit eating pizza for the same reason," said Jimmy. "When I looked at it on my desk every day I knew that even though I didn't have much of a future, I had a past—one that was much better than I often wanted to admit."

"Look at her out there Will. It's almost like she's trying to stay alive. My dad told me once that we build all of our machines to be like us, and in doing so we give them life."

"Pretty heavy stuff."

"I'm serious," Will said pointing out toward the east. "Look at that light. It's like it's trying to see us, and tell us something through that antenna." He turned again to face Jimmy. "It's like an animal in a trap looking up at you . . . saying 'I want to live!'"

"Okay then. Maybe that's our challenge for today."

"I think Aunt Susan is trying to reach us . . . to leave us with a final message . . . 'Stay alive! Enjoy life! Live!'" "Sounds like a plan." The boys looked back over the water and she was gone.

# EPILOGUE

Jack Grayson stood in the center of the Wheeler family plot of the Vermilion cemetery, and looked down on the grave of his wife, Susan Wheeler Grayson. The sun was shining, an invigorating northwest breeze cut across the granite garden, birds were chirping, leaves were fluttering to the ground adding a pastel to the neatly cropped green lawn, and Jack had a loving and contemplative smile upon his face. A scrapbook of memories flooded his mind as he looked upon the inscription carved on Susan's tombstone. Today, he told himself, there would be no more "bitter tears."

"I can't think of a better way to celebrate our 26th wedding anniversary," Jack began. "Than to surround you with our family, the people we love."

Jack looked up and scanned the faces of the people whose joined hands now completely encircled Susan's grave. On his left, Dr. Meagan Palmer was radiant in the bright yellow morning sun that backlit her gleaming black hair and benevolent smiling eyes. On his right hand he etched into his mental scrapbook an image of his son Jimmy that would forever replace the former graveside snapshot that he had so despised. Across from him, Will Daysart was illuminated with a light of serenity that had eluded him since his father's death. Jack reflected quietly upon the miracle of this scrapbook scene. It was a grainy black and white photo that could have been hanging on the walls of the Legionnaire post downtown.

Young Meagan in a weathered KSU sailing team slicker with her roomie's name stenciled on the pocket. Little Willie Daysart wondering over the marvels of the mysterious colored light machine given to him by his father. Jimmy Grayson with his sketch pad and colored pencils creating a world that only he saw clearly. Alone and struggling in the swamp of his self doubt and guilt, Jack had lost sight of these images. Pictures that floated on the water like flotsam from a shipwreck, waiting for someone to gather them up before the wind blew them irretrievably into the abyss.

Now the power of the completed circle gathered and focused the images into a vibrant energetic life force. Jack looked again around the circle. "Old nanna Wheeler always reminded me that we come here on our special occasions, not to wallow in death, but to celebrate life. Susan left us with a reminder to shout out our love rather than weep bitter tears of despair and regret."

Now Jack squeezed his son's hand and looked into his hopeful blue eyes. "Jimmy, I hope you can forgive me for not seeing the beautiful person you are, and have always been. I love you and I want you to know that together we can enjoy the legacy your mother bequeathed us—a lifetime of sharing and caring for each other.

I'll always be here for you. But I hope, in fact I'm asking you now to consider staying here with us so we can make up for lost time—too much lost time—and fight this disease of yours together." Jack wanted desperately to hug his son and to feel the life he had given him coursing through his body, but the circle he decided should not be broken—not yet.

"Will," he said turning his attention directly ahead. "I know things have been tough for you here since your dad died, but you haven't really had much support. I blame myself for that and for much of the trouble we found ourselves in these last few weeks. Please consider staying on here with us. You can run the business or sell the business. You can live in the old house or sell it. Just think about what we've been through and what I've said." Now Jack looked again at Jimmy. "Whatever you boys decide to do I want you to know that we support you and will do whatever we can to help you out."

Jack could see the boy's eyes turn toward Meagan. "Yes, I've asked Meagan to marry me and she has agreed. It seemed to me that this was the best place in the world, and the best time, to make the announcement."

"It's kind of strange isn't it?" said Meagan as she squeezed Jack's hand.

"That we've all come to this place to celebrate our rebirth? The events of the last month have changed us all in fundamental ways . . . good ways, ways that Susan would be proud of."

Meagan looked down at Susan's tombstone and smiled warmly. "I think I knew Susan as well as anyone could. She was the sister I never had, the wife that I had never been, and the mother that I always hoped I could be." She looked up into Jack's eyes with the tears of confession flowing freely down her cheeks. "I think her greatest gift was the ability to make peace and in doing so giving new life to those she helped." Now Meagan looked around the circle.

"Each of us should think about the baggage, hatred and pain we were carrying around a month ago and thank God that he gave us all the strength, determination and courage to get where we are today."

Meagan squeezed Jimmy's hand and looked into his moist eyes. "I know I could never presume to take your mother's place, but I think she would approve of me trying to pick up where she left off."

Jimmy was the first to break the circle. He dropped Will's hand and wheeled around to face Meagan Palmer. As he covered her in a warm embrace he said, "I couldn't do any better. Welcome to the clan."

"Speaking of the clan," said Will. "What are we going to do about Paddy Delaney and his money?"

"After the Coast Guard inquiry over the sinking of Maggie's ship with him on board, and the investigation over the loss of *SEAQUESTOR*, which he technically owned, I think he decided to fold his cards," said Meagan.

"And?" asked Will.

"And the last word I had was a message on my machine telling me had gone back to Ireland for an extended recuperation."

"He did take some pretty big losses in the end," said Jack. "When the Coast Guard couldn't come up with any sign of the sailboat wreckage and no evidence of it's location on the bottom of the lake I think he got awfully frustrated and just gave up."

"I suppose no one will ever know where that sunken treasure is located," said Meagan. "It's probably a mystery that's better left unsolved."

Will and Jimmy were now sifting their thoughts and generating a great deal of brainwave static that poured forth from their eyes. Suddenly Jimmy's eyes brightened. He had it.

"Mom will always know where her boat is," Jimmy said quietly as both Jack and Meagan turned toward him. "Will brought something along with him—something from the ketch."

Will reached into a small duffel bag on the ground beside him and pulled out a plain metal box that looked like the drawer from a safety deposit vault in a bank. Reverently, he loosed the catch and flipped up the hinged lid, then held out the box to Jack. Jack was frozen for a few moments as he looked inside. He reached inside to withdraw the contents then recoiled quickly with second thoughts. Now he looked up into Will's face and met his serious grin with one of his own.

"What do you intend to do with this?"

"It's mom's log book," said Jimmy quietly. "And Will and I thought it was only fitting that she should have it."

"And as her final captain I presume you logged her final resting place?" asked Jack already knowing the answer.

"Which is several miles different than the fix we gave the Coast Guard," said Will.

"Some secrets," Jack said. "Not all, but some, are better taken with us to the grave I guess." Jack looked at Meagan, then Jimmy, and finally Will for some reaction.

Everyone watched silently as Will Daysart interred the demon that had haunted Jack's dreams and plagued Will's life. The same demon, paradoxically, that had allowed Meagan Palmer to cleanse herself, while lighting the way home for Jimmy Grayson. When it was over, Jimmy knelt down and placed a small bouquet of Iris over the freshly replaced sod. "Thanks mom," he said. "I love you."

"Well then," said Jack. "Ednamae has a big Harbour Towne breakfast waiting for all of us."

"That sounds great," said Meagan hungrily. "What will she be serving?"

The three men looked at each other and almost in unison exclaimed, "It's a secret recipe."

*After we have brushed off the dust and chips of life, we will have left only the hard clean question: Was it good or was it evil? Have we done well or ill?*—John Steinbeck

# The End